BY KEITH ROSSON

The Devil by Name
Fever House
Smoke City
Road Seven
The Mercy of the Tide
Folk Songs for Trauma Surgeons

THE DEVIL
BY NAME

RANDOM HOUSE
NEW YORK

THE DEVIL
BY NAME

a novel

KEITH
ROSSON

Copyright © 2024 by Keith Rosson LLC

Published in the United States by Random House,
an imprint and division of Penguin Random House LLC, New York.

RANDOM HOUSE and the HOUSE colophon are registered
trademarks of Penguin Random House LLC.

Library of Congress Cataloging-in-Publication Data
Names: Rosson, Keith (Novelist) author. | Rosson, Keith (Novelist). Fever house.
Title: The devil by name: a novel / Keith Rosson.
Description: First edition. | New York: Random House, 2024.
Identifiers: LCCN 2023050553 (print) | LCCN 2023050554 (ebook) | ISBN
9780593595787 (hardcover; acid-free paper) | ISBN 9780593595794 (ebook)
Subjects: LCGFT: Apocalyptic fiction. | Horror fiction. | Novels.
Classification: LCC PS3618.O853544 D48 2024 (print) |
LCC PS3618.O853544 (ebook) | DDC 813/.6—dc23/eng/20231113
LC record available at https://lccn.loc.gov/2023050553
LC ebook record available at https://lccn.loc.gov/2023050554

Printed in Canada on acid-free paper

randomhousebooks.com

2 4 6 8 9 7 5 3 1

First Edition

THE DEVIL
BY NAME

FEVER HOUSE

(noun, informal)
a government collation center used to contain
afflicted or "fevered" individuals

1
THE SIGHT

NAOMI LAURENT

Nevers, Bourgogne-Franche-Comté region, France

Denis knocks once and steps into her room.

Past her bed and to the window, where he thumbs aside the gauzy curtains. They're on the fourth floor, next to the stairwell. Naomi rises, sits there numbly, sleep still crowding her. She'd been dreaming of her brother.

"Come," Denis says, without turning from the window. "We have to go."

"What's the matter?"

"Nothing's the matter," he says curtly. A tall, wide-shouldered man wearing a black knit cap and a mishmash of scavenged tactical gear. A black hunting rifle slung over his shoulder. A week's worth of beard. "Just get dressed."

"Where's Emilie?"

"Getting breakfast." He steps away from the window.

Naomi rises out of bed, and when he sees she's only in her T-shirt and panties, sees the blocky red glyph on her thigh, somewhere between a birthmark and a brand, he blushes and cuts his eyes away. He steps out of her room, staring at the floor. "Two minutes," he says.

Naomi hunts for her clothes as the door shuts behind her. She's seen Denis kill a trio of fevered from a quarter mile away, patiently ejecting the spent bullet casings from his rifle, the shots measured and even. She's seen him once argue with a shopkeeper over a payment he'd tried to renege on, the two of them getting so heated that Denis had spat at his feet and then dug his knife into the shopkeeper's guts, hoisting him off the floor, the man's toes scrabbling for purchase while his wife had looked on screaming. That's Denis and his broken, funhouse morality: He'll kill a man for looking at him wrong, but Naomi in her underwear is something that will send him running from the room.

She gets dressed, gathers her pack, looks longingly for a moment at the bed, and then steps out into the hallway where she finds Denis and Emilie waiting for her. Denis spends a moment assessing her appearance, her readiness for travel, then hoists the rifle and his pack onto his shoulders. He carries almost all of their supplies. Emilie hands Naomi a muffin slathered in butter and a paper cup full of water.

"Thank you," Naomi murmurs. It's rare, but it happens sometimes: a small, quiet moment of grace between the two of them, a respite against Denis's ceaseless intensities.

They are in the small town of Nevers after days of travel. Denis and Emilie do not know that this is her hometown. She has so few secrets left, but this is one of them. To be here is to hold fiercely to her mother and father once more, to hold tight to little Hugo. She remembers this hotel as a child, its trio of spires on the roof, its arched windows. Her family hadn't been poor, but even if there had ever been a need or opportunity to stay at a hotel in their own town, they couldn't have afforded this one. Now, five years after the Message, everything is different. Much of Nevers remains in ruins, with straggling bands of fevered still roaming its alleyways, trapped in its cellars, thumbs of smoke still occasionally coloring the sky. There are armed guards at the entrances of the hotel, men who had given

Denis a hard time about his guns until he'd paid them, his face drawn tight with resentment.

Now he pushes open the door to the stairwell. Besides the rifle, he carries a pistol on his hip. He doesn't let Emilie have a gun, and would never—never *ever*—let Naomi have one. He thumbs off the pistol's safety, keeps it pointed down.

They don't like stairwells, any of them. It's too easy for bad things to happen, and then you're trapped. Bullets in stairwells, Denis has told her, act sneaky, ricochet in impossible ways. Emilie is the most afraid, and as they begin their journey toward the ground floor, Naomi can hear the woman's breathing become pinched behind her. She wonders what it was that made Emilie afraid like that. Naomi, the cargo, walks in the middle, as always. She takes a bite of her muffin and feels a savage twist of cruelty toward the woman behind her. *You're afraid?* she thinks. *Good. I hope you slip. Crack your skull open.*

At the ground floor, Denis pushes open the door and they step out into the parking lot. Only a few vehicles back here, rust-lashed and likely in the barest working order. Occasionally, if the weather is particularly bad, they'll hitchhike, but Denis insists that relying on a car is too dangerous. There was a stretch where they had tried motorcycles, but the bikes had been loud, had brought the fevered out from the tree lines and the insides of buildings. Now they either ride bicycles or walk. They walk for miles most days. Naomi sometimes wonders how much of the country she's traveled since meeting Denis and can't fathom it. A guard is leaning against the wall, a shotgun on a sling across his chest. He nods as they make their way across the parking lot, let themselves out of the gate.

Denis walks with his pistol still at his side. Something is bothering him. Naomi finishes the last of her muffin and downs the water in her cup in one go. She walks over and sets the empty cup on the windowsill of a building, the window glass broken out. It is the type of thing Denis would normally chastise her for—he pictures a fevered lurching from the darkness of the window, latching onto her arm. A harrier sticking a gun in her face. But he's too distracted this morning, head roving left and right as they walk. Emilie makes a *tsk* of disappointment and that's all.

He's in his mid-forties, she thinks, and beyond his obvious lethality—he is military through and through—Denis is fastidious, punctual, organized. He's managed to keep himself and the two people in his charge alive for this long across the broken wasteland that is France. No easy feat, especially considering what they do to survive.

"Something's wrong with you," Naomi says to his back. She doesn't want it to sound like an accusation, and thankfully, Denis doesn't take it as such.

"It's just a feeling I have," he says.

"What do you want to do?" Emilie asks from behind her. They keep walking, the street wide and quiet.

"Keep moving," he says. "We have an appointment." He looks at his watch. "In two hours. We have a ways to go."

"Is it in town?" Naomi asks.

Denis nods, adjusts his pack on his shoulders. "On the edge of it. A farm."

Naomi secretly thrills at this, even as it cleaves her heart. Walking through her hometown, wondering if there might be a way to lead them past her house. The faint glimmer of an idea moves through her: that her father might have survived all these years, might still be at home somehow. She imagines a light shining in a darkened window of her house, like nothing had ever changed. She knows it's foolish and wishes for it anyway.

Denis holsters his pistol and unslings his rifle, and Naomi's unease kicks up a notch. There is the sense that people are here with them, tucked in the corners of things and watching silently, but it's something only felt, spied barely in her periphery. A flutter of curtain here, a door slowly edging closed. They pass landmarks, so insignificant in her childhood, but charged with loss now, each one like a strike to the chest. Here was where her parents would take her and

Hugo to buy school shoes. Here was where her father had some-times gotten them Thai food on his way home from work. There was the Loire River and the red-tiled roofs of houses, the wide, patch-work quality of the streets. Shrubs once trimmed to offer privacy to people's homes have grown wild and unkempt. Ivy covers some buildings entirely now. They pass a pair of cars in the roadway, fend-ers bent and crumpled together, the windshield of one starred in a constellation of bullet holes. Impossible to tell if the conflict was recent or not.

Naomi walks, thinks, pines—even after all this time—for the way things used to be.

They walk down the narrow rue de Lauzon, little more than an alleyway, the pavement so broken from weather and age that it seems specifically designed to twist an ankle. The shrubbery's grown high enough on each side that it nearly forms a canopy over their heads, save for a small break in the shrubs to her left, where a wrought iron gate has permanently rusted open.

Denis has just passed the open gate when a fevered staggers from it.

A woman. Her hair had once been blond but is now the tint of gunmetal, colored by countless days amid the world's filth. Her hand brushes against Naomi's coat before Denis turns and pops her in the forehead with the stock of his rifle. There is an eye-watering whiff of shit and decay—impossible to tell when she'd been turned, how many years or months back, but she is clearly dead. The woman falls on her ass, jaw snapping shut. "Keep walking," Denis says to Emilie, his voice tight. He is angry that he missed her coming out of the gate. Emilie pushes Naomi onward. She looks back to see Denis slinging his rifle over his shoulder and unsheathing the dark blade of his hunting knife from its scabbard at his thigh, and then she's walk-ing again.

Later, when Denis catches up to them, Naomi says, "I could have done it."

He's in front of her now and doesn't turn. He holds the woman's head in one fist by her filthy hair. The head twists and bumps against his leg as he walks. Drops of thick, jelly-like blood patter on the ground. The face sometimes turns to Naomi. The eyes. Naomi looks away when it happens.

"We have a schedule," is all Denis says.

He believes that the fevered have a rudimentary understanding of language, can decipher warnings, and so, as they step from the mouth of the overgrown street and into a larger thoroughfare, he lifts the head aloft.

"Stay back! Fuck off!"

After eight, ten more blocks of Denis yelling—during which they pass Naomi's school, now a cluster of rubble that looks like it was struck by a bomb—he lays the woman's head in the middle of the street. He spins around once in the roadway, arms splayed wide, as if daring any other fevered to come forth and challenge him.

There will be no going home, she knows then. There will be no light in the window. No tearful reunion with her father.

This is her life: Denis and Emilie ferrying her around. *Do your trick, girl.* To tell the two of them that she grew up here would only cheapen her old life.

No, better that she never goes home again than that Denis step foot inside her house. Goes past the blood-spattered living room, up the stairs. Past Hugo's room with his spill of toys on the floor, the soccer uniforms he insisted on wearing as pajamas. She imagines Denis looking at the totality of her life with those unforgiving, assessing eyes of his. Imagines Emilie pawing through her dead mother's jewelry. Better she never see her home again than see it ransacked like that.

Another hour and they arrive at the farmstead on the outskirts of town. She remembers the place only vaguely; her family never really had cause to come out to this area. In front of the house is a field, an expanse of emerald green. Cows chew contemplatively behind a barbed-wire fence. It's a nice image, idyllic and sweet, and they all spend a moment looking, even Denis. Then they walk the dirt road along the field toward the house, the ditch beside them overrun with weeds and wildflowers. The sun punches through the patchwork of clouds for the first time that day. Emilie coos at the animals, drifts a hand between the wires. It's unusual to see livestock like this. Penned and fed. There are wild animals everywhere, and dogs that rove in packs and will attack. Feral cats, rodents of all types. Birds and deer. Raccoons, possums. But cows? Fenced in like this? It feels like a good omen. Even Denis appears lifted by it, if only because it means the people here are wealthy. Denis likes wealthy clients.

Near the house, the dirt gives way to a paved driveway. Denis turns and offers the two of them a rare smile. "This is the place," he says. There is still a black drip of the dead woman's blood on his cheek. Naomi cannot stop staring at it.

He turns and lifts an arm, calls out "Hello!"

As if in response, a cow moos behind them, and Emilie actually laughs.

JOHN BONNER

Portland, Oregon

Bonner holds the severed hand in his lap.

He's pinned motionless in the garish red dreams it offers, his mind hung there, when his phone begins vibrating on the couch beside him. He gasps and pulls himself away—it's never easy, drawing himself back from its tide—and sets the hand in its box on the floor, clapping the lid shut. He clears his throat, palms sweat from his face, does a five-count in his mind. Picks up the phone.

"Bonner."

"John, it's Kendall."

"Hey Dave," Bonner says.

"Look, we caught a hot one," Kendall says. Never one for small talk. "I need you down there."

"What is it?" Bonner's knee joggles madly. He tries to stay in the moment, on the phone with Dave Kendall, his handler, but the hand's blood-visions of severed limbs, atrocities, dismemberments, drift through his mind like lights in a fog. It calls out to him from its box and Bonner gently pushes the whole thing away with his shoe. Tries to focus on what Kendall's saying.

"Katz got a call from the desk clerk at the Parade."

"The hotel?"

"Yeah. Clerk came up to one of the rooms to evict a tenant, said it looked like a slaughterhouse inside."

"How many bodies?"

"Well, you tell me, John, is what I'm saying."

He scrubs a hand down his face again. "Got it. I'll be there in ten."

He hangs up and breathes. Picks up the box, once again marveling at how light it is. That something so insignificant could be so resoundingly lethal. As one of the three remnants—*the hand the voice the eye*—it is responsible in no small part for the dismantlement of the world. He makes sure that the hasp is closed and locked. The box is lead-lined, the only thing that seems to minutely calm its ugly, clamorous call for violence, and Bonner puts it back in the freezer in the kitchen.

He thinks for the hundredth time, the thousandth: *Destroy it. Throw it in the river.*

Thinks the same thing every time he comes here. Never does it.

It's his sick little treasure. His eternal hair shirt.

Strung out as sure as any addict on the blood-songs it shows him, that red tide he throws himself into.

By the time he's in his car, he feels almost human again. Heart slowed. Panic subsided. Images he saw while holding the hand fading like sick, beautiful dreams.

The Parade Hotel is eight stories tall. Once a bright robin's-egg blue, time has faded it to a sort of featureless gray, and the hotel's first story is now festooned in the graffiti of a thousand warring tags. A tower rising at the edge of Portland's boxed-in industrial southeast, the Parade was erected in the pre-Message years as a kind of stopgap measure for the growing houseless population in the city, and through government mismanagement and funding issues it was only a quarter full when the world exploded. Now, five years later, it's vice central. You want to gamble, you want to pay for sex, you want to buy a gun, the Parade's your first stop. Dope of all kinds moves in sizable quantities through here, and if you want someone shanked, you'll have a line out the door of those willing.

Inside, the clerk's missing from his bulletproof kiosk. The lobby's empty save for a pair of old-timers perched around a card table near the front windows. Bonner walks over, gets cursory nods—he's a known quantity in the fever house. Not liked, but feared enough.

He spends a few moments watching the men play cards, both of them grousing at each other the whole time. They're playing for cigarettes, and Bonner waits until they finish their hand before he flashes his Terradyne badge. It's just for propriety's sake; they already know who he is.

"You guys hear anything about someone dying in here?"

"I'm dying right now," one guy grumbles, scratching his armpit. He's got a bandage on his neck that's seeping orange iodine, and he looks both gruesome and somehow festive because of it. "The dogshit this one passes along, my lord."

"Bite me," mutters the dealer.

"Where's the clerk, gentlemen?" Bonner says.

"Manny? He's upstairs. With that other cop."

"What floor?"

"I don't know, fourth?"

"Third," the dealer says. "Bunch of hacked-up bastards up there, is what I heard."

"Yeah?" Bonner says, interested. "You personally see anything?"

The old-timer shuffles the cards, keeps his eyes down. "Not that I know of."

"I bet you see a lot of things, though. Sitting here and all."

"None of it good," says the bandaged one. He fishes a cigarette out of his shirt pocket and throws it onto the middle of the table. "Ante up."

Bonner takes a pair of his business cards out of his own pocket and hands one to each of the men. "Listen, I might need to talk to you guys when I come back down."

"We're not going anywhere."

"Okay. And that has my number if you think of anything later."

The dealer takes the card from Bonner with two fingers and makes a show of putting it in his shirt pocket, then deals.

Bonner takes the stairs up to the third floor. He smells cigarettes, mold, disinfectant. At the third-floor landing he sees people gathered around a doorway at the end of the hall. He walks over, asks for Manny. A guy turns—a kid, really, has to be in his early twenties, with smeared glasses and a scraggly attempt at a beard, shock still writ large on his face—and raises his hand. Bonner tells him to hold on and then dips his head in the doorway. Katz is standing in the middle of the room, his hands on his hips.

"Katz, you good?"

Katz doesn't even turn. "Oh, I'm fucking fantastic, John. How're you?"

"I'm gonna talk to these guys," he says. "Be right back." Katz waves his hand. Bonner catches the coppery closeness of spilled blood and uses the sleeve of his jacket to shut the door. He turns, and the group in the hall, grown now to maybe eight or nine people, steps back a few paces.

He badges everyone. "Folks, my name's John Bonner. I'm a security officer with Terradyne Industries, and we all know they're our bread and butter in here. I'll need you to step over here and form a line, please."

"Rent-a-cop" drifts soft and quiet from the crowd.

Fury moves through him easy these days, sloppy, and Bonner grins big and wolfish. "Up against the wall here, please. This won't take long."

Murmurs, pointed looks, a few folks grumbling and slowly taking off down the hall, casting glances at him over their shoulders. Daring him. Fuck it, Bonner thinks. In the old days, they'd have had beat cops doing all this, multiple guys knocking on doors, getting names and details. But five years after the Message? After most of the world suddenly started devouring each other? Shit. There're Bonner and Katz and maybe thirty other operatives working the entire city, and that includes maintaining security for the collation center itself, and the city wall. And that's thirty ops all vying for the same broke-ass equipment. The weapons that come in over the wall and move through the Parade are better than the shit they're issued. Jesus, Katz still carries a revolver. Bonner could run down the hall, zip-tie the stragglers, but then what? Like that would inspire folks to cooperate?

He runs down the line, getting everyone's names, where they live in the building, phone numbers if they have them. Most people are forthcoming enough, even if they have little to share.

He does the clerk last. The hallway light sputters for a second and the two of them stare up at it.

Bonner's got his little notebook, clicks his pen. "Who was the room registered to?"

"I looked," the kid says, the pale gleam of the hallway window reflected in the lenses of his glasses. "I couldn't make it out."

"What do you mean?"

"I couldn't read the signature. He told me what his name was when he signed in, but I forgot."

"And you couldn't read his signature?"

"Yeah, it was just, it was like a scribble."

Bonner clicks his pen again, digs a divot into his notebook. "And that doesn't bug you? That your records are illegible? That you got a homicide in your place of business and you don't know who paid for the room? Because that bugs the *piss* out of me, you know?"

The kid swallows so loud his throat clicks. "It's a cash operation, sir. We're, we're not too concerned with stuff like that. I mean, look around."

Bonner points with his pen at the camera above the stairwell, mounted high up, where the wall meets the ceiling. "How about those? Those work?"

"They're just for show. They haven't worked since I been here."

Bonner grins again, a tic he picks up when he gets angry. He wants the hand, wants to be back there. Sitting with it. "Okay. Alright. So what can you tell me about him? The guy that got the room."

"I mean, apart from the eye, he looked like any other dude that comes in here."

A chill walks through Bonner, prickles his scalp. "What do you mean? He had the eye on him?"

Nodding, the clerk holds up his hand. "Yeah, it was right there, burned into each palm."

"So he was with the Sight, is what you're saying."

The clerk shrugs. "I mean, I guess so. That's what they all do to themselves, right?"

Bonner puts his notebook away, lets out a disgusted little chuckle. "Yeah, see, letting me know that first? That would have saved us some time."

He walks back into Room 312, finds Leo Katz still standing amid the charnel howl of the place. There're the blood-stink, and the loosed bowels, yeah, but mostly the room's full of that sort of electric *nearness* of death, something that he will forever associate with the hand, how the hand brings death close to you. Brings you right up to it. The room hums with these people's profound absence, the strange way their bodies take up physical space but offer nothing else. He lets out a breath, shuts the door behind him.

Three corpses in the room. All nude. Two on the bed, one sitting in a chair in the corner.

The rooms in the Parade are flop rooms: a bed, a dresser, a window painted shut. One chair. Nail holes in the walls where pictures used to hang. The two bodies on the bed: A big guy splayed out on his back, chest and stomach furred in hair. The woman beside him is older, worms of varicose veins marbling her legs up to the knees. Gray bob. The sheets, dingy as they are, swallow the brightness of the blood that haloes their heads. Both have been stabbed in the face and neck multiple times. Their eyes are gone, the sockets turned into jellied red craters. Their hands rest at their sides. Bonner turns and stares at the door. He breathes, counts. Tries not to vomit.

"All three got the fucking marks on their hands," Katz says, angry about it, peering down at the second woman, sitting in the chair. "The eyes."

"Yeah," Bonner says. "The clerk ID'd 'em."

Katz, a Portland Police Bureau detective before the Message, doesn't like Bonner and doesn't try to hide it. He thinks Bonner's here because of political strings that his uncle has pulled for him. And he's right.

Katz lifts a shoe toward the woman in the chair, the fanned wings of her blond hair spattered red, obscuring her face. Her torso and breasts are wreathed in gore. Her hands, resting in her lap, are gloved in blood up to the elbow. "She's the doer."

"The knife there?"

"Right here by the chair leg, yep. Kitchen knife, looks like." He points. "So she does the two on the bed, then sits down and does herself."

"I'm not seeing any defensive wounds on either of their hands."

Shaking his head, Katz says, "No defensive wounds if you *want* her to do it."

Bonner wills himself to look back at the bed. "Can you imagine? Just letting someone do that? To your face? And not putting your hands up?"

"Lot of things I can't imagine. Getting a room at the Parade, for one."

"Alright. So what're we calling this?"

Katz snorts. "I don't know, a family reunion? A trio of the dumb-est motherfuckers on earth? It's a non-event."

"Come on. Give me something Kendall will sign off on."

Katz turns and finally looks at him—truly looks, for the first time since Bonner rolled up. Katz is pushing sixty, with a walrus mustache and a steel-gray buzz cut. A nose with the telltale capillaries of a heavy drinker. He laughs at Bonner outright. "I promise you, Dave Kendall will not give a flying shit about this." He fishes a smoke from his shirt pocket.

"Why not?"

"Because it's the Sight."

"There're three hacked-up bodies here, Katz."

He lights his smoke. "That's what you see? Because I see three willing participants."

"You don't know that."

"It's *the Sight*, John. It's what they do."

"Okay. So what now?"

Katz inhales big. "So now Kendall calls a crew to clean this shit up and everyone goes on with their lives."

"Except for these three."

"Well, yes, clearly."

"You don't want to, I don't know, be cops for a minute? Work this?"

Katz blows smoke at the ceiling. "Fuck you, John."

"I'm serious."

Katz points at the woman in the chair with his cigarette. Says loudly, "There's nothing to work. It's a cult. They suicide out like this. It's their thing."

"You don't care about why?"

"If they started doing this shit to other people? Sure, I'd care. But look at this." He gestures again with the smoke, a big arc that en-compasses all the horror in the room. "They're keeping it in their own club. Kendall absolutely will not care, and neither should you. Besides, seems to me like you got other things going on."

"The hell does that mean?"

"It means you look strung out, Bonner. I don't know what trip you're currently on, but you look like dogshit."

"I'm fine."

Katz lets out a little laugh, pulls on his smoke and exhales. Squints at Bonner through the haze. "Yeah, you're something, but fine's a mile away from it."

DEAN HAGGERTY

Drale, Indiana

Ragman, ragman, traverse the run-down world. Dean on his bicycle, calves like softballs after the years of it, the piecemeal trailer rattling along behind him. A thing he'd managed to scavenge and weld together over a period of a week, holed up in a machine shop on the outskirts of Birmingham. Months after the Message, this had been, Dean seeing which way the wind would blow, knowing that cash would be worthless for a long time. It was *things* that would matter in the future. Inventory. He hadn't used a torch since his summers off from college, working in an auto shop for his uncle, but the seams and joints he'd made had held well enough, and six months after the Message ripped its way through everything, Dean had transformed himself into a ragman, a scavenger, trundling his siphoned wares along the skin of the ruined world. Sometimes his cart got bartered down to its barest essence, and Dean's pockets grew flush with cash—five years later and people were starting to use paper money again—and other times it sat heavy with goods.

Anything, he'd discovered, could fetch a price, earn him some sort of trade. It was just a matter of finding the right person and using the right words. He'd worked the graveyard shift at an answering service previous to the Message (Dean thinks of them as the Before Days, with a rose-lit sort of nostalgia that he knows is both pointless and potentially lethal) and had grown used to that sort of solitary life. In spite of everything that had happened to the world, he was shocked to discover that, as a ragman, he *liked* people, liked being around them. His was a life that felt at times like it bounced from heartache to heartache, so to realize that he missed people when he traveled at night, or those times when he traversed rarely used country roads? It was a revelation. As a boy, his mother had told him he was "too loud for his own mouth," and it'd taken until he was forty-nine years old to truly understand how right she'd been: The world now forced him to be cautious of everyone, always, and damn if he didn't still find it hard to keep his guard up all the time.

Today he rides his bicycle and cart along US-460, a drizzling stretch of broken six-lane blacktop that winds its way through the town of Drale, Indiana, a place as unremarkable and beautiful as any other he's wandered through. An area run roughshod with greenery, many of the houses and buildings fallen to a sort of grand and vibrant ruination. Wildflowers pushing through the concrete of the town square in bright purple lines, a wall of vines greening the brick facade of a gas station. Occasionally, as he rides along, Dean will holler in his sonorous baritone, a voice he's perfected over the years, "Ragman, ragman! Goods for sale, goods for barter! Soap! Ammo! Jewelry! Trades okay!" His voice carries through an afternoon grown thick with the promise of rain. His stomach gurgles with hunger—breakfast was a handful of dried apples and some tart, half-ripe blackberries he'd found by the road—but even that meager meal had been a beautiful thing.

A telephone pole, its base hidden by a ring of shin-high weeds and wild grass, has a sign stapled to it, a bright pocket of color in the day's gloom. Blue and red text on a field of white, its message is quietly desperate, and Dean laughs to himself as he pedals past:

AMERICA IS *BACK*!

THE PROVIDENCE INITIATIVE IS FOR
ALL AMERICANS!

LISTEN TO JANE!

BUY, DON'T BARTER!

Jane. The government's newly minted spokesmodel. The new face of America now. Of America's products, America's supposed reformation. A kind of national rebrand, something that Dean profoundly mistrusts and wants zero part of.

He rides on, passes after a while a white clapboard house tucked down a gravel road; in his peripheral vision, he sees a man come out onto the porch and wave him down. Dean lifts a hand in response and turns slowly, careful not to tip the cart over. Down their road he goes, the cart rattling merrily along. That's the sound of promise right there, Dean thinks. Sound of cash money.

The house is small but well kept. The yard is mowed, which must mean a push mower, given the dearness of gas. They have a fence, wisely, and as Dean coasts to a stop, the man is joined on the porch by a woman in a faded floral dress and winter coat, a sleepy-eyed infant at her chest. They stand on their cement stoop and eye him with a mixture of caution and interest. The man has a pistol held loosely in one hand, which isn't a thing Dean finds particularly worrisome anymore. Just the way the world leans now.

"Howdy," he says, hopping off his bicycle, offering them what he hopes is a neighborly grin. It's best not to be too forward out here, particularly when rolling up onto white folks' property, invited or not. He's found that the same high-wire act of loose, easy friendliness and professionalism that worked best running the answering service phones for divorce lawyers and plastic surgeons also works as a ragman. Dean's voice is his greatest tool. "You folks like to take a look at the goods here? Or if you're aiming for anything in particular, I can tell you if it's in stock. I take paper cash or trade."

The woman switches the baby from one arm to the other. Her hair's in a bun, loose strings framing her face; her body's latticed with exhaustion. It's a hard enough world, Dean can't imagine what it's like adding a baby to all of it. "Got any kids' stuff?" she says.

"For the baby there? Oh yes," he says, pushing down a sudden surge of ache, sadness. It's not often that he'll allow his heart to hurt for George, for Nichole, but some things do it of their own volition. A baby's rare enough in the world these days, and seeing one stirs the ashes of his sorrow. He loosens the bungee cords that hold the blue tarp tight over the top of the cart; there's a method to Dean's madness when it comes to packing, an internal storage process that he knows more by intuition at this point, by feel, and he finds the plastic bin that holds the baby and children's goods in seconds.

He gestures at the gate with his free hand and the man says, "Yeah, go ahead," and Dean opens it and walks through the yard, setting the plastic bin down at their feet on the stoop. He heads back to the cart, giving them space. The man crouches, setting the pistol at his feet, and paws through the box while the woman peers down, gently rocking the baby. At the cart, Dean begins calling out things that might interest them.

"Saw you all got electricity here," he says.

"Sometimes," the woman says.

"I got a clock radio, a box of lightbulbs. Brand-new, still taped and everything. Got batteries of all kinds, but they're used; pretty much got to try your luck with those."

"How much for these diapers here?" the woman calls out. Dean looks up, squinting. It's an opened box of Huggies, but almost full.

"We got cloth ones, Melissa," the man says quietly.

"Hush," she says back. "You're not the one does the laundry." And again to Dean, "How much?"

"I can sell 'em to you individually or do the whole box."

"Well, how much is what I'm asking you."

"Depends on if you want to trade or buy."

The man gives the woman a quick, assessing glance and she nods curtly; Dean feels a flurry of emotion, a twist of something like love toward them. These two are tight, he thinks. Making a go of it, working the world together. Raising the baby the best they can.

"We got some canned stuff to trade," the man says.

Dean brightens. "Yeah?"

"Pickles and beets and things."

He grins big at them. "Oh, you are speaking my language, friend."

"We got probably three jars we could give you."

"Two," the woman says, flint in her voice, and again Dean's heart lurches with love.

"Two would be a fine trade," Dean says, and she takes the baby, steps inside. The man crouches down again and thumbs through the bin once more.

"Got some ammunition if you need any. Assuming that's a nine-millimeter you got."

"We're all set with that," the man says.

"Okay. Got some chargers might work for your phones. You got cell service out here?"

The man shrugs, still looking. "Supposed to. Calls dip in and out, though. We signed up for the whole Providence thing last year."

The Providence Initiative. The government supposedly getting a leg up on the crisis—*all* the crises—and getting back to the business of governing. Dean has seen the census-takers with their clipboards and tablets, their green neon vests, accompanied by groups of fever hunters as they went house to house, getting geographical and ethnological information, trying to figure out how many people were even still alive. You could sign up for a ration card, ostensibly get gasoline and food with it, but half the places Dean's come across won't accept them. Whole thing was a mess, indicative of how badly the world was still broken.

"Government's supposed to come back and help us all out, huh?" Dean says.

"Yeah, great fucking job they did the first time around. I got a ration card, but I also got to drive forty miles to a gas station that accepts it. Wind up in the hole worse than I started, you know? Fucking Jane, man."

Dean allows himself a cackle of laughter. "Ah, Jane. It's something, isn't it?"

"And to even get the ration card, I had to sign one of those, the hell is it called, a *loyalty proclamation*."

Dean nods. "Where you say you're an American, pro-America, love everything that Jane stands for? Promise that you're not in a militia or housing a fevered?"

The man nods bitterly, then shakes his head. "You signed it yet?"

"Not me," Dean admits. "But I move around a lot. Don't stay in one place for too long."

"I hear you." The man gathers his pistol and stands up, his knees popping. He puts the handgun in his waistband, leans against the porch's post, his arms crossed. "They're supposed to come back, start providing some kind of law. So they say. Get people working again. Food on the table. Hell, last can of Jane beans we got had a dead roach inside it. And when's the last time you were in an actual grocery store anyway?"

Dean hooks his thumb behind him. "I don't know, I seen a grocery store maybe ten, fifteen miles back down the highway there."

The man nods. "Well, you saw the sign. That's the IGA. I been shopping there since I was a kid. Place was ransacked down to the last onion about three days after the Message. People just sleep there now."

"Whole world's broke down," Dean says, the familiar cadence of mournful commiseration in his voice. It's like putting on a comfortable suit.

"Well, someone broke it," the man counters. "I don't know who, but someone sure did."

"True," Dean offers, ever the diplomat.

"Anyway, yeah." He pushes himself from the post, lifts his chin. "You got any books in there?"

Dean brightens. Books are some of the most useless inventory he trucks in, but for those few readers he encounters, they are gold incarnate. "Looking for fiction, nonfiction?"

The man shrugs. "Honestly? I just want to read a damn book, man."

Dean holds up a finger and accesses that internal database of his. Rifles through the cart and lifts up another bin, brings it over and sets it at the man's feet. "You all done with this one?" he asks, motioning toward the bin of baby things.

"Better wait for Melissa on that."

"Okay," he says, amiably enough. It's beginning to mist, and he goes over and carefully lays the tarp over the cart. "Fever hunters do a lot of sweeps here?"

"Hell no," the man says. "We saw one guy in a green vest and hard hat come out, but he just looked at the power lines for a minute, and then he took off. Most of the hunters, when we do see 'em, they just stick to the highway."

"You get any drifts?"

The man shakes his head, looks out at the middle distance. "Not for probably, what, six months? We'll get a fevered that rolls through every once in a while, maybe a pair of them, but it's only two, three times a month now. They just butt up against the fence, or they keep walking, wind up walking along the road there."

"That's pretty good, I suppose."

"Yeah, well," the man says, and then the woman comes out. She's left the baby inside and carries two jars. One a pint of dark beets and the other a quart of pickles in a variety of greens and yellows. Dean's mouth floods with saliva and he once more crosses the threshold, takes them gratefully. The woman ferries the box of diapers back into the house, gently shutting the door behind her.

"How much for these," the man says, holding a tattered paperback in each hand. Horror novels Dean had traded for some machine parts back in Murfreesboro.

"Oh, you know," Dean says softly, his hands on his hips, still caught up in that good feeling, the decency of these people. "I can just let you have those, friend."

The man pulls his head back, surprised. "You sure?"

"You bet. Not a lot of call for books most times. Go for it."

"Well, I appreciate it."

It hastens the goodwill among them, and the woman comes out with a cup of instant coffee for him. The heat of it, the chipped porcelain mug from a local bank long since gone to ruin. A place he imagines is filled with rats now, and debris, or just straight burned to the ground. It's a nice moment, the three of them, maybe the nicest moment he's had in a while, but Dean is ever cautious of overstaying his welcome. Ten minutes later, he's packed up his cart again, lighter now a bag of some gently used makeup and a roll of duct tape, and heavier a black-bladed hunting knife and another pint of beets. Good trades overall, a good day, and even with the rain finally starting to come down, his heart is light as he pushes the bike around in a semicircle and prepares to make his way back to the highway.

He's gone a few feet down the drive when he hears the squeal of the gate, someone trotting on the gravel behind him, and he realizes some part of him was expecting exactly this. Thinking it was too good to be true. Thinking here it comes.

The man sidles up to him, a pained look on his face. Shoulders hunched against the rain.

"What's up?" Dean asks. A smile on his face that he hopes doesn't look panicked or frightened. He can't see the man's sidearm anywhere; Dean's got a pistol in a small gig bag lashed to the frame of the bike, but there's no way he can reach it in time.

"Listen, I just wanted to tell you," the man says, licking his lips, and it's then that Dean realizes the look on his face is one of discomfort and apology. "There're some folks in the county here that would, well, they'd probably go after you if they saw you. You know what I'm saying?"

Dean nods, a flutter of panic in his ribs. "We talking anything organized, or just folks?"

"Well, they call themselves a militia."

He sucks at his teeth, nods again. "'Course they do."

The man sighs, his restless gaze settling on the highway, the little lines of weeds running up through the cracks in the asphalt, the grass in the ditches. Dean puts him in his late twenties; he tries to remember being that young and can't manage it. The world of Before is like a fairy tale, a thing halved and placed behind glass. So much of its intricacies now blurred or distorted by time. "Point being," the man says, "they got guns and trucks and you can see 'em all up and down the highway here. Nothing to do with Providence, they're their own thing. *Patrolling*," he says, his voice rich with sarcasm. "It's just, it's not a great stretch of road for certain people."

"I'll keep an eye out," Dean says softly, an ember of anger stirring hotly inside him, wanting to flare. He shoves it down. This man is just the messenger. Dean nods goodbye, pushes off and heads down the highway, things at a roil inside. The rain falls hard now, hisses on the fields, hisses on the road, snaps on his shoulders, the hood of the parka he's pulled up. All that goodness in him, that good feeling, vanishes quick as if someone's excised it with a knife. Dean finds himself, in that moment, profoundly eager to get the great grand fuck out of Drale, Indiana.

The whole world's broken down, he knows that. But some places are more broken than others.

TO: ALL ACTIVE TERRADYNE SECURITY PERSONNEL

DATE: MARCH 12, 20XX, 4:00 PM

SUBJECT: REMINDER: PROVIDENCE INITIATIVE PHASE TWO

Principles, Points of Focus, and Objectives of PROVIDENCE INITIATIVE, PHASE TWO

ACTING PRINCIPLES

- Afflicted individuals, if seized and collated with minimum risk to security personnel and local citizenry, and in keeping with government-mandated collation guidelines (see *Phase Two Strategic Objectives*), shall be transported to the nearest collation center for containment.
- The term "fever house" shall not be used in any Terradyne- or government-sanctioned public communications to describe any collation center or its surrounding environs.
- The term "fever" or "fevered" shall not be used in any

Terradyne- or government-sanctioned public communications to describe any afflicted group or individual.

POINTS OF FOCUS

- To reinstate and rebuild vital infrastructure, in keeping with Phase One objectives.
- To provide vital rations such as food, gasoline, and housing, provided that the individual in question can prove citizenhood, and prove to not be aiding an afflicted group or individual, or a member of a non-regulatory militia, and that the individual has signed a loyalty agreement to the United States government.
- To provide citizenry with government-linked and trackable cellular phones and devices, particularly in areas near resources earmarked as in the national interest (collation centers, subsidized farms and production centers, derricks, pipelines, etc.).
- To reinvigorate law enforcement opportunities, particularly at municipal and federal levels, including stringent prosecution and imprisonment of those convicted of criminal activities, as well as political activity deemed detrimental to the mission of Terradyne and the US government.

PHASE TWO STRATEGIC OBJECTIVES

- An acting quotient of 1 in 4 (or 25%) afflicted individuals encountered by security forces shall be removed to the nearest collation center. The remainder (3 out of 4 afflicted, or 75%) may be invalidated.
- To disseminate US government- and Terradyne-approved promotional and ration materials (clothing, tobacco, canned goods and non-perishable foodstuffs, designated alcoholic

items, etc.) that denote Jane as the government's national spokesperson/symbol of national renewal.

OPERATORS SHOULD CONSULT FIELD SUPERVISORS REGARDING SPECIFIC OBJECTIVE PARAMETERS.

MORE TO FOLLOW. AS EVER, THANK YOU ALL FOR YOUR TIRELESS SERVICE AND DEDICATION.

THEO MARSDEN, CEO
TERRADYNE INDUSTRIES

IN PARTNERSHIP WITH THE UNITED STATES GOVERNMENT

JOHN BONNER

Portland, Oregon

Bonner and Dave Kendall, his handler, are standing in Portland's grim industrial southeast as dawn breaks open across the city. They stand at the edge of the docks there, warehouses in long and staggered rows behind them, watching as a barge churns along the dirty surface of the Willamette. Kendall smokes a cigarette and waits for Bonner to talk. He's always been patient like that.

Bonner's tired. Sleep's like a ghost he relentlessly chases, only catching little flits of it here and there. Guilt howls in his blood like cheap dope. That, and years of continued, willful exposure to the hand, has likely scoured any possibility of a decent night's rest from him. He scrubs at his face, smells Kendall's cigarette, the dirty river below them. The barge will stop at one of the loading docks further down the Willamette, and men will move the containers from the barge with cranes, and someone will peel back a section of the vast wall that rings the city to let those containers inside, where the goods inside will be distributed, in their piecemeal way, to keep folks in Portland alive.

Or, maybe, the shipping containers are filled with fevered, and they'll be transported to the collation center, which was once the city's convention center and is now what amounts to a brutally refurbished, reinforced, windowless storage unit. Thousands of bodies shoved in that lightless place, shoulder to shoulder in darkened exhibit halls and cavernous ballrooms. Portland itself, sealed off, acts as the collation center's little spillover area. The walled city a stopgap measure, the way a saucer might catch a cup's spilled tea.

Kendall pulls a flake of tobacco from his tongue. His demands of Bonner have always been simple: Work the gangs, try to halt guns and dope getting over the wall, make sure dockworkers don't start getting popped for the goodies inside the containers. Work your cases, of which Bonner has no shortage. You see a fevered anywhere in the city that isn't in the collation center? There's been a mistake. Kill it or call it in.

His main ask: Keep your ear to the pulse of Portland's rotten heart. Listen. Gather information and relay it. Be a conduit.

Kendall's finally had enough of waiting. He pitches his cigarette over the concrete lip of the dock, down into the froth. "Alright, you win, John. What am I doing here?"

Bonner's been trying to figure out how to say it. "That thing at the Parade yesterday."

"What about it?"

"It's bugging me."

Kendall nods. "Okay. And?"

"It was a murder-suicide."

"Yeah, that's what Katz said."

"It was the Sight."

"I know."

Bonner stares out beyond the docks, watches the ripples of oily scum on top of the water. "What are we going to do about them, Dave?"

It's an interesting look Kendall gives him. Assessing, but Bonner's not sure what it is the man's gauging. Finally, he says, "I don't think we need to do anything."

"Really."

"They're fringe. The only people they hurt are themselves. It's a suicide cult. A fun little by-product of surviving Armageddon."

"Dave, if you'd seen that room—"

Kendall rolls his eyes. "What, I've never seen a body before? You want me to wax poetically about Sarajevo, John? Bosnia? Shit, I was in New York during the Message, you want to talk about a bloodbath. Give me a break."

It's the image of the eye they carve into their skin that keeps snagging at him. How there are three remnants that served as puzzle pieces in ending the world: a severed hand, a recording of a voice, and an eye. He's given the Sight little thought in his time working for Terradyne—Kendall's right, they mostly stay to themselves—but then he's never considered it, either: What if the Sight actually has possession of the eye, one of the remnants?

What if they're using it?

Softer, Kendall says, "They're pariahs, John. Why do you think you never see a Sighted on the street unless they're in packs? Because everybody—us, the gangs, the guy on the street corner digging through the trash, *everybody*—hates them. They're ghosts." It's like Kendall and Leo Katz sat down and went over their bullet points together.

"So there're three people slaughtered in a motel room," Bonner says, "and we just drop it?"

"No," Kendall says. "Crime scene finished working the room this morning. They'll give me the report when they're done. But with no defensive wounds? And a pattern of these types of events by these people? I won't lie, John, I'm not real concerned. What is there to investigate?"

"They could've been drugged. They could've been sleeping—"

"Medical examiner put a pistol in his mouth last month, if you recall, and we're still looking for a replacement. Our focus is on convictions—"

"Juryless convictions."

"—in front of a judge—"

"A Terradyne-appointed judge—"

"—Jesus *Christ*, you are stubborn. *Point being*, we need convictions, which means we need to solve cases that involve actual victims." Kendall's gone all singsongy now, like he's talking to a child. "Those dipshits in the Parade were not victims, John. They wanted to step out, and they did. That's it."

"Alright," Bonner says tightly.

Kendall nods. "We good?"

"Yeah, we're good, boss."

"And you're doing alright?"

Bonner looks at him. "What?"

"You sleeping? You look a little rough."

"Everyone keeps telling me that."

"Look, I know I'm chopping you off at the knees here. Do the best you can. We're all drowning, we just got to help each other stay afloat."

A gull cries and wheels overhead, settles on a post a few feet away from them. Tilts its head and fixes Bonner with one black, depthless eye. The barge's horn booms across the river, makes him flinch. Part of him wants to be back in that dark apartment on Eighty-second, sitting there on the couch, cradling the hand. Swimming in its horrors.

But there's the eye, the eye, the eye to think about.

"No," he says. "No, I hear you."

KATHERINE MORIARTY
Cape Winston, Massachusetts

A hard spit of rain is coming off the cape, the ocean gray and churning, mean little whitecaps in the froth. The jetty sticks out like a broken finger. Early evening, dark already, and Katherine Moriarty walks along the wet sand, leaning into the wind. Navigating twisted washes of gnarled driftwood, she sips at a ceramic mug of tea long gone cold.

They've been gifted with electricity in recent months, under the auspices of the Providence Initiative, something that she and the other residents of Cape Winston, Massachusetts, remain profoundly wary of. Still, to see the haloed streetlights in the little downtown area, there beyond the dunes? The way the rain's lit up beneath those lights, like droplets of white fire falling on the boardwalk? That's a marvel, no denying it.

She sees the limned shape of the burned church some stretch ahead, above a slowly sloping rise of beach dotted with crabgrass and more driftwood. The shape is simply an outline, a small black crag of ink against the darker night sky. She knows it by sight, has made it a habit to walk toward it each night after work.

Wind sends a gray-black shock of her hair into her mouth, her eyes, and she spends a moment tying it back with a rubber band from her pocket. In the five years since the Message, Katherine's grown her hair out, her frame has turned sinewy, catgut. There have been years of lightlessness and hunger and she tells herself she's already lost everything that matters.

She lifts the mug to her lips, drains it, tips the last dregs onto the wet sand. Occasional headlights prowl the coastline road some hundred yards away. She last saw another person twenty minutes before, a man walking his border collie; he'd been bundled in a neon green Jane poncho, a handout from Terradyne workers trying to curry favor with the populace. The two of them had nodded at each other, kept their distance in the dark. She places the empty mug in her satchel.

Another five minutes and the staggered lean of the church has grown closer. Katherine crests the final dune, her feet squeaking in the sand, and then crosses the street and stands before the ruins. There's evidence enough of devils in her life—real ones, actual ones—and still she can't find any sort of lasting interest in God. A God that would lay waste to the world like this? Do what He's done to Katherine and those she loves? It seems proof only of His profound absence, moral or otherwise.

So, her journey: a nightly sojourn to the church. She imagines sometimes that she actually does find God there, all curled inside the charred frame. Imagines what He might say when He's discovered. Imagines what she might say back. But really, this is a nothing-place. A mad tumble of blackened brick, a jigsaw puzzle of scorched timbers. Debris for the rats to run through. Certainly nothing holy.

She turns back without going inside. Tonight will be the same as last night and the night before. She'll visit Nick and then curl up on the couch in her little cottage with a book and a fire. Go to work in the morning. Finish, walk the beach, turn around, go to bed.

Do it again after that.

Katherine heads home.

She makes a fire, drinks more tea, reads a Richard Price novel she'd found in a free library at the bottom of Lark Street. She feels herself drifting off on the couch, the wind pushing against the eaves, when a pocket of sap explodes in a log in the fireplace and she jerks awake. She'd been in a kind of half-dream, remembering Matthew in the townhouse in Chicago, the sound of the pistol shot she'd fired down the hall at the body running toward her.

It bothers her, the dream. She rarely dreams of Matthew and the townhouse these days; it's a section of her life that she has worked hard to compartmentalize, in spite of the obvious reminders. She takes a hot bath—another marvel, that—and then sits on her bed for a while, drying her hair and staring at the wall. There's neither calmness nor terror inside of her, but instead a kind of grand vacuousness, an *unfeeling* that is as close to peace as Katherine gets now. After a while, she stands and dresses herself in a pair of coveralls. A heavy coat, a scarf. Thick winter gloves. Boots. She's careful to tuck the sleeves into the gloves. She looks at the time.

It's 3:17 in the morning, as dead as the night gets.

Katherine walks outside. The rain is gone; the moon's bright enough to see by.

She steps out into her backyard. Green grass and a walking path of paving stones. A pair of hydrangeas that flank the back door— Katherine thinks they're ugly and grandmotherly but maintains them as a kind of homage and thanks to the house's previous owner. Against the rear fence is a corrugated metal shed with a large iron bolt run through a pair of eyelets in the doors. Katherine walks across the yard to slap the doors once, twice, three times.

She fishes the bolt from the eyelets and puts it in her pocket. The doors slowly open.

Her son, Nick, stands there.

He is lashed to a steel post set in the floor. His body is wound in chains, his arms pinned to his sides. Dressed in a filthy T-shirt and black jeans, he sees her and snarls, moonlight smeared across his teeth. His jaws snap shut and open again. His eyes are lifeless and empty as cast-off pieces of plastic and she wants to spend a moment looking for something in them, for some kind of change, some kind of love or at least awareness, but the chains around him hiss and clank as he pulls. He's trying to get at her, jaws clacking like casta-nets.

"Hi, baby," Katherine says softly. "I missed you today."

She fishes two black nylon sacks from her jacket, her fingers clumsy in the gloves, and puts one first over Nick's head. He becomes featureless, shapeless beneath it. Then she pulls the second one over her own head, the world going black, so that they might share the same world of darkness. In this way she might join him, be the same as him. Just for a little while.

Maybe I've gone mad, she thinks. Considers one more time that perhaps the heart just wasn't made for this sort of thing.

She lays her arms around him.

Katherine hugs her boy, her fevered son, and talks to him in that shared darkness. Her words muffled against the fabric. She tells him how much she loves him, how proud she is of him, how good a man he remains. Even now. The cold shape of him bucks and writhes against her. The clack of his teeth by her ear. The chains clink and hiss as she holds his strange, furious body against her own. Katherine's heart breaks once again, breaks a million times, breaks forever as she touches the heatless curve of his skull and tells him again and again he is *good*, he is *loved*, she's so sorry, he is a good man, a good boy.

FROM: JACK BONNER
<J.BONNER@TERRADYNE.GOV>

TO: THEO MARSDEN <T.MARSDEN@TERRADYNE.GOV>

DATE: OCTOBER 18, 20XX, 5:29 PM

SUBJECT: MESSAGE TRANSCRIPTION / CLASSIFIED

Theo,

Yes, you already have copies of this in your files, but I figured a digital version would be easier to send out to your team. I know we've long been running with a skeleton crew here—doing the impossible, really, which is especially impressive, given everything we've managed to accomplish—but all of my intel indicates that the recording (i.e., Matthew Coffin's voice that was captured on David Lundy's thumb drive) has been permanently lost. I blame myself, of course. Those post-Message hours were insane, as I'm sure you remember. If the drive, or the original source material, *is* somehow discovered, it's unlikely that it can ever be broadcast with any significance again. Of course, the odds of that might change once we meet Providence's eventual infrastructure goals. We'll cross that bridge, etc.

Anyway, looking forward to when we can actually get down to brass tacks and start investigating how all this happened. Believe me when I say I had a very specific target list of places for the Message to be broadcast, and I still don't know how the equipment—or that damn engineer—could have made such a massive targeting error. It weighs on me.

That said, here's the transcript of the recording that was broadcast. It reads like gobbledygook to me, like a man having a breakdown, but clearly there's no denying its effectiveness as an aural weapon.

Safe to say that you should keep this close to your vest and not share with the whole world, newly encrypted government email system or not.

Also goes without saying, but in spite of everything, I'm proud to be working on this project with you. Providence is an apt name for what we're doing, friend.

Best,
Jack

**RESTRICTED—HIGHLY CLASSIFIED—
INTER-GOVERNMENTAL USE ONLY—CLOSED**
DATE: XX/XX/XXXX

PROPERTY OF TERRADYNE INDUSTRIES
TERRADYNE ARCHIVES

RE: OPERATION: HEAVY LIGHT
RESTRICTED—CLOSED—CLASSIFIED IN-AGENCY
PERSONNEL ONLY—DESTROY UPON RECEIPT

(S/NF/CL-INTEL-CLOSED) Below is a transcript of a field re-cording discovered, purportedly, on an unused hard drive located in Dynar Laboratories in Beaverton, Oregon, a suburb of Portland. Dynar Laboratories was, at the time of discovery, headed by Dr. Je-rome Finch. Finch and his team were working under the command of ARC Agency Director David Lundy, within the confluence of the OPERATION: HEAVY LIGHT program. At the time of the re-cording's discovery, one of HEAVY LIGHT's mission objectives was the exploration of sonic warfare/psychological control opportu-nities through sound modulation experiments.

(S/NF/CL-INTEL-CLOSED) It is believed that the subject speak-ing here is Matthew Coffin. (See Addendum A-34 for an informa-tional link to Matthew Coffin's files.) As noted, both Director Finch and Director Lundy are now deceased and no longer available for questioning (see Memorandum A-19/13 for more information).

(S/NF/CL-INTEL-CLOSED) The recording is 00:59 seconds in duration. A single "bump" in volume can be heard approximately 00:09 seconds into the recording; investigators have surmised this might have been caused by the Subject bumping the microphone or someone dropping something near the recording device. The Subject speaks in a monotone; linguists have noted inflections in certain words and glottal stops, as well as an overall "accent," that place the speaker as residing and having spent significant time in the Pacific Northwest, though this remains speculative. Based on a variety of factors, it is believed that the voice throughout the en-tirety of the recording—as well as the Subject weeping from 00:29 to 00:50—belongs to a single individual, though, again, it remains possible that other nonspeaking individuals were present.

(S/NF/CL-INTEL-CLOSED) See Departmental Report PRI-3321-6, *Physiognomic and Physical Effects of Base Field Recording on Subjects* and numerous memorandums and reports regarding the effect the broadcasted recording had on the global populace.

(S/NF/CL-INTEL-CLOSED) Transcript of the recording in its entirety is as follows. Recording begins mid-sentence.

00:00–00:29:—if I tell you to sever the head of your neighbor, yes, to dine in the bowl of their skull, you do it, and we might call that fealty. If I tell you to make me a necklace from the heads of your children, to make me a red veil from their latticed veins that I might lay on my brow, you'll curtsy on bloody knees and crow, "Yes, Father!" and you'll ready the knife. And we might call that fealty as well. I say cut out your eye, you slice away. Take your hand off at the wrist, you whet the blade and get to work. That too is fealty. You understand? Yes? Make me a king's house from this whole place. How I use your voice now, how I speak through you, the sorrowful jaw working just so. How you might remake the world for me. A king's house among all the leaning world. You shall make me a house of fever and wounds. A house of beetle and crow. A house of worms. A house of hounds that savage forever at the belly of love and take root there, devouring.

00:29–00:50: SUBJECT weeps.

00:51–00:59: Cut here, here, here. Avail yourself to me. Make me a house of fever and wounds, where all rooms are ghastly and dark. Do it. Make me a king's house, and you will have all you ever wanted.

(S/NF/CL-INTEL-CLOSED) END RECORDING
PROPERTY OF TERRADYNE INDUSTRIES
FOR GOVERNMENTAL USE ONLY

THEO MARSDEN

Rolla, Missouri

Theo Marsden, CEO of Terradyne Industries, walks through the front entrance of what had once been the Agriculture Building of the Missouri University of Science and Technology in Rolla, Missouri. The man's suit is pressed and tailored. He carries a briefcase in one hand—always been a briefcase man, Marsden, always loved the theater of it, the *ostentation,* and finds himself in this moment profoundly, ridiculously grateful for the opportunity to be a briefcase man again. His polished oxfords clack smartly on the floor. Through the lobby and down a number of hallways, he eventually comes to a conference room and nods at the security flanking the door, a pair of hard-faced boys in Terradyne fatigues, assault rifles slung across their chests. There's a badge on a lanyard around Marsden's neck that he's used to get into the building, and this too is a thing that he's grateful for. No, Christ, he's grateful for *all* of it: the badge, the lanyard, the clean floors, the smell of fresh paint still in the air. The sense of *industry* here, movement. These stoic boys with their guns, their willingness to protect this place and the bodies that populate it. To protect men like Marsden. How could he not be grateful for that? How could he not be moved? It all means the same thing: The world is finally stopping its wayward lean.

I'm righting this ship, he thinks. At last.

One of the boys—Derrick Eastman, his personal security—opens the door for him. Marsden winks, steps inside, Eastman shutting the door behind him. Decent-sized room, and it's been swept for bugs, he's been told, though if any of the cratered shitholes that once made up their enemy nations actually have the capability for that level of subterfuge these days, Marsden would be surprised. The past five years have done a lot to cool off the world's geopolitical problems. An apocalypse will do that. Most other supposed superpowers, according to reports, are currently a seething miasma of famine and fevered right now.

Marsden's greeted by a number of familiar faces. Some he's known for decades, long before the Message—Jack Bonner, for instance, his partner at Terradyne, he's known for nearly fifty years, since they were kids at UCLA. Nearly everyone present is an older man like himself, and dressed sharply in their own suit. Marsden looks on approvingly. It's only after having it all taken away that you forget about things like this. The fit of a jacket over your shoulders, how it lands just so. The precise knotting of a tie. Gleam of a wingtip. It simply means more now.

The men sit at a U-shaped set of tables, while against one wall is a smaller table set up with packets of instant coffee, pitchers of water. A twelve-pack of Jane cola. Fresh muffins.

God, he loves it. Moved to his core by the sanctity of a paper cup, a stir straw. Hot water! How much literal death have they all waded through to be here, to marvel at an electric kettle of hot water?

Twenty people in the room. The United States government's Providence Committee. Tasked with rebuilding the country, simply put, with Marsden and Jack Bonner leading the way. The Committee's a quilting of senators and congressmen, national security advisors, and former members of Terradyne's board of directors, men who have managed to navigate the past half decade without getting killed or made fevered. Twenty figureheads in the merger that brought together the fractured remains of the government and Terradyne, the largest defense contractor on the planet. Twenty people who are remaking the world.

Marsden takes a seat at the head of the table—what's the point in playing it humble? He's never minimized his ambition, why start now?

"The president couldn't make it, unfortunately," he says, smoothing down his tie, earning a decent-sized laugh from the group. He waits, gives Jack a small smile where he sits to Marsden's right, and everyone slowly settles, their faces bright and expectant. Jack, he's sure, probably considers the dig at President Yardley a cheap shot, but it's all intentional, all curated. He wants this committee to feel insular, self-contained, confident. And the simple fact is, he truly doubts Preston Yardley will ever leave Washington, DC, again. The man is terrified, and lives in his own delicately crafted Oz, yelling bold proclamations from behind his curtain. Even with his obsession with Matthew Coffin and the remnants, he's more likely to handcuff himself to a fevered than ever get on a plane to Missouri. Still, Jack surprises Marsden and offers him a nod. He understands what the man is doing, even if he doesn't approve. Neither of them are stupid.

"Jokes aside," Marsden says, serious now, "I want to thank you all for coming. I know getting here for our first in-person meeting was not easy. Not everyone's got personal air travel at their disposal." He fixes Dan Fitzpatrick—Wyoming senator and billionaire beef tycoon, a man who's managed to maintain a fleet of private planes through all of this—with a wolfish grin.

Fitzpatrick puffs up at the attention, lifts a hand in recognition. "Happy to help out any other Committee member that needs it, Theo. We're all working toward the same thing here."

Steve Stater, who'd been a House member in Montana in the Before times, and has somehow lost two fingers on his right hand in the preceding years, says, "Might just take you up on that, Dan."

"Let's talk after the meeting, my friend."

Marsden sits there for a moment, letting that feeling wash over him. The room is filled with good intentions and men with the willingness to do what's necessary.

"Alright," he says, "let's get started. There's a lot to tackle, and we'll need everyone with clear eyes on this. Jack," he says, "can you give us a rundown on where we're at with Providence? We've officially entered Phase Two, and there're quite a few moving parts to consider."

Bonner stands up. He's still a spry man, though both he and Marsden are within breathing reach of seventy. He walks over to a blank screen mounted on the wall and someone dims the lights. The projector springs on, and Bonner starts his pitch. Despite his call for clearheadedness and attention, Marsden almost immediately feels his eyes begin to droop. Jack's their numbers man, but he's never been much of a public speaker. Marsden stands and goes to make himself a cup of coffee; he and Jack have gone over the Providence objectives so often, he could recite them in his sleep. All the pieces are in place. There will, of course, be the inevitable hiccups: The militias have taken root in a way that's surprised them all, and Jane as national spokesperson, an image of American resiliency, has yet to catch on with folks the way she had in the focus groups. Still, you put the paddles to a country's heart to kick-start it again, there's bound to be some discomfort at first.

He comes back to himself, hears Jack's voice, a little more sonorous now, having warmed up to his presentation: ". . . so all these other objectives aside, we're now looking at a one-in-four collation number, per Dr. Suarez's report. Meaning one in four afflicted individuals is to be detained and shipped to the nearest collation center, where they'll be tagged and monitored and pretty much shoved out of sight."

"And that'll be enough to ensure an adequate pool of subjects for the vaccine?" someone asks.

"Absolutely. Looked over the paperwork myself. Everything seems sound." Marsden winces at Jack's use of *seems*. Words like that, they're like chum in the water. He should know better. "So let's talk about the other seventy-five percent of the afflicted."

"Light 'em up," Fitzpatrick crows. Laughter popcorns around the darkened room.

Jack clears his throat; even in the dark, Marsden can read his discomfort. They've never seen eye to eye on the one-in-four ratio. It's a divide that's reflected not only in this room, but across the country. They were people, the fevered, and now they're not. Now they're both more than that, and vastly less than. They're monsters, Marsden thinks, though Jack still believes a vaccine will be able to pull them back from whatever hellish amber they've been put in.

Focus groups are divided. Some look at a fevered and see their loved one trapped inside, and others simply see the monster. But Marsden wishes Jack could comprehend a simple truth: It doesn't matter what the focus groups think. It matters what the *Committee* thinks. They've all gotten here by their abject willingness to kill, and they want killers to lead them. If Jack vies for the gentler approach, he'll lose, every time.

"*Light 'em up* is the general idea, yes," Jack says stiffly. "Hunter teams have been notified that three out of four afflicted are to be dispatched. 'Invalidation' is the term we're using in the literature."

"And you're fine with that," says Alan Brentsworth, a heavyset man with a gray mustache. He'd been a senior deputy at the NSA, and Marsden realizes that Brentsworth is giving Jack a chance to voice his displeasure. He makes a point to keep an eye on the two of them.

"I am," Jack says, after only the briefest pause. "For now. We all understand how volatile the situation is. It's pointless to try and grow corn and tobacco and whatnot, grow these crops or run a cannery, give out food to a starving populace, if you have to worry about the damn farmers getting overrun by a drift in the first place."

There's a moment where everyone considers it. "Any questions?" Jack asks. There aren't, so he walks over and turns the light on, twenty old men blinking owlishly in the light.

"Now that we've gotten that out of the way," he says, "I'd like to ask Dr. Anita Suarez to come in." He opens the door. Dr. Suarez is a

small-boned Latina woman with cat's-eye glasses and a black pony-
tail. Marsden expects her to be wearing a lab coat like she has during
every one of their previous interactions, but she walks into the conference room in a green silk blouse and smart, tapered charcoal pants.
If she's concerned about being the only woman in the room—and
the youngest by twenty years, probably—it doesn't show.

"Doctor," Jack says, sitting back down in his chair, Marsden still
at his perch in front of the coffee. "Now that Phase Two of the Initiative has begun, I was hoping you might debrief us on matters
pertaining to the vaccine." Jack showboating a little, hamming it up
in front of the pretty lady.

"You bet, Mr. Bonner, thank you." Dr. Suarez takes a deep breath
and smiles. "Hello, everyone," she says. "I'll begin by noting that, in
regards to our work on the vaccine, the one-in-four ratio that we've
established is well suited for an adequate subject pool. But in my
opinion, it doesn't address the more humane issue of it all."

"Oh Christ. She's a scientist *and* a liberal, Jack?" This from Steve
Stater.

Suarez looks to Jack for help, but before he can say anything,
Marsden says, "Doctor, I mean this with all due respect, but you're
out of line. The moral repercussions of the ratio rest squarely on this
committee's shoulders."

"Mr. Marsden—"

"Enough. Please. Continue with your presentation."

"And spare us the proselytizing," Stater mutters.

Suarez walks over and turns off the lights. When she starts speaking, her words are precise and clipped with anger. "Gentlemen, I
have mixed news for you. The good news is, a vaccine—we're calling
it IVAR-5—has been developed."

Murmurs throughout the room.

Here Suarez nods at Jack and another slide appears on the wall of
the conference room, a pie chart of multicolored wedges.

"As of now," she says, "IVAR-5 has a fourteen percent efficacy
rate."

"Jesus Christ," someone mutters.

"I won't get into the math," she says, "given the breadth of this committee's interest in such things, but I will say that we are obviously not meeting the projected benchmarks necessary for Phase Three's success at this time. And to be clear, a fourteen percent efficacy rate does not mean that we're injecting a hundred afflicted with the vaccine and fourteen are cured. Far from it. It means," and here another slide flashes on the wall, "that we're meeting fourteen percent of the mental, physical and physiological touchpoints for what we consider a 'cured' patient."

Here, Jack opens a binder and begins passing out booklets to each of the men seated at the conference table. A few thumb through them while most stare glassy-eyed at the square of light on the wall. "None of the major benchmarks—cognitive function, pain reception, basic speech—have yet to be met. Even minor goals, things independent of cognition—reduction of ophthalmoplegia, for example—we're still far behind on."

Fitzpatrick, one arm slung over the back of his chair, says, "So in what way *are* they being cured?"

Suarez's shadow is massive behind her, flung up onto the wall and part of the slide. She sees this and takes a step back. "In nearly every subject, an injection of IVAR-5 elicits no change. No physiognomic differences, nothing physical, electrical. The afflicted's blood, even, is as viscous as ever. But in those that IVAR-5 *does* affect—and we're talking less than half a percent of test subjects here, gentlemen— the vaccine shows an initial, definable improvement to a number of touchpoints. A marked change in brain function, particularly notable given the inflammation the 'fever' wreaks upon the myelin coating of the nerves in their brains and spinal cords. There's marked physiognomic improvement. Heartbeat returns to somewhat normal levels. Ophthalmoplegia—that telltale 'deadness' or lack of movement in the eyes—diminishes. Some pain receptors even begin working again."

"Great," Stater says. "But only fourteen percent? Seems to me the simple question is, how do we raise that number. Right?"

Suarez pauses, looks to Jack Bonner again for support. Another little something Marsden would do well to keep his eye on.

"The difficulty is that for the small percentage of subjects who do experience these improvements, it lasts for an average of eighty-two to ninety-two seconds."

Silence in the room, the men trying to decipher that.

"Okay," says Fitzpatrick, drawing the word out, "so what happens after ninety-two seconds?"

Unflinching, Suarez says, "Roughly half the subjects return back to their afflicted state, and the rest, so far, have expired."

"What do you mean, expired?"

"I mean they died."

The room quiets again, everyone sitting with it.

"Hell," Fitzpatrick finally says, "it's not much of a goddamn vaccine then, is it? Sounds more like a weapon to me."

"Expensive-ass bullet," someone mutters.

"It's damn well not anything we can sell people on," Marsden says at the side of the room. A few heads turn his way in the dark. "We need a hell of a lot more, Doctor, than half a percent of them getting cured for, what? A minute and a half? Jesus wept."

"I understand," says Dr. Suarez.

Fitzpatrick tosses his booklet on the table. "I think we all know what's going on here."

"What's that, Fitzy?" Stater says.

"It's obvious to me and anyone else with an ounce of faith. We're trying to use science to cure the devil's doing."

"Hear, hear," Stater says.

"I mean, we all appreciate what you did, Jack. Portland was being overrun by these things, and if Russia or China or who the hell ever had gotten wind of it? We'd have been nuked back to the Stone Age, I have no doubt. You made an impossible call and leveled the playing field before that could happen. But let's be honest. That recording y'all played? That's the devil talking, and these things left over are born of the devil, and I am of the opinion that prayer and decisive, lethal action are the only things that will solve any of this."

"Dan," Jack says. "Research and study are our best bets for solving this—"

"Come on over to Carey Avenue. The Financial Building over in Cheyenne. That's our little containment center. Come smell five thousand of these things shoved in a building, Jack, tell me how good your research is working out."

"We're getting off track here," Jack says, rising and turning on the lights again.

Fitzpatrick taps a finger against Suarez's report. "I'm just informing you of what the rest of us already know. You're trying to fit the damn devil in a test tube, Jack, when a bullet is what you need."

"What the hell was that," Jack hisses, loosening his tie. He and Marsden are walking across the courtyard to their offices while a cold wind blows through the promenade, sending up little whirlwinds of dead leaves. There's scaffolding everywhere, tied-off piles of lumber under tarps; refurbishment of the college has been slow going, due to both lack of manpower and scarcity of supplies.

"What do you mean," Marsden says, playing dumb, getting a little thrill from Jack's fury. They've finished their glad-handing with the rest of the Committee; once Marsden gets to his office, he'll call President Yardley and fill him in on the Initiative's progress, or lack thereof. It's very likely that Yardley will hear Suarez's dismal numbers and shitcan the entire vaccine program. He knows Jack's worried about that same scenario.

"Where were you?" Jack says beside him. "You left Anita in the wind, Theo. She was dying up there."

"Oh, it's 'Anita' now?"

"Go to hell," Jack spits.

The last of the winter snow lies in delicate, gritty fantails on the campus grass. Another gust of wind buffets them and Marsden dips his head down against it, smiling into the collar of his coat. "The numbers are what killed the vaccine, Jack. Not me."

"The Committee needs to present a united front to Yardley," Jack says. "We need to show faith in Suarez's capabilities. Belief in the process. And you're letting Fitzpatrick run his mouth about the *devil,* for Christ's sake."

Coyly, Marsden says, "You think he's wrong?"

"Goddamnit, Theo."

"Look, you should be happy. If I called Yardley up and suggested we move forward with total eradication of the afflicted, what do you think he'd say?"

Jack draws back from him, horrified. "They're *people,* Theo. Your *children* were turned! Your grandchildren! What would Barbara have said if she heard you talking like that in there—"

Marsden turns, all slyness gone. Puts a finger in Jack's face. "Not another word about Barbara."

Jack's mouth opens and closes, too stunned to talk.

Marsden's unmoved. "I'm just being honest with you. Yardley wants a handle on these things and hunter teams are way more viable and *clearly* more effective than a vaccine. That's just the truth of it."

"Theo—"

Marsden starts ticking things off on his fingers. "He wants a strong military and renewed law enforcement presence. He wants taxes, lights that work, football games on TV. He wants convictions in courtrooms of troublesome individuals. Any dissent needs to be dealt with now, not later. The fucking militias have already got too big a foothold as it is, politically and otherwise. He wants to consider annexation, either north or south. Not today, not this year, but eventually."

Marsden steps toward him, lowers his voice. "And you should be prepared for an eventuality that includes shutting down the vaccine program, Jack. You know what Yardley wants to do."

"Wipe out the fevered."

"Wipe out the fevered, yes. And use all seventeen of those cities as prisons. Eventually get those folks inside doing some sort of labor, something to better the country. But we can't have any kind of upheaval going on. Country's too fragile for it. We convict anyone who doesn't toe the line, doesn't pull their weight, put 'em behind those walls. Let that be a lesson to everyone else. And, Jack, he wants us to do something with the man in the box."

In that moment, Marsden can see the young man Jack had been at UCLA, there on the beach in Venice, both of them laughing, tanned, stoned more likely than not, watching the girls pass by. He remembers the conflict he'd seen writ large on Jack's face when Terradyne had brokered their first deal—a dozen Stinger missiles sold to an admittedly questionable rebel group in Guyana, the two of them not even twenty-five years old at the time. Jack, always and forever with that look of carefully measured consideration about him. Marsden knows that the Message haunts him, murders his sleep at night. But he also knows—knew then, even—that sometimes you just have to shut your eyes and jump if you want to get things done.

"You can't be picking and choosing at this point, Jack. Not anymore. The world ended because of you."

"Fuck you, Theo," he says with surprising heat. "I don't *know* what happened. It wasn't the order I gave and you know it."

"I'm just saying. Here we are. Choices were made. You want to rebuild the world? You want to help people? They need to feel safe again."

"I am absolutely against any use of the Coffin asset," Jack says. "I won't allow it. I'll tell Preston that too. Coffin can rot in that box for all I care."

Marsden smiles; Jack showing a bit of spine. "You know Yardley can override you." Unspoken, but implied: *You know I can too.*

Jack shrugs, looks out at some interminable point, turns back to him. "Then I'll quit."

"What good will that do?"

"We don't even know *what the hell he is,* Theo."

Marsden moves a step closer, tries to bridge the gap between them. Putting a hand on Jack's shoulder, he says in a conciliatory tone, "What's the idea we've always operated under? Terradyne's first tenet?"

Jack shakes his head, looks out at the skeletal trees, the staggered lean of materials in their loose piles. "He's not human, Theo. The afflicted, they're one thing. They're people, deep down. They might be able to be changed back somehow. But Matthew Coffin, he's different."

"What's the one thing, Jack? That we've always worked under?"

Jack sighs, looks out at the trees again. "If we don't make the sale," he says, "someone else will."

"That's right. Same goes for Coffin. We have this *thing,* Jack. This strange, dangerous, tremendously powerful *thing.*" Marsden squeezes his shoulder and says softly, "We need to use him while we can."

NAOMI LAURENT

Nevers, Bourgogne-Franche-Comté region, France

Always, always, there is the barter to be considered.

Denis loves the barter.

The table where they're seated, a large and rustic wooden thing, the top of it glossed smooth and dark by years of use, sits in the middle of the kitchen. Naomi wonders if the rest of the house is like this: well worn, but beautifully curated. She wouldn't know—she, Denis and Emilie were ferried from a side door straight to the kitchen, their sense of being interlopers confirmed by the way the bulk of the house is closed off to them. The woman who'd greeted them at the door—mid-thirties, dour, wispy auburn hair shot through with gray—has retreated elsewhere after asking them to wait. Naomi wonders how old the table is, how many thousands of meals have been taken here. As ever, Denis offers no information about who these people are, how they've contacted him. Naomi is not an equal; she is a tool. The table stands in stark contrast to the brushed-steel appliances on the counters, the oak-topped island. It's a massive kitchen, clean, with a picture window that overlooks the

road and the idyllic green field and its cows. You'd never know, looking out there, what sort of world it's become on the other side of the
glass.

The woman comes back with a man in tow. There's a lean and
hunted look about him, and Naomi recognizes it immediately for
what it is: He's desperate.

"Thank you for coming," he says. His eyes bounce between Denis
and Emilie, as if afraid of what might happen should he stare at
Naomi too long.

Denis pushes off the wall and offers a hand. The man takes it, and
when Denis asks him to tell what happened, the man's face floods
with a mixture of emotions. She sees fear, confusion, guilt, sorrow.
All in a span of seconds.

"Does it matter?" the woman asks, and then dips her head after
the man turns and gives her a sharp look. She walks past Naomi to a
carafe on the kitchen counter, pours herself some water. Naomi's
stomach gurgles, but she says nothing; propriety is as much a part of
the barter as anything else. She'll get her food and water after she's
done.

The man is thin and haggard; he might be handsome, but the
depth of those feelings inside him have turned him into something
else. He needs a haircut, Naomi thinks. They all need haircuts.

Denis quietly assures the woman that everything matters.

The man tucks a hank of hair behind his ear and then shoves his
hands in the pockets of his jeans, stares at the floor. "We lived in
Nice," he says. "His mother and me." Naomi's eyes cut to the woman,
who in turn looks to the floor. She's not the mother then, she and the
man coming together after. "When the Message came, Antoine—
that's his name—was just an infant. Thirteen months. I was outside,
readying the garden." He shakes his head. "Just, you know, messing
around. It was a thing that calmed me, gardening."

"Sure," Denis says softly.

"Amanda—my wife—she was the one that got the call." He looks out the window and then steels himself to finish. "She answered it. She was affected, of course." Naomi feels a thudding sense of inevitability to this. The mirroring of her own horrors.

"I'm sorry," Denis says. He does this sometimes—surprises Naomi with his diplomacy. Denis is a killer, but he is political with his kindnesses.

"I, we—Amanda didn't survive. So it was just me and Antoine. Just me and this baby."

Naomi thinks of her mother in their living room, sun-shot and bright, Naomi dizzy with the flu as she'd trod down the stairway of their little house. Seeing her brother Hugo's twitching fingers on the floor. The inhuman sounds her mother had made. The widening pool of blood on the floor.

"We survived in Nice as long as we could, but the city got too dangerous. Me with a baby? Trying to find formula? Find food, with raiders and murderers everywhere? There were so many fevered there, and Antoine, he was always crying."

Naomi's throat clicks. She shuts her eyes. No one pays any attention to her.

"Outside of Planfoy—God, I was so fucking tired by then, so frightened—I left him to go wash myself. It was just a moment. There was a little creek bed there, just a moment to myself, he was sleeping, bundled up, and I heard him cry out," his voice cracking now, "I was so fast, it wasn't more than a second, but a woman, a woman was leaning over him, biting him, biting at his arms—" His voice has a rushed, brittle cadence to it, like each word is a splintered thing being forced from his throat.

"He changed," the man says, still staring at the floor. "He's so small, it was only minutes later."

"I'm so sorry," Emilie says, and she sounds sincere.

"I came here," he says, gesturing toward the woman, "to Lisette's home, and here we've been."

Denis says, "You brought your baby from Planfoy to Nevers?"

"On foot, yes."

"That must be two hundred fifty kilometers. And he was turned?"

"I put him in my pack." The man scrubs at his mouth. "I put a bandanna over his face." He cracks a single, unlovely laugh. "He has six teeth. They're very small." He fixes them with a smile that's as close to madness as any she's seen. "And so," he says brightly, "we have heard of you," gesturing at Denis, "and we've heard of her, and what she can do."

"You know our prices?"

"You told me a working gun, a week's worth of food for three, or a thousand euros."

Denis nods. "Which do you prefer?"

"But can she do it? Can she—"

"She can do it. Which do you prefer?"

The man spares a glance at Lisette—his sister? An old lover, one taken before his wife died?—and then walks through the doorway, comes back with a stack of currency. He hands it to Denis, who counts it and puts it in one of the pockets of his pants. The hotel last night had cost them twelve euros for two rooms and the breakfast.

"Where's the baby?"

The man shuts his eyes for a moment and then motions them toward the doorway, further into the house. Denis holds up a hand to Emilie, who sits back down, hurt. Perhaps he doesn't want Naomi to be too crowded down there. God only knows what rattles around in Denis's brain.

They're led through the living room, all dark wood and a scatter of framed photos on the walls, faces passing by too fast to see. He brings them to a stairwell. The stairs creak beneath their feet, and Naomi is enveloped in the press of mold and damp walls. The sound of the generator grows louder as they descend. They step into a large, sunken basement with a few naked bulbs throwing out yellow light. Support beams carve up the open space. Yes, this woman Lisette, this man, they certainly do have resources, don't they? Cows. Propane. A thousand euros ready to give away. Naomi sees a pair of wine racks, each filled with dozens of bottles.

Somewhere down here, the baby lets out a screech, and Naomi's heart floods with ice.

The man leads them to a small alcove where Denis's head brushes one of the overhead bulbs and the room is lit in a mad swing of illumination, shadows bending and twisting all around them.

Naomi has seen people come up with countless entrapments meant to contain the fevered, who don't seem to feel any pain. She's seen a fevered man turn his own hands into a red, boneless mess in an attempt to free himself from a pair of handcuffs. You put a fevered in a room with a living person and a thousand blades between them, the fevered will cut herself to ribbons trying to get through. Trying to contain them is like trying to capture the wind. They're elemental, of singular intention. They can be held captive, they can be dismembered, but short of beheading or some kind of vital brain interruption, they will not be stopped. Naomi's seen any number of terrible, unforgettable things over the past five years.

But she's never seen a fevered baby.

There's no need to lash this one down or lock it up.

It's too small for such things.

The man has simply stacked some cardboard boxes in front of the doorway to block any escape. The alcove is roughly four-by-four feet. Size of a closet. There's a blanket on the floor. Naomi sees toys on the ground too—a stuffed elephant, a plastic baby book, a rattle—and feels some vital part of her heart come unmoored. She thinks of Hugo and suddenly wants to vomit.

The baby is gray. He wears a matted onesie black with filth. He lies on his back, kicking and gurgling, and when he sees them, his eyes widen and he begins rocking until he manages to turn himself over. He crawls to the stack of boxes and pulls himself up. Blood vessels have bloomed red in the whites of his eyes. His mouth opens, little nubs in the gray gums. His jaw snaps shut and he reaches for them.

She turns and presses her hand to her lips. Swallows the nausea down. The generator chugs and kicks over, the lights flickering for an instant.

"He hasn't grown," the man says. "Not in five years. He doesn't cry, he doesn't sleep. Just lies there, and when he sees me, he tries to bite." He's weeping now. "Six teeth. You wear your gloves, you wear your heavy shirt." He scrubs at his eyes. "I try to hold him sometimes and he just pushes and bites."

Denis puts a stilling hand on the other man's shoulder, and it might look like a gesture of comfort, but Naomi knows that it isn't. He's gently steering him back away from the alcove.

"She needs to be alone with the child," Denis says, and this is new, new and decidedly untrue, and some part of her, even as she catalogs the quiet horrors of the situation, some part of her *knows* what Denis is doing. The part of her that saw the wine bottles, the cows, the generator, the money, some part of her *knows,* and still she reaches down for the child, reaches to touch him, to change him back, a larger part of her insisting *Denis won't do it, not with the woman upstairs, he's not that crazy.*

And *still* she screams at the sound of the gunshot, bright in the closed-in space of the basement.

She is still screaming, in fact, as the child's little jaws snap at her, as her fingers graze the cold crown of his head. Denis pulls her from the alcove.

"Don't bother," he says in her ear.

Naomi is babbling. "Please, Denis, please, it's a *baby,* let me help the baby, I can change him back," but he pulls her over the man's body and up the stairs. He drags her by one arm as she screams. He pushes through the door upstairs and through the living room and to the kitchen, where Emilie looks at the two of them wild-eyed, the butcher knife still dripping in her hand. Blood stippling her face. The woman—Lisette, was it?—splayed in a red pool on the tile at her feet. Slash marks on those pale hands.

"I heard the shots," Emilie says, sounding stunned, pulled from some dream. "I thought this was right."

"Well done," Denis says. It is as close to praise as he's ever come with either of them, and Naomi decides to just keep screaming forever.

DEAN HAGGERTY

Bent Valley, Kentucky

They get him at dusk.

Dean's on Highway 80 when it happens, half an hour past the unfortunately named town of Stab, Kentucky. He's passing over a crack-slabbed bridge with greenery choking both sides of the drop-off when he hears a vehicle behind him. Here it is, he thinks. The bridge is free of cars, but the cart will make a quick escape impossible.

He coasts to a stop at the far end of the bridge, gets off the bike and turns around. Turns out it's actually two trucks, big-wheeled, gleaming. One's black, the other a vibrant Day-Glo orange so ugly it's beautiful. The headlights pin him. His heart slamming in his throat, Dean slowly reaches into the saddlebag hung on the frame of his bike. There's a small seven-round Ruger pistol in there; he's brandished the thing more times than he can count and never once fired it at anyone. Couple guys are standing in the truck beds, limned by the headlights. Dean squints against the light, pistol hanging loosely at his side.

"Howdy," one of them calls out. So friendly. Every shit-kicking racist he's ever met has used that same tone.

"Hey there," Dean says. "What's this all about?"

"You want to do yourself a favor and make sure that pistol stays pointed at the ground."

"Definitely won't do nothing if I don't have a reason to."

This earns a few guffaws; men happy, perhaps, at his gall.

"What brings you out here at night, friend?"

Dean shrugs. "I'm a ragman. Just passing through."

"Yeah? Just passing through, huh?"

"Heading east." He's aiming for a light, conversational tone. Guys talking around a keg. "If I haul ass all night, might be able to make it to Virginia by morning."

"Yeah? Well, boy, we do like the idea of you getting the fuck out of here, that's for sure."

It's the *boy* that crystallizes everything. Dean might as well raise his pistol now, start firing. There's no getting out of this. No appealing to their virtue, their kindness. White men with guns call you *boy*, you either run or someone comes away bleeding.

"See, we heard complaints of a Black fella looks like you stealing stuff."

Bull-fucking-shit, Dean thinks. I could be in a suit selling Bibles next to Jesus himself and *Black fella stealing stuff* would still be tumbling out of your mouths. "This in Stab that you hear this?"

"All over."

"Drale?"

"Like I said, all over the place," the voice says, even flatter this time.

"Wherever I might be, is what you're saying."

A few chuckles. "Pretty much. You and your friends."

Dean nods, trying to tamp that coil of rage inside him, trying to remind himself that pride's what kills you faster than anything, but he can't help himself. "You all make a habit of this?"

"What's that?"

"Running people out of town."

A spanning silence now, the energy changing. The pistol in his hand feels plastic, inconsequential.

"We make a habit of running criminals out of town, hell yes we do. Except you and your smart mouth just graduated."

"How's that?"

"Well, now you get to leave all your shit here. Bike and all."

Heat all through him. Everything in that cart, five years' worth of hardscrabble survival. He still has two jars of pickles left, for Christ's sake. Just the cart alone, all the work it took making it.

Dean grins his *ah-shit* grin, the grin that's allowed him to squeeze—before the Message and after—in and out of countless situations with white people, and with it he tucks his pistol in the back of his jeans and then slowly raises his hands in the air and says, "You know what, I'm gonna go ahead and take off. Y'all have a good night."

He's got a leg hoisted over the bike when the first shot rings out. He steps off, pivots, and then he's running through the gloom, more gunshots coming now, Dean pulling the pistol from his waistband and firing once behind him, the men hooting and laughing. Dean thinking even as he scrambles down the embankment, blackberry brambles pulling red lines across his face, his arms, that he's not done with these men, not by a long shot.

JOHN BONNER

Portland, Oregon

Bonner in the parking lot of the apartment building, thinking of the hand. Thinking how badly he wants to go up there, sit with it. Pining for the way it scours away all of his guilt with arias of blood and fury and death. More than once he's found himself up there on the couch, seized by the hand's power, only to find that he's pressed his pistol underneath the soft tissue of his jaw, his finger testing the trigger's give.

He knows it's poisoning him. That he should get rid of it.

Torn between what he wants and what's right, Bonner's desperate for a distraction. He exhales, nearly weeping with frustration, lifts his hips, fishes his phone from his pocket. Dials Katherine—anything to keep from going upstairs.

He's surprised when she picks up; they haven't talked in a while. It's painful for them both, particularly her. Too many sorrows unspooled between them, too little of the present to pull them together.

"John?" she says, unable to keep the surprise from her voice.

"Hey." He pinches the bridge of his nose, instantly regretting the call. This poor woman and how he's failed her.

"Hey," she says. And then, when Bonner doesn't say anything: "Is everything— What's going on?"

"Uh, I was just calling to see how things are. How you're doing."

Silence, then: "I mean, I'm fine. We're— Yeah, everything's fine."

"Yeah, no, I hear you—"

"I'm just getting through the best I can, you know?"

"Yeah," Bonner says, running his free hand, suddenly sweat-slicked, down the length of his pants, almost frantic to get off the phone. What the fuck was he thinking? Calling her? "How's Nick?" he says, wincing right after and pressing a fist against his forehead.

Even through the phone, he hears her sharp inhalation. A sound like he's punched her.

"He's the same," she says.

"Yeah," he says, practically sputtering. "Yeah, I hear you, Katherine. Listen, I've got to run, I'll talk to you later. Was good talking to you." Hangs up, cursing. Tosses the phone on the passenger seat. Spends a minute with the palms of his hands pressed against his eyes. Always looking for ways he might absolve himself. As if Katherine was ever going to tell him it was okay.

He still thinks he could have saved Nick, if he'd had more time. Just a few more seconds.

He steps out of the car into the rainy afternoon. Angry now. At himself, at a world that's freighted him with these guilts. He's so frantic now to outrun these feelings moving through him that he bolts across the parking lot, up the stairs to the second floor. Sweet Christ, he called *Katherine*?

Most of the building's windows are free of glass. Doors gone or hanging on hinges; the wood salvaged for burning, or kicked in by folks looting the apartments. But not that corner one on the upper floor. That door's locked tight, reinforced on the inside, the windows boarded with heavy plywood. Bonner, years back, making a day of it, fortifying the place.

Even with that, he's gotten stupidly lucky here. He knows it. So much so that he wonders sometimes if luck is truly the navigating force that's kept the place safe, when every other apartment's been scavenged, picked clean. Wiring pulled out of the walls. People have squatted in this building, shat on the floors. He found a body in a ground-floor bathtub last year, wrapped in a bloody shower curtain. Every time he walks these steps, he expects to find that front door busted open.

But he gets lucky—if that's what it is—one more time. Door's closed and the key fits. The deadbolt turns, thunks home.

As soon as he steps inside, that glottal *thumping* rises up in the way-back meat of his brain. The familiar stridency to it, the eagerness, along with the first nattering of a headache, there along the scar at his temple.

It's like drowning, being near the thing. It's a sensation he's come to love.

He flips the light switch, notes for the hundredth time the galaxy of dead flies in the bowl of the light fixture, the way it throws a warped chiaroscuro of shadows on the walls. Here's the broken coffee table, its contents spilled onto the carpet. The grimy couch with its spatter of old bloodstains. He walks into the kitchen, his fingers grazing the handle of the freezer. Its pale yellow surface, a five-year-old phone bill held up with a magnet that shows a vintage cutout of a housewife drinking a cup of coffee. DON'T TALK TO BABY 'TIL SHE'S HAD HER JUICE!, it says in bubbly letters. The hand flexes in his brain. Bonner wants to puke. He wants to run screaming. He wants to open the freezer and sink to the filthy linoleum and curl the hand to his chest until he dies of thirst.

The dichotomy of the remnants. The three remnants: the eye, the hand, the voice. Bonner has the hand, lost ownership of the eye in the screaming aftermath of the Message. No one knows where the recording of the voice went. All three used together will—*did*—create something of unimaginable power.

Bonner considers calling Dave Kendall, telling him everything. Spilling forth all this poisonous history. It'd be like lancing a wound. How Matthew Coffin, heartbroken and self-obsessed, had fallen in thrall to something, and had been convinced, years ago, to perform some dark ritual of dismemberment upon himself. And how Coffin's remnants—his hand, his eye, the recording of his voice—were made, and how the recording of his voice drove anyone who heard it instantly blood-crazed and murderous. How that recording was broadcast, thanks to Terradyne and his uncle Jack, across virtually every phone signal on the planet; anyone who made the mistake of picking up was driven mad in a matter of seconds.

It's these two parts of himself that are continually warring—how Bonner's grown sickly protective of Coffin's hand over the years, *greedy* for it—and how the guilt over his involvement in the Message has absolutely decimated his life.

For years now, he's managed to do what previous agencies couldn't, what Terradyne couldn't, what the US government failed so miserably at: He's held the hand captive. Kept it isolated, kept it from doing more damage than it already has.

What if he can do it with the eye as well?

What if the Sight does actually have it in their possession? Shouldn't he try to get it back?

Christ, isn't he obligated to?

What if—a big *what if*—he somehow gets ownership of *all three* of the remnants? And then destroys them? He could do that, right? Manage that when the time came?

Bonner opens the freezer. Takes out the box and walks to the living room. Exultant, horrified, eager. Hating himself.

Thing is, he *understands* the hand, in some dim, animalistic way. Understands it's a thing that wants to move, wants to *travel*. It revels in movement, in transition, in creating as wide a swath of chaos and violence as possible.

And he's managed to keep it captive in this apartment for years.

But sometimes?

Well, the hand's like an animal. You got to let the thing *walk*.

The box feels warm to the touch somehow. Bonner's wondered what these visits have done to him over the years. What changes

THE DEVIL BY NAME

these exposures to the hand have cost him. If things as specific as brain synapses, chemicals, neurons, have been altered in some vital way. He imagines the brachial trees of his veins all stunted and black-laced with rot. His heart curling with char in his chest. Nothing that dramatic, perhaps, but years of swimming in the bloody mental chum the hand offers simply can't be good for him. Matthew Coffin fell under the sway of something when he was still alive—isn't it possible that some vestige of that same thing lives on in his hand, this severed appendage?

Bonner's way past stopping, though.

Destroy it, he thinks again.

"Five minutes," he tells himself. "And then I'm out."

He opens the lid.

An hour later he's back in the parking lot, his head resting against the steering wheel. Caught in that half-lit space where the hand's pull has diminished but not left him entirely. All these afterimages seared behind his eyes, like he's been staring into the sun.

His phone rings and he dreamily slaps at his pockets. Finds it.

"Yeah."

"Where are you?" Kendall barks.

Bonner lifts his head, tries to blink away the visions. "I'm about to lean on a guy in the Crooked Wheel crew," he lies. "They're pushing dope through a room in the Parade."

"Yeah, no," says Kendall. "That's not happening. I need you over here." Bonner catches the constrained fury in his voice. "Right fucking now, John."

"What's up?"

"Here's the address," Kendall says.

It's a ranch-style place out in Foster-Powell, with a wild overgrowth of yellowed front yard behind a chain-link fence and cardboard over at least half the windows. He sees Katz leaning against a Terradyne unit parked at the curb. He's in a white dress shirt, the sleeves rolled to the elbows, revolver in a holster at his waist. He's smoking a cigarette and he grins big when he sees Bonner walking across the street. He tilts his head at the house. "Oh, you're fucked, son."

Bonner walks up the driveway, pulls open the screen door. Smell of blood right there, first thing. The rich stink of it.

A short hallway and there's Kendall standing in the living room, scratching an eyebrow.

The room's gloomy, with crazed little shards of sunlight cutting through the cardboard and falling onto the carpet. Two bodies are splayed out on the floor, both men. One's been hacked at, his limbs a chopped-up scribble of meat and bone. His head's been chopped at too, with eyes and a nose that are mostly implications among all the red. Burned, raised glyphs of eyes are visible among the ruin of his arms. One hand is upturned and Bonner sees the eye burned there in the palm. Same glyphs on the other body—the doer, Bonner thinks—but this one just chopped at his own wrists, bled out that way. But not before he managed to write a message on the wall.

REGAL JOHN BONNER, it says.

Right there in blood on the wall above the couch, letters a foot high.

A fly lands on the back of Bonner's hand, bites. He slaps at it.

Kendall looks at him with scared, angry eyes.

"What the fuck is this, John?"

Bonner, standing there with the fear walking big through him. Taking up all the space inside.

Because he knows what it means.

KATHERINE MORIARTY

Cape Winston, Massachusetts

She hangs up the phone, turns it off. She doesn't want to hear it
if it rings again.

John Bonner calling her? Reaching out to ask *how she's doing?*
How *Nick's* doing? The audacity of it. Like since the last time they
spoke, God had reached down from a fucking cloud and feathered
her kid's brow with a glowing, benevolent hand? Turned him back
into the man he had been? Her hands are shaking and she stares at
them until they stop.

She's eating an early dinner at Augustine's, Cape Winston's sole
café. The skeletal, scorched remains of the church sit on its little
sand-swept rise only a few blocks away. Katherine's drinking a bottle
of Jane beer and trying to slough off the day's ferocities. Or had been,
anyway, before Bonner had called, rattling the chains of her past,
stirring up all this old hurt within her. He's one of the few people
alive who remember Nick the way he was before. And thinking of
Nick makes her think of her husband, all the ways she and Matthew
failed each other over the years.

She's just finished her shift. Like everyone else with a ration card, Katherine does her bit for the Providence Initiative. Something she, with more than a little bitterness, considers America's post-apocalyptic happy dance version of the New Deal. Get folks working while also rebuilding the country's infrastructure, which had been shattered like a flung plate. She'd signed her Terradyne loyalty agreements under an assumed identity—Katherine Moriarty was now Katherine Sunderson; she could thank Bonner for that. Once her fake ID had gone through, she'd worked hard at throwing away every vestige of her old life. Any paperwork, mementos, old IDs. She was Katherine Sunderson now, with Nick the only anchor to the woman she had been.

Honestly, she knows Bonner means well, but a part of her hates him, and always will. He was the last person to see Nick before he was turned, and Katherine can't help feeling that whatever Bonner tried to do to save him wasn't enough.

Katherine's job is in outreach, cold-calling phone numbers from a list she's given every day. Her job is part interview, part scold, part snitch-work. It's terrible, but you can't buck your Providence obligation or you'll go to get food somewhere and your card won't run. Everyone in Cape Winston lives in fear of getting their card pulled, and paper cash hasn't really caught on here again.

So four days a week she walks the fifteen minutes from her house to what was once a Best Buy in a strip mall. She signs in, sits down at a computer station amid a dozen others. Puts on her headset. Gets her list of numbers from her manager and calls folks, reading from a pre-printed questionnaire and collecting the answers in a spreadsheet. The questions are a mixture of the mundane and the harrowing:

When was the last time you saw, in person,
an afflicted individual?

• Less than a day ago
• Less than a week ago

- Less than a month ago
- More than a month ago

Describe the encounter.

*How well does the Providence Initiative's rationing
(such as gasoline, cell phone, foodstuffs) meet your needs?*

- Providence Initiative rationing meets all of my needs
- Providence Initiative rationing meets some of my needs but
  not all of them
- Providence Initiative rationing meets none of my needs

Explain your answer.

*Please describe, in as many words as you'd like, your
experience during the events that transpired during
XX/XX/XXXX, colloquially known as "the Message."*

All this is done in an attempt to understand, in some baseline way, how people have changed since the end of the world. Most folks grudgingly speak to her—no one wants their card pulled. Still, some are happy to cuss her out, shouting about government overreach, liberty, sovereignty, the Constitution. Terradyne, the government and Jane are called every terrible thing, and these calls almost invariably end with some threat or insult directed at Katherine herself, though neither she nor the caller really know anything about each other, and likely aren't even in the same state.

Now, though, it's a fine spring day, and her shift is over. Bonner's call has rattled her, yeah, but it's not like he's sitting across from her. Still, his question—*How's Nick?*—stirs up so much inside. Longing, sorrow, anger. Guilt, buckets of it. Between that and the dream the previous night—Matthew in that townhouse, the body running at her down the hallway—she feels punch-drunk, nervy. She hardly ever dreams of her husband anymore, and it feels like a dark portent, like bad shit is heading her way.

Still, here she is. Sunlight punches through the tatter of clouds overhead. Through the front window, between buildings, she spies a wedge of gray-green sea. There's the gentle clatter of cutlery against plates, a few murmured conversations around her. Lena, the café's old mastiff, sighs and settles herself on the rug by the doorway.

She's finishing the last of her soup when a pair of fever hunters walk into the café, the bell above the door jingling and announcing their arrival. Their faces are red and blotched, their black balaclavas held in their fists. The room doesn't entirely quiet, but some new, charged quality hangs in the air.

They strut up to the counter, past Katherine's table. Bootheels clacking on the wooden floor, rifles hanging from slings. She catches a whiff of alcohol as they pass.

She thinks of Nick in the shed, his jaws snapping shut and opening again. How these boys—and they are, they're boys—how they would gun him down in a second if they saw him. She imagines they were teens when the Message came through, and once again asks herself what allure killing the fevered offers these people. Is it the security offered by working for the government? The misguided notion that they're doing some good in the world? Or the act of killing itself?

The café's owner, Augustine, steps up to the counter. "What can I do for you," he says, sounding unhappy. The hunters wear hardened collars around their throats to protect from bites, plastic guards around their forearms. The pockets of their fatigues bristle with gear—tourniquets, flares, magazines for their rifles.

The taller one, gangly and redheaded, with a buzz cut that shows a long, curving scar along the back of his skull, seems to sense Katherine's gaze. He turns and looks at her, smirking. He's twenty years old, if that. He readjusts his rifle sling and says to her, "What's up?" She realizes the kid's hammered. Sees it in the way his eyes drift a bit before settling on her.

"Not a thing," she says, and lifts her beer bottle. Looks out the window. Her cheeks flush with anger.

"Well, you look like you have something you want to say to me."

"No guns in my place," Augustine says at the counter, trying to veer the kid's attention back to him, but it's like he hasn't spoken at all.

"Do you?" the kid asks.

"Do I what?" Katherine says.

"Do you have something you want to fucking say to me."

"Hey," Augustine says, louder, "you want to order, or you want to take a walk," and the other hunter tells him to shut the fuck up, and the café goes tight with tension. The redheaded boy moves closer to her table and crouches down, his rifle resting across his thighs.

"You got nothing to say? Now that I'm in front of you?"

She turns in her chair to face him. She clasps her hands between her knees, tucks her hair behind an ear. They're at eye level with each other. "You're wrong," she says.

The kid's face opens in joy. "I am?"

"Killing them is wrong," Katherine says.

The other hunter leans against the counter. He folds his arms and snorts. "Shit, dude. Here we go."

That glittering look in his eyes, each word coming out slow and intentional, dense with mockery, the kid in front of her says, "Killing them is wrong?"

"I'm sorry, but you guys need to leave," Augustine calls out.

"They're people," Katherine says. "Half the fevered you drop are people that used to live here. Neighbors." Her heart snags in her throat, thickens her words. "People's children."

The other hunter chortles at the counter. "They're *children,* dude. Won't you think of people's *children?*" Something about his face, the way he laughs; she realizes the two of them are brothers.

"Listen to me," the hunter crouched before her says. His eyes are bloodshot, the irises flecked with green. Again, that alcohol fog, like he's sweating it out. "There is nothing in there. There's fucking nothing left of them. They're not *human*, they don't *feel*. They don't, they don't *love* you."

"Fuck you," Katherine spits.

His face darkens. "No, fuck you. Fuck you, lady. For being stupid. And weak. They're not even animals. Animals can *think*."

Augustine makes some new gesture behind the counter—Katherine can't see what it is, her eyes are locked on the kid's—but the hunter at the counter says, "One move and they'll carry you out of here in a bag, swear to God," and this makes the hunter that's looking at her smile big.

He says to Katherine, "You ever talk to me like that again, lady, and you won't be walking around afterwards."

Everything in her goes electric. She leans toward it, toward that banked rage inside her. Nick in the shed, Matthew, her escape from Chicago in the hours after the Message, all of it. "What does that mean," she says flatly.

If he's taken aback, he doesn't show it. "You don't want to know."

"No, I do," Katherine says. "Tell me what you mean."

"Get the fuck out of here," Augustine yells, and Lena stands up, lets out a low growl from her place by the door.

"We're leaving," the hunter says, standing up, not taking his eyes from Katherine. "That dog takes a step toward me, I'm shooting it in the face."

Augustine calls Lena behind the counter.

Katherine's expecting some show as they make their exit—knocking something over, kicking in a window. But they don't look back. Just the sound of their bootheels on the floor, the squeal of the front door as it opens and swings shut.

FROM THE ARCHIVAL NOTEBOOKS
OF MATTHEW COFFIN

Ah, hell, here we are. That sense of boundless possibility inherent in a cheap-ass notebook and a Bic pen you found in a junk drawer! The sense of wonder in it, like any wild-ass thing might be revealed!

Katherine and I, shockingly, are on the outs. Again, I mean. Split. Maybe for good, but how many times have I said that before? This one was less me taking a little unannounced sojourn away from the family home and more her just absolutely exhausted with us as a couple and finally telling me to get the fuck out. Here we are, everything fractured and cratered one more time. It's nuts how two people can run up against these same arguments over and over again, *for years,* and each time you find yourself looking in the mirror, like, "Golly, how did I *get* here?" Like Katherine and I haven't been tilling the same endless battlefields for a very long time. Same things we've always struggled with—my supposed distancing, her insistence on constantly, endlessly ingesting my air. This sense of pressure, of everyone, forever, at any conceivable moment, up in my shit. How sometimes you just have to *breathe,* and she doesn't get that. I turn around and there she is. I go in another room, there's the kid. These two need-machines right there, vying endlessly for my attention. Is it something Katherine will ever truly understand? I mean, Nick wasn't even *born* when the two of us started ramming our heads against this wall. Katherine all "Why won't you talk to me?" And me being like "If I have to navigate this apartment with you in it for one more minute, I'm gonna jump out the window." Seriously—had I known that marriage would be this goddamnably hard? That father-hood's supposed rewards would often feel pretty fucking minimal in comparison to its cost? Christ.

So Katherine's told me to jet for the hundredth time. And I have done so with profound relief.

Francis is on tour, my buddy Francis the Beast, and he's lent me his loft. Happy to do it, he says, provided I keep an eye on the place. It's in the Pearl District, and if I had to guess, I'd say it was an auto shop or something back in the day. It's been refurbished— what hasn't in this neighborhood—and the ground floor is huge, wide open, with these giant-ass rafters that crisscross the ceiling nearly two stories up, and a couple steel bay doors that have been welded shut. Glossy cement floors, repurposed planks on the walls that look, I don't know, oiled, somehow. The kitchen takes up one wall. Whole place looks like a gloomy bar you can hardly afford to drink in, honestly. There's a ladder that leads up to a little sleeping area upstairs, and off from the main room is a little broom closet of a bathroom, with a toilet and a standing-room shower stall, a big industrial sink. No tub. Still, it seems as good a place as any to get my shit straight. Decide if I'm finally going to do it. Either ditch Katherine for good, let the D-word tumble from thine lips and then move on down the road, or try once again to rebuild this dried-out scarecrow of a marriage.

Nick came over last night. The first time I've seen him since I left. Kid was quiet, kept mostly to Francis's couch, which folds out into a futon. It felt weird, the whole thing; Nick's fifteen and just read his book while I listened to tapes and wrote. I've discovered Francis's boombox and a stack of his cassettes, and I've taken some comfort in these dead-ass formats. The two of us listening to Gregorian chants and Appalachian blues and shit, not really talking. Felt like we were roommates that didn't particularly care for each other's company. I tried to engage with him every once in a while, but nothing really landed. This quiet little stranger that I helped make. Living so much in his own head.

We got that in common, I guess.

Finally I got sick of the silence and we went out for sushi at Shoyou, the place with the plates that run around on a conveyor belt. Nick was glum, radiating a quiet confusion. I was withdrawn, preoccupied; I've been doing a decent amount of coke lately and am feeling more than a little strung out, truth be told. When I take a minute and honestly think about it, how else could I expect him to act? His parents are split—or at least in the process of splitting—and he's a teenager on top of that. Confusion and rage are like a *requirement* at fifteen. See, when I write it, I can recognize why he is the way he is, but at the time, watching him picking at his California rolls with a pair of chopsticks, all petulant, not even eating? Just mashing the stuff into a paste? It pissed me off. Like I need a sullen teenager attached to my leg while I'm going through my own shit, right? I laid into him, and he looked up at me with those big, trembling cow eyes, tears just ready to spill out.

"What is your fucking problem," I said, right there in the restaurant. Not quietly, either. A couple people turned their heads my way, and I stared at them until they looked down at their plates. Then I turned back to Nick.

"I don't know," he said, all timid, which made me even more pissed.

"Do me a favor," I said, trying hard not to jab my chopsticks at him, "try to avoid sitting there moping like some sad-sack motherfucker, okay? You do that for me? I just bought you dinner, man. You got a roof, clothes, you'll always have money. The fuck do you have to complain about, Nicholas?" Knowing full well he had plenty. But the moment, it grabs me sometimes. (I was crashing a bit too, not gonna lie. Jittery, a headache. Not sure how bad the coke had been stepped on, but it felt like someone had shoved Drano into my sinus cavities.)

"I don't know," he said again, his voice even smaller. He hoisted a piece of sushi to his mouth and chewed, looking down at his plate.

And then there's me, just feeling like an asshole.

I wanted to tell him I was sorry, I should have, but instead I stood up and went to the bathroom, did my last bump in a stall to calm down.

Nick managed one night here then went back home. Again, can't blame him. But when he left it was the weirdest thing. Maybe it was guilt or—probably—just being strung out, I don't know, but when he left I still had this sense that there was someone in the loft with me. The place had *pull*, that was for sure.

Pull, a Matthew Coffin creation, thank you very much, is like how a place—a room, a street, a venue, even an entire city—will have a certain *feeling* to it. The way it affects you. And the pull of the loft had changed after Nick left. Not something that I'm gonna be broadcasting around, but it felt like there was a new fullness to the place. Like, sound here felt damped a little bit, the way it is when there's more furniture in a room. I walked the perimeter of the loft—which was not tough, given that it's basically a big-ass square. But also I went into the bathroom, peered behind the shower curtain, looked in Francis's big steamer trunk that he uses for storage. Opened the kitchen cupboards, even. Nothing. But that *pull* was still here. Freaked me out enough that I said fuck it, put on my coat. Went out for a couple drinks, made some calls for another bag, but of course—because bad luck always rolls downhill—it turns out my connect's out of town.

This was yesterday. Last night, I mean. I came home from the bar—Mercy's, with the Christmas lights everywhere—after getting 86'd. Little embarrassed to even write that part. I was cut off after getting lippy with the bartender. It started because I dumped a ten-dollar bill into the jukebox so I could play both the Blank Letters albums back-to-back. I just wanted to sit in my feelings a little, how the songs made me think of the best parts of Katherine. The best parts of myself. But the bartender turned the jukebox off halfway through "I Won't Forget It," and I kind of went off on him. Might have crowed about how I was, sweet Christ, "the greatest American guitarist of the past thirty years." Might have even thrown my pint glass on the ground. Lucky I didn't snap an ankle, the way the cook, who was not a small dude, tossed me out. I started walking home, doing the Stagger of Shame, all swerve and zombie-stomp, but then had to backtrack ten or fifteen blocks when I realized I was in fact walking toward my old apartment and not Francis's place.

I eventually made it back and crawled up the ladder to the sleeping loft. The sheets were musty, just *stinking* of mold, something I hadn't noticed before. That feeling of pressed-in closeness was going off big-time up there. I got the spins. Remembering how the bartender's face closed up like a fist when I threw my glass down. If I was a better man, I thought, I'd pick up a guitar, work shit out that way. If I was a better man, I'd call my wife. Try to understand my son, extend him some grace. But I just lay there, resisting the urge to barf on Francis's whatever-thread-count sheets that smelled like they'd been dragged through dogshit, my eyes cinched tight against it all.

And then I felt the creak, the pressure. The implied *shift*.

Someone had sat down at the end of the bed.

Had to take a second. Just the audacity of writing something like that. But yeah, it's a sensation that's hard to miss. The pressure of a body as it bends the mattress down? The weight? I froze, my heart suddenly parked up near my eyeballs, but finally, the spins got so bad—I didn't want to, but I did—I opened my eyes and looked. Of course there was no one there. But the pressure didn't leave.

I kicked out, touched nothing, and sat up, staggered off the mattress and down the ladder, palms all sweat-slicked on the rungs, just about falling two or three times. I *almost* made it to the bathroom when I puked all over the floor. Stepped around it, heaved some more in the toilet, rinsed my mouth out and then staggered over to Francis's couch, that red leather monstrosity that Nick had slept on the night before. I lay down and my head felt worse than before.

I swear, before I passed out again, I could see someone crouched at the edge of the upper loft. This shape peering down at me.

Francis's place has bad fucking pull, that's for sure.

In the morning the feeling was gone and I felt better. Well, I felt like death had cracked open the top half of my head and taken a bodacious shit inside, and then cinched the cap of my skull back on with roofing nails, but that sense of being watched seemed goofy in the daylight. I've spent all day today cleaning up my messes, drinking tea, looking at my phone, and pointedly listening to Francis's cassettes, music that does not in any way remind me of Katherine or the band. Feeling way less freaked.

After all, it's not like there *is* something here in Francis's loft. I believe places can hold their histories, good or bad, can distill it down into a feeling—that's what *pull* is, really—but the idea that that history can manifest into something physical? Nah. I've courted enough of that shit throughout the years—a lifetime of hitting up psychics and participating in séances and all that—that if there *was* something to break through, I'd be fine with it. Thrilled, even. But the thing is, there's nothing out there. There's no God, there's no devil. There's just us. Our bodies, our voices. Our errors and our mistakes and urges. Our endless fuckups. That's all.

A week now in the loft.

Francis called me last night from somewhere in Denmark. The line kept cutting in and out, but he sounded drunk and happy. "How's shit working out, brother?" Francis calls everyone brother, a kind of forced camaraderie as he steamrolls over you with his opinions, his drinks, his bass-playing. I've known the guy for twenty years and he's always been like this. But the fact remains, I'd needed a place, desperately so, and he'd hooked me up without a second thought. I owed him. "You keeping the rats out?"

"You got rats here?" I asked.

"I mean figuratively, my man. Spiritually. The rats in your *mind.*"

The thing on the bed had seemed very far away then. "How's the old Continent?" I asked.

"Europe, baby," Francis crowed. "Europe is *insane.* Every show's been packed. Boston Bob got held up at the border; he mouthed off to some Estonian border patrol guy who pulled a fucking pistol on him. Bob just about shit. Sasha had to talk the guy down, pay him off, it was crazy." Francis and his band and their crew all pushing fifty years old and still holding tight to the trappings of rock music, like that shit was sustainable. I guess maybe it was, for him. Myself, I felt like I was long past the time I could bang women I'd just done shots with and then hit a stall and do lines and not wake up just, you know, dead. But talking with Francis, the desire suddenly ripped through me. That was another thing about being out of the apartment and on my own—I was free to indulge in my most destructive of traits. Maybe that was it—maybe I was just tired of being a dad and a husband. Maybe I just wanted to get fucked up.

"Hey, Francis, you got a connect here?" I asked him.

"What, for blow?"

"Yeah, or whatever." Since the bumps I'd done in Shoyou the week before, I'd run out, and my regular guy kept claiming to be unavailable, with no one to put me in touch with. Everyone was dry, he said.

The line crackled with a burst of static and I didn't hear all of what Francis said, but I heard the name Lydia.

"Who," I said. "Hippie Lydia?"

"Yeah." *Crackle. Cut.* "Gypsy Lydia."

"Don't say gypsy, dude, it's not the eighties anymore."

Francis laughed. "From the man asking me for cocaine like he's in a Belushi movie."

"She still got that little place on Lombard? By the Dairy Queen?"

"Yeah, that's the place."

"Do I need to say anything?"

Crackle. "Yeah, you say 'Hey, Lydia, might I buy some cocaine from you?'"

"Come on."

"Just, you know, tell her I sent you."

"I appreciate it."

"No problem."

"Listen, Francis, I don't want to keep you, but I was wondering, you ever felt anything weird in here?"

Crackle. "—the loft?"

"Yeah."

"Like what?"

"I don't know, man." I *didn't* know. I still don't. "Just something weird. A presence."

Francis laughed. "Yeah, my ex-wife haunts the place. The second one. Just say 'Get thee behind me' and she'll tickle your balls."

We said our goodbyes, I looked up Lydia's place on my phone— she runs a little consignment shop over in North Portland. Opens at ten tomorrow.

And that's that. My phone's sitting right in front of me as I write this. I could call Katherine. Try to ford that river once again.

Or I could go to the corner store and buy some beer. Listen to music and seethe inside my own mind for a while.

Choices, choices.

THEO MARSDEN

Rolla, Missouri — Washington, DC

Two weeks after their dismal debriefing with Suarez, Theo and Jack Bonner fly to Washington, where President Yardley's called a meeting.

The two of them and their security details are escorted onto a cavernous DC-10 (the ghost of the FedEx logo still visible on the fuselage if you get close enough). They bounce along the tarmac, and then comes the incredible, familiar arc and rise as the plane takes off.

The flight is uneventful, and wonderful for that. It's a relatively new thing for Terradyne, planes in the air again. Jack is tight-lipped, presumably still stung about the thing with Suarez, and nervous about Coffin. Some part of him must know that that's what this palaver with Yardley's all about, but neither of them mention it.

They land at Andrews Air Force Base, which shows promising signs of activity, even though a massive amount of the architecture on the southern side has burned to the ground, and a giant passenger jet rests wheelless on one of the airstrips, smoke-blackened.

They deplane and are escorted to a pair of waiting military SUVs; Jack in one, Marsden in another. As ever, Eastman rides with him.

DC's desolate. A large part of Phase One had been focused on the most basic of infrastructure improvements: getting shit off the roads, particularly in and out of DC and Rolla. The freeways have slowly been cleared of years' worth of abandoned vehicles. There had been massive, miles-long traffic jams after the Message, everyone trying to flee the Beltway. Now oceans of dead cars fill parking garages, and long unbroken lines of them line the sides of roads. Eventually they'll be disassembled, smelted, the materials reused. For now, they're out of the way and that's good.

It's a cold, dry day, and the city feels abandoned. Government and Terradyne personnel are roughly split between here and Rolla, but this city's so big in comparison. Marsden surprises himself by pining for the busyness of the college. Their convoy passes a turret-mounted Humvee parked at the side of the road, the young machine-gunner's head tracking their passage, his eyes impassive behind dark shades.

They're escorted through the rotunda of the National Archives Building; where once sat the Constitution, the Declaration of Independence and the Bill of Rights, now stands a phalanx of soldiers bristling with weapons. Yardley's personal security detail. Marsden, Jack and Eastman are led through the detail by an aide and brought down a series of endlessly branching windowless halls to a numberless office door. The aide knocks twice, and they're told to come in.

And there sits President Preston Yardley. Stationed behind some long-gone peon's desk of compressed particleboard, a single window behind him, its blinds cinched tight. The carpet is wine-bottle green and the room is just large enough for a single bookcase and a pair of rolling office chairs that sit in front of his desk. Eastman moves to the hallway and shuts the door behind him. Yardley stands up and bends over the desk, shaking each of their hands. Marsden notes that he's still dying his hair black.

"Quite the office, Mr. President," Jack says with a touch of gentle mockery that makes Yardley cough out a chop of laughter.

He sits back down. "Yeah, well, the Oval Office is a pile of rubble last I checked, Jack. Besides, I like being in the maze here. Every day or two, different office, different building. Keep 'em guessing. Have a seat, gentlemen."

They do. There's a lot of throat-clearing, unbuttoning of jackets, crossing of legs. Then, before Theo or Jack can start talking, Yardley puts an elbow on the desk and points a blunt finger at them. He's an old man, grown older since all of this, but there's no waver or tremble there. "Before our whole big dance starts, I want to know where my assets are."

"We're still working on it, Mr. President," Marsden says.

"So you got no idea, is what you're telling me."

"We know that one asset—Saint Michael, as he was called—died on an airplane as the ARC team fled Portland, hours before the Message. Michael's last big act was apparently pulping David Lundy's head with his bare hands."

"I know all about that, Theo. I want to know about the hand, and the recording, and this supposed eye. The *remnants*. The key to all of this is the remnants, and what my man in the box might be capable of."

Jack opens his mouth to speak but Yardley holds up a hand. "I'm sure you've got plenty of excuses ready as to why you haven't found them, Jack. I'm not interested. Keep looking."

"Yes, sir."

"Meanwhile." Yardley fixes Jack with a pointed gaze, his eyes hooded as a lizard's. "Theo tells me the vaccine is not exactly cruising along."

Jack glances at Theo, looks back. "We're working on it."

"You working on it seems to be code for you having no clue."

"Mr. President—"

"I'm giving you three months to come up with something significant and then I'm cutting the vaccine program for good and we'll proceed with Phase Three of the Initiative. I think that's fair. I want things buttoned down. We kill off the fevered, put the damn insurgents and militants and activists behind the walls. Put them to work for once in their lives. Let it be a lesson to everyone else."

Here we are, Marsden thinks.

Jack shuts his eyes. Jack Bonner, never letting go of the guilt over what happened. Over his part in it. And still hoping that a vaccine might serve as some redemptive arc for the world. As if that was how things worked. "Mr. President," he says, "we're working as fast as we can."

"Great. You get three months. Then we move forward with eradication. One hundred percent of them, none of this three-quarters bull. Wipe the slate clean and start over. That's always been the cornerstone of Phase Three, unless your pipe dream of a vaccine worked out. Which it sounds like it hasn't."

Jack shuts his eyes, and Marsden feels a little thrill at his squeamishness. If he falters now, Marsden and Yardley will roll right over him.

Yardley leans back, drums his fingers on the desktop. "Good deal, gentlemen. Which brings me to my next point."

Here it is, Marsden thinks. In his periphery, he sees Jack's hands tighten on the armrests of his seat.

"You are well aware that I want the remnants, yes? That I believe they—and Matthew Coffin—are the key to making the United States the governing force on the planet. And you don't have any remnants for me. So, think carefully, gentlemen. What *exactly* is our plan with the man in the box? He's the one piece of the puzzle that we have ownership of."

Yardley waits, hands folded. Neither he nor Jack say a thing.

"Nothing to say?" Yardley says. "Let me make it clear for you. I want to move forward with activation. I want to let him loose."

"Mr. President—"

"If that thing in the box is an angel or a devil or *whatever,* I want to know about it. I want to see what his capabilities are."

"Sir," Jack says, "I just, I don't think it's a good idea."

"Preston," Marsden says, hoping the use of the president's first name feels appropriately totemic, lends the appropriate gravity, "in theory I agree with you, but—"

"But what?"

"Sir," Jack says, "we're in this position because we vastly underestimated the parameters of these assets. Messing with Matthew Coffin before we know what he can *do*—"

Yardley leans forward. "Let me stop you right there. We're in this position, Jack, because you had your engineers broadcast that message over everyone's goddamn phones. You—*specifically* you, Jack—are the one that screwed us. You and I had a target list of countries that *I* approved—China, Russia, Saudi Arabia—and instead, you went whole-pie on me. You put the Message out *everywhere*. I feel the need to remind you how lucky you are to be sitting here right now. Theo talked me out of a firing squad."

"Yes sir," Jack says, swallowing so hard Marsden can hear his throat click. "This is the exact reason why I think study is so important—"

"How do you propose that we understand this asset if we don't let him stretch his legs? What's the process look like? Because every day we just hold him in that box and comment on how scary he looks? That's a day wasted. A day we offer other nations time to regroup. This country's still vulnerable as hell. Have either of you prayed about it? Prayed for guidance in this matter? Neither of you?" Yardley shakes his head. "*Do it.* God provides. Make no mistake, God's hand is more fierce than man's. Always will be. Stronger than any eye, any recording of the devil's foolishness." He opens a drawer and takes out a stack of documents in yellow TOP SECRET folders, pushes one to each of them. "Meanwhile, I want you to look at this. And then tell me with a straight face that we should just sit back and wait to see what happens with Matthew Coffin."

Marsden opens the file, thumbs through the photographs first— aerial photos of what looks like a farm, a few outbuildings, a road. Cows in a field. Then, close-ups of some faces, figures framed in the large picture window of a white farmhouse. In the window stands a broad-shouldered man holding a rifle. He's in tac gear but bearded, dirty. A thin, hard-faced woman next to him. Lastly, a dark-haired girl, high school age probably, but with that emaciated, bird-boned look people get from a long time on the road. He skims the accompanying intel report and freezes.

"What is this?" Jack says.

"Could be nothing," says Yardley. "But we poached that off DGSI, French intelligence, yesterday. Those photos were taken on the outskirts of a town called Nevers, and we're finding an enormous amount of local chatter about these three, particularly the girl. I want to move on this before DGSI scoops them up."

"French?" Jack says. "How do we even have intelligence capabilities in France?"

"I know what you're going to say, Jack. Don't even bother."

"I mean, are they French citizens?" he asks. "I hate to be that person, Mr. President, but do we believe in national sovereignty or not?"

"Get out of my office," Yardley says. When Jack doesn't move, he snaps his fingers and says, "You think I'm joking? Get out."

Jack looks at Marsden for a moment and then he walks out, the door clicking softly behind him.

Yardley folds his hands, puts them on his desk. Exhales. "At some point, Theo, there will be an impasse between you two that you will find insurmountable. I guarantee it. And you'll have to make a decision."

"Yes, sir."

Yardley taps a finger on the folder. "I'm sending a team here."

"When DGSI finds out we poached their intel—"

"When they find out we poached their intel, they might finally install some security protocols. Let me worry about DGSI. If the girl can actually do what this report seems to imply, I want her in a US facility by the end of the week. I'm tempted to bring her here. But what do *you* want, Theo?"

Marsden has worked with President Yardley long enough to

know that when he asks a question like this, it's not a question at all. It's a command, and one that he would do well to accept.

"We want her in Rolla," Marsden says. "I want her. Please."

"Good. And *I* want a substantive, on-paper definition of what we have in the box, you understand me? The United States government didn't align ourselves with Terradyne because of your looks. You *provide,* Theo, or you and Jack are out on your asses, you understand?"

"Absolutely, sir."

"Good. I want an extraction team heading out to that farm ASAP. And then you let Matthew Coffin stretch his legs a little and tell me how it goes."

"Yes, sir."

"I'm not asking you, Theo. This is all I think about. These are your priorities."

"I understand."

Yardley rolls his shoulders. "Alright then. Keep that folder. And will you do me a favor?"

"What's that, sir?"

"Pray on it. Seek answers there. Jack and his sovereignty bull, that's old thinking. If Coffin is as powerful as I think he is and this girl can do what it seems like she might? This nation can act as the sword of God, Theo. I have petitioned the Lord at great length, *great* length, and He has told me the answer lies with the remnants, and the girl, and that fellow you got there in your little bunker. With him as a weapon and that girl as the salve? We can rule the entire globe in His name."

2
MORSE CODE
FOR THE DAMNED

NAOMI LAURENT

Nevers, Bourgogne-Franche-Comté region, France

She was eleven, home sick from school, when her mother had answered the phone. Naomi was watching cartoons up in her room, maybe too old for them by then, but when you get sick like that, and feverish, you want to curl into yourself, fall back into the child you once were. She was watching her old shows on her tablet, the one with the crack in the screen from when she'd accidentally knocked it off her desk, and then her mother had started screaming downstairs.

The Message had come through in the early afternoon. Her father was at work in the town center—he did something at a bank, she had never understood what exactly. He was neither particularly high nor low in the scheme of things, she knew that, and it had caused arguments between her parents sometimes. He was American, her father, and it was part of why her parents saw things differently. But in the five years since the Message, Naomi has pictured him countless times in the last minutes of his lunch break, maybe finishing off a coffee at that café he liked near the bank. The most bland, normal-looking man in the world, with his glasses and slight double chin and kind brown eyes. Normal-looking, boring even, save for the tattoo of a winged knife on the inside of one forearm. One that he was always sheepish and self-effacing about—*I wanted something that looked tough, Nomo*—and that led him to wear long-sleeve shirts on all but the hottest days. Yes, in the years following the Message, she has imagined him peering down at the screen of his phone, only mildly surprised to be receiving a phone call during his break. Accepting it, probably, with a slide of his thumb. How it was that easy to go from a person to not one.

It's what Naomi's mother had done. Naomi wouldn't learn this for a long time, of course, wouldn't know that it was a message relayed over all of the telephones at once that had driven everyone suddenly, terribly mad. All she'd known was that her mother had begun screaming downstairs, these pained and torturous shrieks that chilled Naomi's blood as she rocketed up in bed, the tablet clattering to the floor. She'd run down the stairs to the living room, one hand lightly tracing the banister, where she'd found her mother on her knees in the middle of the floor, her back bent like an old woman's. She could hear, distantly, music playing over her mother's phone. A rock band. Naomi at eleven had liked pop songs—Black M, LGS, Gabrielle Goulet, nice singers like that—and this sounded harsh to her, a woman yowling in English. Naomi had felt a coldness settle over her, seeing her mother contorted like that.

"Mom?"

Her mother had turned at the sound of her voice, wild-eyed.

Blood on her chin, smeared around her mouth.

Naomi saw then that she was bent over Hugo's body. His little fingers tapping a rhythm on the floor.

Her mother had pivoted on her knees to look at her, and Naomi had frozen when she saw the wet piss-mark at the crotch of her mother's pants.

"Mama?" she'd croaked, swaying a little. Her terror reducing her again to some younger version of herself.

Her mother had been shoeless, and in her haste to rise up, she'd slammed her shins against the coffee table, a glass tumbling off—her brother only recently deemed old enough to drink from big-people glasses—and shattering on the hardwood floor.

Naomi would remember forever the way her mother had righted herself and stepped on the shards of glass as she sprung at her. Not registering the pain. Hands curled into claws, a ribbon of bloody saliva falling from her jaws.

Her little brother's body on the floor, fingers still twitching madly.

Beneath Naomi's scream, the song on her mother's phone had played on.

Now, here. The farmhouse.

Where the cows are all dead.

She stands at the kitchen table looking out the window. The sun is bright this morning; steam rises across the expanse of the field. The wildflowers, the grasses, the cragged mountains far beyond, blue with distance. But the cows: Even from here she can see the flies harrying their humped black shapes. They'd been crying in the night—she'd told Denis that they probably needed to be milked, and Denis, drunk, had stalked out into the field and shot every one of them.

The bodies have been there for days. They've taken on the motionless, monolithic shape of the landscape, save for the trembling green sheen of flies upon them. The smell drifts into the house when the wind shifts. Denis and Emilie are somewhere on the upper floor, oblivious, twisted in their sheets, sweating out the dead couple's wine. She thinks of that poor woman hung up on the blade of Emilie's knife, of the man in the basement with Denis's bullet ricocheting in the bowl of his skull. The shallow graves Denis dug for them in the back field.

There are ants on the counter now, and a mad black circle of them in the honey left smeared on a plate. She wets a sponge and wipes them up, spends a moment stacking the dirty dishes in the sink. They have been here over two weeks now, seventeen days, and dread grows larger inside her every morning.

She starts washing the dishes, occasionally turning and looking out at the black shapes of the dead cows.

Run, she thinks for the millionth time. *Run.*

But no. That might have been an option before. It isn't now.

The clatter of dishes, the warm water on her hands. There's a well here, and a generator, and propane. The three of them have luxuriated in hot showers. In a stocked pantry, in beds, the wine. "I'm amazed no one raided them before us," Denis told her. "They were completely unprepared," he'd said, as if they'd brought death on themselves.

She gathers a bucket of food scraps and empty tins. Denis, complaining of fruit flies, has insisted she throw everything outside. She takes the compost bucket and goes to the back door, stepping carefully over the black drag-marks of blood there on the porch. When she comes back in she finds Emilie in the kitchen, her hair matted, face still puffy with alcohol and sleep. She pads past Naomi and fills a glass with water, then stands before the picture window. For the briefest moment, Naomi feels a sense of kinship with this woman, the horrors they have faced like some kind of connective tissue between them. But then the moment passes without a word, and Naomi goes back to the dishes. It's rare that Denis allows the two of them to be alone for any length of time. Perhaps, she muses, Emilie has killed him. Perhaps he's had a heart attack, dead in his new bed. She allows herself a brief moment of fantasy that it's so.

And then the baby starts crying, the sound drifting down the hall, Naomi coming back to herself.

"Better quiet him," Emilie says softly, the glass to her chest, still looking out the window.

Naomi goes into her bedroom and picks the baby up from his makeshift crib, a cardboard box lined with blankets. She lifts him, rocks him until he lets out a single hiccupping sob and then settles into her, making nonsense words. She walks slowly around the room, one hand on his back, and Denis leans in, his hair corkscrewed, fixing her with a single baleful stare. A look freighted with so much: with loathing and fury and a resentment at how intrinsically he's tied himself to her.

Two nights after he'd buried the man and woman in the field, Naomi had snuck down into the basement. Denis and Emilie were already passed out upstairs, still triumphant over their newly gained riches. She'd crept through the darkness, reluctant to even turn on the light until she got further from the stairwell, and then pulled on the chain of a single bulb near the child's alcove. The pull-chain wavered, casting a twisting shadow on the wall.

The baby's gaze, unfocused at first, had settled on her, his arms spasming. He lay on his back and opened his mouth, showing her a tiny scattering of teeth. A soundless, gray-skinned child with, she would find, a pair of filthy, adult-sized bite marks on his left forearm.

"Hi, Antoine," she'd whispered, thinking about her mother hunched over Hugo on the living room floor.

She had waited until the lightbulb on its chain had stopped its minute revolutions, then moved forward and picked him up. He'd writhed in her grasp and she held him at arm's length. There was, as ever, no specific feeling in her. There was nothing cosmic in the doing, nothing holy. There was no sense of *power* that moved through her. She simply turned him around, his back to her chest, and placed a hand upon his cold crown while he silently bucked. She held him to her like that for some interminable time.

A pastiche of images unspooled behind her eyes, a kind of shifting library of the child's life. His father staring down at him, concern etched upon his face. The horizon dipping and rising as he was carried somewhere. It's always been like this: She takes on some sort of psychic weight from the people she turns, catching these shuddering glimpses of their lives as they're pulled back—but for a child so young, there'd hardly been anything to make note of. Antoine's had been a small life.

No images of him while fevered. No images of the alcove, of his box. The darkened years he'd spent in the basement. There never are. It's as if no memories are formed in that darkness. As if the fever pauses everything, halts it.

At some point his small spasms had settled down.

She'd turned him around then, looked in his eyes, and saw the weight of life in him, the new awareness. His skin was already changing, even. Blood once again thrumming inside him. A heart returned to its familiar drumbeat. She held him to her chest as his first feeble cries began; he grasped her finger with one hand and squeezed.

She thought, Try and take him from me.

Try, and see what happens.

Naomi was twelve when Denis came into her life. She'd spent the year after the Message scavenging throughout central France, half-heartedly looking for her father until she was kidnapped by a group of reavers who'd made it their business to sell children. She was housed in a horse trailer with eight other boys and girls who ranged in ages from three to fourteen, all of them lashed together at the ankles to make escape more difficult. Denis's group—a bedraggled, bearded group of AWOL soldiers who still wore the uniforms of the French Army—had raided the reavers' encampment one night, making quick work of them. The children had watched the reavers die through a slat in the plywood that covered the trailer windows, the night briefly lit up with gunfire. Few of the children made any sound at all.

Denis's unit—it'd been him and four other men—had taken them away still in their leg-cuffs. They were led deep into a wooded area miles away from the encampment the reavers had made. Their leg-cuffs were cut and each child was paired with another, and they were put in tents that did little to dispel the chill. Still, Naomi's tent had felt luxurious compared to the horse trailer. She was put in there with a seven-year-old named Marie, who cried inconsolably about how hungry she was until she fell asleep with her thumb in her mouth. The plan, Naomi overheard the men talking around the fire, was to sell the children to an outfit in Melun, some forty-five kilometers outside of Paris. So they were just slavers killing other slavers, then. Stealing what had already been stolen.

All of Europe had trembled under the weight of the fevered in that first year. Crazed figures that ambled across the countryside, that flooded cities, that made more fevered wherever they went. Denis and the other soldiers, she would learn later, had abandoned their unit, which had been tasked with taking back Paris after it had been overrun.

They walked toward Melun for three days, making poor time. Fevered were everywhere, and the children made mistakes. One boy screamed when he stepped on a nail in the street, and a fevered rose up from behind a parked car as if drawn to him by a string. The ensuing gunfire brought more of them, and in the end, two of the youngest children and one of Denis's soldiers were dead.

Two days later and Melun was finally close. It was early, raining fiercely outside, still dark but heading toward dawn, when a drift found them.

The group had been sleeping in an industrial building at the edge of an overgrown, rock-studded field. The soldier tasked with guard duty had fallen asleep, and by the time he woke up, it was too late. The drift had discovered him, and as they fell on him the building's door had been pushed open. Within seconds, they filled the room.

Screams, bodies rising confused in the half-light. Fevered falling upon sleeping children. Gunshots pinging off the building's metal interior. Muzzle flash, bullets punching through flesh. Screams. Naomi had stood up and promptly tripped over someone's feet, skinning her hands on the cement floor. And then Denis had been beside her, pulling her up, shouldering aside a fevered who bit down on the sleeve of his uniform. Denis ran his knife into the man's eye and twisted, and he and Naomi ran out into the breaking dawn, her hands still stinging from her fall. They sprinted through the rutted field, and then farther to the tree line. At one point Naomi looked back and saw dozens more fevered staggering around the building. Screams echoed inside.

"Fuck," Denis had hissed—she hadn't known his name then, simply knew him as one of the captors who'd taken her after murdering her previous captors—and unslung his rifle, laying himself prone on the ground. "Don't run," he said, "or they'll get you."

She should have, though. She should have run through the trees, run until her legs gave out beneath her, until the building was a silver speck on the horizon. But fear rooted her there. She was twelve years old, and he was an angry adult with a gun, and he had told her to stay.

She remembers the percussive quality of his weapon, how quiet it seemed in the vastness of that field. Denis splayed in the mud, spacing his shots, dropping fevered as they milled around the building. She kneeled there beside him, thinking of Marie, crying with her thumb in her mouth. Thinking of the boy who had stepped on a nail. And Hugo, always Hugo. Denis dropping four, five, six of them without pause or breath, and even at twelve years old she marveled at his accuracy. The rain that fell on them was warm, like bathwater; the screams in the building were beginning to lessen.

Neither she nor Denis heard the fevered man stagger up behind them until he fell upon the length of Denis's body, latching onto his neck, biting at that fat ridge of tendon behind his ear. Denis had bellowed and flipped over, both men scrambling to get upright. Denis, the faster of the two, drove his hunting knife up through the man's jaw and pulled the blade to the side so that the jaw half-hung there in a tumble of sinew and yellow bone. And still the man had come after him, until Denis put the blade through the crown of his skull. Denis clasping a muddy hand to his own neck then, and when he turned to her, she saw the fear of the fever. Of knowing it would happen, but not what it would be like.

"Come with me," Naomi said, three words that she's regretted every day in the four years that have followed. So much could have been different had she let him turn. But she'd said it, and something in her voice made Denis follow her, and no fevered had come after them. She led him through the rain some forty, fifty meters away to a rock wall under the canopy of trees, and she had him sit and lean against it.

Where had the knowledge come from? The implicit understanding that she could do this? She'd thought of her father and the conversation they'd had the year before the Message. There had been a surety inside her, a sudden, dirt-deep understanding that were she to touch this man, she could help him. She kneeled beside Denis, who was breathing fast, his hand still pressed to the jetting wound at his neck. She'd reached out and gently pulled his hand down. She'd touched the wound there, her own hand trembling, and Denis had gasped, tried to push her away. She put her hand back as he stared at her, his face trying to settle on a single expression.

God, the images she had seen when she touched him. The things this man had done, and had done to him.

Why had she healed him like that? This killer. This man willing to sell children.

Because, she thought, if you can save someone, you should.

And if you can't save the right person, you'll spend forever trying to save everyone else.

Denis had looked up at her, his back against the stone. She had taken her hand away from his neck and there was understanding on his face: He was healed. She had healed him. He was still bleeding, and the wound was filthy, but she had pulled the fever from him before it had had a chance to take root.

"You need to clean it," she said. "Put a bandage on."

"What the fuck are you?" he'd whispered.

Naomi had thought of her father's tattoo. The strange mark on her own thigh.

"I don't know," she said, and that had been the truth.

———

Denis, upon hearing the sound of the squalling, newly healed baby in the basement, had stormed downstairs in his underwear, his pale body a riddle of scars, and had struck Naomi in the face. A looping roundhouse that she knew he'd pulled even as she was sent sprawling to the concrete floor. She'd curled around the baby to protect him, her vision a galaxy of dark stars when her head hit the floor. Denis had stood over her, Antoine screaming.

"I should smash your fucking brains in," Denis said. "What have you done?"

Naomi watched as Emilie's legs appeared at the top of the steps, her footfalls cautious. After a moment she had turned, the legs disappearing again.

Denis held out a hand. "Give him to me, Naomi."

"No," she said.

His jaw had snapped shut, loud enough that it made a sound. She had seen him kill people for less.

"Give me that child. Now."

Still curled on the floor, the baby writhing in her arms, Naomi had peered up at him and said, "No." Had said, "If you hurt him, I'll stop doing it for you."

She remembers the look on his face, how he'd never considered such a thing.

"If you stop doing it, you're useless to me."

"Then I die."

"Then you both die," Denis countered. "What's the point of that?"

Naomi had sat up; the movement seemed to revitalize the baby, who screamed even louder. As if he knew his fate was being decided.

She'd begun rocking him then, still sitting on the cold floor. "You think there's a point to any of this?" She spat it, like an accusation. "The point is, if he dies, Denis, I stop. And if I stop, what will you be? Another fucking bandit on the road."

He surprised her by smiling. "Watch yourself."

Then he'd looked around the dismal room, the dusty, shadow-choked corners. He rubbed absently at a scar on his chest.

"If he keeps me awake—" he said.

"He'll keep you awake sometimes, Denis. He's a baby. He'll cry."

Denis's face darkened again, his goodwill gone. "I survived without you, girl. What makes you think I can't do it again?"

"You did survive," Naomi said, her heart a fist in her throat. Knowing this gambit was a dangerous one. "But look around you. What kind of life was it on your own?"

He'd stared at her until she looked away. Then he cursed under his breath and stomped back upstairs.

She comes from her room after quieting Antoine to find Denis hunched over a bowl of cereal at the kitchen table, the black shapes of the dead cows in the field behind him. He tells her they have an appointment at ten-thirty.

Naomi distractedly pushes her own cereal around with her spoon. It is tasteless, old, from the stockpile in the pantry. Antoine slept poorly last night, and Naomi, tired, feels all the rough edges of herself brought into sharp relief. "Is it here, or do we have to go there?"

"Here," says Denis, wiping his mouth with the back of his hand. His hair has grown long enough that it sticks up now. He puts a thumbnail between two teeth and says, "And that baby better not make a goddamn sound while it happens."

Naomi rises, pushes her half-finished bowl over to him—no wasting food allowed—and he sneers and says, "And why don't you take a shower beforehand. You smell like shit."

Eyes shut, Naomi nods in agreement. Every time she thinks she can no longer be cut by this man, he manages to find a way.

Antoine is still sleeping in her room when the visitors arrive. Protocol dictates that she is to stay in the house while Denis negotiates. She and Emilie sit at the kitchen table. The clouds have broken open and bees trundle about in the wildflowers. The dead cows lie there like the leftovers of some bad dream. She swears she can hear the hum of the flies through the open front door.

A pair of men walk up the road beside the field. A fevered man is lashed between them; ropes have been tied around his midsection, pinning his arms to his sides. Black netting is wrapped around his head, and one man drags him along while the other guides him with a stick if he begins to go off course into the ditch. Denis waits on the porch, sipping from a coffee cup full of wine, his pistol on the railing. His rifle leans against the kitchen wall, by the window.

When the men get to where the paved section of the driveway begins, Denis tells them to stop. They do, the one with the rope yanking on the fevered man to still him.

"So who is he?" Denis calls out.

The one with the rope says, "He's a friend of ours."

Denis laughs and sips from his cup. "You treat a friend like that?"

What other option is there, Naomi thinks. The fever carves out any allegiance, any love, any consideration. Of course they have to tie him up, put netting over his face.

"Well, he bites if we don't, sir," the one with the rope manages.

"All night long, all day," the other one says.

"How long's he had the fever," Denis asks.

"A year, maybe."

"We kept him in the garage."

She can hear the smile in Denis's voice. "And he's just been in there all this time."

"What else were we supposed to do? He's our friend." This causes Denis to bray a single gunshot of laughter, and she realizes he's already drunk. Ten-thirty in the morning. He's coming undone, she thinks.

"You have the money?"

The two men trade glances. They are disheveled, ageless and begrimed. Friends, lovers, brothers. Who knows. Naomi has long stopped trying to discern people's relationships. She touches the fevered and the fever is pulled from them. Denis gets his money, his guns, his food, and Naomi gets to continue living some sort of life. Gets to take care of Antoine.

"We heard you would take other things," one man says.

Denis drains his cup. Naomi can see the silvery stretch of scar tissue behind his ear where he was bitten. "Like what?"

"We have gold."

Denis waits a beat, then says, "You have gold."

"We raided the treasury of a bank some towns over," one starts saying, but Denis is already walking down the porch toward them, tucking his pistol into his waistband.

The fevered becomes briefly animated at Denis's arrival, snapping and pulling against the rope. His head is a featureless black sphere in its cocoon of netting. He wears stained gray dress pants and a rolled-up long-sleeve shirt stiff with grime, and finally the one with the stick tires of his pulling and rears back and strikes the back of his knees. The fevered falls to the ground, where he rolls on his back and writhes. It's then that Naomi sees the mark on the inside of his forearm and all her breath is pulled from her throat.

A tattoo of a winged knife. Was that what it was? She'd only seen it for a second.

A whisper against the window glass, pulled from her almost against her will: "Papa?"

She stands up, takes a few halting steps toward the door.

"What are you doing," Emilie says, but Naomi hardly hears her. Remembers her mother's back, her bent body. Hugo's twitching fingers. Her father had left for work that morning and she was sick so he just called out to her through her door that he loved her and she never got to say goodbye. But the tattoo. She could heal him, she could *heal* him and then—

"What is his name?" she calls out from the porch, and Denis's head whips around at the sound of her voice, his eyes cutting and furious.

"What?" one of the men says.

"Get your ass back inside," Denis calls out. "Now." Naomi takes her first step down the porch, her hand on the smooth banister, and the man with the stick seems to trip on nothing, his feet tangling around each other as he falls to the ground.

She stops at the bottom of the porch, the world taking on the taffy-slow cadence of a dream. The fevered man begins worming over to the fallen body, the man with the stick—who now, Naomi sees, has a red flower of blood on his back—while Denis pivots and begins running low back toward the house, firing his pistol blindly behind him. The big picture window that she's spent so much time staring out of the past month shatters with a sound that's almost musical.

Denis, only a few feet away from her now, staggers and falls. He grunts like someone has punched him and then scrambles up the stairs, grabbing her roughly by the arm and pulling her inside. He slams the front door shut, locks it.

Through the starred, broken front window, Naomi sees men step out from the scrim of trees beyond the field. Dressed in green camouflage, holding weapons, moving in tandem. Naomi can't breathe.

Denis, gasping, seizing his rifle, tells Naomi and Emilie to get upstairs, to the closet in his bedroom. Hide there.

"I have to get my father," Naomi says woodenly, watching the fevered man on the driveway try uselessly to bite at the dead man's face through his mask of netting.

Denis casts her a wild, crazed look. "What?"

"That's my father out there."

"Who is?"

"The fevered one."

Somehow she missed it, but the other man, the man with the rope, lies dead in the driveway now as well. His body splayed out, facedown.

"The fevered one?" Denis repeats, and even as he pushes past her, goes to the window, she knows what he'll do. What else could she ever expect from him? It is the only thing Denis knows.

He braces the barrel of the rifle against the trim of the window and fires. Her father—if it had truly been him—lies still now, the top of his head pulped and glistening.

Denis, always a lethal shot.

Naomi screams. She claws at him and he shoves her away. She catches a glimpse of the men in camouflage as they break and spread toward the edges of the property like drifting smoke. One of them drops behind the body of a cow in the field and fires a burst that marches across the front of the house, sending a rain of splinters and bits of insulation drifting down upon the three of them.

"Christ, get her upstairs," Denis bellows.

Naomi runs to her bedroom and grabs Antoine from his meager crib and then follows Emilie up the stairwell.

In the bedroom that Denis and Emilie share—the unmade bed, clothes on the floor, wine bottles on every surface, all of Denis's military fastidiousness vanished—they hide in the closet. The fusty odor of hanging clothes, of dust. The most normal smell in the world. The sound of gunfire beneath them, bullets punching through lathe and wood, twanging off stonework. The baby screaming through all of it.

Some interminable, unknowable amount of time later, the shooting stops. Emilie is a hunched, pressed shape against her. The smell of Antoine's shit fills the tiny space, and then the closet door opens and the room is filled with the blinding and terrible daylight of that late morning. One of the men in camouflage stands there. A black balaclava over his face, the bore of his pistol roving between them.

"Who can heal?" the man asks in American-accented French. "Which of you is the healer?"

Emilie pushes herself up from the closet floor, saying in a mad rush, "She is, she's the one, it's unnatural, she's an abomination," and the man tells her to step back. Naomi stands, her legs screaming from being in the same position for so long.

"Is this your baby?" he asks her.

"Yes," she says.

"It's not," Emilie says, "it's one she brought back from the dead, a fevered, an abomination as well," and the man turns and raises the rifle at her and she shrieks and shrinks down with her hands over her head. He zip-ties Emilie's hands, and Naomi feels one of those rare rushes of pity for the woman.

"Come with me," the soldier says to Naomi, motioning her forward with his gloved hands. He zip-ties her as well, in the front, and carefully, so that she can still hold Antoine. He leads her out of the bedroom and down the hall.

"What about me?" Emilie cries. The soldier ignores her.

Downstairs, the farmhouse teems with activity. A half dozen men in camouflage are walking around, the walls littered with bullet holes. Everyone wears those black masks. Their fatigues bear no insignia.

Denis lies dead in the kitchen.

On the tile floor, his face is untouched, his eyes gazing up at the ceiling as if deep in concentration. His feet are crossed at the ankle. His torso is a red valley of bullet holes, the coppery reek of blood close in the room.

The soldier puts a hand on her shoulder. "Look over here."

"I want to see him like this," she says, and he takes his hand away. Antoine reaches up and pulls her hair.

Another soldier approaches and the one who walked her down the stairs says, in English, "Left, upstairs bedroom."

The soldier nods, walks away.

Moments later she hears the gunshot just as the sound of a chopper begins filling the world outside the shattered windows.

THEO MARSDEN

Rolla, Missouri

Plenty of reasons why they chose Rolla. The Mississippi River only a hundred miles to the east, and Rolla with a highway transport hub available to every corner of the country. A working military airport a dozen miles away. Being in the Midwest, it'd hopefully be a bit tougher for any Chinese or Russian ICBMs to make their way over, though he knows that's mostly wishful thinking. Besides, it seems the days of nuclear threats are done, at least for the time being; Russia's apparently a wasteland of Cold War concrete and rusting infrastructure, and China's fevered population outnumbers the living three to one.

Mostly, though, it's optics. They're going for a rebrand, culturally and economically. DC puts a bitter taste in people's mouths.

Rolla offers an antidote to Washington's grimness and, let's face it, to Yardley's evangelism and now-entrenched hermeticism. Rolla's the new face. Rolla gives off a small-town feel, bunting and parades and red barns and apple festivals. The old world's dead, Rolla says, and the nation's relentless cynicism shall die with it. For now, Yardley's on board. There will come a time when he and the president will have to ford the chasm of differences between them, even if it's only geographically, but for now, Yardley sees Rolla as valuable. Worthwhile.

But mostly? It's because of the labyrinth.

The labyrinth's the *real* reason why Marsden picked Rolla.

The university has its own microgrid that, thank jumped-up Jesus Christ, has been up and running, fully functional and staffed by qualified personnel for some time now. Which means that the new Capitol has its own self-sustaining power source, even during blackouts. It'd been part of the school's engineering program back in the day. Replete with a number of laboratories and research spaces, the labyrinth's a closed-off, insular microcosm complete with a grand total of two entry and exit points—an elevator and a stairwell— making it an ideal containment facility from a security standpoint.

You have something dangerous you want to hold captive? Like Matthew Coffin?

Keep him eighty feet underground.

Marsden and Eastman follow a soldier out of the elevator and down a hallway. Everything is glossed and quiet down here, just the hum of the overhead lights, the sharp snap of their footfalls. The place is hushed with a sense of seriousness, of industry, which is another reason why Marsden loves it here. Important things are being done. At the end of the hall, he swipes his badge along a pad by the steel door that leads to the laboratory and research areas.

The main area of the labyrinth is huge, so large that it gives their voices a certain hollowness when they speak. High cement ceilings and that unspoken sense of pressure from all that earth above them. He badges open another door that leads to a smaller antechamber, this time motioning for Eastman to hang back. It's a decent-sized room of rough-hewn rock walls and empty save for one thing: a man standing inside a glass-fronted box. Marsden takes a number of deep, calming breaths as the pneumatic door whirs shut behind him. Shuts his eyes. Tries to calm himself. Matthew Coffin—whatever he is now—is suffused with this strange magnetism, a cruel allure. Marsden comes down here often, more often than strictly necessary. And more than once he's considered breaking the box's glass front and doing something terrible with the shards, using a pale green piece to slit his own throat. Or bringing a handful of it to his mouth and biting down, swallowing, turning his whole mouth into a red hole, the glorious burn of it, the pulping of his tongue, blood pouring between his teeth like water through a grate—

"Jesus wept," Marsden hisses, running a hand across his brow. They keep the labyrinth monitored and air-controlled, but being near Coffin like this, his body always feels like it's fluctuating between hot and absolutely chilling.

And yet he comes here, stays long after other matters require his attention. Coffin, somehow, eases his troubles. Distracts him. Marsden almost *luxuriates* in the bloody, miasmic quicksand that are his thoughts when he's down here. How he finds himself reduced to something animalistic, his thoughts muddled and warm, like the dragging of a knife against a throat—

He opens his eyes and looks up to find Matthew Coffin staring at him.

Marsden grins, shakes a finger at him. "Oh, you're a tricky one, you." The box they've housed him in is an oblong thing. A casket, essentially. Eight feet tall, three sides of tempered steel, with the box-face itself made up of three-inch resistant glass, supposedly shatter-proof. Should hold back a fucking tank, is what the techs have told him. You want to take him out of the box, you have to open it via the electronic pad at the side, which takes another badge—and the only ones with clearance for that are him, Yardley and Jack Bonner.

The glass has a sea-green cast to it and it gives Coffin the ghastly, drawn countenance of a movie monster. He finds himself enrapt with the wreckage of the man's body. His skin looks rotted, gray, and Marsden knows he weighs one hundred and sixty-six pounds, a weight that has not fluctuated an ounce in all the years he's been held here. His hair is an oily, clotted black that brushes the back of his neck. He is missing two toenails on his right foot that have never grown back. Derrick Eastman's squad found him in a townhouse in Chicago during a recon mission a month after the Message; Coffin had clicked his tongueless mouth, just once, and Eastman's squad had turned their rifles on each other, with Derrick the only survivor. Since that time, there've been no episodes, no speech, no movement. They've kept him in what amounts to a storage unit and he hasn't done shit. Stands and stares and that's it.

A missing hand, with a grisly yellow-black ring of meat at the wrist.

An eyelid that hangs limply over the dark hollow of a missing eye.

That dry slot where the tongue used to be.

The owner of the remnants.

Shit, the *supplier* of the remnants.

There are dozens of glyphs carved into his flesh; many of them are illegible, given that they're warring with a number of large wounds that researchers believe are due to boat blades, from the man's time spent in the Willamette River some fifteen years back. No one on Marsden's research team can tell him anything about the glyphs themselves—they're not aligned with any lexicon or language of note. Circles, triangles, perhaps something that looks like an eye. Large entrance and exit wounds are scattered along his torso and upper arms, the result of Coffin getting chewed up by gunfire from Eastman's team.

Matthew Coffin. Founding member of the Blank Letters, the band who penned the song "I Won't Forget It," which was also used as cover for the recorded message that essentially ended the known world.

Matthew Coffin. The man in the box.

Pray for guidance, my ass.

"What *are* you?" Marsden murmurs now, taking a single step forward, lifting his chin to peer up into Coffin's remaining eye. Unlike the fevered, this eye glitters with a cold intelligence. A cunning, and,

THE DEVIL BY NAME

Marsden thinks, a clear contempt. Coffin's lips part, his head tilting like an inquisitive dog. Marsden catches a glimpse of that red-black cavity that used to hold his tongue. Their eyes form this bridge, some kind of electric, transitory thing, Marsden falling back into those dark waters again, his brain churning with gore, when there's a sharp knock on the door and he gasps, brought back to himself.

He walks over and badges the door, his vision still a little blurred.

"Sir," Eastman says, "I just received word from the office." *Office* being code for Terradyne's network of intelligence analysts.

Muddied thoughts clear a little. He sees Eastman's eyes jump over his shoulder to Matthew Coffin in his box and then back to Marsden's face.

"Okay," he says, impatient. "And?"

"The retrieval in Nevers was successful."

"The girl?"

Eastman nods. "They're on their way here with her."

"Does Jack know?"

"I don't know, sir."

"Alright. Don't say a word to him."

"Yes, sir." The briefest jitter of Eastman's eyes moving from Coffin and back to him again. They certainly have a history, these two. "Sir, there's one more thing."

"What's that?"

"She has a baby with her."

Marsden pauses. "A baby. There wasn't any baby mentioned in the report we got from Yardley."

"Yes, sir."

Marsden pinches the bridge of his nose and steps out of Coffin's cell, relief and loss somehow both snaking their way through him at the sound of the door hissing closed. His mind clears almost immediately.

They make their way back to the elevator and Marsden badges the pad. "Make a note, Derrick."

"Sir."

"No one talks to that girl until I do. She can be welcomed, given food and water, scanned to see if she's fevered, whatever. But no one talks to her until I do. Not Jack, Suarez, not anyone. Me."

"Yes, sir."

KATHERINE MORIARTY

Cape Winston, Massachusetts

Sound of the ocean, the wind howling against her. The star-smeared sky above. The blackened frame of the church there in the distance, Katherine walking to it again. Drawn to it in spite of herself. Unwilling to try and discern the meaning behind the desire. Petitioning God, loathing God, furious at God. She walks, mourns Nick, tries not to think of him as dead, as broken, as lost. Tries to moor herself in the memories of him as a boy, as the man he'd been before he turned.

What else can she do? Her heart's been broken a million times already. You'd think it would get easier, but she keeps finding new rooms for the heartache to lie down in.

She had been afraid that Matthew would be angry when he learned she was pregnant. Would leave. But he had surprised her. That was his one constant: The man could always surprise her. He'd surprised her that time with his joy. My old man was a shit, he said, and vowed to be different. For a long time, she believed him, and they'd forged a life together. The three of them—no, the five of them, truly, with Arthur and Doogy, the other members of the Blank Letters. Nick had toured with them, had grown up in the van on the road; by the time he was four he was up on stage in industrial-strength ear protection and a little toy guitar, pretending to play along with the band during their encores. He was a kind and patient and quiet kid, and after Matthew's death, when Katherine's fear of the world had narrowed her life down to the smallest of apertures, he'd moved in with her. Took care of her. Protected her.

Ah, God.

The vast unfairness of it. She has managed to compartmentalize any guilt about the Message itself—she sure as hell didn't write the song that was used with that intention in mind. Nick, though. That's another story. That her son should be reduced to this. Because of Matthew Coffin's weaknesses. And because, when you get down to it, because of her. If she had just done better, done more.

Seen Mathew for what he was.

But he hadn't always been that way, had he? Arrogant, yes. Insecure and self-centered at times, but also . . .

She walks the beach and remembers Matthew putting Nick's chubby little fingers on the frets of a guitar, the boy plinking out his first awkward chords.

Sees Nick bringing him a card he'd made Matthew in class, first grade, maybe—a band of ladybugs with mohawks. *HAPY FATHRS' DAY.*

His first job as a teenager, part-time at a record store, a thing that Matthew had lined up for him, the string-pulling a perpetual embarrassment to Nick in the few years he worked there after school.

And Nick's voice on the phone when she was taken, forcibly, to Chicago. The last time she spoke to him, before he'd . . .

Well, before.

Just before.

There are times when the ache and the loss are so profound that she wonders how it is she'll go on. She marvels at how the heart just stupidly keeps pushing its tired blood along. How she still needs to piss, eat, sleep. The stupid, pointless bravery in standing up. In put-

ting one foot down and lifting another, navigating the constant em-
battlements of the world. She has considered more than once just
offering Nick her arm out there in the shed. And she too could be
lost forever in whatever fog he's been cast in.

Matthew had been her husband and then he had been an anchor
around her, dragging her and Nick down with his furies, his infideli-
ties, the ever-fluctuating, mercurial nature of his love.

And now he is her jailer. Her heart's been cleaved from her because this stupid, selfish pact he made with whatever monster seized
upon him—that made him whatever wretched, fucked-up thing he
is now—wound up turning Nick. Nick, the one thing she had left to
moor her to the earth.

A man on the phone had told her today that she should be
ashamed for her fealty to a murderous government, and there is a
part of her that agrees. It's Terradyne that hires the fever hunters,
allows them to run slipshod and mad across the countryside. Killing
all the afflicted—she likes that word, it makes sense to her, it fits well
with the thing that's happened to Nick—or shipping them off somewhere to be shoved in a box.

But isn't that what you've done, Katherine? With your own son?

She crests the rise and crosses the street and there stands at the
burned remains of the church.

She keeps coming back here. Like some answer will reveal itself.
If there's a devil—and surely that's what Matthew's become now,
what he was in Chicago—then there must be some God. Right?
Some equivalent? What she saw in the townhouse wasn't an aberra-
tion, or some scientific anomaly. It was undead, all river-brine and
resurrected gray flesh, reaching for her with the only hand it had left.
Where had God been during all of that?

She crosses the street and walks up the concrete steps into the
ruins, grit rasping underfoot. Her parents had never been religious;
there was a time when Katherine was young, where for a brief period
she'd fallen in with a neighbor girl whose parents had taken Katherine to church for a month or two of Sundays. She had even been

gifted a small faux-leather Bible with onionskin pages, its type so small and confusing her seven-year-old mind could hardly decipher it. But she remembers the book feeling totemic, full of some unspoken magic. Katherine's mother had tolerated it with a bemused sort of benevolence until Katherine claimed to have dreamt of an angel in her room, a man-shaped thing with fanned wings that shifted color like an iridescent puddle of gasoline. The angel—she was convinced it was some kind of angel—had told her things of great importance, things that always seemed on the cusp of being pinned down and remembered upon waking, but the knowledge always managed to flit away. After a few mornings of talk about angels with shining wings, her mother had put a stop to church.

And that had been God to her: a small Bible with a pebbled orange cover and some strange dreams. Nothing she saw after that—in her life or the world itself—made her lean toward the notion of a loving God. In fact, the opposite happened; the world's boundless cruelty seemed tantamount proof of holy absence.

At the rear of the church is a swath of floor mostly cleared of debris. She feels her footsteps change as she walks across this space. She stops, steps again, strikes her heel against the floor. Again, that hollowness.

Katherine crouches down, arms on her knees. Peers in the gloom.

She sees an iron ring inlaid into the floor, then a three-by-three-foot section of flooring, the seams darker against the already-dark floor.

Katherine touches the ring.

"Why the hell not," she says, and pulls.

The hatch opens with a squeal, a drift of dust and ash falling down into the mouth of the hole. She steps back, waiting for something to burst forth, but nothing does. There's a set of gray wooden stairs and cement walls, and beyond that, nothing. A dark cave. Some subcellar. She has no flashlight; her phone offers little illumination.

She closes the hatch again, softly, and stands. Makes her way out of the ruins. She's happened upon one of the hidden, forgotten spaces of the world—there are more of them now, obviously, but it's always good to know another.

She goes out to the shed with her mug, the two black bags for their heads in the pocket of her jacket. Her backyard is fenced; Lark Street is mostly empty anyway, a few neighbors at the end of the block, the houses bracing her on each side quietly falling into themselves.

Nick bucks and strains against his chains when he sees her. His eyes widen. Every single time, some part of her hopes it's in recognition. That he *sees* her.

But it's not love, nothing like it.

He sees prey, is all.

Katherine puts a fist to her lips. She's crying again. Can't help it. He strains toward her, his jaws clacking. Tendons on his neck taut as wires. "What, that's all I am to you," she says in a terrible Boston accent, "a piece'a chopped liver?" and somewhere beneath her voice is madness and the great, profound sorrow rooted at the heart of it all. No one should have to live through this. Goddamn you, Matthew. Make me see our kid like this and I still have to go about my life?

She knuckles her tears away. She breathes. Picks up her mug and sips her tea. A foot of space between them. The ocean is a white noise machine at her back. The chains hiss as he strains, relaxes, strains, relaxes.

"I could kill you," she says. "Maybe I should. Would that be better?"

"Shit, I'll do it," a voice says behind her, and Katherine spins, the mug falling from her hands onto the grass.

The fever hunter is there—the redheaded one with the curving scar at his ear. She sees two things right away: He's raising a pistol at her, and he is swaying with drunkenness. The other hunter, his brother, is even closer. That one's pistol is lowered at his thigh, and he holds out what is probably meant to be a calming hand toward her. Had they followed her? How had she not heard them?

"Get away from him," the hunter close to her says, and she knows, just by looking at their faces, what they'll do. They'll shoot Nick where he stands, and she'll be robbed of her son twice—the first time when he was turned, and now, here, in a volley of bullets, wrapped in the chains she's put him in.

The three of them in this frieze, until Katherine screams—screams *loud,* years of banked rage and fear behind it—and takes the iron bolt from her pocket and strikes the closest hunter cleanly across the temple. The sound is meaty, significant, and he drops, and the drunk one—*They don't* feel, *they don't* love *you*—staggers toward her, his pistol suddenly bucking in his fist. Loud cracks, muzzle-flash that lights up the ugly snarl of his face. Katherine screams again, some dim part of her hearing the twang of a round punching through the corrugated steel of the shed and she runs toward him just as someone tackles him from behind, her small backyard suddenly rife with movement.

The redheaded hunter's on the ground, dazed, a short distance from his brother, and Katherine reaches down and picks up his pistol, her palm slick with sweat. He's pushing himself up when the man who tackled him—a Black man with hair graying at the temples, eyes wide with panic—hooks a heel in his ribs and pushes him down to the ground again. "Yeah, why don't you stay put until we get this shit figured out," he says. Then he sees Katherine aiming the pistol at him and his arms rise skyward fast.

"I heard the screams," he says. "Just trying to help. And, uh, trying not to get shot too if we can manage that."

DEAN HAGGERTY

Stab, Kentucky — Cape Winston, Massachusetts

Christ, how many years since you smelled the sea air? Dean's asking himself this as he pedals along the sidewalk that braces the windswept beach of this little ocean town, the gray jetty leaning out there in the chop like a roofing nail.

How long since you walked on the sand somewhere, heard the pounding of the surf? Not since those summer weeks at Nags Head, he and George playing in the surf, Nichole reading on the beach, those big shades on, that sun hat, him picking up his boy and whirling him around, seawater jeweled on his arms. George screaming with glee, how *light* he'd been, his head lifted back, feet trailing the surf. Him and Nichole saving up all year, him working graveyard and hardly seeing either of them, felt like, but there were always those two weeks in some Nags Head seaside house, often smaller than their apartment back home, all they could afford, but with the ocean right there. George and his sandcastles, his digging, his wrestling with Dad. Never tired, the boy. All this before Dean's heart got whittled out of his chest.

Along with this memory comes a brutal flare of loss, a sudden throbbing ache for his kid, his wife, for the whole long-gone world. Son dead, wife gone, all before the Message, and now the world reduced to the road behind him and the road in front. Even his cubicle at the answering service, with its sickly cactus and glitchy mouse, is spied these days through the ache of nostalgia, and he *knows* that job was mostly bullshit. Still, here he is, smelling the ocean for the first time in decades. Happy to be alive and mourning the whole damn world all at once.

He pedals on, unsure of where to go next. He's hungry, he's broke, his cart's inventory is at its barest since he anointed himself a ragman all those years back. Most importantly, those boys back in Kentucky seem to have carved some essential bravery out of him. He's ridden hard for days, weeks, trying to distance himself from them. He knows that they're long gone—men like that don't generally venture far from home, prefer to lord it over folks via a familiar locale—but his heart still flinches at the memory. He'd mostly traveled at night, slept during the day, set back from the road.

That night, he'd dove into the underbrush at the end of the bridge as the Kentucky boys fired their guns. They'd had no spotlights, thankfully, and he was able to crawl back up and peer out of the gloom and watch them in the garish illumination of their own headlights as they examined his cart. Heartsick at the quickness with which they threw his entire inventory into the back of a truck bed. All his carefully labeled bins. His entire life.

He listened to them, a trio of bearded men in baseball caps and plaid button-ups, standing around their trucks. Watched them guzzle white cans of Jane beer while one of them rooted around in the bins, casually throwing his shit on the ground.

"You guys want the bike? Seems in decent shape."

"Hell, I got no shortage of bicycles."

"What about this cart thing he's got?"

"Rickety-looking," one of them had murmured.

"I dunno, seems pretty solid to me. These welds look handmade. Did a good job."

"Yeah, listen to Ricky here. Master welder."

"Masturbator."

"Oh, kiss my ass."

"We could scrap it."

Groans all around. "I'm so sick of scrapping shit. You all can do it, but I'm out."

"So no bike, no cart?"

"Fuck him, long as he keeps his ass out of town."

"Guy can probably hear you right now."

"Shit, that boy left a hole in the trees over there like the goddamn Kool-Aid Man. He's in the next county."

"Well, I ain't leaving it for him to come running back to."

"I hear you."

"Load it up?"

"Fuck it, why not."

They put the bike and cart in one truck, the bins in the other, and turned back the way they'd come, back toward Stab. Headlights twisting through the dark as they pulled U-turns, and then Dean had been alone. Him and the bugs and thorns, the burble of the creek down below.

He stood, brushed mud from his pants, tried to calm his heart. Push the fear down. His choices were equally simple and terrible.

He could leave it all, count himself lucky he'd escaped with his life.

Or he could go after them. Get everything back. God, even get some of it back. Where would he ever find a torch to do welds like that again? And scarcity or not, it was still years' worth of inventory in the back of that pickup, countless hours' worth of careful salvage.

Dean was a ragman. Without his inventory, he was a man with a gun walking the world, alone. A ragman brought out the best in people. Brought out the wonderment, the notion that not all was lost. A ragman pulled the joy from found things, made them new again.

A ragman ate.

A man with a gun just took and took, courted death every minute. It wasn't even a choice.

He started walking the way he'd come. Back toward Stab.

Turned out it was easy to find them.

In town, he saw that orange truck, bright as a safety cone, parked in a doorless garage next to a fenced-in area full of chained-up dogs. Drums of machine parts, broken appliances, and rotting two-by-fours dotted the yard. For all their talk of not wanting to scrap, they seemed to traffic in exactly that.

The retrieval of his gear had not gone well. Had turned lethal, in fact. The dogs had alerted them to his arrival, and Dean is pretty sure at least one of the men died after he'd left him pitched against an oil drum full of bent rebar, the man kicking frantically at the muddy ground as blood poured black from a bullet wound in his neck. The bellows of the man's friends in the dark, the frenzied dogs, the clatter of the empty cart behind him as he'd jumped on his bike and hauled ass back out of town. Got the cart, and a miracle that he was able to hook it to the bike, but his inventory was gone. No retrieving that.

Two days later, he'd walked the bike and cart off the road and through a thin stand of scrub oaks. Dean needed to sleep. He was exhausted and thirsty and too afraid to try and salvage anything for the cart yet—Stab still felt too close. He'd pushed everything through the trees and came to a small clearing. The ground there was trod flat and in the middle of the space was a fevered lashed to a mud-clotted office chair.

He had been tied to the chair with loop after loop of barbed wire. His arms and torso were a rubbery, scalloped horror of torn flesh where the barbs had become snared in the skin. The wheels and lower chassis of the chair had been buried in the ground so that only the chair itself stuck out. There were no discerning features to the man's face anymore; it was a caved-in thing, chopped at and broken. The eyes had been removed and the sockets filled with dirt and pebbles. A scorched, blackened hole where the nose had been. The man sensed him, though, and lifted his face toward the tops of the oaks, toward the sky. His fingers had been chopped off, but Dean had watched as the backs of his hands flexed and pulled at the wire that bound him. Bullet holes were scattered across his body, and a number of black wounds pocked the man's shins and the tops of his feet, as if they'd used a drill. Nails large and small stuck out of him in odd clusters.

Worst of all, they'd somehow run a rust-speckled sawblade, big as a dinner plate, between his jaws and almost all the way through the back of the skull, through the spine but *not quite,* then left it there and lashed more barbed wire all around it all, so it was this crazed amalgam of ruined face and hanging jaw and sawblade and wire, this cage of hell encompassing the man's head, the jaw crooked and ripped and set at a different angle than the rest of his skull. The whole thing was mostly bloodless. There were hardly any flies.

It seemed the man had been there for a long time. The wire was rusty in places, the fabric of the chair that was not mudded had faded to a dull, washed-out gray. It'd been sunny that day, and on the light-dappled ground beneath the trees, Dean saw evidence of the torture that had been wrought upon him. Flattened ammo boxes, a gasoline canister, its plastic faded to pink. Beer bottles, the labels peeled off. One waxy green shotgun shell. A rusted wrench half-buried in the damp earth that the ragman in him categorized in a single second as unsalvageable, an act he did against his own will, some automatic thing that he'd honed in himself over the years and in this moment hated himself for. The man was nude and Dean looked away from his genitals, afraid of seeing what brutalities had been done there.

Like a fucking fevered Pez dispenser, he'd thought, and when he turned and vomited, nothing had come out, not even bile. He tried to imagine who it was that might be coming out to this little clearing in the trees whenever the hurt or boredom or desire struck them— whatever the screaming blue fuck it was that drove people to do this. The man was making small clicking sounds behind him and it took

Dean a moment to realize it was the steel of the sawblade clicking against the man's spine as he tried to buck in the chair, to get at him. A bird twittered in the trees and Dean started crying then, and his body seemed to resent even this, because no tears came. Just dry, ugly sobs.

He took the Ruger from his waistband and aimed it at the man's head. Since the shoot-out in Stab, he had one bullet left—he'd checked a dozen times since then, like more might suddenly appear in the magazine if he was quick enough.

His hand shook. He'd let out a little hiss of disgust with himself and steadied his aim and even took a step forward. Still the fevered's fingerless hands flexed, those shattered feet digging their divots in the earth. Little dribbles of dirt spilled from the eye sockets.

Dean couldn't pull the trigger. Couldn't do it. He put the Ruger back in his waistband and swiped furiously at his still-dry eyes.

He tried to say *I'm sorry* but all that came out was a husky croak. Tried to say *I can't spare the bullet*, and there was nothing. He walked out of the clearing, pushed the bike and cart back to the road and pedaled furiously. He'd ridden for three more hours until he came to with the bike rattling on the gravel shoulder, the world suddenly dimmed, and Dean realizing he was about to pass out. He pulled everything into a grass-choked ditch, not caring who saw him, and fell asleep exhausted beside his empty cart. And it hardly mattered because his dreams were filled with the man in the chair anyway. He woke with the sun going down bloody against the horizon and it was like no time had passed at all for how tired he still was. And he knew that he had found a terrible thing that would stay with him forever.

Later, the days and nights merging together into one long half-dream, he's pedaling along the boardwalk that laces the beachside of this little town, moonlight carving the surface of the water into shards of rippling, reflected light. CAPE WINSTON, the sign had said on the outskirts some way back. In the distance, he sees the charred remains of a church, a blackened spire cutting through the night sky. He'll sleep in this town somewhere, figure out his next move in the morning.

The street rises after the promenade, a short stretch of businesses, mostly empty storefronts. A Jane convenience store, a café. Lines of small houses that rise up into the hills—the promenade is lit, and here and there he sees lamps in windows. A township rewarded with the Providence Initiative's electricity, then.

He turns on a whim and heads up one of the hillside blocks. He'll find an abandoned house, sleep inside, or in a backyard. The hill steepens considerably and Dean steps off the bike, begins pushing it up the hill, when he hears a woman's scream close by, just around the side of the cottage he's in front of. His immediate thought: A fevered has wandered by. Dean is halfway around the side of the house when he hears the gunshots echoing from the backyard. There's a moment, no denying it, of ball-tightening terror and the considerable urge to run away. Whatever this is, it is not my problem. But—in a moment just as quick—he remembers the fevered with the sawblade through his head. You can be the person who brings that madness into the world, or you can do the other, better thing.

What he sees when he pushes through the backyard gate: a woman with her hands raised, standing before a shed that's cloaked in shadow. Closer still: a fever hunter in Terradyne fatigues firing a pistol at her. Dean doesn't think. Just moves. Knocks the man to the ground. The man tries to get up—he's strong and wiry—and Dean puts a boot to his ribs and tells him to stay down.

When he looks up, the woman's raised the pistol his way. Bore of that barrel looks big as a goddamned eyeball, he thinks, like his whole future rests inside that black circle.

And then Dean sees that there *is* a fevered. Chained up in the shed.

The fuck have I got myself into, he thinks.

———

"I figure you got two choices," he says. "Shoot 'em or let 'em go."

"I'm thinking," the woman says. Katherine, her name is, and she's got one hunter's pistol in her waistband and the other in her fist. This lean, almost emaciated woman with long gray-black hair and a hard, chiseled face. All those guns on her, Wild West shit.

The two Terradyne ops—they're kids, really, probably in high school when the Message came through—are now sitting on the concrete steps of her back porch. The rangy redheaded kid, smelling of booze, glowers at them like he's got flat murder in his heart. The other kid looks like he wants to go to sleep. He's got one of Katherine's dish towels turning red at his temple. He holds it there and dips his head down between his knees.

"You fractured his skull," the redhead says. "When you hit him."

"I'm okay," the other says, but he says it dreamily.

It's a hell of a scene, what Dean's walked into. These two and then this fierce woman and the fevered still rattling its chains in the shed over there. They're trying to talk and the thing is pulling, straining to get at them. It's distracting. Dean holds his own little Ruger against his thigh. Not a chance he's telling any of these people he's got a single bullet left. Which reminds him.

"Hey," he says, "where's your rifles at? All you hunters carry those big-ass rifles. Where's yours?"

"We turned them in."

"What do you mean, you turned them in."

The one with the dish towel pressed against the gash at his skull peers up at him, squinting. "We turn them in after our shifts."

Dean is incredulous. "The fuck you doing in this woman's back-yard if you're not on your shift?"

"That's a fair point," Katherine says.

The hunters shut up.

"For real, what're you doing?" Dean says. "Getting drunk and fol-lowing this lady around? What exactly was the plan, gentlemen?"

"We got a report there was a fevered around here." The redhead says this, lifts his chin toward the shed.

"That's bullshit," Katherine says.

Dean asks him what his name is.

"Chris," the redhead says, all sullen.

"Who's this?"

"Jason," says the other one, his chin between his knees again.

"Chris and Jason. Jason and Chris." He looks over at Katherine. "Yeah, you got to shoot 'em or let 'em go. I'm leaning hard toward letting them go, personally. Had enough killing to last me. And you don't want the heat of two dead Terradyne hunters on you."

She takes a deep breath and lets it out. Without a word, she turns and goes to the shed and closes the doors. Runs a heavy-looking peg through the eyelets. Locks that fevered in there.

"You know that's illegal," Chris calls out.

Dean laughs, amazed. "Shut the fuck up, dude. Choose silence right now."

Katherine comes back and points at her gate. "Get out of here."

They seem reluctant, as if waiting for some trick, or maybe the booze and the head wound have made them logy. For whatever reason, they don't stand up until Katherine starts to raise the pistol their way.

The redhead—Chris—leads the other one. When he gets to the gate, he looks over his shoulder, his eyes settling on Katherine. "I'll see you around."

Dean raises his hands, walks forward. "No, no, no. We're not doing that shit. We're not doing the, like, proclamations and threats and all that. Get the fuck out, man. You got bested. Get that head wound checked out."

Katherine and Dean follow them around the front of the house where Dean's bike and cart still sit. It seems like hours have passed since he stopped here, but it's been what? Ten minutes, maybe?

The hunters walk down the hill, turn the corner. To their credit, they don't look back.

Dean and Katherine watch them go. Dean crosses to his bike, pushes it toward the sidewalk. Careful, now that the danger's over, that he's not encroaching on this woman's space. "Why *do* you have a fevered locked up in your shed there?" he asks. "You don't mind me asking."

Katherine considers him. "It's Dean, right?"

"Yeah."

"That's my son in there. In the shed."

He sucks at his teeth, nods. "I'm sorry to hear it."

Katherine sighs, tucks a hank of hair behind her ear. Looks up and down the street. "I figure Cape Winston's pretty much done for me."

"Maybe so," Dean says.

"You hungry? I got a favor to ask you, but it's probably best to ask on a full stomach."

"I'm mostly thirsty," he admits. "You give me some water, I'll do whatever, pretty much."

She nods at the Ruger still in his hand. "You mind taking the magazine out of your gun there?"

"I don't mind."

"You mind handing it to me?"

"How about I just put the mag in this other pocket?"

"That's fine," she says.

He pushes his bike and cart back into her front yard and they step inside her house. Dean thinks of the man out in the shed. Her son, chained in darkness. He can't tell if it reads as an act of love or something else. He keeps thinking of the sawblade man. The horror of someone doing that to what is still, to some degree, a person.

Katherine's kitchen is small and narrow. She takes a glass from the cupboard and pours him water from the tap. He drinks it down and she pours him another. He gasps like a child when he's done.

"You got running water here. Electricity."

"All the amenities," Katherine admits, wiggling both hands in the air. "Praise Terradyne."

"Ha," Dean says. "Just got to sign that loyalty card."

Katherine nods, and then her face darkens with some certain

awareness and she walks past him to a kitchen table with a scatter of paperwork on top. She rifles through stacks—he sees the Terradyne logo on some of the pages, a xeroxed pamphlet with a woman smiling and wearing a headset—and she turns to him.

"They took my shit."

"What?"

"They took my ID. My ration card and my ID. They broke into my house."

Dean's confused. "You don't keep your ID on you?"

"No. It's a long story." Katherine stares at the table, puts a thumbnail between her teeth. Finally, she looks up at him and says, "Look, I need your help."

"I told you, I'm in."

"I need to move him."

"From the shed?"

Katherine nods.

"Where to?"

"I got a place," she says.

Dean thinks of his bike and cart out front. Thinks of those two young men, sobering up. Feeling belittled, aggrieved, emasculated. What would he do if George had lived enough to make it through the Message? What would he have done if George got bit? Same thing as this woman, probably. "You think they'll come back?"

"Oh, I think they'll raid this place at the very least. And soon."

He's grateful for a moment—it levels him, that gratitude—but he's glad that George never made it to a world where you had to decide how to spend your last bullet. Where he never had to see something like the sawblade man.

"You want to protect him," Dean says.

"I'm his mother."

Like chasing after the men who took his cart—it's the easiest decision.

"Let's go," he says.

CHRIS CANINO

Cape Winston, Massachusetts

Jason's loopy as hell as they trek back to the garage, that dish towel the woman had given them already soaked. Chris is scared to look, but the wound at Jason's temple had looked *soft* when he'd seen it earlier. Mushy. He holds Jason up as they walk. It's a long-ass way back to the garage and Jason's eyes are mostly closed.

She took their pistols. *Shit.*

It's not like they were going to do anything serious. Him and Jason were done with their shifts, had already turned in their rifles and were back walking home. Chris pretty hammered via a flask of vodka he kept in his vest. They'd been heading home to the three-bedroom house they'd taken over at the south edge of town, when Jason had seen the woman from the café stepping out of the rubble of the burned-down church. Seemed shady as hell, man. What was she doing? They both remembered her straightaway, and shared a look—brother-telepathy, same look they'd shared a thousand times, right before they did something that would inevitably get one of Dad's beat cops knocking on the door a few hours later. It was a look that said, Yeah, let's just fuck with her a little bit. Just a *little* bit. Her talking about the fevered being *people's children*, like she had a clue. Both of them thinking of Jamie, how the drift fell on him, took him apart, him being the smallest and always lagging behind, the sound of his screams still haunting years later. And this chick having the audacity to talk about *people's children*. Like she knew a fucking thing about anything at all.

"Come on," he says, getting pissed about it all over again. Touching the arcing scar that curls up around his ear. There'll be guys at the garage who know what to do. Nearest hospital's twenty miles away, and neither of them have a car.

Jason, in a sleepy voice, says, "I want to go home, dude."

"I'm taking you to the garage, Jay."

"I'm tired, man."

"I know. A little bit longer."

People's children my ass.

His buzz is fading to a kind of background hum, and instead the fear's starting to bubble up. Fear and a hangover headache. Their supervisor will of course shit an absolute brick. Not just at their seized pistols, but if the lady files a complaint—what would happen? Would they get court-martialed? Him and Jason were pretty fast and loose with the protocols, all the hunters were, but if it got out that they'd actually broken into the lady's house, well, that'd make Jason getting smacked in the head look like self-defense, right? Even if there *was* a fevered chained up in a shed in the backyard. I might have fucked up, he thinks. And to top it off, here's his brother, nineteen years old and still as reliant on him as he was when Chris was eight and learning to microwave instant noodles and chicken nuggets and shit for all three of them. Dad either on a shift or sleeping in his bedroom with the blackout curtains and the white noise machine, a deathly *do not disturb the old man or else* pall hanging over the entire house. Taking the food out a second before the microwave dinged, careful not to scrape your fork too loud against the plate, because if Joe Canino got woken up before he had to strap on his gun belt and badge, you could rest assured that every ear in the house would be getting cuffed. As the oldest, Chris carried his brothers' weight, caught the most grief, and he's realizing now how badly he's fucked up. He wants to puke.

"My head hurts like shit," Jason mumbles.

"We'll get you to the garage, man. Chuck can help."

"She nailed me, dude."

"We'll get her," Chris says. "We'll fucking get her, Jay." He means it.

The town's hunters work out of an old garage at the end of town. Chris feels a mixture of relief and fear when he sees the open bay doors, other guys walking around inside. This little beacon of light and activity. The night shift supervisor, an old Marine in his fifties named Chuck, has always treated Chris and Jason like they were more than a few bricks short a load, and any bullshit that Chris tries to run past him will get sniffed out in seconds. Best to just be straight with it, or straight as possible.

Chris steps inside, passes a few guys gearing up, putting on their Kevlar vests, strapping the bite guards on their arms. Their eyes go big when they take in Jason, and in the garish electric light of the garage, the blood on the towel looks black. In that moment, a part of him recoils at all of it—at the grand responsibility that's been placed on him. He's twenty-two, been in and out of trouble since he was a kid, tasked with raising two half-feral brothers on his own because of his magical disappearing mom and piece-of-shit dad, and look at what he's managed to do with it all—

Chuck looks up from his desk in his office, the overhead lights shining through his flattop. "The hell is this?" he barks.

"Chuck," Chris says, willing his voice steady, "we fucked up."

Chuck stands up, walks around his desk. It's a long, narrow office, runs the length of the garage. There's a cluster of folding chairs around a card table at the far wall, and Chris walks Jason over and sets him down in one of the chairs. Chuck hisses when he crouches before Jason and gently pulls the towel away, sees the wound at his temple.

"The fuck happened?" he says, and it's not the anger that Chris was expecting. It's sadness, shock. Even fear, a little bit. Still, Chris is so relieved that Chuck isn't angry at him, he wants to start bawling.

"This fucking chick brained him with a, like a, steel peg. She was keeping a fevered in a shed and we followed her and when we tried to smoke the fevered, she dropped him." This, then, is how to play it. It's the truth shone through a slightly better light. "She got our pistols."

Chuck, still crouched before his brother, gently tilts Jason's chin so that the wound is lifted up to the light. There's blood, clearly, but mostly it's that sense of *softness*, the flesh beside his eye swollen and toward his ear all smooshed in and ripped. The wound is already purpling. Whole thing makes Chris's stomach lurch.

"How many fingers am I holding up?" Chuck says.

Jason's eyes drift open a little. "My dick."

"I'm serious, how many?"

"Mmmm," Jason says, and then closes his eyes again.

Chuck stands, his knees popping. "We got to get him to the hospital in Sackton. Hopefully they have a doctor there today. I'll call one of the trucks in." His big bulldog face starts to bloom red—the anger Chris was expecting has finally arrived. "You come with me," he hisses, and Chris leaves his brother sitting in the chair. He dutifully follows Chuck back to his desk at the other end of the room, their boots scuffing along the cement floor.

Chuck gets on the CB to call one of the hunter teams. They confirm they're on their way back to the office, give him a ten-minute ETA.

Chuck sets the handset down and folds his arms. He eyeballs Chris. Those laser eyes. Tell-me-the-truth eyes. Every cop he's ever talked to, his dad included, had those same eyes.

"What. Happened."

Chris stares at the floor. "I told you, we seen this lady doing suspicious shit so we followed her and it turned out she had a fucking *fevered* locked up in her shed, and when we tried to invalidate it, she brained Jason with this rod that she used to, like, lock the shed. Then this dude rolled up and got the drop on us and they took our pistols."

"Took your pistols," Chuck says flatly. He blinks. "This dude rolled up and took your pistols."

How many times in his life has he been in this position? Some adult looking at him, disappointed? Expecting more from him than what had actually happened, like Chris might just magically pull better choices out of his ass. Stonily, he says, "They got the drop on us, is what I'm saying."

"You'd already turned in your rifles, right? This was after your shift?"

"Yeah."

"Well, thank sweet baby Jesus for that. You been drinking, Chris? It smells like your parents fucked in a distillery."

"I might have had a little vodka."

"Jesus. Who was the woman?"

Chris shrugs, tries to look aggrieved. "I don't know."

"Where's the fevered?"

"She's got this house on Lark Street. It was in a shed in the back. We got her ID."

Chuck bristles, tongues a molar for a second before he says, "How's that?"

"What do you mean?"

"How the fuck did you get her ID, genius? She hand it over to you?"

Chris cuts his eyes away.

"I asked you a question."

"We took it."

"What, like you mugged her? Took her purse?"

"It was in her house."

A beat. "You went into her *house*?"

"She was acting suspicious."

"Yeah, right," Chuck says. "'Course she was. Give it to me."

Chris reaches into his fatigues and takes out the woman's ID and her laminated loyalty card with its magnetic stripe across the back, the one that doubles as her ration card. Chuck frowns at the picture on the ID, then stuffs both of them in his shirt pocket. "You are in the shit, son. You and your brother both. But if there's a fevered in this town, I want to know about it. We'll get your brother to the ER in Sackton and then you and me and a couple of the boys are going to that house."

Relief worms through him. There might be a way out after all.

Chuck stands up and walks toward the back of the room.

He makes it halfway there and goes still.

Still in a way that tells Chris everything.

The world kind of stops. Sounds get big. The thud of his blood in his ears, clack of his boots across the floor as he hurries over there, moves past Chuck. One of the guys in the garage drops something metallic on the floor next door and it clangs.

Jason sits there on the chair splay-legged. Head thrown back. Overhead light reflected in the curve of his open eyes. The bloodied towel come to rest on the floor beneath his fingertips.

Chris thinks of Jamie, his and Jason's little brother. His father had looked so disgusted after the drift had gotten him, gotten Jamie, the old man weeping, saying so bitterly, *You fucking* ran, *Chris. You and your shit-ass brother, you* ran *and you let my boy die, you let them fucking* eat *him.* He thinks of all the dead that have strode through his life.

His brother's dead. Jason sitting there, dead in that folding chair.

There's no one left now.

She killed him.

That woman, she killed him.

JOHN BONNER

Portland, Oregon

Bonner had been in Nick Coffin's apartment when the Message came through. His uncle Jack had warned him that the Message—or something like it—might happen. It'd been him and Nick and this guy named Rachmann in the apartment. Rachmann had been an Austrian or German freelance operative, something like that, a guy Nick had hired to help get his mother back from ARC, the black ops agency that Bonner had worked for. They'd kidnapped her in an attempt to wrangle ownership of the hand from Nick. The whole thing was, finely put, a yowling clusterfuck from an intelligence standpoint. Only minutes earlier, Bonner had discovered a cache of Matthew Coffin's paperwork—old notebooks, correspondence, song lyrics from his days in the Blank Letters—and one notebook in particular had seemed to document the man's downward spiral into what folks at the time had presumed was simply madness.

Now, Bonner knows different.

But in the meantime, Nick and Rachmann, they'd had this fucking *box*, right? Darkly oiled wood, everything gilded in gold leaf.

And Bonner had wanted to see what was inside. Not *compulsively*, like the way the hand would ultimately wind up working him over. He just wanted to see, was all.

That'd always been Bonner's problem: the absolute inability to leave well enough alone.

So he'd sat Nick and Rachmann down on the couch in the living room and taken that gold-leaf box from them, and just as he'd opened it, all their cell phones had rung at once.

Rachmann had sneered at him, urged him to look inside. What was it he'd said? *Take a good look, motherfucker. Tell me what you see in there.*

And Bonner had looked in the box and Rachmann had answered his cell phone, and heard the Message, and gone insane.

Bonner had put two rounds through the guy's mouth, shards of jawbone and European bridgework falling to the floor in a red spill, but not before Rachmann had lunged forward and bitten Nick Coffin on the hand. Rachmann had pitched over the couch, dead, while Nick cradled his hand to his chest. Chanting *Oh fuck, oh fuck* like a mantra. Rachmann's cell phone still going on the floor, Bonner hearing a snatch of that famous Blank Letters song before he stomped the screen in.

"Just stay calm," Bonner had said, his own head a maelstrom of panic.

Nick had looked up at him with threads of blood running between his fingers. "He fucking bit me, dude. Ah, God."

"It's okay," Bonner said. "We'll figure it out."

So reassuring. As if he'd had a clue.

Each remnant has its own unique power, and the eye, it told you the manner of your death. And what had Bonner seen when he looked upon it?

Well. He'd seen darkness shot through with a wavering scatter of a light, something he recognized as a flashlight beam, or maybe a lantern. He had seen Katherine Moriarty with blood stippling her face, her expression one of drawn, sustained horror. He saw a Black man with a tight afro and a hand, gloved in blood, at his throat.

Bonner saw his own hands covered in blood too, darkening his lap.

There was a lot of fucking blood everywhere, honestly.

He saw a dark-haired girl. Saw a baby, of all things.

They were in a room and all around them were a sea of people.

No, not people. Not entirely. Fevered.

Most strange of all, he saw the hand itself, saw the eye in its box, and something else—something *fluttering*. A clot of dark string, something trailing in a wind.

These broken-glass puzzle pieces, and with it a bomb-blast of understanding: *This is how you'll die, John.*

A vision like that, though? You got time to *consider*. To try and twist it, to look at each facet like some gem held beneath a jeweler's loupe.

You got time to try and barter for your own life. To put up blockades against your own mortality:

If I never see Katherine Moriarty again, I'll never die.

If I avoid, what? A Black man with blood on his hand? I do that, I won't be hurt.

I never go into a dark room, I'll live forever.

Avoid dark-haired girls and babies.

It got ridiculous after a while. And yet—banking on the notion that the eye told the truth, that it wasn't full of shit, wasn't a devil's sleight of hand—it offered its own sense of protection. No shiv-bearing skinhead could lay him down. No barroom brawl or errant bullet between two warring gangs would end his life. No cultist from the Sight would put him in the earth. In this way, a part of him *wanted* to believe the eye, because believing in the eye made him untouchable.

REGAL JOHN BONNER, written in blood.

He parks in front of the building, reluctant to leave his car. He hasn't been here in years, since he got Nick out after the Message. The Regal Arms was already an old building before the Message and the interceding years have done it no favors. The exterior's trashed; the windows on the ground floor have all been busted in, with an ankle-high drift of leaves and garbage lying across the open entranceway door. No lights shine inside. Still, he knows it's the right place. Feels it.

Dead leaves crackle underfoot as Bonner marches beneath the arched doorway, the rusted, weeping letters that say *Regal Arms Apartments*, then through the foyer and up the steps to the main landing. REGAL JOHN BONNER, so cute. He'd known immediately what it meant. Kendall had been enraged, frightened; the Sight's insular killings not quite so insular, now that Bonner's name had been scrawled on a wall in someone's blood. *I don't know what the fuck this means, but take care of it,* had been Kendall's order.

The further inside the building, the darker it gets, but through the lobby and up the stairwell there's enough errant light from the shattered windows to see by. He pauses at the landing of each floor to test for sounds, gauging for fevered or any other variety of danger. That kind of near-psychic radar that you build up by working in the city long enough.

The fourth floor then, and down the hall to the apartment that Katherine Moriarty had shared with her son. The ceiling sags with decay, the hallway thick with a fierce reek of mold. The carpet squishes, and chunks of fallen plaster litter the hallway in big swaths.

Their apartment door is open. Bonner sees the cold white light of an electric lantern spilling into the hall. He takes out his Glock—this kind of darkness-shot-through-with-light is similar enough to what he saw in the eye to give him pause. And clearly someone's expecting him. He raps the pistol on the doorjamb. "Knock knock," he says, and steps inside.

The place is quiet, somehow heavy with silence. Framed Blank Letters posters still hang on the walls. A section of the ceiling near the kitchen has buckled in, rainwater darkening that part of the floor, muddying the molding, but beyond that the place is surprisingly unbothered. An LP jacket rests face-up next to the turntable, the Clash's *Give 'Em Enough Rope*. He runs a finger along the cover, makes a line in the dust.

He can't go in the bathroom. Just can't manage it. Can't think of those terrible hours after the Message when they'd agreed that he should lock Nick inside. The building by then had been heaving with screams, the sound of things breaking around them. Sirens ripped apart the night. He and Nick talking through the door until Nick had finally turned and couldn't speak anymore, couldn't form words. Bonner blocking it with furniture.

He walks into Nick's bedroom, sees the casual disarray of a guy who hadn't planned on his world ending. Clothes on the floor, window left open. The wall beneath it a riot of mold and rain tracks.

Matthew Coffin's papers lie in a scatter next to a cardboard box on Nick's bed.

Bonner's mouth goes dry. The last time he was here, years back—funneling a fevered Nick out of the bathroom and into a waiting SUV to be taken to Katherine—everything he'd hidden had been gone. Ransacked. The hand, the eye, the archives, all of it missing. The hand he'd stumbled across in the interceding years, but the rest he'd written off.

And now he's being called back here?

And the archives are sitting on the fucking bed?

What the hell is going on?

He sets the Glock on the bed and hurriedly shoves all the papers and folders and spiral-bound notebooks into the box. He's folding the box flaps shut when someone behind him says, "Hello John," and Bonner gasps and scrabbles for the pistol. Pivots, *stupid stupid*, finger pulling on the trigger, close, *close* to firing.

The man in the doorway falls to the ground, tries to scramble away, letting out a noise somewhere between a shriek and a laugh.

He's thin, with an unruly mop of brown curls and heavy-framed glasses. "John, John, wait! You got our message!"

Bonner stalks forward, heart in his throat, terrified. He'd heard nothing, had no indication someone had come in behind him. Drawn so deep into the well of himself. "Your message," he says, talking loud, the fear making him lean over the man. "You mean the bodies in that fucking house? My name written in their blood? *That* message?"

The guy's turtled up on the floor, a hand shielding his face. Bonner sees the eye burned into his palm. Sees this one's got eyes carved all over him. His arms, his cheeks, his neck. Bonner blinks, breathes.

"Well, here I am," he says. "The fuck do you want?"

The man drops his hand, peers at Bonner. "We want to give you the eye, John."

He blinks. "What?"

"It was foretold."

He lowers his pistol. The man seems to take his silence for approval; he slowly sits up, crawls from the doorway over to the couch. Sits in the very spot where Nick Coffin had sat. "You're the messenger," the man says. He sounds happy about it. Like he's a guy sharing some fantastic news.

"Wait. You *have* the eye?"

He grins, and Bonner spies a sort of gleeful madness at work there. "We do! And we want to give it to you. You're the one that will bring us forth, John. You're the messenger, the harbinger—"

"Hold up."

"—it's you that will bring about the house of wounds, the house of the worm. We've done everything we've been told, crept down every dark road the eye showed us, and it's showed us *you*, John, now it's *you* that needs the eye, *you* that will be the harbinger—"

"Stop."

"—*you* that will open the doors to the house of the devoured world—"

Bonner steps big out of Nick's room and into the living room and he smacks the guy, hard, on the top of the head with the barrel of the Glock. The pistol's mostly plastic, only weighs a few pounds loaded. It still shuts him up. But when he lifts his head, he's grinning up at Bonner like a supplicant who's been gifted with something divine.

It's hot in Bonner's blood, this idea that he might possess the hand, the eye and Coffin's archives. Katherine has told him about Chicago, the night of the Message—Matthew Coffin's reanimated body staggering toward her, brought back to some brutal, undead half-life in a batshit-mad attempt at reconciliation after death. And his uncle Jack has told him about Rolla, Missouri—how Coffin's being held there in stasis. Unmoving behind glass. Bonner knows, in some guttural, intrinsic way, that Coffin is still the linchpin to all this wretchedness. The architect of the Message. So if Bonner has Coffin's remnants and his notebooks that document his ruination, *how* it all happened? Well, then Bonner holds all the cards, doesn't he? And if he ever gathers the courage to actually destroy the remnants, well—it's maybe even enough to kill Coffin, whatever he is now. Terradyne might want to keep him around in a nice little box, some ghoulish trophy, but if a recording of his voice was enough to decimate the planet? It's better to end him.

Bonner says again, "You have the eye?"

"Of course," the man cries like a carnival barker. "It's in the kitchen! It's waiting for you."

He touches Bonner's wrist; his hand is slicked with sweat. Bonner pulls back in disgust. "We were led here," the man says. "Years ago. We took the hand, the eye, the papers. We've held it for you all this time, we *waited*, we performed the eye's visions when it told us to, shed our blood when it told us to, *we called you*, John! We did this for *you, you* are the harbinger—"

"I'm the harbinger," he asks woodenly, and it sounds as if his voice comes from far away. Because a part of him knows. Has always known.

"Yes! We would give you the hand too, John, but it got away from us some years before. The hand is a tricky thing. Deceitful, demand-ing movement."

It's true enough. Bonner's been reunited with it, has been swim-ming in its blood-visions for years now. He knows all about its de-mands.

"Motherfucker, *I* was the one who hid these things here. Don't act like you're helping me out."

A look of wide-eyed shock. "I didn't— We didn't—"

"So why are you giving me this shit back now?"

The man laces his fingers around Bonner's wrist again. "Don't you understand? It's shown us our death, John. Shown us *all*. That John Bonner's the harbinger, the one who brings about the devoured world. You open the door *all the way* this time, John." He licks his flaking lips, grasps Bonner's wrist with both hands now. Laughs up at him, gleeful.

"He's coming *here*," the man says. "We've been shown. Oh, he's coming *here*, John, and you will be the one to open hell's door for him."

KATHERINE MORIARTY

Cape Winston, Massachusetts

They fold him in Dean's cart, wrapped in his chains, and lash the tarp over it all to hide him.

Another indignity to her kid, stacked on years of them.

There's no one out at this hour, but there are lights on in windows, and the pair of them leading a fevered by a chain down the street would certainly cause attention. So, this.

They reach the church with its blackened framework and Katherine turns and scans the horizon. Cape Winston looks as it always has—a tiny enclave huddled against the dark. The two of them hoist Nick from the cart and onto the floor of the church, Dean holding tight to his chain. Katherine stops when she gets to the cleared area at the rear of the church, pulls open the hatch. Dean comes over to see.

"You got to keep an eye on him," she says.

"I got his chain wrapped around a post over there." The two of them stare into the black mouth of the space, the stairs leading down into darkness.

Dean seems doubtful. "You really gonna put him down there?"

"I have to. They're coming back for me. For him. Shit, probably for you."

"I know it," he says. "It's just a hard road, is all. Hard to do this to someone."

"Better than them shooting him in the face and sawing his head off," she says. And how different is this from the shed, really? Sorrow bounds in her like quicksilver.

They hoist him up and Katherine puts the bag over his head and leads him down the narrow flight of concrete steps. He leans against her in his chains, teeth clacking. The room is small, with a low ceiling and weeping concrete walls. On one wall is a stack of boxes sitting on a pallet. A storage facility for the church. This close to sea level? She wonders if it ever floods, if Nick would survive that. There is a light socket in the ceiling with no lightbulb. It's a hollow space beneath a burned building and that's all.

Her vision blurs; she's crying.

"You okay?" Dean calls down.

"Can I have a minute," she says, her voice thick, and she sees, at the top of the stairwell, Dean's legs walk away.

Nick presses against her and there's nothing to lash his chain to down here. She stiff-arms him to keep him away. Still—always—the jaw snapping beneath that black bag.

Nick at six years old, losing both of his front teeth within days of each other, showing off the gap to any person he came across.

Nick, coming home from his shift at the record store, talking excitedly to her about a band that he'd discovered, and the look of conflict and then disgust when she told him that the Blank Letters had done a string of festival dates with the band in Europe years back and the guitarist had a penchant for bringing underage fans to his dressing room.

Nick at fifteen, sullen and bomb-blasted with grief and confusion at Matthew's funeral. His hair gelled, wearing a suit too big for him, his Adam's apple working as he stared at the coffin.

Her kid.

Her boy.

Nick.

Early on, in those months after the Message, before Bonner had arranged the flight that reunited her with her son, when she was alone on the East Coast, trying like hell just to stay alive, she thought of Matthew as a man who had simply made too many bad decisions. She pitied him. Even when Bonner told her about the threaded, subliminal message—of *him talking*—that had somehow been used as a weapon to rip the world apart. Even then she thought of him as weak, mostly.

But then she saw Nick and what the Message had done to him, and now it's just bitterness all the way down. Bitterness and rage at Matthew.

She leaves Nick in that concrete hole in the ground and walks up the stairs, and then shuts the hatch. She and Dean push some wreckage over the seams of the doorway, dirty it up. Under the ground like that—it feels different than the shed. It feels like a burial.

They walk back down the boardwalk. Dean keeps a respectful distance as Katherine weeps with a fist pressed to her mouth.

Everything was so fragile, it turned out. Her life for years now has rested on a knife edge, and in minutes those two boys from Terradyne broke it all. And now they have her forged ID, the thing her entire past rests on.

They scope out her place first from the overgrown pathway between two houses across the street. All seems quiet. Dean seems unsure of what to do next. So does Katherine, truthfully. All she knows is that a great wheel has been set in motion and she has to run.

But run where?

"You won't tell," she says, and it's impossible to hide the note of pleading in her voice.

"Not me," Dean says softly. He looks down the street and then back at her. "What are you going to do?"

Katherine laughs. It's better than weeping. "I mean, pack my shit and go. It's not safe here anymore."

"Yeah," Dean says. "Figure I kind of lost my shot at a warm welcome when I helped kick the shit out of two fever hunters the second I roll into town." He tilts his head a little, and Katherine knows what's coming next. "Where you think you're headed?"

"I don't know," she answers. "Apart from putting my life in a backpack, I really don't know what to do next."

He lifts his chin toward her house. "Well, you want some help packing, at least?"

NAOMI LAURENT

Nevers, Bourgogne-Franche-Comté region, France— Rolla, Missouri

A man in fatigues enters, a rifle across his chest.

"I want the baby," Naomi says.

A man in a suit brings her a bottle of water, his face a carefully painted canvas of benevolence.

"I want the baby," Naomi says.

A man in a lab coat tries to take her temperature.

She holds up a hand. "I want the baby."

The mantra, the anchor, those four words.

She says it in French, in English, puts it down in both languages after she mimes writing and they fetch her a piece of paper and a pen. It is both her truest thing and the wire that roots her to the ground. Antoine will not meet the same fate as Hugo. There will be no woman bent over him, no spasming tiny fingers. No pool of blood on the floor. She's returned Antoine to the world, and now she will keep him safe.

The soldiers had brought her to the chopper. One of them had wrested Antoine from her and she'd tried to fight back until she saw him gently place the child inside a box lined with blankets, even putting a pair of oversized headphones over his ears. The chopper had flown over Nevers, her hometown reduced to a kaleidoscopic pastiche at that angle. Even as they slalomed over the countryside, a part of her was already insisting that it wasn't her father she'd seen. No. Plenty of men had tattoos on their arms. She probably hadn't seen it clearly.

They'd landed somewhere north of the city at a small stretch of road that was being used as a makeshift runway. They transferred to a small plane and flew for some time—they didn't cover her eyes but the windows of the plane were blacked out. They landed at a windswept military-style airfield. Perhaps it was in Paris, perhaps not. She'd heard that the city had finally been liberated from the fevered, though what she saw at the airfield made her wonder; it had the air of desolation about it. A radio tower in the distance stood smoke-blackened, pocked with what looked like mortar rounds. A large section of the hurricane fencing had been pulled down. There were dead bodies outside the fence, their stillness reminding her of the cows. Someone handed her the baby. The soldiers spoke quietly in English to each other and didn't address her at all unless they were telling her to move somewhere. They wore gloves and seemed reluctant to touch her or Antoine.

They boarded a larger airplane. The soldiers sat up front, near the cockpit. Before they'd taken off, one of them had crouched down and said to her in English, "Don't touch anything. Just sit here or I'll take him and I'll tie you to your seat. Do you understand?"

She did. She'd gone only to the bathroom at the back of the plane, taking the baby with her, cleaning them both up as best she could.

Later, the soldier—or another one, they still wore their masks—brought her a handful of nutritional bars and a can of orange slices. She peeled the lid and fed most of the latter to the baby with her zip-tied hands. Drank the syrup herself. Ate all the bars. She told the soldier Antoine needed to be changed, and he said, "Oh shit, sorry," and brought her a box of diapers. This was when she realized that something was happening. Diapers were nearly impossible to find anymore. Had become almost pointless luxuries in a world like this.

They flew over the water for a long time.

She slept, woke, slept.

Hours later, bending toward evening, and Naomi in her half-sleep looked out the window and thought she recognized the American White House, one side of it charred and buckled, and then it was gone. An image from movies, gone so fast she wondered if she'd dreamt it. Some minutes later, the plane landed, taxiing to a stop on another airfield, this one with a bevy of vehicles roving about, people running; she'd even seen another, larger airplane preparing to take off. It felt surreal, that the world was capable of these movements again, and her sudden strange proximity to them.

They sat on the runway for a long time, Antoine restless and fussy, Naomi's fear and exhaustion lending everything a gritty, blighted texture. She could smell herself, the sour fear-sweat that had been wrung from her. A soldier eventually brought her a blanket and said, "I can take him, if you want." They had removed their masks now and something in his face spoke to her.

"Don't let them take him from me."

"Okay," he said, and lifted Antoine, still careful not to touch her, and she caught a few more hours of fitful, broken sleep on the plane, a sleep shot through with bad dreams: Denis and Emilie and their leering faces, the man with the tattoo and the bag on his head, the man who was definitely not her father. The cows crying to be milked in the dark. She kept waking, afraid that Antoine was gone, but then she would hear his burbling laughter, lean over and see a pair of soldiers playing with him up near the cockpit.

Hours after that, a tanker appeared and refueled the plane and they took off again. She asked the soldier if she could stand and stretch her legs and he nodded. She hated herself in that moment for being grateful to him.

Sometime later she was told to sit again. The soldier came back to her without Antoine and when she asked for him, he said the baby needed to be up front during the landing.

"You fucker," she spat.

He was unbothered and held up a black bag for her to put over her head. She refused and they had to hold her down to put it on her. Then they cinched her zip-tied hands into some sort of mesh bags that cut tightly into her wrists, Naomi bucking and screaming at them, the soldiers cursing and still careful not to touch her skin. Her throat hoarse, Antoine bawling somewhere close by.

Time bent after that. Fractured and broke. The plane skidded, landed. She was led outside and, after hours in the plane, sensed in the darkness the expansiveness of the world. She tried to go limp and was held by both arms, pulled along, her shoulders wrenched painfully. The inside of the bag grew slick with moisture, with her panic. She was put in a vehicle and then brought from the vehicle to a building. She cried out, and in English a man at her ear told her wearily to shut up. There'd been the faintest sheen of light through the woven fabric of the bag and once she heard the telltale ding of an elevator, though she couldn't tell if they were going up or down.

Then a room, where she was seated, not particularly gently. She tried to flex and pull the bags from her hands but couldn't manage it. Eventually someone came in and took the bag from her head, a soldier with plastic gloves and a filtered mask. He left the bag on the table in front of her.

Cement walls painted a mint green. No windows, a heavy steel door. Underground, maybe. A flimsy card table, like something you'd find in a church basement, and on the other side of it a folding chair like her own. A rack of them standing in the corner. No adornments on the walls, nothing to indicate where she might be.

She has no idea how long she's sat there when the door opens once again and an old man walks in, gently shutting the door behind him.

"I want the baby," she says in English. "And I have to piss."

His face is cragged with age, and he has a head of fine, thick white hair, the slightest jowls. He wears a dark blue suit with a maroon tie and a white dress shirt. But it's the eyes that give Naomi pause: fully present and calculating in the same darkly mirthful, assessing way that Denis's were. His face splits open in a grin.

"Your English is fantastic. You learned in school?"

She doesn't tell him about her father being American. Just says again that she wants the baby.

"I promise you, you'll see him soon," the old man says. He sits across from her and lays his hands on the table. They are big-knuckled, slowly bending their way toward arthritis like her grandfather's had. But there's nothing grandfatherly about him. His eyes crawl across her face like she's a math problem he's trying to solve.

"What is this place?" she says. Naomi's broken her own vow—speak only of Antoine until they give her the baby—but she's trying to tamp the panic down.

The man says, "You're in the Capitol, dear."

"The what?"

An indulgent smile. "You're in the new Capitol of the United States. The *interim* Capitol, is the language we're using, but if I'm being honest, we're here to stay." And then, brightly, "You're one of our first guests."

Naomi licks her lips. "I saw your White House. We passed over it. It was burned."

"I know, isn't that terrible?"

"You can't hold me here. I'm French. I was born in Bourges. This is against the law."

"I'm sorry," he says, "but the old laws do not apply." He shakes his head as if regretful at the fact of it.

And then he leans back, folds his hands across his stomach. "My name is Theo Marsden, dear, and I run this place. The whole thing. If you want to see that baby again, tell me everything about your gift. Right now."

THEO MARSDEN
Rolla, Missouri

H e says this and her face closes up, goes blank. She demands the
child again, and Marsden, truly, has to stop himself from leaning over the table and kissing her. In those four words—*I want the
baby*—the girl has given away her entire heart. It won't take a gun or
a knife to get what he wants. Won't take a pair of pliers held up before her eyes.

It will take the baby, and that's all.

"Of course," he says, pushing his chair back. "We'll talk about the
baby, and about your incredible ability. But first, the bathroom, yes?"
He rises, knocks on the door twice. Eastman opens it. At Marsden's
order, he takes a knife from its scabbard at his thigh and cuts the
girl's zip ties.

"Keep her hands covered in those bags."

"Yes, sir."

"How am I supposed to wash them?" the girl asks.

Marsden smiles. "We're not taking them off, dear. You can manage."

She seems more relaxed when she comes back. In her absence,

Marsden has gotten her a bottle of water. She drinks the entire thing, sets it down carefully on the table between them.

"What's your name?" Marsden asks.

"I want the baby."

"How old are you?"

She blinks. "I want the baby."

Marsden leans back again, rests an ankle on a knee. Drums a rhythm with his fingertips on his shin. She's only just arrived, he tells himself. He hasn't even debriefed the team that extracted her yet. What little he's heard was essentially a retelling of the DGSI analysis: She was in the company of a man and woman, possibly relatives, more likely her captors. Both of them had been executed after a firefight with the extraction team; the man had clearly had some level of military experience. Rumors had been circulating through the area that she was capable of turning the fevered back, pulling out the infection—or whatever the hell it is—from the afflicted.

"Who was the man you were with?"

The girl swallows, cuts her eyes away for just a second. "I want the baby."

"Tell me about him," Marsden says. "Whose baby is it?"

"I'm not telling you anything until I see him."

The girl jumps at a knock at the door. Marsden curses inwardly. His time alone with her is gone. Whatever he might have gleaned— about the baby, about the girl's abilities—will belong to everyone now.

Jack Bonner and Anita Suarez step inside, Jack looking disheveled and angry. They each take a folding chair from the rack and now there are four of them in the small room, each flanking a side of the table.

Suarez is practically salivating. "Hello," she says, leaning forward with her hands clasped between her knees. "I'm Anita Suarez, the acting deputy director of medicine here in the Capitol," the whole thing trailing off awkwardly when she notices the bags cinched around the girl's hands. She turns to him.

"Are those necessary?"

"They are."

Jack, ever the fool, stands up and smooths down his tie with one hand. "Young lady, my name's Jack Bonner. I'm the CFO of Terra-dyne Industries, which has joined forces with the acting United States government during this difficult and exciting time—"

"Jack," Marsden says, his grin belying his fury at being inter-rupted. "It's not a sales pitch." Jack sits down, embarrassed, and Marsden feels their divide widen. Fine. Let it happen.

"Now that we've all met," Marsden says, with a *Can you get a load of these people?* roll of his eyes toward the girl, "I want to let you know that we're committed to helping you and the child you came here with."

"I want the baby," she says again. "Now."

"Who exactly *is* the baby?" Suarez says. "Is he your child? What's his name?"

The girl seems to consider answering, but hunkers back down in her chair and crosses her arms, face impassive.

"We want to help you," Marsden says. "We do. But you'll have to help us as well. That's just the way of it, dear." He folds his hands and waits. The girl meets his gaze, her eyes hooded and challenging.

"I want the baby," she says once more, and Marsden feels some-thing inside him come unzipped, just a bit, at her audacity and stubbornness.

"We heard intelligence chatter," he says, "that you can bring the fevered back to life. You've made quite a name for yourself. Do you want to know what your DGSI calls you? Your French military?"

"I want the baby."

Marsden leans forward and hisses, "I'll bring you that baby's fuck-ing *head,* how's that?"

Both Jack and Suarez look at him sharply, their eyes widened in surprise. He takes a moment, lets the words hang there, then leans back again. "Now. As I said. Do you want to know what they call you in Paris, dear?"

The girl's dead-eyed look of contempt could still water, could shatter stone. If she's afraid, that fear is stuffed deeply within her. Audacious or no, part of him admires her for it.

"What do they call me in Paris, old man?"

Marsden smiles. "They call you the Witch." He nods. "They say you pull the fever from people, bring them back, and that your father makes you do it."

Her jaw works for a moment before she says, "He wasn't my father." She is working so hard at giving nothing away. But she is young, and tired, and terribly alone, and Marsden has been seated at bargaining tables like this for most of his life.

"The baby's one, isn't he? You brought him back."

"I need to leave," she says in a husky whisper.

"You're not leaving."

"Do you know what will happen," the girl says, "if I touch you?"

"No," Marsden says. He steeples his hands and rests his chin on them. "Tell me."

"Theo," Jack says. Marsden ignores him.

"Go ahead," he says. "What happens if you touch me?"

She stares at him—she doesn't bend, he's got to give her that, and her eyes stay true. "I'll make you rot," she says finally.

"Well, we don't want to do *that*," he says, the last word singsongy and drawn out. He doubts that it's true—he feels like they'd have heard that in the DGSI chatter—but certainly isn't about to call her bluff.

"We want to help," Suarez says soothingly, trying to salvage some vestige of the girl's allegiance. "And if it's true, if you really can bring the afflicted back to some measure of *quantifiable* life, well." She lets out a little exhale. "It could change the world. That's not hyperbole, that . . . It's incredible."

"And you want that, don't you, young lady?" says Marsden. "Because you know what happens to that baby if you don't."

Jack turns to him, half standing.

THE DEVIL BY NAME

"Theo," he says tightly, "a moment outside, please."

Still staring at the girl, Marsden says, "Jack, for once in your life, sit down and shut the fuck up."

Jack sits, his face twisted. Suarez draws into herself, her hands crossing protectively over her stomach.

"So what's it going to be, my little witch?" says Marsden, rapping his knuckles twice on the table. "Will you cooperate? Answer our questions? Or would you like me to bring you a foot? A little hand?"

The girl's face tightens; she looks away, and Marsden thinks, *I win.* In a small, husky voice, she says, "I want to see the baby first."

"We can arrange that," Marsden says, "and we will. But first, *you answer me.* Is he your child?"

"No."

"Whose baby is he?"

"He doesn't have anyone else."

"That's not an answer."

"His father, the man who lived in that house, took care of him. The baby, he was bit. He was fevered for years. We made a trade. *Denis* made a trade. That's what we did, we traded for guns and food and things. And Antoine, I brought him back," her voice growing thick now, "and Denis killed his father and now he has no one else but me."

"Denis is the man you were with?"

"Yes."

"Antoine is the child's name?"

"Yes." She angrily swipes a tear away.

"What's your name?"

"My name is Naomi Laurent."

Jack Bonner slaps the tabletop and the girl jumps. "Theo," he says. "You're done."

Marsden stands and says to Naomi, softly, benevolent, "Dr. Suarez will take you to your room, and she'll be sure to bring, what is it, Antoine to you."

Suarez escorts the girl out. Jack waits until the door closes behind them and then points a finger at Marsden, his lips pulled back. "Have you lost your goddamn mind?"

Marsden plays it up, looks confused. "What?"

"Threatening to cut up a *baby*? That's who we are now?"

Marsden chuckles.

"What?" Jack says.

"Your hypocrisy is maddening, Jack."

"What's that supposed to mean?"

"It means I'll threaten her and more. Without question. If that girl can do what French intelligence thinks she can do? Hell, you can line the babies up and I will take them apart if it means we get what we want."

Jack looks at him with horror. "You're insane."

"What, it's insane to try to reclaim this country, Jack? To fight for what's ours?"

"You've overstepped your bounds."

"This is a mandate. Yardley's on board."

"Bullshit."

"It's true."

"The president approved you threatening a prime asset with the dismemberment of a baby. You're out of your fucking mind."

"Jack, if this girl can actually *bring them back*," Marsden whispers fiercely. "*And* we have Coffin, whose voice started all this? We have the poison *and* the antidote." He taps the table with a finger. "The vaccine is a joke. It's never happening. We both know it. But with these two? We run the world."

Jack's lips tremble. Finally, he deflates, his anger gone. "We should be courting her with kindness," he says, "if even one-tenth of what you're saying is true. You get more bees with honey, Theo."

"We don't have time for honey."

"Is that Yardley saying that, or you?"

"Both."

Jack inhales, his eyes roving Marsden's face. "You've changed," he says.

"With the times, Jack, yes. We have a grand opportunity here—"

"To what? Seize power? Run a, I don't know, a *fiefdom*? The two of you already want to turn the fever houses into goddamn *prison cities,* Theo! Now this? With you and Yardley as what, lords of the domain? That's the world you want?"

"You've lost the thread here," Marsden says.

Jack laughs bitterly and walks out. Marsden's sitting there in the ensuing silence when his cell phone rings.

"Yes," he says.

"Yeah, hello, Mr. Marsden. My name's Chuck Bunty, I'm the district supervisor for the collation program over here in Plymouth County." The man sounds nervous, flustered with the officiality of the call. "That's in Massachusetts, sir, a town called Cape Winston, and, well, we've got a unique situation here."

"Okay," Marsden says. Smiling a little, grateful for the distraction.

"So, we had a lady who assaulted one of my hunters pretty bad. Well, killed him, to be honest. And we were able to get her ID—her loyalty pledge and her ID card and all that—and when I ran it through our program, it got flagged."

"Okay," Marsden says again. "And why did it get flagged?"

"Well, normally we got folks at our loyalty centers that do all the data entry and stuff when someone signs up for their pledges, gets their ration cards issued and all that. Except *this* ID, I ran it and it was set up by someone who only did this one entry, and he works for Terradyne, but in security. Not at one of our loyalty centers, and nowhere near Massachusetts. Anyway, I ran it up the chain because I thought it was odd, this guy just entering this one ID, and finally folks I was talking to told me to call you."

"Alright. What's the woman's name, my friend?"

"Katherine Sunderson."

"Not ringing a bell."

"Yes, sir, that's not what made us flag it. It's the guy that entered it."

"Alright, I'll bite. Who is it?"

"Uh, a fella named John Bonner. A security officer in Portland, Oregon, I guess."

A pause. "Really."

"Yes, sir. Which was confusing to me, because what's he got to do with us out here in Cape Winston—"

"This Sunderson woman," Marsden says. "You happen to have her ID photo on file?"

"I do, sir. We can send it right over. Heck, I can send it to your phone, if you want."

"Please do."

The supervisor hangs up and Marsden sits. Jack can wait. The girl can wait. All of it. If this woman is who he thinks she is, she's almost as valuable as a remnant, given what she might know. What she might be able to do.

Or make Matthew Coffin do.

His phone pings. There it is.

Grainy, pixelated, but unmistakably her.

It's Katherine Moriarty's face looking back at him.

There are four or five remnant-adjacent people that Terradyne is still interested in. Katherine Moriarty. Her son, Nick Coffin. A few others.

And here's Katherine Moriarty—Matthew Coffin's goddamned *wife*—staring right back at him. Still alive.

He calls the supervisor back. Puts honey in his voice.

"My friend, where was it you were calling from again?"

FROM THE ARCHIVAL NOTEBOOKS
OF MATTHEW COFFIN

Scoring at Lydia's was a bust, to put it mildly. I cabbed out to her place, restless and haggard from some seriously shitty dreams the night before.

Everything around Lydia's little storefront was beat to hell. Tagged, entrances grated, a city garbage service that seemed to take the whole "pick up the garbage" thing pretty casually. But Lydia's place—*Curiosities*, it was called, done up in cursive script in the window—she'd fixed it up nice. A bell jingled when I walked in, and right away the smell of incense hit me, the kind Katherine burns at home, and I had to push down this sudden weepiness. I was so tired.

The store was small, narrow. Racks of vintage clothes in the middle, bric-a-brac on shelves on each side. Framed posters and paintings on the walls. Lydia came out from the back and I could see right away the gears shifting, her trying to place me. Any other time that would've pissed me off—the Blank Letters still have *some* kind of cultural currency, for Christ's sake—but right now, I just had that itch. Booze wasn't cutting it. I needed to get up and out and *away* from myself. Not just because of the stuff with Katherine, but from the loft too.

"Marcus, right?" Lydia said. She wore a sleeveless dress with wild swirls of neon color and a narrowing white belt at the hips. A dress crafted seconds after the invention of color. The thing scraped against my eyes; I felt a ripple of a headache coming on.

I said, "Matthew, actually," all pissy.

Just for a second, her face tightened in distaste. "Ah, that's right. Matthew. How are you?"

I stood on tiptoes, peering around a rack of sweaters and jackets, then turned back to her. There was no one else in the store. "Lydia, I'll just come out with it. Francis the Beast told me I could score from you."

Lydia stood there, her head tilted quizzically. Processing what I'd just said.

Then she tucked a hank of mouse-brown hair over one ear and did that thing where a person smiles and frowns at the same time. "What did you just say?"

"That's a no, I take it."

"That's a get the hell out of my store, is what that is. My *God.*" She pointed at the door behind me. "I mean it. Get out."

"I'm not well," I said, like that was some sort of apology and a joke at the same time. I turned around to go outside, cursing Francis in my head. I looked down at my hand as it reached for the front door and it, I don't know, it looked far away. Looked like someone else's hand. There was a sudden rip of pain through my head and I almost gasped.

"And you're talking to me about *Francis?*" said Lydia behind me, animated in her outrage. "I haven't seen Francis in, Jesus, two years? He told you I deal *coke?* Get the hell out of here."

I was at the door, had my hand on the doorknob, Lydia still railing behind me—she'd done coke twice in her life and certainly never dealt it, she informed me, she believed in the healing properties of *some* hallucinogens but certainly not cocaine, how dare I—when in my peripheral, a blue-tinted glass jar of marbles on a nearby shelf suddenly tipped itself over. I watched it happen. It was like some unseen person ten feet away reached up and pushed it over. Lydia's scream was *loud*.

Hundreds of marbles exploded across her floor, and then Lydia let loose a weird, animal kind of chuffing noise as they all rolled toward me. With that serpentine clicking sound—seriously, you ever heard two marbles click together? Picture that times a thousand— they all formed a kind of ululating, trembling circle. Right around my feet.

Lydia had her hand covering her mouth, still making that weird panting, chuffing noise. The marbles trembled but none of them broke the circle they'd formed.

I just stood there, afraid to move. I looked over at Lydia, like she might be able to give me some guidance. But she just stood there, a fist pressed against her mouth. Strangely, the need to score intensi- fied; I caught another whiff of Katherine's incense, and I felt this starburst of intense longing for my son. And then an image flitted through my mind, veered around like a bird trapped in a garage: Nick in the booth at Shoyou, holding chopsticks, with guitar strings wound tight around his neck, and me twisting and twisting them until blood ran in threads down his collarbones.

"I'm sorry," I said. I still don't know if I was talking to Lydia or myself or Nick. To all of us, maybe.

Finally I went to step over the marbles, too fucking scared *not* to by then, and that's when Lydia *truly* screamed; it sounded like some- thing in her throat had ripped loose. I caught a flash of something in my periphery and turned.

In the corner of the store, she'd set up a full-length standing mir- ror, the frame all carefully wrought dark wood, the whole thing look- ing very 1970s-Jacuzzi-key party.

And in the mirror was a twisting, fog-like shape over my shoul- der.

Gray and writhing, it wreathed my shoulders, twined itself above my head. I could see the far wall through it, but only a little. My personal little whirlwind.

I turned and fully faced the mirror then, and the mirror immediately starred with cracks, as if someone had just smacked it with a hammer. The marbles began that serpentine hiss even louder, all of them jumping minutely on the cement floor. You ever heard a flurry of hail falling real sudden on the street? This was that a hundred times over.

I took an abrupt step out of the circle, stupid with terror at that point, and the marbles stopped jittering and rolled apart, rolled loose. Whatever had been binding them together was gone. The fog-shape was gone. Through the starburst in the mirror, I could see a broken funhouse version of Lydia's drawn, stricken face behind me.

I staggered—that's the only word for it—down the sidewalk, nearly knocking over an old woman pushing her groceries in a little cart. She called after me—in Russian, I think now—but her voice sounded guttural and clotted, like more than one tongue was forming the words.

I made it to Sandy Boulevard and walked west for miles, my head swimming. It felt dreamlike, that walk. At one point, I started smacking myself, beating my head and shoulders as rain began to fall. Convinced the thing had attached itself to me, that it was snared in the fabric of my clothes, the collar of my coat.

Came to some pub, don't even remember which one, and stepped inside with rain dripping from my hair. Ordered a whiskey, called a cab. My hands still shook. I was afraid to sit at the bar, afraid of what I might see twisting above my shoulders in the bar mirror, so I sat down at a booth and waited. Made it maybe five minutes before I just couldn't be in there anymore, so I went and stood outside, counting my breaths until the cab pulled to the curb.

So here we are. Back at Francis's scarred kitchen table with two six-packs of imported IPAs and a fifth of Jameson. The overhead rafters throwing weird shadows on the floor because the lights keep flickering and popping. There's some almost-discernible pattern to it, like if I could decipher it, something important would be revealed. Morse code for the damned.

Well.

Kind of came to in the middle of the night. Pulled back into myself. I'm sleeping on the couch, of course. Fog-man, unseen-man, the good old boy that permeates this space? He owns the loft upstairs. I'm just house-sitting. I don't go up there.

Tried calling Francis earlier, the phone just keeps crackling. I think I got ahold of him, but I'm not sure. There's just so much noise. I swear there are *almost* words buried beneath the sound of it, the static.

I am clearly drunk, yes.

Why don't I leave? I could be in a hotel in half an hour. With lights that actually lit up the room. Lights that didn't flick-flick-flick. The dark just keeps pushing in here. Even the sound of traffic gets eaten up sometimes.

I fell asleep on the couch, and when I woke, I was sitting upright.

I see pictures I hear sounds.
I see people gagged and bound.
Little poem for you Katherine.

Whiskey's empty. I'm fucking hammered.

I don't know what's happening to me.

So I woke again, okay, and saw that I'd been walking a circle in the floor, around and around the table here, just these endless revolutions, and I only came out of it when I whacked my shin hard enough on Francis's wooden chair—this heavy-ass thing that looks like it was made for some stern hausfrau in the 1800s and weighs about as much as a guitar cab. Shin felt like it'd been cracked in two. Head throbbing. My tongue like cotton batting in my mouth. And I was dimly aware that I'd been making some kind of *noise* while I walked.

Something simple, guttural, like an incantation. It felt *good*, I re-member that, but I couldn't quite place the sounds or the rhythm.

The house of the worm, maybe? Was that what I was saying? Some-thing like it.

The circles I make around the table, they're not *bad*, Katherine. It's not *bad*, what I do.

Back at the table now. Writing, playing a Springsteen tape on the little boombox Francis left behind. I keep wanting to look up at the loft, up that ladder. See the fog-man. Mister marble-jumper himself. But I'm too afraid.

Caught myself walking around the table again. I don't know if days are passing or minutes. Seems like it's always night outside the little windows of the bay door.

This time I *knew* the words in my mouth, could still feel the shape of them in there.

The name of my wife, name of my son.

Saying their names again and again.

The circles, Katherine, they're not *bad*.

Francis called, and I chewed him out over Lydia. He was less than receptive. Francis's tour is going badly. The drummer broke his hand doing some motorcycle stunt on one of their days off, and rather than cancel the rest of the tour, they've sent him home and hired a fill-in. So now Francis, instead of partying, gets to teach the songs to the new drummer.

"You don't like it," he told me sourly, "you can get the hell out of my place."

"No," I said. "It's cool. It's just, Francis, she told me she'd done coke twice in her life. It was embarrassing, dude."

Francis snorted. "Yeah, Lydia's done coke twice, just for ten years each time," he said. "Maybe you spooked her."

Did I tell him about the mirror then? Or the marbles?

Did I tell him about the fog-man?

Did I say how I'm pretty sure I can feel it now? How it's *hooked* on me, like some kind of suckerfish?

Nah. I didn't tell Francis nothing. I told him thanks and hung up.

When's the last time I saw Nick? Katherine? When's the last time I ate anything? Took a shower? I just write and walk circles and talk and write. Listen to tapes. I must go out; the alcohol keeps appearing. But I don't remember buying it.

Did the circles again—*house of fever house of wounds* in my mouth again and again, ten thousand times—and woke up and found that I'd carved something into my arm with one of Francis's mean little serrated steak knives. This ragged-ass picture. An eyeball or something. A rough circle with a mark inside. I'd bled all over the floor.

I can see it now, in the corner of my vision. Definitively.

Some shape up there in the loft. Shifting, twisting, but wholly present. Sitting patiently.

Waiting.

So yeah. Okay.

I know it now.

There's definitely something in here with me.

JOHN BONNER

National Guard base, thirty miles north of Gearhart, Oregon—Portland, Oregon

The Message happened so fast, it was like a light being turned off. Massive power failures across the globe because the front-line workers for basic services, accustomed to being ready to problem-solve at all hours, had answered their phones in the middle of the night and, whoops, suddenly gone batshit. There was the total and immediate decimation of supply chains. Military, law enforcement, medical and civic infrastructure, all halted in a matter of moments. Global economy? Turned to dust in an eyeblink. Moments after the Message, organized society itself had pretty much become a cute idea. A fond memory.

And to top it off?

Suddenly your loved one's a monster that wants to eat you.

Cruelty's the engine that runs the world. Bonner knows it. Has known it for years. That Terradyne—Christ, that his *uncle*—could choose to be the orchestrator of said cruelty, *that* still floors him sometimes. Terradyne didn't start all the madness with the remnants—they'd been sought after long before Terradyne got ahold of that recording. But oh, Uncle Jack and Theo Marsden had sure capitalized on it when they had the chance, hadn't they? And they've been capitalizing on it ever since. What Terradyne's doing is like shooting someone and then offering to clean up the blood, as long as they get to keep all the stuff that belonged to the dead guy.

Which, when he thinks about it, is exactly what the Providence Initiative is all about. Cleaning up the mess, but making sure only certain people benefit. The Providence Committee, for one.

And here's Bonner in the middle of it.

Terradyne's eternal yes-man.

He's been involved in some aspect of government intelligence for the entirety of his adult life, a decent amount of it spent either undercover or in dark ops. *And yet.* And yet he couldn't reconcile it inside himself, what Jack had done. Get your hands on this profoundly powerful, lethal weapon, which is what the Message was, a recording that could drive any listener rageful and mad in a matter of seconds, and just . . . carpet bomb the fucking planet with it.

Jack Bonner's always been insulated by his education, his wealth, his age—he was the oldest sibling, Bonner's own mother four years younger. He was built with the unique mental gymnastics needed to be CFO of the largest defense firm on the planet—Bonner understood that you have to be at least a little mad, a little power hungry, to fend off the guilt that comes with selling weapons on a global scale. But this desire to acquire the recording, and then the will to play it across the world? That was the part that he couldn't let go of. The part that broke his heart, and the part that had led him to storm one of Terradyne's earliest Providence planning sessions, back when it consisted of a ragged-ass group of a few congressmen and some scared-as-shit Terradyne board members and their bodyguards. The group had cleared out the conference room of a Holiday Inn in Vancouver, Washington; a year after the Message, it was a town still thronged with fevered, though nowhere near as bad as Portland, where the first desperate inkling of the wall was being pieced together. Bonner remembered the quailing, uneasy look on these powerful men's faces as he'd strode in with his fists in his pockets, a smile on his face that had bought him a few precious seconds. All the meatheads on Terradyne's payroll tasked with protecting these soft-ass execs had grown too slow, too logy on their calorie-rich rations. Food production was at a standstill, and famine was striding big through the country at that time. You heard about entire platoons gone AWOL, how they'd started ransacking towns, eating people. Shit was dire. But if you worked for Terradyne, you got your bottled water and your twenty-two hundred calories every day, even if they were gag-worthy military MREs.

Bonner, furious, had threaded his way past these beefy, slow motherfuckers, and up to Uncle Jack, who even then had been far from a young man. Bonner had dropped him with a single, brutal liver punch that had sent the old man retching and sinking to the floor. Moments later the strongmen had sprung into action, and Bonner's beating had been swift and thorough.

He was transferred as a prisoner to a National Guard base over at the northwestern tip of Oregon. Sent there in a three-truck convoy, which meant he was important. The fevered were *everywhere* then. Clots of them drifting across the highway, chasing the convoy like murderous dogs. They'd passed a rest area somewhere on Highway 26 and saw a mother and child on top of the building there, surrounded by a drift a thousand deep, easily. They were screaming for help. The gunner in the rear Humvee laid down a few bursts from the M240 as they sped past and that was it. *Good luck, ladies.* Bonner grew numb at the idea of how quickly and irrevocably they'd screwed themselves, screwed the entire world. Jack Bonner was a madman.

The National Guard post was a pretty bare-bones affair by the time they arrived. Most soldiers had either been deployed somewhere— getting chewed up in Portland, Eugene, and Salem most likely—while others, rumor had it, had stripped off their uniforms and beat feet, headed out into the maelstrom of the world to find their families or navigate this new, terrible landscape without Uncle Sam's demands hanging over their heads. It wasn't an official military prison that they threw him in—nothing much could be considered official anymore—just some empty barracks filled with monuments to the immediacy of what had happened: footlockers still left open, magazines splayed out on beds.

Apart from the profound guilt he felt over Nick Coffin, about not being fast enough, about leaving him alone in Portland, Bonner had appreciated his time there. Precious days to ruminate on what he might have done. The barracks had beds, a door that closed, a generator that still worked. Someone brought him food. It was not a bad place to be as the world ground to a stop.

He'd been on his bunk, reading a tattered paperback copy of *The Stand,* when his uncle came to see him. The old man, in spite of everything, still looked like a guy used to sipping good cocktails on a vast expanse of manicured lawn somewhere, a man who might enjoy nine holes anywhere in the world without needing to call ahead. Bonner was halfway surprised he didn't have a pastel sweater tied around his neck.

"Uncle Jack," Bonner said, standing in the doorway, hands on his hips. He cast a quick glance over Jack's shoulder. Nothing but chain link and razor wire out there, a single manned guard booth. A sniper's post high up in the yard. Bonner couldn't tell if anyone was even in it. And what did it matter? Where was there to go?

"Hell of a shot," Jack said by way of hello, and stepped past him. He looked around the room like it was a piece of real estate he'd had his eye on for a while. He tapped a bedpost with his wingtip, as if testing its solidity.

"Come on in," Bonner managed.

"Truly, hell of a shot you got me with, John. I pissed blood for three days, did anyone tell you that?"

"I haven't been getting my reports, I guess."

Jack let out a little laugh. "I hear you," he said. "Point being, I'd have done the same thing. I truly don't know what happened."

A stitch of anger unthreaded inside him. "Well, what happened was, you bought a recording of Matthew Coffin speaking a bunch of gibberish off someone after David Lundy died and then you used it to end the world."

Jack held up a hand, his eyes shut, and Bonner had seen something of his mother in this shared familial gesture. He felt a sudden, unexpected pang of homesickness rip through him. Neither he nor Jack had been able to contact her following the Message and Bonner was still trying to adjust to the knowledge that she was almost surely dead.

"You don't know what you're talking about," Jack said.

"You're the one that sent me to ARC, remember? An agency whose only job was holding on to the remnants. I'd say I know more about it than most."

"Look," Jack said, "I'll just come right out and say it. We're moving you. You've been enlisted to do security."

Bonner nodded in mock seriousness. "Enlisted. Got it. Where have I been enlisted?"

"Well, Portland, John."

He laughed. "Aren't you building a fucking *wall* around the city right now? That's what it looked like to me."

"We are, yes. And a collation center for the afflicted. The first one."

"The fuck is a collation center, Jack?"

"A containment facility."

"Ah. And who greenlit that?"

His uncle shrugged. "Everyone. Everyone who matters. Theo. Yardley."

"Appreciate it, but I'll have to decline."

"Even before all this, John, you went where you were told to go. This isn't new. You should be grateful."

Bonner laughed, looked at the wall.

"Sending you there, believe me, is a compromise," Jack said. "Theo wanted you out of the picture."

"What does that mean?"

"It means a firing squad was discussed."

Bonner sputtered, threw his arms wide. "*You* played the recording, Jack. *You* bought it, *you* played it—"

"Look, once we get on top of this—"

"Jack, I love you, but you're a fucking idiot if you think you're ever getting on top of this."

"—once we get on top of this, once we get some, some vestige of operational security again, we'll need people that will stay the line. You, John, are *far* from meeting those requirements right now. You're unpredictable."

"Theo Marsden can go fuck himself, Jack. How's that for unpredictable?"

"I'd say it's pretty telling, honestly."

"Man, you are unbelievable."

"What you know about the *history* of all this, John? About Matthew Coffin, this Katherine Moriarty woman? Their son? About the remnants? That *alone* makes you susceptible to bribery, blackmail, interrogation. Coupled with your *clear* contempt for any sort of remaining authority? You're a risk."

"I'm your nephew."

Jack had waved his hand as if an insect was harrying him. "Oh, Christ. Your mother was too pragmatic to have raised you like that."

"So you're making me a screw in this new walled-in prison city of yours."

"Again, it's not a prison. It's a holding facility."

"Can I leave if I want to?"

Jack cut his eyes away. "We want personnel to focus on—"

"See? It's a prison."

His uncle had scratched at an eyebrow. "It's that or the other thing." Then he said, in a conciliatory tone that surprised Bonner, "We need operatives there, John. Desperately. We're on the cusp of getting things up and running. We need people to put their ears to the ground. *Particularly* there."

"Jesus, Jack. You're still playing God."

"Really. How do you figure?"

"You ripped the world in half, and now you're rebuilding it. And who gets to wear the crown? You and Theo?"

"That's not remotely fair. Or accurate."

"I'm not interested. Get someone else."

"Believe it or not," Jack said, "I'm trying to do what's right here. Theo and Yardley? They're pushing for eradication. 'Total reduction of afflicted population to zero' is the language being used. So far, the men we're working with, this interim committee, they're reluctant to sign off on that. But it'll happen. Not this year, not next, but eventually. Theo, he just wears people down. At least with these, these *storage* facilities, if there's a vaccine, we can turn them back."

"So you stick them in a cell and then wall up the city and you want a merit badge." Bonner had made to slow-clap but the look of pain on his uncle's face made him stop.

"You think so lowly of me, John."

"You played the recording over the entire fucking globe—"

"I didn't mean to!" Jack suddenly bellowed, lurching toward him, his veneer shattered. His voice cracking, those old man hands drawn up into claws. Here was a man kneecapped by anguish, by guilt, and Bonner felt like a fool for not having seen it earlier. "Something went *wrong*! My orders were *outlined*, the protocols were in place to *just* send the Message to an *allotted number* of targets, targets that Yardley approved—"

"Yeah, even that's fucked up, Jack. You don't see that?"

"It's so easy to sit on your little throne and judge me, isn't it?" His gaze was manic, blazing. "You've never had to categorize, assess, *choose* between bad scenarios and terrible ones. Where every outcome has a cost."

"That's half a field agent's job."

"Right," Jack said, nodding. "And the last time you got jammed up, the last time you made a bad call, what happened?"

Bonner could only gaze at him with a mix of revulsion and awe. Nothing was off-limits with him.

"What happened, John? I'll tell you what happened. You killed a protester on the Williamsburg Bridge. And who helped you?"

"You did," Bonner said softly.

"*I* did, that's right. *Me.* And now you judge me, like your hands are so clean. Like you're so pure. You think I'm not scrambling every *goddamn* day to right this ship? To fix my mistake?" He swiped a hand across his mouth. "I didn't invent the Message, John."

"Look, let me ask you something," Bonner said.

"What?"

"You really want to save people? I mean, really?"

"Of course I do."

"No matter what?"

"Don't patronize me, John. I'm too tired for it."

"Listen to me," Bonner said. "I'll go be your prison guard, your cop, your snitch, whatever you want. *If* you do something for me, Jack. And if you never tell a soul. You do that, and I'll help you." It'd been a gamble, but he didn't know what else to do.

"Fine."

"You don't want to hear what it is first?"

"No," Jack said. "I don't care."

"Okay," Bonner said. He let out a long, shaky breath. He sat down on the bed, scrubbed at his face. "I need you to help me get Matthew Coffin's son to his mother."

Jack frowned. "His son?"

"Nick Coffin."

"Where is he?"

"He's in Portland, and Katherine Moriarty's on the East Coast."

"Jesus."

"You help me get them together, reunite them, I'll do what you want."

The moment hung there, and Bonner forged ahead. "And you can't let anyone at Terradyne know about it, Jack. Ever. Not Yardley, definitely not Theo Marsden." Pragmatic or not, he had banked everything on the notion that Jack's belief in blood, in family, meant something. That his *guilt* meant something.

A beat. "Fine," Jack said. He laughed, pinched his nose. "We found Coffin, did I tell you that? Found him in a townhouse in Chicago. He's . . . he's not like the rest of the fevered."

Bonner thought of what Katherine had told him. Coffin reaching toward her in that bathroom, worms in his hair. Gray and chopped and somehow alive.

"We have a place," Jack continues, "where we're keeping him. Underground. In a box, essentially. He's terrifying. But if Yardley finds out where the boy is, where his mother is, he won't stop. He'll keep looking for them. The man's obsessed."

"I believe you," Bonner said. "And there's a hitch."

"There usually is," says Jack.

"He's stuck in a bathroom."

"What?"

"I go there every once in a while to see how he's doing. Check on him."

Bonner could see his uncle doing the math, figuring it out.

"He's afflicted?"

"Yes."

"How long's he been in there?"

"Oh, a while."

So Jack had helped him move Nick. Even as he feared Nick Coffin might have lucked into some of Matthew's abilities after becoming fevered, Jack kept his word. When Bonner came back to the Regal Arms with a handful of Jack's men, ready to corral Nick and send him to his mother, he discovered that his entire little hoard—Coffin's archives, the hand, the eye—was gone, taken from Nick's closet. Someone had come into the apartment—been led in? called in?—and taken them. He kept his mouth shut, tried to stuff the panic down. Didn't want to alert the Terradyne ops Jack had sent him with.

Nick was still in the bathroom, Katherine's giant dresser leaning in front of the door. They moved it, then broke the door down and gathered Nick. No one was bit, but seeing the kid fevered like that, knowing he'd paced that little room for a fucking *year*, it did something to Bonner. It seemed almost worse than dying.

They bound Nick and put him in the belly of a plane in a body bag. It was one of the first post-Message flights in the country, and Bonner and Nick were met by a weeping, furious Katherine on a stretch of tarmac on Cape Cod, near the little town he'd helped her settle in after Chicago. He drove the two of them from the airfield to her house in an SUV Jack had arranged. Jack, truly, had arranged everything. Paying off the pilot, getting the car. The world was still maddened with the fevered then and they had to sleep overnight in the SUV, with Nick in the bag in the trunk, and he could tell it was driving Katherine mad, the nearness of him, how changed he was, but what else was there to do? She had a house on an empty street in a town called Cape Winston and in the backyard was a shed and that's where they put him. They didn't say goodbye and there was a moment where he wanted to fling himself to the earth and beg her to forgive him, if he had just been a moment faster, if Rachmann hadn't answered his fucking phone—

Later he would set her up with a fake ID and loyalty card, everything under an assumed name. The point being, kill Katherine Moriarty. Become someone else. Stay small, stay quiet. He would try to help her, occasionally call, see how she was doing. Underneath it all was the throb and pulse of guilt.

To his credit, Jack never spoke of it. Bonner and his uncle agreeing tacitly that Jack could never be told where Katherine Moriarty—Katherine *Sunderson* now—actually was. That it was better for him not to know. It was then, finally, that he believed his uncle might have some modicum of regret hung up within him. Maybe he really hadn't known what had gone wrong with the Message. Maybe they were both animated by their guilt.

Fate accepted, Bonner headed back to Portland, got to work. Word got out fast. He was one of the first ops working the city, and soon everyone knew who he was. Knew that Terradyne backed him. Knew that Bonner cultivated information, and could be counted on to trade rumors or names for a few extra smokes, a beer.

A couple months after getting Nick back to Katherine, he rediscovered the hand. Literally just happened upon it. Driving aimlessly throughout the city, trying to get his resentments and furies under control, trying to do the job, he drove across an overpass and felt that brief but familiar blip of death-song in his brain. He almost put the car into the guardrail. Reversed, backtracked, got out of the car and walked around, homing in on the thing. Found the hand in a choke of weeds in a culvert beneath the overpass. The odds of it all.

He's thought it before, how little luck seems to be involved, how it feels at times like something else. Something intentional.

Fate.

Doom, maybe.

It was when he found the hand again and hid it in the apartment on Eighty-second that everything went south for him. When he started visiting it, sitting with the thing, letting its currents move through him.

There were still a lot of fevered in the city back then, running loose and getting into shit, which meant half his job was cleanup and containment. Gathering them, getting them placed in the fever house—he refused to call it a "collation center"—in the old convention center. He would never be entirely respected by folks here, but he was a guy who tried to make things happen for people, and that got picked up on. He worked crime scenes, actually filed his reports, which in the early days meant doing everything by hand. He tried to get the right guys in a room together to quash gang beefs, and he leaned on husbands and boyfriends when claims of DV filtered through the grapevine. He became, in his own way, a sort of shot-caller, if only because he was an op with Terradyne's weight behind him. The whole thing was a trip, and he was surprised to discover he didn't mind working the city. It felt redemptive. Like the good he did was tangible, something he could seize in his fist, mark on the wall. Even as the hand's darkness began to twist through his brain.

Now he sits in his car outside the apartment on Eighty-second with Matthew Coffin's eye resting in its box in the trunk. The hand is upstairs and he swears he can feel it. Hear it. There's been—he sees it now, sees how obvious it is—this acclimation, this *lean*, toward it over the years after he'd found it again. Or been led to it. Feeling bad? Feeling sorry for yourself about Nick and Rachmann and Sean Pernicio, the dead kid on the Williamsburg Bridge? Got the ghosts of past mistakes pissing on your head? Poor guy, go sit with the hand for a while.

Feeling *good*? Oh, same thing.

Close a case? Feeling stuck? Restless? Sit with the hand.

He's *hooked,* is what it is. Has been.

He wants to go up there so bad. Take those stairs and unlock that door and fall into those dark red dreams.

You are the harbinger, the one who brings about the devoured world. The one that opens the door.

He'd been tasked with protecting a place, protecting its people. He'd lost sight of it. He'd done this instead. Done perhaps a decent job of it, but there's no denying the fucking thing's twisted him up like a corkscrew over the years.

What kind of man would he be now if he'd never laid eyes on it at all? Never spent these countless, sick, sad hours with it? All these days?

You are the harbinger.

The hand's up in the apartment. Bonner's pistol in his lap. He stares at it. Thinks again that he ought to destroy the thing, but there's no weight to it. A threat grown gossamer-thin.

You are the harbinger. He remembers how happy the man had been when he'd said it.

Bonner lifts the pistol, turns it so the muzzle is pointed at his face. Considers the oily, plastic taste should he actually put the barrel in his mouth.

He sets it back in his lap, looks at the box in his passenger seat. Police reports, Coffin's old correspondence. Battered notebooks.

I should keep the remnants so that I can bury them. Hide them. Make sure no one uses them, so nothing like the Message ever happens again.

Bonner smiles down at the pistol. You're a fucking liar, he thinks. That's not why you want them. You want them because you're drawn to them, same as everyone else.

He puts the Glock in its holster. Thinks of the hand upstairs. Calling out.

You will be the one to open hell's door for him.

Him meaning Matthew Coffin, or whatever unknowable thing moves through Coffin these days. There in his box underground.

He's coming here, according to the Sight—according to the *eye*—and John Bonner fucking helps him?

"Nah," Bonner says. "Not me. It's not happening."

He reverses, leaves the hand up there, tires screaming. Pulls out of the parking lot in a boil of smoke.

THEO MARSDEN

Rolla, Missouri

He and Eastman in the labyrinth, before the door of Coffin's room. Marsden is furious, muttering, pacing the halls. *Fucking Yardley.* Unbelievable. Of all the years the president's been holed up in DC, wafting through the emptied city like it's his own little mausoleum, he's finally gone and done it.

He's actually leaving.

The old bastard's actually getting on a plane and coming *here.*

It was the girl that did it. She was the catalyst. Marsden's just gotten off the phone with Yardley and he's pacing, massaging his chest, trying to quell the thunder of his heart. The rage and fear threatening to bubble up.

"I changed my mind," Yardley had said. "I want to see her do it with my own eyes. Her and Coffin."

"We haven't gotten that far yet, Mr. President—"

"Theo, God has placed this girl in our care, and she must be dealt with firmly and with no appeals to, to softness. This is a matter of divinity, of God's will. He will not be swayed and neither will I. She's been given to us and we must use her."

"I totally agree, sir—"

"I'll be there when I can. A few hours."

Marsden opened his mouth to say something, but Yardley had already hung up. The panic had bloomed in him then. Everything he had—the girl, but mostly Coffin, the hours he spent with Coffin there in the labyrinth, the sense of unbridled *power* he felt there, that cloying, beautiful, bloody feeling of *enclosure*—all that seemed suddenly on the cusp of being taken away from him.

At least Yardley didn't know about Katherine Moriarty.

The potential discovery of the Moriarty woman in Massachusetts was an incredible thing. So much mystery surrounds Matthew Coffin, what he can do, how he came to be the way he is. Moriarty's one of the few people on earth who may have answers.

"What's this hunter's name again?" he says to Eastman, trying to calm himself. "The one who discovered her?"

"Canino," Eastman says. "Chris Canino. The other hunter he was with died."

"Died?"

"That's what the report says, sir. His brother, I guess. She killed him."

"Moriarty? Jesus."

"I guess a squad raided her house an hour ago and both her and the fevered were gone."

"It's Nick Coffin," Marsden says.

"What's that, sir?"

"It's her son. Bet you a million dollars, Derrick. Bet you a steak."

"Yes, sir. Anyway, Canino's already in the air. Should be here soon."

"She hid him somewhere," Marsden says, but he's clearly talking to himself, and Eastman doesn't reply. "Smart." The fact that Nick Coffin is afflicted changes things. Narrows their options: Nick can't be debriefed, for one. Can't tell them anything about his father. And so it makes finding Katherine all the more important. She's now the only true connective point left to Matthew Coffin.

"Wait out here," Marsden says, and Eastman nods.

He badges the door and steps inside, waits for the door to close before he steps up to Matthew Coffin's box. Gazes up at that stilled face. He feels the familiar sense of envelopment, and it soothes his heart, allays his fear a little.

He's considered what it is he'll say. He breathes deep, exhales. "I grew up," he says, "in a strict home. My father was in the military. I was small and quiet until I got provoked, and then I would explode. Often scared the hell out of people, this little eighty-, ninety-pound maniac. It generally amused my father, these fights, until I was teased by the son of an officer on base who held a higher rank than him, and I beat the boy up. He'd been teasing me for months, this boy, cornering me, and I snapped. It was an ugly thing, nothing brave about it. I hit him across the face with a stick, broke the orbital bone. The bone around the eye." Marsden blinks, flung back into the memory of it. Such things happen around Coffin; being near him means churning the dark soil of your own unhappiness. "My father beat me in turn, and then paraded me before the boy's father with my nose still bleeding, like some sort of proof that justice had been done. It was the only time he ever struck me. And then he brought me back home, his big hand around my neck, and put me in my room and shut the door. I sat there on my bed. For hours. I didn't cry. Didn't move. The blood on my face dried but I didn't itch it. Didn't wipe it away. When he came in later that night, I knew he was surprised to see me still sitting there. He crouched in front of me, tried to speak calmly. Sensibly. He was a veteran, had seen and done things in war that haunted him. Like many of us, he was a man who could compress and section off his own history and be quite reasonable most of the time. He told me that there was a hierarchy to things, and what I had done had broken that hierarchy. In doing so, I had put my family in danger. He could not technically be demoted for what I did, but the boy's father could make things difficult for him. It was a formative event for me. My nose throbbed where he'd hit me. I felt betrayed by him, and I don't think that feeling of betrayal ever entirely went away. I still loved him, sometimes against my will, but I learned to parse out that love, and things were never the same between us."

He stares into Coffin's face, puts his hands behind his back, tries to still his hammering heart. Destiny is in the room here with them. He feels it. As if his fate trembles on a knifepoint.

"I tell you this, Matthew, as a son and a father. I tell you this with the belief that you can hear me, understand me. I had two children of my own—two girls—and they died after the Message, but I like to think they died trusting me. Loving me. That that rage in me had been whittled down enough that my own children did not feel the betrayal that I felt. I don't know exactly what you are, or what you are capable of, or if you are just some, some *automaton* fulfilling an unknown purpose. But I'm here to tell you that if there is something you've been brought here to do? You'd better do it quickly. Forces—men—are conspiring to push you forward in a way you might not prefer. And we have a girl here who can turn your fevered back, turn them away from how you've made them. Your son Nick has been turned. We are close to finding Katherine—"

It's the sound of their names, he thinks, that does it.

Coffin crouches down on one knee and, with his remaining hand, tents his fingers against the glass.

Marsden lets out a little yip of surprise, his veins flooding with ice. Years spent in this box and Coffin's never moved, not once. A savage rip of joy moves through him. I *fucking got him* moving, *Jack, when you never could, were too afraid to—*

"Yes, Katherine, we're looking for her now," Marsden gibbers, taking a step back and then forcing himself forward. Moving through the fear. This is what Yardley's demanded, after all—Coffin moving. Coffin *acting.*

He approaches the box and peers up into that ruined face.

"Your wife and son," he says. "We're looking for them now. There's a hunter that's coming here. He's seen her in person." Marsden's hand floats up, traces the green glass. He feels buoyed, adrift. Fear suddenly gone in the gaze of that eye.

Coffin blinks, then opens his mouth, widening it until Marsden sees something pale and glistening inside. Marsden lets out a little hiss of air, equal parts exultant and horrified, as Coffin slides his hand over to the side where the ID reader sits. All this while holding his gaze and images rise through the murk of Marsden's brain. Some of them are the standard horrors that being near Coffin inspires: a limbless torso bobbing in a red sea, a severed eye cupped in a palm and turning, a border of severed heads on pikes. But some are new: Coffin with his hand around a woman's throat. A pair of unfurling, black-veined wings. A sea of fevered filling a street. A skyline on fire.

Marsden sees his own hand rising, pressing his badge to the reader. Some distant part of him is telling him to run, to get away, that he's made a mistake. That Yardley's a fool. And then there's a hiss of pneumatics and a rush of rotten, fetid air. A claxon alarm goes off, filling the room. There is a handle on the side of the box and Marsden struggles with it; it is, after all, too late to turn back. The glass face of the box opens.

Matthew Coffin clambers out.

"You want your wife," Marsden breathes. "Of course, yes, I understand, I—"

Coffin lurches forward, bare feet slapping against the floor, wildly faster than Marsden could have imagined. Coffin reaches for him and he backpedals, screeching, slapping his badge at the door's ID reader and just as it opens, Coffin hooks an arm around his neck and brings him close, mashes their lips together.

The taste of the grave floods his mouth.

Dirt. Stagnant water. Rot.

The cold press of him against Marsden's body. He screams, and perhaps there is the slightest feeling of something entering his mouth, writhing over his tongue, though that might just be the panic that's seized him. He slaps uselessly at Coffin's shoulders.

And then Eastman is there, and from an arm's length away he fires a burst from his rifle and Coffin lets go, staggers back a bit. Gunfire impossibly, painfully loud in the room. Dark clots of Coffin—the rounds got him through the side, the ribs—patter wetly to the ground. Still, Coffin regains his footing and surges forth. Christ, he's so *fast*. Even as Eastman's rifle chatters again, Coffin hooks his fingers into Eastman's mouth and *pulls,* the flesh between the jaws horrifically *elastic* for a moment before the lower jaw comes off in a red spray, a crack of bone. Eastman screams, his weapon clattering to the floor, Marsden's mouth still filled with that graveyard-wet, that taste of clotted earth, and then Coffin follows Eastman to the ground, straddles him and leans all of his weight on his single gray hand with Eastman's head pinned beneath it. The soldier's body bucking, the alarm howling overhead, great fantails of blood painting the floor, until Eastman's head caves in with a deep crack, a spray of brain pulp. Marsden, screaming, scoops up Eastman's rifle and stumbles over on legs that feel like they belong to someone else. He puts the barrel to Coffin's temple, and Coffin looks up, and there is something in his gaze, in that single eye, that looks *different,* looks human in a way that it never has before, like something has changed, like there's some measure of mercy and gratitude in what Marsden's about to do—

He pulls the trigger, and Matthew Coffin's head explodes in a tumble of blood and brain, his lifeless body staying upright for just a moment before its inevitable trek to the floor.

KATHERINE MORIARTY

Highway 195, west of Cape Winston, Massachusetts

The moon scours the world with light. They're off the highway, in the backyard of a two-story house with a wraparound porch and a roof that's caving in on the northeast side. They've chosen the place mostly because of how the driveway's choked in greenery, the house itself mostly hidden away. They set up camp in the overgrown backyard—Dean says he doesn't like sleeping indoors if he can help it. The place is fenced in on three sides, with narrow walkways on each side of the house. He's already pulled up his bike and cart by the back porch and yanked up a circle of overgrown grass to make space for the evening's fire.

They sit with the fire between them, Dean feeding it small twigs. Beside him is a stack of old roofing shakes he's found in a stack by the fence, cast-off pieces that are tinder-dry and will burn hot.

Katherine reaches into her pack and fishes out two cans of chicken noodle soup. By the time she's able to puncture the cans with the tip of Dean's knife, the flames are crackling, Dean himself reduced to a shape, the whites of his eyes glowing.

"Probably let this die down a little, yeah?"

Dean nods. "Yep. Get some coals going."

They wait. Katherine fills the silence by reaching into her pocket and pulling out a pack of cigarettes. Jane's face, red and blue printing on white paper, FULL-FLAVOR CIGARETTES emblazoned above. She offers him the pack, and Dean leans across the fire, takes one.

Katherine hasn't had a cigarette in, what? Thirty years? Jesus. Since she found out she was pregnant with Nick. Not even when the Blank Letters toured and all three of her bandmates smoked like chimneys. But these she's kept in a drawer at home, unopened, and they made it into her slapdash packing as they hustled to leave the house.

Her throat starts to tighten at the memory of it—putting Nick in a fucking cart, down into the ground—and as tears well up, she bends down and cups the cigarette to a match. Blinks them back. She passes the matchbook to Dean, and then closes her eyes against the sudden head rush.

"Haven't smoked in a long time," Dean said.

"Me neither."

"Got no clue why I'd start now, but here we are."

She shrugs. "Why not, right?"

"Guess so. You lived in that town for a long time?"

"Cape Winston? No. Couple years."

The fire pops. Katherine hears bats flitting by overhead. "How old's your son?"

She stiffens. "He'd be thirty. He is thirty, I guess." Katherine blows a jet of smoke up to the sky, blinks.

"You don't want to talk about it. That's cool."

"It's nothing personal."

"No, I hear you. I'm sorry."

"I want to thank you for helping me, though. I was in deep shit. You still got that gun on you?"

"This little Ruger, yeah."

"You want another one?"

"A pistol?"

"Yeah."

Even in the dim light, Dean looks surprised. "I would not turn down a free pistol."

Katherine stands, dizzy from the cigarette, and hands over one of the hunters' guns from her jacket pocket, handle first. "Please don't make me regret that."

He hesitates before taking the gun, Katherine's arm stretched to meet his across their little fire. "No plan to," he says.

She sits back down, takes another big drag. More silence, the pops of the fire, and then Dean says, "You think they're gonna be looking for us? Outside of town, I mean."

A moment, then, to tell him the truth. That she's been living under a fake name, that she's intrinsically bound to all of this madness. That Terradyne in its entirety will likely be looking for her now. But then he would leave, and she is afraid of being alone. "Well," Katherine says cautiously, loathing herself for this weak and partial truth, "probably best to keep a low profile for a while. You never know."

She puts the soup cans in the fire and the two of them watch the coals flare and dim in the breeze. "So that cart out there," she says. "What's that all about?"

"I'm a ragman. I was, anyway. I was recently, uh, liberated from my wares."

"What's a ragman do?"

"Ragman divvies up the goods of the bygone world," he says, fanning his hands out at each side of his face like a showman.

"So, scavenging."

"Well, yeah," he says, unbothered by her frankness. "But it's more than that. It's a question of knowing what to scavenge and what to ignore. Who to approach, and how to talk to 'em. Lot of things at play." He taps a finger to his temple. "There's an art to it."

"You like it?"

"I love it. I love finding things that still work. Things people can find meaning in." Pushing the coals around a little with a hank of scrap wood, he says, "What about you? If you had your loyalty card, I guess that means they had you working."

"I did interviews. Gauged the loyalty of others, I guess you'd say."

"What do you mean?"

Katherine stubs her cigarette out in the dirt and tosses it in the fire. "I called people who signed up for the Providence Initiative and asked them a bunch of questions. Like a survey. Essentially asking people if they were happy with the services Terradyne provided."

Dean's mouth splits open in a grin. "You did not."

"Absolutely did. Pretty much asked people to give the Message one to five stars and why."

He leans over, clapping his hands softly. "Holy shit, man."

They settle then into a more companionable silence. Katherine has another cigarette, Dean shaking his head when she offers him the pack.

"So," she says after a while, "we might as well get the big question over with."

"What's that?" Dean says warily.

"Where were you when the Message came through?"

He nods. "St. Louis. How about you?"

"Chicago."

"Chicago couldn't have been pretty."

Katherine sits up on her knees, reaches in and picks up one of the cans of soup with a rag. Peers at it, sets it back on the coals. "I don't think anywhere was, really. What'd you do before the Message?"

"Worked at an answering service, if you can believe that."

She smiles. "They still had those?"

"They did. What about you?"

She curses herself—such a dipshit move. Leaving herself open like that. First he'll say, *Oh, you're a musician? What do you play?* And then she can either lie or tell the truth, and both are messy. She's already skirting around the truth with this man in regard to her stolen ID and all that it means. "You know," she says. "Bounced around.

Raised my kid, mostly. What about you? Family?" She sees the look on his face and curses again.

"At one time, yes," he says, nodding. "A wife and a son."

"I'm sorry."

"Don't be. This was all before the Message. Long time ago. My boy would be, what? Seventeen years old now. Was six when he died."

"Christ, Dean. I'm an idiot."

"Nah," he says, screwing up his face, shaking his head. "George, his name was, after my wife's father. So funny, so wild. Slept maybe four hours a night, seemed like. Hummed like a telephone wire. Him and his mama got in a car accident. Drunk driver." He smiles, drawn into himself.

"I don't know what to say, man."

"You don't got to say nothing, Katherine. I've had years to mourn it. Hell, my wife left two years later because all we could do was mourn, and that's a singular thing. Hard to do together. But I want you to know, *I* know what it's like to hurt for a son. That big hollow space inside. How you blame yourself, how that blame becomes like a third foot, some extra shirt you always wear. Just this new and terrible part of you. And how days keep coming at you and you just don't know the why of it. Like it's outrageous that you're expected to move through them with all this hurt inside."

"I miss him so fucking bad," Katherine says, her voice cracking. Tears blur her vision.

"Your boy? 'Course you do. It's a heart-killer, losing a child."

There's nothing after that for a while. The crackling of the fire. Bubbling of the cans in the coals. They pick the cans up with their rags and eat while steam twists around their heads.

Katherine finishes her soup, sets the can aside. Both of them with their sorrows twined around them. *If this was a date, I'd say we were trauma bonding*, she thinks, and is just so fucking sick of herself. Sick of Matthew, sick of his memory, sick of hating him. Sick of fearing the thing he'd become, there in Chicago. Sick of wondering if she'll wake up some night and see that, that *remainder* of him, looming over her like a fucking ghoul. She smokes another cigarette, then takes a roll of toilet paper from her pack and excuses herself. Pees around the corner of the house. Sleep tugs at her, finally. Weariness. When she returns, Dean kicks the fire apart and bids her good night, the two of them in their sleeping bags with the dim coals and the black smear of the firepit.

Katherine shuts her eyes and before she can begin to mourn Nick again, before she can run through the devilish, heartbreaking catalog of what was and what is, sleep is pulling her down with both hands.

Chicago.

Matthew's grayed hand pushes the shower door aside. He lurches forward, feet slapping on the floor, and puts his hand around her throat.

There is a dark-haired girl in the corner, her mouth frozen in a scream.

She thinks she hears the distant squall of a baby too, and then Matthew is leaning toward her, opening his mouth, perhaps so that they might kiss, and then his head begins splitting wetly down the middle, with glistening purls of flesh tumbling off to reveal what Katherine understands is his somehow *truer* face, the face he has hidden, and then great pale wings burst from her periphery and wrap themselves around her head.

He's changed, she thinks, *oh God this is what he is now*, and then her nose fills with the scent of cigarette smoke and dirt—

She bucks herself awake on the hard ground to find Dean with his hand over her mouth, his eyes wide and white in the dark, she fucking *knew* it, she reaches for her pistol and can't find it, hand scrabbling in the grass, the terror of the dream still gumming her mind.

"Drift," Dean hisses, taking his hand from her mouth. He stands at a crouch.

She slaps at him, scoots away. "What?"

He points at the house and whispers, "*Drift.*"

She can hear it then, a somehow tidal sound. An ocean of sighs, of feet scraping against road. Her scalp tightens.

Dean hoists her up by the armpit and Katherine finds her pistol and they crawl like babies up the back porch. He crouches, has his knife, is ready to shimmy open the door if need be, but Katherine reaches out and twists the doorknob and it opens with a creak that makes them both wince.

They step into the darkness of the house just as an errant fevered staggers around the corner into the backyard. It's an older woman, naked save for a pair of panties, her hair now a gray clot matted to her skull, her fish-white body a crosshatched nightmare of bloodless abrasions. *Barbed wire,* Katherine thinks wildly, eyeing the woman through the wedge of the open door. Even in her terror, Katherine feels a wild surge of empathy for this woman who made the eternal mistake of answering a midnight phone call in nothing but her underwear. Dean exhales silently and slowly closes the door. The old woman with her back to them, her hands flexing at her sides. Her jaw clacking together in little flurries.

Dean and Katherine stand there in the dark, staring at each other.

She can hear the drift passing by in front of the house, beyond that choke of greenery. Slowly, slowly, Dean locks the back door. Katherine creeps through the dark of the house, crouches before a wedge of curtain in the front room. Smell of mold, dust. Dean settles beside her. She smells too the acrid tang of his fear, or maybe her own.

It's a fucking tide of them out there. The largest drift she's ever seen. They stretch so far back they've become a silvered line around the highway's bend. Moonlight on their shoulders, the occasional snarl or croak of ill-used vocal cords when one agitates another, bumps or halts the progress of the group. They wend around stalled cars like water around a rock. They are colorless with age and ruin, their bodies reduced to a simpler palette. Slathered in blood and filth and then poorly rinsed by the elements. Before the Message, in movies or on TV, she'd always thought the palette of the undead was an affectation, everyone always done up in muted duns and grays and browns. Earth tones. Surely some of them would have been bitten in a floral print dress, she'd thought at the time. Where were the zombies in neon-green booty shorts? And there may have been such things at the beginning, but they're all the color of sand and earth now. The world grinds and dims and dirties everything. Time takes it all from you.

The snarl and sigh of them, their footfalls on the road. She imagines Nick somewhere in that drift. He'd be just another drop of water around the rock.

It's a moment of reckoning for her. There won't be any returning from this, she thinks. No vaccine will bring him back. No magical potion to make it all better.

She turns and sits on the couch. Covers her face with her hands and weeps. Dean puts a warm hand on her back and then takes it away.

There will be no happy, revived world. No cosmic hand reaching down from the sky and righting things.

There will be no saving Nick.

He's gone.

Her son, lost to her forever, and who's at fault?

Matthew. Matthew, the architect of that fucking *recording*, dismembering himself in some insane *ritual,* and coming to her in some kind of half-death in Chicago, petitioning for her love.

Like anything might ever be the way it was.

Matthew's the one that did this.

FROM THE ARCHIVAL NOTEBOOKS
OF MATTHEW COFFIN

Something here for sure
Crazy I ever doubted it
The loft the kitchen the floor
Around the table I go ho ho ho
a circle in the floor, a circle to make a ring

the house of the tongue the eye the hand
the house where I shall live again. House of
    wounds, house of the worm. The pact I made.
The house of second chances and the devoured world

the hand the eye the voice
the wife the son the light
wed the wife crown the son devour the light

then will be the house of fever and wounds house of beetle
house of crow
a king's house where you will remake the world

You talk talk alk

You fucking talk like you know me. You don't know me.

Alright.

Jesus.

Honestly? Honestly, I am just profoundly tired most of the time. Looking at what I wrote here, I have zero memory of actually writing that shit. None of it. I have *vague* memories of sitting down, drinking whiskey at the table, my hand moving across the page like one of those spiritual mediums way back when. Is that what I've become? Some vessel for something? Something that's seized on my grief over this life I'd just absolutely laid waste to? I keep finding empty bottles on the table, the couch. Cigarette butts everywhere. I must be going out and buying them, but that's just more guesswork.

I'm absolutely covered in these glyphs now, my little steak-knife runes. I come to—wake up, whatever the hell it is—scabbed and aching and terrified, but in a very detached sort of way. And then I fall right back into it.

Talked to Francis last night.

I was in the dark on the couch. The static on the call was so heavy it was like snakes hissing in a bag.

"I'll be home in a week," Francis said.

"Okay," I said.

"I appreciate you looking after the place."

I glanced around. Entire constellations of empty bottles. Dirty clothes like dead skins on the floor; I discovered some time back that I have a tendency to piss myself in those walking trances of mine. When I come to, I take a shower, try to clean my clothes in the bathtub. Apart from my mystery booze-runs, I don't know the last time I left this place.

"Thank you," I said to Francis, or to the hissing snakes that were Francis. I wasn't even sure I was talking to Francis at all. After we hung up, I leaned back against the couch and winced. I could feel the wool blanket I slept with getting stuck to the fresh glyphs on my back. How could I even make those? Put those markings on myself? What, a blade on a stick? How?

That's all bullshit, anyway.
I mean, I know what's happening. I know who he is.
He started in the loft, now he struts around like he owns the
    place.
And to think, at one point I actually wondered, *ha ha,* if this
    place had bad pull.
Whole fucking place is bad pull.
Francis went and somehow got himself one shitty roommate.
Or he's been with me a while and just announced himself once
    I was alone.

HOUSE OF THE WORM
HOUSE OF THE WORM
HOUSE OF THE WORM
HOUSE OF FEVER HOUSE OF WOUNDS

The part I forgot to say was that when Francis and I were talking on the phone, when he was telling me he was coming home, I put the phone on speaker and ran over to his boombox and put in a mixtape he'd made, something in big block letters on the label that said DEVIL ROCK. Francis and his tapes! I marveled at the synchronicity of it. *Sly,* man. Then I put the boombox next to my cell phone and pressed RECORD.

We talked and I stood there and when I came out of it, I had some new shit carved into me. And then I remembered DEVIL ROCK, remembered wanting to see if there were words in the snake-hiss sounds, words buried beneath what Francis and I were talking about.

I rewound the tape and pressed PLAY and it wasn't Francis on there at all.

It was this. It was a voice saying *this*, I copied it down word for word:

If I tell you to sever the head of your neighbor, yes, to dine in the bowl of their skull, you do it, and we might call that fealty. If I tell you to make me a necklace from the heads of your children, to make me a red veil from their latticed veins that I might lay on my brow, you'll curtsy on bloody knees and crow, "Yes, Father!" and you'll ready the knife. And we might call that fealty as well. I say cut out your eye, you slice away. Take your hand off at the wrist, you whet the blade and get to work. That too is fealty. You understand? Yes? Make me a king's house from this whole place. You understand? How I use your voice now, how I speak through you, the sorrowful jaw working just so. How you might remake the world for me. A king's house among all the leaning world. You shall make me a house of fever and wounds. A house of beetle and crow. A house of worms. A house of hounds that savage forever at the belly of love and take root there, devouring.

It was that, and then me crying.

And then the voice saying:

Cut here, here, here. Avail yourself to me. Make me a house of fever and wounds, where all rooms are ghastly and dark. Do it. Make me a king's house, and you will have all you ever wanted.

It was my own voice on the tape.

Just me, chatting away. Muttering full-blown insanities. The whole phone call with Francis apparently imagined. Just me talking to myself.

And I pressed STOP and said okay okay okay for a while and smoked a cigarette. Smoked a *bunch* of cigarettes. And then I threw up in the bathroom and it was just a fist twisting inside me. There was nothing to get out. And the thing is, the truth is?

The truth is, a second chance sounds good to me. Another time to get it right. With Katherine. The kid.

 With my whole life.

 I believe he tells me true. Why would he lie?

The hand the tongue the eye house of fever house of wounds
 wed the wife crown the son devour the light
 and I might remake the world for him and do things better
 Do things true
 Cut here here here
 Avail yourself
 This one more time to try and not fucking ruin everything

Katherine I'm writing this for you so you'll know
 Katherine
 Katherine
 listen
 I really am sorry for the whole thing

3
THE MAN IN THE BOX

THEO MARSDEN

Rolla, Missouri

In Suarez's office, down in the labyrinth, Marsden takes a proffered bottle of water with a hand still shaking. It's his second bottle; he can't seem to wash that foul taste of dirt from his mouth. His sleeves are rolled up, his suit jacket flung over Suarez's chair. Coffin's blood, black as ink, stipples one of his shirtsleeves. Suarez's office is a place of stark utility—white cement walls, a pair of monitors, filing cabinets. Jack stands at the office door looking stricken and terrified. He's even forgotten his tie somewhere. Someone has finally shut the alarms off. Marsden feels bomb-blasted. The world pulled from beneath him.

"Can you tell us what happened?" says Suarez. She's checked the pulse in his wrist; everything else he's begged off. The labyrinth is on a closed-circuit loop. There's no audio, only video, but it's only a matter of time before a tech gets the bright idea to pull up the footage. What they'll see, he knows, is damning: Coffin bending down in his little glass cage, Marsden badging open the box for him. Then Coffin pressing his mouth to Marsden's. And then all that with Eastman, the poor kid, and Marsden emptying their most valuable asset's brains out on the floor.

Still, there's something about that final moment, how Coffin's eye had lost that deathly cast. As if something in him had changed, some vital, terrible thing going away. Or perhaps, Marsden's mind whispers, had been transferred to someone else, say by putting his mouth over yours—

"I'm fine," Marsden says. "Truly." He turns to Jack. "Has that hunter made it here? Canino?"

"He's here," Jack says, "but Jesus, we have other things to discuss, Theo. Yardley's plane just touched down, your security detail got his head flattened like a goddamn penny beneath a train, and our *last remaining asset* is suddenly invalidated—"

"Not our last asset."

"Excuse me?"

"There's still the girl, remember? And the baby. We still have things of value, Jack." Marsden is telling himself this as much as anyone. Everything feels on the cusp of falling apart. All these years of effort, suddenly unmoored by a single bad decision? No, he can still fix this. Somehow.

Marsden's phone begins chirping in his pants pocket. He makes no move to answer it.

Jack smiles tightly, and says, "Dr. Suarez, will you excuse us for a minute?"

They step out into the hall. Marsden's legs are still watery, loose with panic. The place is now abuzz with activity; security emptying out the labyrinth until an investigation takes place—Jack's decision. Marsden himself is in shock, but it's one of those things where knowing it doesn't do anything to stop it. For the time being, Jack Bonner has taken the wheel.

Jack leads him past a room with an open door—Marsden catches a glimpse of a thin, shorn-headed young man in Terradyne fatigues. Canino, presumably. They go into the next room, which turns out to be a storage closet. Shelves and boxes, smell of cleaning fluid, snap of the overhead lights. They're close enough that he can see the pores on Jack's nose, the map of wrinkles around his eyes.

"Theo, what the hell happened in there?"

"I don't know." Then, cagily, "Have you seen the footage?"

"We're getting someone to pull it up now. It's on a server upstairs. Do you remember anything?"

Before Marsden can answer, Jack's phone begins vibrating. He frowns and takes it out of his pocket. His face tightens and he brings the phone to his ear.

"Mr. President," he says. "Yes. Yes, sir, it's true. We're still looking into what happened. I've got Theo here now and—" He stops, nods. "Yes, sir." He holds the phone out to Marsden. "He wants to talk to you."

Marsden takes Jack's phone. Puts it to his own ear. "Mr. President."

Yardley says, "I'm about ten minutes away, Theo. I just want to know one thing. No bluster or bullshit. Did we just lose Matthew Coffin?"

"Preston, I—"

"Yes or no, Theo."

"Yes," Marsden says. Saying it feels like breaking his own finger. Five years of work, tremendous sacrifices—ones that most people couldn't even comprehend—and it's all undone in a moment.

"It appears I have made a grave miscalculation in judgment," Yardley says. "I've hitched my cart to the wrong horse."

Marsden doesn't understand. "Mr. President?"

"I told you there would come a time when you and Jack would reach an impasse, and I was right. Theo, I am hereby relieving you of your governmental duties, both within the Providence Initiative and Terradyne's day-to-day operations."

"Preston, you can't—"

"The hell I can't," Yardley says. "Don't you *move* until I get there. Don't you dare talk to that girl. I want a debrief on *exactly* what happened when I arrive. Put Jack on the phone."

But Marsden doesn't. He tastes dirt in his mouth, feels his panic growing and the low throb of a headache start somewhere above his left eye. He thumbs Jack's phone off. There is the sense of standing on a high place and being pushed off; he is living in that second before gravity seizes him, pulls him down. My entire life in service to this, he thinks. And it's being taken away from me.

Jack says, "I'm sorry, Theo."

Marsden smiles. "You know it's not your fault, don't you?"

Jack frowns. "What isn't?"

Dirt in his mouth, Jesus.

"The Message," Marsden says. "The programming error? The engineer? You poor dumb bastard. How that all must have weighed on you."

Jack tilts his head, confused, and Marsden brings the edge of the phone down onto Jack's face. His nose breaks, and he staggers against a shelf. Marsden pushes him down, Jack turtling up as Marsden puts a supporting hand on the wall and kicks him in the face two, three, six times. Stomps on Jack's head, readjusts, does it again. Again. He drops Jack's phone to the floor and steps over him, gasping. A thought flits through him and he bends down—wheezing like an old man, Christ—and slaps at Jack's pockets until he finds what he's looking for: Katherine Moriarty's loyalty card and ID. *Katherine Sunderson* printed on both of them. He turns the light off and quickly opens the door and shuts it behind him. Smooths his hair back, nods at one of Suarez's researchers as she passes by, carrying a box of her stuff.

He walks to the room where the hunter sits, waiting. Opens the door.

The young man looks up, his face carefully blank.

"You're the one who found Katherine Moriarty?"

"Whatever the fuck her name is," the hunter says. "Yeah."

"What's *your* name, son?"

"Chris Canino."

"Did she really kill your brother?"

He blinks, nods.

"How'd you like to get her back?"

"It's the only thing I want."

"Good. Come with me."

Canino stands up. The way he moves, he hums with a kind of distilled rage that Marsden finds thrilling, even a little frightening. He's a few inches taller than Marsden.

"Do you have a weapon?"

"No, sir."

He leads Canino quickly past Suarez's office, down another hall, and they pass a soldier in Terradyne fatigues. Marsden lifts a hand and the soldier stops.

"Son," he says, "give this man your sidearm."

"Uh, sir?"

It's still a thing that can be fixed, he thinks. All of this. "Emergency acquisition," he says, and offers a smile he's used at so many boardroom meetings, so many conferences and hearings. The soldier unsnaps his holster and hands Canino his pistol.

Marsden claps the man on the shoulder and they keep going.

"That fit in your holster there?" he asks quietly.

"Yes, sir," says Canino.

Another hallway. Time is narrowing down, grains of sand through an hourglass. When Yardley arrives, Marsden's power is gone, evaporated. He badges the room where they're keeping the baby. "Pick that child up," he says.

It's in a bassinet, a plastic thing, and Canino walks in and lifts it awkwardly. Marsden says, "Just the baby, son, not the whole thing."

Next, Canino with the baby pressed to his chest, they walk the hall to the girl's room. Marsden badges it. Windowless, cement walls. A bed, a folding table and chair. She's sitting on the bed with those bags still on her hands, her face puffy.

"Get up."

"Why?"

"Because I told you to."

"Where are we going?"

"No more questions. Stand up."

She stands, her eyes settling on the baby. "Give him to me." Canino pauses, but when Marsden nods, he hands her the child with palpable relief.

If anyone thinks it strange that the baby and this girl with the bags on her hands are being taken aboveground, no one says it. He is Theo Marsden, after all. Second in line only to the president. Bloody shirt or not, Rolla is his.

They take the elevator up and exit into the grand lobby of the Capitol amid all the displaced researchers, the baby beginning to squall in the girl's arms. It's dark beyond the windows, and their little group steps outside. The night's chill touches his face. People mill about, unsure what to do, but Marsden grips the girl's arm and they keep walking.

"Do you know who I am," he asks Canino as he leads their small group around the building, toward the motor pool.

"No," Canino says.

"I'm Theo Marsden."

After a beat, Canino says, "Okay."

"I run Terradyne. I started the Providence Initiative."

Canino's face, already white, goes ghost-pale. He looks to the girl and back to Marsden. "Am I in trouble? Me and Jason saw the fevered and—"

"No, son. You're not. Come with me."

The motor pool—the college's old maintenance building, now with a series of makeshift carports erected next to it—turns out to be pretty slim pickings. It's been a slow process, finding working military vehicles scattered throughout the area and bringing enough of them back here to form a decent armory. Still, they come to a trio of Humvees in one of the carports.

He opens the door on the first one and leans in. Working in

THE DEVIL BY NAME **217**

weapons sales this long has taught him a decent amount—in this case, that Humvees don't have keys. He flips on the ignition switch and sets it to RUN; the battery light goes on. He waits, the baby beginning to fuss behind him again, and then the light turns green and he flips the ignition switch. The Humvee rattles to life.

A soldier in fatigues comes trotting out from the building next door. He's got a walkie-talkie in his hand, oil smeared on one cheek.

Canino's fast. Not as fast as Matthew was, but he moves with an efficiency that's impressive. Two quick steps and he puts a mean right cross against the man's eyebrow. The mechanic falls back onto the pavement, the walkie-talkie clattering away. Naomi screams and Marsden pushes her and the child into the backseat.

Marsden gets behind the wheel, his phone in his lap. Time is an arrow that eventually has to land. Yardley's getting close now, he knows it. I can still fix this, goddamnit. Before it's taken from me. He dials, tells Canino to get in the back with the girl.

The op who picks up on the other end asks for Marsden's name and then a numeric code—a password. Eventually, that password will change or be revoked entirely—Jack and Yardley will see to that—but not yet.

His password is accepted and the op says, "What can I do for you, sir?"

Marsden pulls out of the maintenance parking lot and begins navigating toward surface streets that lead to the highway. He puts his phone on speaker, sets it in the console.

"If I give you the ID number on a loyalty card, can you pull up the phone number registered to that account?"

"Yes, sir," the op says. "Go ahead and give me that pledge number when you have it."

He lifts his hip and takes out Katherine's ID. Hands it over his shoulder to Canino. "I left my glasses in my coat. Read these numbers out."

Canino leans over the seat, reads the numbers from the Katherine Sunderson ID.

"Got it, sir. You ready for the contact info?"

"Can you text it to me?"

"Yes, sir." Marsden hears a ping, an incoming message. Lifts up his phone, squints at it. There it is. Moriarty's phone number.

"Son, can you tell when a call was last made from that phone?"

"Looks like it hasn't been used in a while, sir. Last call was received a while ago, from Portland, Oregon."

Katherine and John Bonner touching base. He'd bet on it. Who else from Moriarty's past is in Portland anymore? Certainly not her husband or son.

"Can you triangulate where the phone is right now?"

"Hold on a sec, sir."

"Where are we going?" Naomi says from the backseat.

No one responds.

Keyboard clicks on the other end of the line, and then the op says, "Our system pings every Terradyne-issued phone every thirty minutes. The last ping on that line showed it about, oh, six miles inland from a town called Cape Winston, in Massachusetts."

So she's still on the coast, but moving inland.

Question is, where has she hidden her son? And if the father is capable of something as powerful as the Message just by talking, what might the son be able to do?

I can still fix this, Marsden thinks. I have everything. The girl, the baby, the hunter who saw Katherine Moriarty with his own eyes. I have Moriarty's ID. Her last known location.

"One more thing. I need the phone number for a security officer in Portland, Oregon. John Bonner." He spells out the last name.

"Would you like me to text that one to you as well?"

"Please."

Another ping.

Marsden thanks him, hangs up. They're on the highway now and he opens up the Humvee's engine a little, wanting some distance from Rolla. Not a minute later they pass a string of headlights all tightly packed, some half dozen of them, and Marsden thinks, *There's Preston's motorcade. All these years and he finally got off his ass and came out here. Enjoy the mess, Mr. President.*

After a while he has to roll down his window and spit.

Just cannot get the taste of dirt out of his mouth.

DEAN HAGGERTY

Highway 195, west of Cape Winston, Massachusetts

They spend the rest of the night in the house. Dean sleeps on the floor, and calling it fitful sleep would be generous. Eyeballing the hugest drift he's ever seen in his life will make a man a little uneasy. Eventually he'd fallen into some sort of gritty half-consciousness while Katherine tossed and turned on the couch, the springs complaining every time. They woke to morning light spilling through the curtains, both of them irritable and tired. It was the kind of sleep that felt almost worthless, like you might as well have just stayed up and gotten shit done.

He stretches and goes to the back door, carefully unlocking it, peering out to see if there're any stragglers. There aren't—the poor old lady in her panties has wandered off—so he creeps out into the dew-dappled yard, songbirds singing in the trees, and retrieves their sleeping bags and backpacks.

When he walks back into the living room, Katherine is sitting up on the couch, hair hanging in her eyes, still as a doll.

"Hey," he says. "I just realized I should put these on the porch to dry."

"You don't have to do that," Katherine says. Her voice is a husky croak.

"It's fine."

"Don't do it, is what I'm saying." She holds out her hand and Dean hands her the damp sleeping bag. There's a *whish* and *zip* of fabric as she lies back down on the couch and covers herself with it.

Dean stands there, unsurety stilling him. Wondering just what his allegiance to this woman actually is, now that their immediate danger—the drift, the fever hunters—has been put to the side, at least momentarily. Yes, her fevered son dredges up memories of George, but that's neither here nor there. There's nothing in the world stopping him from getting on his bike and moving on down the road. No one would put an ounce of blame on him for it. And there's a not inconsiderable part of Dean that knows it would just be easier.

Not knowing what else to do, he spends an hour quietly scavenging the house, building up a bit of inventory. It's soothing, and Dean's pleasantly surprised by some of the things he discovers. There are a few plastic tubs in a hall closet and he empties them of their linens and begins quietly making his way from room to room, filling them up. It feels good.

He finds, in the back room they'd first hidden in, a butane stove and a pair of sealed fuel canisters—a rarity, right there—as well as tents, a pristine pair of women's rubber boots, and a small hand ax that fits in his palm as if it had been made for him. Upstairs, he comes first to a teenager's room, where he stands for a moment in something akin to prayer. It's such an intimate moment, stepping into these final days, into people's lives that ended like someone hitting pause on a film. The bedroom window is shattered, a scrabble of tree branch poking through, and a skid of moss and leaves carpets the floor. He finds a bookshelf full of fantasy novels. A portable stereo and a nylon case of cassettes and a folder of CDs. Black Flag, the Misfits, the Clash. Dead Prez, the Coup. Some are burned CDs, some are blank tapes with handmade covers. Dean smiles, leafing through it all, the sudden pulse of sadness for that bygone world threatening to close his throat.

The books are mold-flowered on their spines but he takes the music and stereo and puts it all in one of the tubs. In the kitchen he finds a French press, some lightweight cookware, a toolbox under the sink with some decent tools inside. By the time he's loaded up a third of his cart, the sun is starting to shine through the windows.

He steps back into the living room. Katherine is a mounded shape beneath her blue sleeping bag.

"I'm gonna go now," he says softly.

For a moment there's nothing. Then she says, "Wait," and maybe ten seconds later, heaves herself up into a sitting position. She looks exhausted, blue circles under her eyes. "I'm up."

"Katherine, you don't have to do this. You want to, you know, sleep, do whatever, you go for it. It's your life."

She pinches the bridge of her nose with two fingers then stands up, the sleeping bag wrapped around her shoulders like a cape. She turns and stares out at the wedge of front yard through the curtains. She palms sleep from her eyes and says, "Sweet Jesus, I miss coffee sometimes."

They stand at the highway, Dean gazing down at the scatter the drift has left behind: a filthy rag, a shoelace, spatters of blood. He swears there's a tinge of rot still hanging in the air, but maybe that's just his imagination.

Katherine adjusts her pack, looks back at the canopy of green that all but obscures the house. "Can't go east," Dean says, scuffing his shoe on the ground. "That's back the way we came. And I don't want to go north, just to be bumping up against that drift."

"West," Katherine says.

"Yeah, or south. Sunny Florida and all that."

"I want to go west," she says, and there's something there— something so steeled compared to her earlier inertia—that Dean simply nods. Grateful for the initiative. "Alright, then." He tilts his head toward the cart. "You can always get in this if you don't want to walk."

She smiles. "That shit's undignified, Dean. I'm a lady of culture."

Laughing, Dean says, "Clearly."

"You know what would be faster, though," she says.

"I can't do much without a ration card," the attendant says.

He's a young man with a poorly fitted glass eye and a pair of grease-stained coveralls. Oily locks of hair brush his shoulders, spilling out from beneath a filthy baseball cap. He stands before the pumps at a Jane filling station, and his tone isn't argumentative. He's just stating a fact.

They'd gone west, like Katherine said, and only a mile from the house they'd found an '80s-model Toyota pickup the color of stewed tomatoes with the keys still in the ignition. Lucky in and of itself, and with enough gas to put them fifty miles inland before the tank had gone dry. Dean had refused to give up the bike and trailer entirely—"Put too much blood into it for that," he said—but he'd allowed for it to be loaded up in the truck bed. Dean had driven, and he'd spent most of those fifty miles grinding gears and muttering about just how rusty he'd gotten driving a stick. Large sections of the highway were choked with cars, and more than once they'd had to dip into ditches and adjacent fields in order to keep moving.

"I gave you my name and my ID number," Katherine says now. "I have a loyalty card, I just forgot it."

The guy shrugs. He's got a seamed, weatherworn face, even while Dean puts him at maybe thirty. The new world ages you. The guy grips the half-moon bill of his ball cap and adjusts it on his head.

"I hear you, and that's a bummer. But I need the actual card."

"Look, it's not like it's *your* gas, right? Doesn't Terradyne run all these stations?"

"It's a Jane station, yeah, but, ma'am, without the actual card—"

And then Katherine slowly reaches back and takes the hunter's pistol from her waistband. Aims it at the ground.

"Hey, now," Dean murmurs.

Katherine lifts her chin toward the reader hanging from a belt loop at the man's waist. "Run the fucking number."

"The reader needs a card, I'm telling you."

"There's an override. I know you can enter the number manually."

The guy adjusts his cap again, lets out a chuff of irritated laughter. He shakes his head. "So it's a strongarm-type situation? Couple of swinging dicks over here, huh?"

"I guess we are."

"Give me the damn number," the attendant says.

Katherine recites the digits and the man dutifully punches them in. Dean watches as the reader beeps, the screen flashing red.

The guy holds up the reader. "Card's denied. Your account's frozen."

Katherine looks at Dean. He can't tell what's at work there behind her eyes, but fear's a big part of it. Fear and anger.

"That happen a lot?" Dean asks. He feels like a fool—they should have seen this a mile away. A woman holding a fevered captive? Assaulting a fever hunter? Of course they're gonna freeze her account.

"I don't know," the man shrugs unhappily. "Y'all do something wrong? A lot of times they freeze your account if they think you did something wrong." He eyes Katherine's pistol, holds up a palm. "Not saying you did or anything."

"Look, we still need the gas," Katherine says.

"Let's just get another truck down the road," Dean says. "Try our luck later."

"No," Katherine says. "Look, it's nothing personal." She lifts the pistol, aims it at the eye that isn't glass. "But I need you to fill that tank."

NAOMI LAURENT

I-44, outside of Sanders Bend, Missouri

In those early months with Denis, before Emilie, she'd dreamt of her little brother all the time. Of her mother. The memories of what had happened to them were closed-off things in her waking hours, things she dared not examine too closely in the light of day. But her dreams were a place where those monsters were allowed to roam. The dreams were fractious and ugly and hyper-lit, where the worst hours of her life played out: Her mother's bloody footprints as she chased Naomi back up to her room. Naomi screaming and locking her door, her mother pounding and snarling on the other side. How Naomi hid there for three days, pissing in her closet, growing weak with thirst and hunger, until she crept out onto the second-floor landing and saw the smearing of blood where Hugo had been. How her heart seemed to shudder to a stop when she saw that his little body was gone. The front door was open and she could smell fire-smoke and something like burning plastic on the breeze. She walked downstairs and out onto the lawn where she saw her mother's body facedown on the grass. Her mother's hair was wet with blood and she dared not turn her over to see the injustices wrought upon her face, be it by blade or gunshot or fist. She was dead.

Hugo, she never saw again.

One particular night, she'd dreamt of the living room, her mother's bent back, Hugo's thrumming fingers on the floor, and when her mother had turned her face to Naomi, it hadn't been her mother's face at all. It had been her own. Her own dead eyes. Her mouth wreathed in her brother's blood.

She cried out that time and someone had slapped her awake. She cried out again and was struck again, her hands covering her head. She and Denis had been sleeping in a storage shack at a trainyard and he was slapping at her arms, her legs. The room was stiflingly hot and still and Denis was hissing at her to shut the fuck up.

"You want to bring the entire world down on us?"

"Sorry," Naomi said, blinking.

He had turned on their lantern then—it was an oil lantern, and almost empty—and was staring at her.

In the heat, she had kicked her leg out of her sleeping bag. Denis's eye settled on the mark on her thigh, that strange marking; a rectangle of heavy red lines with something—a ridge of saw-toothed mountains? fanned wings?—inside.

"What the hell is that, Naomi? That mark on you."

"Nothing. A birthmark."

"Pssh. You think I'm stupid?"

"No."

He had glared at her some more—balefully, resentfully, Denis's two central emotions. And then he'd turned off the lamp and lain back down.

Years now since she's ridden in a vehicle.

Denis was always too paranoid, too afraid of roadblocks or empty gas tanks. Being stuck inside a steel box with nowhere to run. But how *normal* it already feels to be sitting in one again, as if no time's passed at all. How she would accompany her mother to buy groceries, or her father on a weekend errand to the hardware store, him whistling snippets of tunes, occasionally raising two fingers off the steering wheel in acknowledgment of some other driver's small kindness. Hugo in his car seat in the back, calling out things he saw. Asking things the way only children could: *Mommy, what do dogs dream of? Nomo*—his name for her that her parents had gleefully seized on—*how old will I be to be a grown-up? Papa, do fish have shoulders?* That last one said solemnly on a family trip to the beach, how it made everyone in the car laugh, her father giggling so hard that tears had actually spilled from behind his glasses and he had to pull over for a moment. Hugo, now and forever like an arrow that can pierce her with a sharpened grief. The enormity of her mother's death is like a large shape in a dark room, something to be eternally navigated around, but Hugo—and her father too, who may have survived— they're questions without answers.

They drive through the dark. She cradles Antoine in her lap, willing her arms not to get tired. The wind buffets the interior of the Humvee and somehow the baby manages to sleep through it. The redheaded soldier sits next to her, looking out of the black sheen of his window. The old man, Marsden, drives. Both men radiate badness in their own ways—it is the soldier that unnerves her the most. His is a jittery, twitchy energy, like a downed wire sparking the pavement.

Morning reveals a sky like sheet metal. Trees and fields line each side of the highway, and through the dawn's light she sees burned or desolate buildings, a warehouse ringed in abandoned vehicles, their sides littered with bullet holes. Her family had once traveled to Mobile, Alabama, where her father was from, but she had been young and Hugo had just been a baby; she hardly remembers it and wishes she'd formed more significant memories for comparison to what she sees now. They pass a billboard of a woman flexing her arm and giving the peace symbol, English words above it that go by too fast for her to read. They pass a gas station with a large picture of that same woman, her face crossed out with red paint in the window.

Bodies, sometimes, in the road. Things to drive around.

On they go, past a storage facility with all the doors of the units open, people living inside. Past a car on the shoulder with hundreds of potted plants sitting on its roof and hood and trunk. A half dozen outbuildings in the distance, their road-facing walls all painted in white to say the same thing: I MISS YOU, RORY. The sun comes out, fine and pure above them.

There are no diapers, she thinks. No food for this baby. No car seat. She feels the crushing weight of the past hours. Naomi had always felt alone with Denis and Emilie, but that aloneness was a known quantity. Here, with these two, it feels depthless.

"Where are you taking me?" she asks. Antoine's eyes open, search her face. His arms flop at his sides, once, twice, three times. Resettled, he calms, stills. She says it again, louder this time.

"Just shut up," the soldier says, annoyed, then turns back to his window.

Fury strides through her—Denis at his worst at least answered her questions, even if only to curse at her.

She leans forward and slaps the back of Marsden's head, her body moving without thinking. The soldier explodes out of his seat, one hand pressing the side of her skull against her window. With his other hand he puts his pistol to her head, pins her against the glass. Screaming at her. Naomi screams then too, and Antoine does as well, a kind of off-key, terrorized show tune. Wildly, somehow, she's still holding on to him.

"All's well, all's well," Marsden croons over his shoulder, slowing down but still moving. "Take that pistol away, son." He turns forward again. "She won't do anything. She wants that little boy to live, after all." Marsden finds her face in the rearview mirror and smiles. "Don't you, dear?"

They drive until dusk, Marsden emptying the canisters of gasoline mounted on the back of the Humvee into the tank. Sometimes they have to backtrack or take a side road to get past a choke of stalled cars. Occasionally they pass a fevered standing in the weed-choked median, or in a nearby field. If they have a clear destination, the old man doesn't say.

Finally, Marsden announces that he's tired and they pull into the lot of what looks to be an abandoned motel. A few rusted, dust-rimmed cars at the far edge of the parking lot. He parks near the front of the motel and they step out into a hushed, silent world, save for the soughing of the wind through the grasses. In its way, it's pretty here, the sun falling just so, the beauty made all the more meaning-less by her proximity to these men.

Naomi stretches her legs, sets Antoine on the ground so that he might move his poor body around. She tries to shake the adrenaline and terror from her limbs—the way the soldier had leapt on her, pushed that pistol against her ear.

Marsden stretches, squints at the motel.

"Chris."

"Yes, sir?"

He points at the doorway with OFFICE in dead neon script above it. "Why don't you go ahead and get us two rooms, son."

"Yes, sir," Canino says, and walks over to the door, a crazed pastiche of buckled glass. Canino pushes against it, the frame scraping against the pebbles of glass on the ground. Taking his pistol from its holster, he disappears into the gloom.

Marsden looks out at the middle distance beyond the road and seems to freeze, like an appliance that's come unplugged. It only lasts for a moment, and then he comes back to himself, blinking. He smiles and says, "How's the baby?"

She tries to reconcile this Marsden with the man who only hours before had threatened to have Antoine pulled apart. The man in front of her now seems old, confused, like he just woke from a nap.

"He needs to be changed," she says.

Antoine finds a stone on the ground and she swipes it out of his hands before he can put it in his mouth. The baby grunts in protest, eyes already spilling with tears at the injustice of it. Marsden smiles down at the child like some benevolent grandfather.

"Yes," he says. "He'll get a rash, won't he?"

He walks over and opens the back of the Humvee. She can hear bats squeaking in the gloaming above them. Antoine tugs on her pant leg, pulling himself up, then flops back down. There are dark plastic containers in the back of the vehicle and Marsden begins cracking them open, looking inside. He finds a shirt and pants, a set of camouflage fatigues, and hands them to her.

"What am I supposed to do with this?"

He shrugs. His eyes are red and puffy. "Change him, I imagine."

She holds up her bagged hands.

Marsden stares at her for a moment and sighs. "Will I regret this? If I take them off?"

"No," Naomi says.

"No 'making me rot,' nothing like that?"

"No."

He seizes one wrist and unties the cord lashed around it. Does the same with the other one. Her hands feel strange, exposed to the air, and she spends a moment flexing them, sensation returning. Marsden tosses the bags in the back of the Humvee and sits on the lip of the trunk. He takes out his phone and frowns at it, his face underlit. He puts it back in his pocket.

"Why did you take me?" Naomi asks. "Why didn't I stay there? In that building."

"Because you're more useful out here than you are in there."

"Why—"

Marsden lifts his chin toward the baby. "Go change him. He stinks."

She picks Antoine up, and brings him over to the wild grass at the edge of the parking lot. She takes his outfit off, uses the pants to clean him as best she can manage. Then she wraps him in the voluminous shirt, cinches it into a kind of ridiculous jumper. This giant wad of fabric with a pair of little arms and a baby's face sticking out of it. She throws the mess, including his old outfit, in an overflowing dumpster at the side of the building, and looks out at the field beyond. It's dark now, and frogs croak all around them. She wonders what Marsden and the soldier would do if she tried to run away with Antoine. Shoot her? Tie her up? Let her go? How deep could the soldier's allegiance to this strange old man possibly run? It seems like they just met.

She comes back to the Humvee and Marsden hands her a tan, vacuum-sealed package.

"What's this?"

"An MRE."

"A what?"

"It's food."

"But what is it?"

Marsden sighs and takes the package back from her. He brings it close to his face, squinting. "That's macaroni and cheese."

"I can't feed him this."

"Why not?"

"He'll shit."

Marsden shrugs and steps aside. "That's what we have. There's a little heater in there to make it warm."

"You've eaten these?"

"Oh, I've eaten all kinds of things, dear."

She sets Antoine in the Humvee's trunk bed and breaks the seal on the MRE. Rummages around inside the bag, pulling out its various pouches. She hands Antoine the plastic spoon, which he immediately puts in his mouth. In one of the pouches she finds a square of stony, featureless bread. "This is disgusting."

"That's a cinnamon roll. My old assistant, Derrick Eastman?" Marsden smiles at her. "Derrick said they would nearly knife each other over the cinnamon rolls back when they were in the field."

She stares at him, uncertain what to say. This man veers around. It's a juxtaposition she never had to deal with in her time with Denis, who was *always* sullen and angry. She hands Antoine the piece of bread. He squishes it in his fist, peers in wonder down at his hand. Puts his fist in his mouth and hoots at the taste.

She and Marsden turn at the grating sound of the office door being pushed open—Canino, jingling a key ring in one hand. The sound carries across the parking lot. Then something in the soldier's face darkens. The old man understands it before Naomi does; he turns, steps around to the front of the Humvee. She follows.

There, across the highway, his body ghastly white against the darkness of the fields, a fevered man shambles toward them.

Emaciated, shirtless, one arm broken and nearly severed at the shoulder.

"Naomi," Marsden purrs. The chopped-arm man clambers awkwardly over the concrete median, his gaze never moving away from them. "Naomi, why don't you show us your trick."

She looks from the fevered man to Marsden and back. Licking her flaking lips, she glances at the little bundle of child eating his bread in the back of the Humvee. Her mouth floods with saliva, goes electric with fear.

"I can't."

Marsden lets out a little laugh. "Oh, now is not a good time to use the word 'can't,' dear. Not with me." The fevered man keeps coming. Now that he's on the road and off the grass, she realizes she can hear him approaching. Hear the *shrrrp-clack, shrrrp-clack* as he drags one shoeless foot across the pavement. He's close enough now for her to see that that foot is caked with filth and blood, and she knows he'll walk on it until there is no flesh left, nothing but yellow bone, and if he falls, he'll keep crawling after that.

"But if I do it, he'll be like that," she says. "He'll be alive, but his arm will be cut like that, his foot, he'll just die all over again—"

"Oh, for God's sake," Marsden says wearily, and walks over to Canino, holds out his hand. Canino hands him his pistol. Marsden strides forward, the gun held at arm's length until the chopped-arm man has nearly walked face-first into the barrel.

The shot peals through the night.

Marsden frowns down at the body and then walks back to the Humvee. He gives the gun back to Canino, then turns to Naomi. His look is one of disappointment. A principal whose star student has been called in for discipline.

"Naomi," he says, "you're here because you have a valuable gift. Do you understand me?"

"Yes."

"You do?"

"Yes."

"Because at some point, if you continue to refuse to do *that which makes you valuable*? Well, that value diminishes." He rubs at a spot above his left eye and then holds his palms out, like *You understand?*

"Yes," Naomi says. "I understand." Antoine is curled in the bed of the Humvee, crying now. He is still holding the plastic spoon in one tiny fist, his other hand covered in sugar and breadcrumbs, and some animal part of her thinks, If I had a knife, I'd stab this man in the heart.

Stab him and run through the dark with this child.

But where is there to go?

"Good," Marsden says. "Now that we understand each other, let's go take a look at your room."

FROM: JACK BONNER
<J.BONNER@TERRADYNE.GOV>

TO: THEO MARSDEN <T.MARSDEN@TERRADYNE.GOV>

DATE: FEBRUARY 2, 20XX, 3:04 AM

SUBJECT: MESSAGE TRANSCRIPTION / CLASSIFIED

Theo,

Finally have something for you regarding the question you asked during lunch the other day. One of the few remaining interview excerpts I could find with the "Saint Michael" asset. Given the level of interest the president's shown in getting Matthew Coffin up and doing whatever it is he does, I thought this excerpt was especially pertinent.

   We're both familiar with the mystery that surrounds this Saint Michael character. *Supposedly* discovered in the '80s on a military base in Greenland or Iceland—the stories vary—he was purportedly able to "remote view" various events—i.e., see events without being anywhere near them, events that often hadn't happened yet. He was shuffled around from agency to agency until he landed in David Lundy's lap. Lundy—again, conjecture, hearsay, etc.—essentially tortured him for information for the next thirty years or so, using Michael's "gifts" as the bedrock to build ARC, his own little dark ops counterterrorism program funded by the Pentagon. Michael grew more and more ill over time, and eventually Lundy's treatment of him backfired, as Michael's final act, as we both know, was apparently squeezing Lundy's brains out of his head. (There were also the rumors that Michael was some sort of angel, with wings that Lundy continually hacked off, something this interview does not exactly dispel.)

Anyway, there's a point to my history lesson. I don't think he really picked up on it at the time, but Michael, it seems to me, is alluding to Matthew Coffin here, or something very similar to Coffin, and this may be the first time the remnants are mentioned. If not *our* remnants, then something pretty damn close. Yet another reason we'd do well to move with great caution and consideration when figuring out how to deal with our friend in the box.

Jack

OPERATION: HEAVY LIGHT
S/NF/CL-INTEL A-13/22—SECRET TRANSCRIPT—EXCERPT

DATE: XX/XX/XXXX

Q: Michael, it's David Lundy. How're you feeling?
A: . . .

Q: I heard you gave the techs a hard time yesterday. Wouldn't answer their questions.

A: . . .

Q: You don't want to talk? Are you upset with me?

A: You hurt me, David Lundy. You had them cut me again.

Q: Well, yes, Michael, I did. This is our deal. You provide me with information with visions, and we use them to catch the bad guys. If you choose not to provide me with information, you get prompted to do so. And sometimes those prompts can be real uncomfortable, can't they?

A: . . .

Q: So you're just not talking? Gonna be pissy today?

A: Do you ever consider—

Q: What?

A: Do you ever consider you may have done something wrong? If a decision you made will have consequences you did not see.

Q: Well, no, Michael, not really. I'm entirely confident in the decisions I've made. Why, do *you* question a decision I've made recently? Is that what you'd like to talk about?

A: . . .

Q: Alright, fuck, man, I'm gonna go. If you don't have anything you'd like to relay to me, I will bid you farewell. As the saying goes, I got shit to do.

A: I made a decision once and I think it was the right one, but I'm not sure now. Doubt is unusual for me.

Q: What is this all about?

A: . . .

Q: Jesus. Come on.

A: There are ones nesting on the edges of the order of things, David Lundy. Ones that skirt the structure of light and dark, that twist beneath it. Birthed of the structure but no longer of the structure. Ones that gain power through blood and trickery and fealty. And they may conceal themselves, and deceive, with the hopes of pushing forward to dismantle all of it, light and dark both. If you knew this, knew the depth of the ruination it would cause, what it meant, would you stop it?

Q: I don't even . . . What the fuck are you talking about, Michael? *Skirt the structure of light and dark?* I don't follow.

A: Never mind.

Q: No, no, tell me. It seems important.

A: It tricks them into dismantling themselves. They offer up an eye, a finger, a jawbone, and it in turn imbues those things with power. It appeals to their small hearts, their small terrors and desires. It promises them things, and a blood-pact is made.

Q: A what is made?

A: . . .

Q: I'm invested now, come on. If you're not going to give me info on a dope run at the border or a truck-bombing or some shit, tell me about, whatever, jawbones and fingers.

A: I stepped forward, David Lundy, instead of merely watching. To stop it. That is where I doubt. I still don't know if what I did was right. The choice I made, with the man. With the light to come. I . . . I don't know.

Q: . . .

A: . . .

Q: See, this is the type of shit I'm talking about, Michael. This is why we take the saw to you sometimes. You talk in fucking riddles if we don't. Talk gibberish. I'm coming back later this afternoon, Michael, and if you don't give me some intel I can *use,* something concrete I can pass on to DOJ, you'll be wishing you fucking *stepped forward,* you understand me?

CHRIS CANINO

I-44, outside of Sanders Bend, Missouri

He's on the bed closest to the door, the girl and the baby on the far one, by the bathroom. No running water out here, no lights. They've got a couple stick-on LED lights that the old man found in the bin with the MREs. He put one on the little table in front of the window and now the two of them sit on their beds and stare at it like it's some dipshit campfire. Jason's murder sits in his brain like a black hole. So big he can't feel the edges of it. Afraid to think of him. Afraid to think that every mile he travels with this weird old man is maybe further from the right thing to do.

"Do you have any water?" the girl says.

"I don't know," he says.

"Can you see?"

He walks out into the parking lot. Roots through the bins in the back of the Humvee and comes back.

"I can't find any."

She sits on the bed and rifles through the little containers from the MRE, squinting at the words in the dim light. Finding a sleeve of crackers, she feeds them to the baby, still wrapped in his giant shirt. It feels insane, having a baby here, and then Chris thinks of Jason again and Jamie, them as little kids. How he was scared of them as babies but then they grew bigger and had idolized him, like he was just the coolest, most perfect big brother on earth, and a kind of choking fury zippers all through him. Makes his hands hot. He doesn't know how to hold all that fury inside his body.

When I find you, Chris thinks.

There's a knock on the door and the baby jumps and then his face clinches shut and he starts crying. Chris opens the door and Marsden stands there, his dress shirt unbuttoned, showing a pale wedge of silvery-white chest hair.

"A word," he says.

Chris steps out, shuts the door behind him. He follows Marsden over to the Humvee. The night is cool. He hears frogs. He looks out at the empty parking lot, the lines of weeds popping up through the asphalt.

"I'd like the pistol, please," Marsden says, and Chris unholsters it and hands it over.

"Holster too."

Canino passes it to him.

"Thank you. We'll look for another for you."

"Okay."

Marsden clips the holster on, fits the pistol inside. He inhales, runs a hand along the hood of the Humvee, peers down at the dust on his palm.

"Tell me about Katherine."

"Who?" Chris says. The look on Marsden's face—there and gone—is the same one he's seen a thousand times from Joe Canino, from his teachers and his friends' parents: *Goddamn, this kid is stupid.*

"The woman who killed your brother, son."

"Right," Chris says, angry. Angry at this old man. The girl and the baby. At the woman. At Jason for being stupid enough to let himself get close to her. Angry at the fevered that just took a round through the forehead. Angry at long-gone Jamie. His old man, his mom. Angry at himself, even.

"She was just some lady," he says. "We seen her in a restaurant and had some words. Couple days later I seen her in town and she was acting all suspicious, so we followed her to her house."

"Suspicious how?"

"She went into a church."

Marsden shakes his head.

"It was burned down," Chris says. "She was, like, walking around in there. We seen her and were like, 'Let's just mess with her a little bit.' So we followed her."

"And there was a fevered in the house?"

"In a shed in the back."

After a beat, Marsden says, "What did it look like?"

"The fevered? I mean, just regular. Just another one of them."

"Man, woman?"

"Man. Skinny."

"And she hit your brother."

"With, like, a big peg, yeah, that she used to lock the shed with. He died about an hour later."

The old man scratches his nose and looks out beyond the parking lot. There are a few minute roving blips of light—headlights further down the highway—but beyond that, it's pure dark. He turns back to Chris. "How does that make you feel?"

Chris's heart gallops. Again, the enormity of it—both of his brothers dead now, his dad. He swallows and his throat clicks. "How do you mean?"

"Do you want to *get* her, Chris? Do you want to help me find her? This Katherine Moriarty?"

"That wasn't the name on the ID."

"It's her real name."

"It was a fake ID?"

"You're missing the point, son. Do you want to get her or no?"

"That's all I want."

Marsden nods. "I had a man who helped me. Derrick. He'd been with Terradyne a long time. Been with *me* a long time. He was re-assigned, though, and I'm looking for someone new to help me. Would you like to do that, Chris?" He says it like it's some great gift he's bestowing. Something in Chris recoils against that, but he tells himself he's closer to killing the woman with this old man than without him. Tries to convince himself of it. "I do, yeah."

"Good," Marsden says. Reaches up and squeezes his shoulder. "Don't let that girl leave tonight, no matter what you do."

Back in the room, the girl, Naomi, is lying on her bed, one hand resting on the baby's back while he sits up, looking around. "If you touch me," she says, "I'll kill you. I can do it."

His face twists in disgust. "I'm not gonna fucking touch you, dude. What are you, twelve?"

She doesn't answer. Chris lies down.

He wants to think about other things—where they're going, how this Moriarty woman—or Sunderson, of whatever her name is—came to be in Cape Winston, why she had a fevered locked up in her shed, how she had a fake ID in the first place—but all he can see is that soft part of his brother's head where he got hit. The way the garage lights curved across his eyeballs. He stares up at the ceiling, hands flexing in the darkness, seeing Jason's stilled body again and again, vengeance making him hot, making it feel like sleep will never come.

THEO MARSDEN

I-80, outside of Big Springs, Nebraska

After speaking to Canino, he gets into bed and sleeps for sixteen hours. He wakes, finally, with his phone buzzing on the nightstand, a glowing white rectangle in the dark. He thumbs it open to see a string of missed calls.

"This is Marsden."

A beat, then Yardley, almost conversational, says, "You took the girl."

Marsden coughs, sits up. Pinches the bridge of his nose. "Yes."

"Why?"

"Preston, I built Terradyne from the ground up. One sale at a time. Providence is mine as much as yours. You can't just decide on a whim to come to Rolla and erase all that."

"Jack Bonner's brain is swelling up. He might lose an eyeball. That's the man you started Terradyne with, and you're talking to me about building things?"

"I won't let you take it all away from me."

"I saw the footage, Theo. I saw Coffin attack you, kill your security detail. I don't blame you, understand? But you attacked Jack and now you're off running around with our last remaining asset, torching the whole program—"

"I'm not torching anything," Marsden says. "I'm saving it."

"Theo, if you don't come back to Rolla with the girl and that child right now, you will rue the damn day. I will strike you with all of God's fury behind—"

Marsden ends the call. He realizes how profoundly lucky—and sloppy—he's been up until now. He finds a pen and a pad of moldering motel stationery on the nightstand by the bed and spends a few minutes copying down phone numbers from his phone onto a piece of paper. John Bonner's, Yardley's, the operator he spoke to. Katherine's.

Then he drops the phone, stomps on it.

They'll need to keep moving from now on.

West, a part of him quietly insists, and it feels right. *We go west.*

They're heading down the highway five minutes later when he sees a column of headlights in the rearview far behind them. Could be nothing, could be a Terradyne shock team mobilizing after Yardley pinged *his* location.

There's still a way to get everything he wants, there has to be. And he wants it all, he realizes. There's no going back to Rolla after what he's done to Jack, not yet. Terradyne as it was before is dead now. So why not let his ambition match his beliefs?

He wants *Yardley's* spot.

He wants to run the entire show.

Why not? He's been hampered at every turn—by Jack and his naive insistence on a vaccine, by Preston Yardley's boundless paranoia and fear.

Not anymore.

He rubs at that spot above his eye, the pulsing throb of a headache starting to come back.

———

They drive until the tank is on E and a pall of wildfire smoke hangs in the air. They've rolled up the windows and still the smoke gets in. The girl occasionally asks where they're going, and Canino wearily tells her to shut up. She says that she and the baby have to eat, have to drink. "You're right," Marsden finally says. He has a treasure here, the two of them, and that treasure will not be lost or rendered unusable while in his care.

They stop at a Jane station. A pair of pumps and a small storefront, the signs in the windows all pre-Message, sun-faded to illegibility.

"Stay here," Marsden says to her, and he and Canino get out.

They gas up and then go inside and browse. Marsden moved once more at the breadth of Jane goods becoming available. Soup and corn chips and pasta. Bottled water, crackers and cheese, bags of candy. Everything done up in Jane's red, white and blue packaging. They bring their snacks and water up to the counter and the proprietor wordlessly rings them up. *West,* Marsden thinks again.

"You have baby food?" Canino asks.

"Nope."

"Or like formula or anything? For babies?"

The man lifts his head toward the back. "Got some milk in the back cooler you couldn't pay me to drink."

"Alright. Diapers?"

"Nope," the proprietor says.

"None?"

"This ain't a baby store, you know?"

Canino's face darkens, ever fast to take offense. "The fuck's a baby store?"

"Look, we got some shammies for wiping the car down, found a box of those in the garage. There's some clothespins in that aisle right there. You were creative, you might be able to make some kind of caveman diaper-type deal."

"Go get them," Marsden says, and Canino turns, muttering, wanders down an aisle. Marsden touches his brow again—the throb there sharpening as the day progresses—and asks the man if he has any aspirin.

"Nope."

"No pain relievers at all?"

"Got a hammer down here, smack yourself in the head with it."

Marsden laughs. "You don't care for us very much, do you?"

The proprietor's mouth works for a moment, trying to decide what to say. "That fella back there's a fever hunter, isn't he?"

"He is."

"Figured so. Not a huge fan of Terradyne, no."

"And yet you run a Jane store," Marsden says.

"Look, friend," the man says, leaning forward a little. "My wife got bit. Four months ago, this was. I'd just got this place up and running, jumped through all the governmental hoops. I was in the back, doing inventory, she was up here, running the register, when a pair of fevered come running in. All shackled up, wrists chained, but they didn't have anything over their mouths, right? They crash through the door and fall on her. And then some Terradyne fellas come running in, dressed in a uniform just like your man back there, yelling and all that. Had a whole bunch of fevered in an APC, apparently, and these two got loose. They gathered 'em up, all sorry, but Tabitha had already been bit to hell. Crying, bleeding. And you know what happened?"

"There's a ratio—" Marsden starts.

The man holds up a finger. "You know what happened? They gathered those two back up and they shot Tabitha. Right outside there." He bares his teeth, the bottom row like little tombstones. "I tried to fight them, but they just shot her, around the corner from where I'm standing right here. I didn't even get to say goodbye. Thirty-three years of marriage. And that's what they told me right before they did it. That we all knew what was going to happen to her in an hour, a day, and they had a ratio they had to stick to."

"I'm sorry—"

"Oh, they told me they were sorry too. You'd be amazed at how little it helped."

"If you have names or badge numbers of these operators, I'd be happy to look into it."

The proprietor stares at him, indignant at Marsden's lack of understanding. "I don't know who you are, or who you think you are, but you are missing the point. She's *gone,* is what I'm telling you. And in the most profoundly stupid way. Kill some of them and not all of them? What kind of plan is that? My wife caught *flies* and let them outside, that was the gentleness she had in her. And now, because Terradyne's too chickenshit to do what needs to be done, I had to pay the neighbor boys to haul her body over to the house, bury her in our field there. Thirty-three years."

Canino, with the shammies and clothespins and a six-pack of Jane beer, has come up to the counter and stands there watching them. Marsden's surprised at himself. He'd have thought he was impervious to things like this, emotionally insulated from them. But the man's pain is like radiation; Marsden feels shame, a moment of sorrow for what he did to Jack Bonner, and his heart shrinks away from it.

"Oh shit," Canino says at his side.

Marsden looks at him, then follows his gaze to the window.

To the pumps outside, where the Humvee's door is open.

The empty backseat.

Canino's eyes go big, all fear and outrage. He runs outside, sets the bag of groceries on the hood, where they spill onto the cement, and sprints around the side of the gas station. Seconds later, Marsden hears the girl screaming.

He finds them in the field behind the building. The girl stands before Canino, clutching the gasping, red-faced baby in one arm. In her other hand she holds a stone. Both she and the hunter are crouched in the dead grass like linebackers.

"Do it," Canino's saying. "Try to hit me. Be the last thing you ever do, promise."

Marsden sighs. Weary of all of it. This fucking headache of his, and the driving just to drive, and the new itch of west in his mind, and the understanding that Canino is probably less useful than he'd first imagined. He must begin to move wisely, rather than solely to get away. He has to be smart.

He raises the pistol into the air and fires. Everyone jumps, turns.

"Get in the damn car," he calls out.

For a moment, no one moves. He says it again, louder, and both Canino and the girl start to trudge forward.

He walks back into the store, the proprietor spooked by the gunshot.

"I forgot to mention. I'll need your phone, please."

Cornfields brace the road, soy fields, wheat fields, the crops magically uniform, magically straight, all on these expansive parcels of fenced land. People can be seen through the fences with their backs bent, working. Razor wire, guard towers, Terradyne ops with shotguns striding the perimeters. Marsden drives, beaming like a proud father. This is what he's built. What he's remade from pure will.

Naomi seethes in the backseat, wipes away tears. Marsden's told Canino to sit up front with him now, and the soldier occasionally turns and spears the girl with burning, baleful looks.

They drive until nightfall, when they find a Jane motel off the highway, run by a soft-faced proprietor in her fifties with a bouffant of apple-red hair and a pair of handguns on her hips like some comic book pistolero.

In the parking lot, he keeps one room key, gives the other to Canino, lays a fatherly hand on the young man's shoulder. "Don't let her do that again."

"Yes, sir," Canino says, jaw set. Staring hard at the ground.

Marsden leans into the open window of the Humvee, where

Naomi still sits. "If you run again, I won't be able to stop him from whatever happens next. Boy is wound wire-tight."

Silence from the girl. The baby stands up in the seat, cooing and gurgling against the girl's shoulder. Reaching toward Marsden with his other hand.

"You understand me?"

Nothing. He sighs—he could push the issue, but he knows from raising his own children that no parent ever wins in a pissing match. He goes to his room, that dull ache in his head almost physical now, a skull filled with concrete. The room is middling and inoffensive: clean sheets and lights that work. Good enough for him. There's a television and a DVD player, a scattering of discs as old as the girl he's traveling with. Still, it's certainly a move up from the night before.

Marsden thumbs the television on with the remote. Stares at the blue startup screen. There's something comforting in it. Calming.

He returns to himself with no idea how long he's stood there. Wiping a string of saliva from his chin, he pivots, suddenly animated again. These strange fugues he's dipping in. Happened in the parking lot the day before too. And this insistence on going west. Was it *actually* the mention of Katherine, he thinks now, that had finally made Coffin move in that glass box? Was it the mention of his wife and son? Or had it been something else?

Something about Naomi, maybe?

So strange: As soon as he thinks of it, that graveyard taste fills his mouth again.

He takes the proprietor's phone from his pocket and unfolds the piece of paper with all of his numbers.

He squints one eye against his headache and calls Katherine Moriarty.

Something like intuition—intuition *but not quite*—driving him to do so.

"John?" someone answers. A woman's voice.

That small thing, that small voice inside him, it suddenly uncoils.

Looms larger. Is it Matthew? Or something else? Whatever it is, this thing is separate from him, and it *leans* toward the voice on the phone, with Marsden too stunned to react.

"John?" she says again, and Marsden's throat—his throat but not *his* voice, no—looses a sad little croak.

"Katherine," he says. The word strange in his mouth, as if formed by a tongue used to not speaking.

A pause. "Who is this?"

"Katherine, you and your son, are you going home?"

"Who the fuck is this?"

"I'm going there too. I'll meet you." It sounds, even to his ears, like a threat, jolly and menacing. Both his voice and not his voice.

"Matthew," she says, her voice cracking. "Is that you? Huh? Well, I'll meet you there, motherfucker. How's that?" Her voice climbs. "How about I put a hammer through your other eyeball, how's that? What you did to *Nick*—"

Marsden, coming back to himself, frightened, hangs up. Walks on thrumming legs to the bathroom, fear and confusion flooding through him now, his heart shuddering. He turns on the light, gazes in the mirror. Gray pouches beneath his eyes—the stabbing pain there. That wild cap of white hair.

Looking in the mirror for any vestiges of Coffin, Marsden sees only himself.

That was your wife, wasn't it? he thinks.

Silence.

Is all this about her, Matthew? Are you coming back for her?

Silence.

Doubt flits through him. How much of this has just been his own exhausted mind leaping at shadows that aren't there.

And then a distinct voice, so different from his own and wholly separate from him:

Yes.

Yes for her.

The voice is greedy, furtive.

Marsden's breath catches. He squints, leans forward. His head suddenly *pulses* with pain, a burst of it, a galaxy; he staggers against the counter, gasping. In the mirror, he blinks rapidly, and watches horrified as his left eye clouds with blood.

A single pink tear spills down his face. Trembles and hangs at his jaw before dropping to the counter.

JOHN BONNER

Portland, Oregon

He's got a place on Alberta, a narrow two-bedroom house with a sizable backyard that he's forever telling himself he'll clean up. Blond hardwoods inside, massive bookcases in every room. Big windows that let the light in. Coffin's archives are all spread out on his kitchen table. He needs the space. The sense of claustrophobia—this closed-in, cloying sense of oppression in the papers, in one notebook in particular—is tremendous. Thumbing through this shit feels like trying to stay motionless in a grave while someone tosses dirt on you. He can't imagine trying to parse through all of it in the Eighty-second Avenue apartment, with the hand just in the other room. He'd lose his mind. There's a glass patio door that looks out from the kitchen onto the wild greenery of the backyard. Bonner, rifling through everything, trying to gather the courage to go through that one notebook, will occasionally look out at the yard for relief, like he's sipping water on a hot day. There's an almost tangible feel to that one journal, a kind of psychic hiss. He half expects the cardboard cover to flip open on its own.

You are the harbinger. We did this for you, John.

Reading its entries is like putting your fingers to a stove burner and then turning it on low. It's a measured discomfort that slowly builds into outright horror, and Bonner, finally giving in to it, wonders if perhaps even Coffin's written testimonies have been imbued with some kind of power. If a recording of his voice can drive people mad in a matter of seconds, what about reading his words? Why not?

Even if it's not the case, the chronology of Matthew Coffin's descent is striking for its quickness, the violence inherent in it. Coffin was, by his own admission, far from the greatest of people. Profoundly toxic, insecure. Self-obsessed. Shitty to his son, his wife.

Still didn't mean he deserved what happened to him.

It's spelled out right there—something had latched onto him inside that loft. Why it chose him and not this—Bonner rifles through the notebook until he finds the guy's name—not this Francis, the owner of the place, Bonner doesn't know. Maybe Matthew brought the thing with him. But whatever it was, it saw an opportunity in Coffin.

Now, with the eye and the hand in Bonner's possession, does he have a way to fight it, whatever it is? If there really *is* anything to the Sight's claims that Bonner will royally, maybe cosmically, fuck things up at some point and open a doorway for whatever Coffin's become, can he put a stop to it?

His phone buzzes. He jumps a little, cursing under his breath. Runs a hand down his face. It's Katherine.

"Guess who I just fucking talked to," she says, and for a moment he can't speak—he remembers the frayed, anguished quality of their brief call five years ago. This woman sounds different. This woman sounds like fury's put steel in her backbone.

"Katherine? Are you okay?"

"Oh, I'm a lot of things, John. Okay's not one of them. I just talked to Matthew."

He can't help it, he lets out a little chuff of laughter. The ridiculousness of it. "You what?"

"It was him. The way he said things, the way he talked, it was the same. Same voice. Inflection. The way he got mocking and all snotty when he was pissed. He said, 'Katherine, you and your son, are you going home?' And then he said he'd meet me there."

"Who was it? I mean—"

Katherine resolute, manic: "I just told you that."

"But I mean, how do you know it was him?"

"Do you think I give my number out to people, John? You think I got a lot of friends, do book clubs, go on dates? You told me, when you got me my new ID, that Katherine Moriarty had to die. And I did that. I stuffed it all down. Didn't talk to anyone. Kept the phone for emergencies."

"Katherine—"

"It was him."

"Okay, I just, I don't know how that could be."

"Look, shit has happened since I last talked to you. I'm on the run."

"Why? What happened?"

"Long story short, someone from Terradyne grabbed my ID."

Shit. If they run her card—and he's sure they have—it's almost surely going to come back to him.

And Jack, maybe. He and Jack were careful, but it doesn't mean that Preston Yardley won't press him about it. Meanwhile, Terradyne will be throwing everything they have at Katherine. She's the last remaining puzzle piece to the mystery that was Matthew Coffin.

"I'm going to kill him," she says.

"Katherine, he's in a catacomb eighty feet underground in Missouri, for Christ's sake. How are you—"

"No, he's not."

"What?"

"He said he's coming home. Said he'd meet me there. We both know where that is."

One of the few things he saw in the eye, saw clearly in that vision, was Katherine. And with Katherine coming here, and what that man in the Sight told him, about him opening the door to hell?

It's happening.

Death—and who knows what else—is moving toward him.

He licks his lips and says, "Do you have the number?"

"Of the guy who called?"

"Yeah." She gives it to him, Bonner writing it in the margin of a notebook page. "How far away are you?"

"I don't know. We're still pretty far east."

"We?"

"I'm with someone. My friend Dean."

He touches the page of the notebook—*HOUSE OF THE WORM* written there below the phone number—and tries to calm his heart. How fast everything seems to be moving now. "So you want to kill him. Matthew."

"Yes."

He doesn't ask why. Doesn't need to. Knew the first time that he saw her, even as terrified as she was, that there was something intractable in her. And he remembers getting Nick out of the bathroom, the death-blank eyes, the snarling, leaping form.

She wants revenge.

"Alright," he says.

"You'll help?"

"Of course I'll help." Thinking *I'm no harbinger. Not me.* How soothing the hand would be right now, the grand distraction of its blood-songs. Sit there, forget about everything. He says, "Katherine, do you remember where the loft is? Where you saw Matthew the day before he died?"

Her turn to pause now, consider. "Why?"

"I need to know. It's important, I think."

She gives him a street name, a description of the building. He knows the place, has passed it a hundred times in his years here, never thought twice about it.

"Look, Katherine, you need to run."

"I told you, I'm already gone."

"Keep moving," he says. "And you need to get rid of your phone."

A beat. "They can do that? Track me?"

"I'm sure they already are. Ditch it. Throw it in a field. Put it in someone's car. They think you know something about Matthew, about what he can do. You and Nick."

"I don't know shit," she says.

"It doesn't matter."

He's about to say more, to reassure her, to apologize once again for Nick, to tell her that he's ready—even if it's a lie—but he doesn't get the chance. Because he looks at the glass door and there's Leo Katz standing on his back patio. His revolver is against his leg. He has a hand at his brow while he leans against the glass.

He sees Bonner and waves with the gun.

The three of them sit in Bonner's living room, him and Katz and Dave Kendall. The photographs of the previous owners stare down at him—at Christmas, on a boat with life jackets on, the two of them as groomsmen at a friend's wedding, grinning big in their plum-colored suits.

Katz leans forward, squints at a photo on the mantel. "These guys your brothers or something?"

"They used to live here," Bonner says. He's sitting on the couch, Dave Kendall drinking a coffee cup of water in the love seat opposite. Katz's revolver is put away, but Bonner gets it. It's a shakedown, and there are motions to go through. This is the dance.

"They dead, these two?"

"I don't know," Bonner says. "Probably."

"But you keep their pictures up?"

"It's a respect thing. Like, thanks for the house."

"Weird. At least decorate the place yourself, you know? It's not like these guys give a shit at this point."

"I'll keep it in mind."

Katz places the photo back on the mantel, smirks. "Yeah, why don't you consider it, John. Why don't you percolate on it."

Kendall sets his mug down. Leans forward, his hands clasped between his knees.

Their cue to start the show.

"So what happened at that house, John? Why is the Sight writing your name in blood before they chop their eyes out?"

Bonner shrugs, exhales. "I wish I knew, Dave. Scared the crap out of me, but that's it."

"You're a shit-ass liar," Katz says, his arms crossed.

Bonner cranes his neck, looks back at him. "I'm being straight with you. I haven't turned up anything. Maybe the Sight got word you and I were working the Parade thing, Katz, and they were trying to scare me off. I don't know. Just as easily could have been your name up there, way I figure it."

Katz looks over at Kendall like *This fucking guy.*

"Did you know," Kendall says, "that your uncle Jack got his head stomped in a bit ago?"

Bonner darkens. "What?"

Kendall shrugs. "Yeah. I guess Theo Marsden stomped an eyeball out of his head and then took off. They got him on life support, which, you know, that's impressive. Not an easy thing these days. But with him out of commission and Marsden in the wind, Yardley's running point on everything Providence-related for the time being. You know anything about any of that?"

"It's news to me."

Kendall nods and says, "Alright. Well, *tangentially to this,* John, is there any chance that the name Katherine Sunderson rings a bell?"

Bonner keeps his face blank, but like he's thinking about it. "No. Nothing's coming to mind."

Katz, from behind him: "Give me five minutes with this guy, Dave," but Kendall holds up a hand.

Panic's starting to creep in, the room feeling small and close. All of a sudden, things are moving too fast to keep up with. And there's all this damning stuff in his house—Coffin's notebook in the kitchen, the eyeball in its box in his bedroom, Katherine's number in his phone. He's got to get these guys out of here.

Katz walks around, crouches down in front of him. "Here's the deal, John," he says, a little heat to his voice now. "I don't like you. I never have. You lucked out and got coverage because your uncle had the juice to put you here. You didn't earn it. I was a detective for thirty years before all this shit."

"Yeah, and now you sleepwalk through your cases, very impressive."

Katz looks over at Dave Kendall. "Five minutes, man. Please."

"Enough," Kendall says, pinching the bridge of his nose. "John, where the hell is Katherine Moriarty?"

He aims for outrage, confusion. "How would I know? I heard she was being held in Chicago before the Message. The last I heard."

Almost imperceptibly, Kendall nods.

Leo Katz is big and slow—Bonner could be up and putting a fist in his throat by the time the guy makes a move. But blood will get them out of here faster. Katz stands up. His hook is mean, right in the nose. He doesn't pull it, and Bonner's vision bursts black. He rocks back against the couch. Blood running down his face, that penny taste in the back of his throat, cartilage crackling in his head.

Kendall sighs. "We know you got her set up, John. I don't know why you'd lie about something so obvious."

"Well yeah," he says, probing the bridge of his nose, tears running down his cheeks, "I did that. Years ago, though. Lots of ops do it." He sounds nasal, petulant.

"Not with high-value assets," Kendall says. "Not with people on Terradyne's Persons of Interest lists. Why are you protecting her?"

"That's classified. You'll need to ask Yardley."

Katz has gone over to the mantel again. He picks up another

framed photo—the owners in ski gear, windburned and smiling on top of a mountain—and examines it. "You dumb fuck. We just told you, Yardley's the one that sent us here."

"Where is she?" Kendall says. "Where's her son?"

"I haven't seen her in years. Haven't seen either of them."

Kendall leans forward, his face solemn, hands clasped between his knees. An appeal, it seems, to Bonner's reasonableness, his logic. "John, I know strong-arm stuff doesn't work. We both know it. It didn't work in the Cold War, didn't work in Kabul, it won't work with you. But at some point, I hear too much bullshit and I stop listening. So our next step, if you keep this up? Our next step is the convention center."

Panic pushing in, crowding the edges of things.

"We'll put you in the bag, John," Katz says from behind him, and Bonner can tell that he's smiling.

"Dave," Bonner says, all subterfuge scoured from him now. "She doesn't know anything."

"You understand I can't take your word for that, right?"

"I can't tell you where she is. I don't know."

Katz, behind him: "The bag, man, it's got this *stink* to it, all the sweat and piss of all the guys before you—"

Coffin's notebooks on the kitchen table. Katherine's number in his phone. The eye in its box in his bedroom. The hand still captive in that apartment off Eighty-second.

Get these two out of here.

But the bag? Christ, no, not that.

Bonner, pleading now, blood on his teeth: "What, do you want me to make something up, Dave? I'll make something up."

"Where is she?"

"I don't know—"

Kendall sighs and stands up. Katz's hand falls like fucking doom on Bonner's shoulder.

KATHERINE MORIARTY

Highway 40, outside of Summerford, Ohio

O n a ragged two-lane highway, grasses grown wild up to the shoulder, and they've just gone through the small and seemingly desolate town of Summerford. Population 601, claimed the bullet-pocked sign they passed, like something from a movie. Now they're among overgrown fields and rusting, scattered outbuildings on each side of the road. The brush-smear of foothills, and beyond that, the orange horizon as the sun begins falling. Katherine drives with the visor down, the setting sun bisecting her at the throat. She drives with Nick in her mind, steeping herself in rage, spending the miles sitting with him in familiar places—the record store he worked at, the greenrooms of a million venues the Blank Letters played at, his third-grade playground, the auditorium of his high school graduation where he was reluctant to walk. She imagines him mostly in their shared apartment, him taking care of her, helping her navigate her terror of the outside world. She imagines him at thirty-five, at fifty, at seventy, the man he might have been.

It's mourning, is what it is. She's letting Nick go. It's the salve she needs for vengeance, for whatever will happen in Portland. Still doesn't stop it from hurting like her heart's getting scooped from her chest.

There's a tape deck in the truck and Dean's taken out the small travel rack of cassettes that he found this morning while scavenging. They're listening to them one by one, and perhaps some of her mourning is aided by the soundtrack. It's impossible to listen to *London Calling* or *Walk Among Us* and *not* think about her childhood, her early years with Matthew. Touring. Pregnancy. Buying the apartment. Nick. Every song with its accompanying cavalcade of ghosts.

At one point Dean looks over and gives her an odd smile. "You really like this stuff?" They're listening to one of the mixtapes—Black Flag's *Damaged* and *My War* on one side, a bunch of early Bad Religion records on the other.

"I love it. I grew up on it."

"Shit makes me nervous, man. That guitar's like listening to a dentist drill."

"That's part of it," Katherine admits. "Part of why I like it. The nervous part."

"I'm more into, like, stuff that doesn't give you a headache."

"We can turn it off if you want."

"Nah," Dean says, "that's cool. I mean, I like thinking about these stressed-out dudes. Bunch of young kids who can hardly play their shit, so they got to work extra hard at coming up with something different. George would have loved it, though."

"Yeah?"

"Oh, yeah," Dean smiles. "He'd be climbing the walls, listening to this. Boy just loved *loud*, you know? Louder the better, he—"

They crest a rise and see a roadblock on the highway up ahead.

A pair of Terradyne trucks are parked crossways in the road, narrowing everything down to a single lane. A sawhorse has been placed between the trucks, the dusk up there alive with the zip and scatter of flashlight beams. Three or four cars in the line, waiting. Terradyne ops can be seen opening up trunks, peering beneath vehicles. They're maybe a quarter mile away, and Katherine comes to a stop on the shoulder.

"That's for us," she says.

"You don't know for sure."

"Dean, come on."

For a moment she thinks of calling Bonner again, asking him what to do—but then remembers she threw her phone into a tangle of blackberry bushes hours back.

"Turn the headlights off," Dean says.

"That'll make us stand out even more."

Dean reaches into the glove compartment, takes out the hunter's pistol. Chambers a round. Katherine turns the tape deck off.

"We can go around. Or just go right on through," he says.

Cursing, she slowly reverses. Turns around and gently slaloms through the overgrown ditch between the northbound and south-bound lanes, the tall grass whickering against the undercarriage. "I saw another highway off-ramp there in Summerford," she says. "We'll take that."

There were those times being held in custody by agents in the hours before the Message, where Katherine had been immobile with fear. Rooted to the ground, and honestly a little amazed that a body could experience that much sustained panic and not succumb to it. That her heart hadn't exploded like a worn tire. Then, in a safe house in Chicago, it had simply been time to *move*—there was no other choice, so she'd found the ability within herself. She'd moved, and gotten free, and sworn that she'd never be frozen like that again. Never let herself be ferried around like cargo again, like a pawn, her throat so tight with fear that every breath seemed hard-fought.

Better to make a terrible move than no move at all.

They jounce through the ditch and start back toward Summer-ford.

It was the wrong thing to do: Dean looks out the rear window. "Yeah, they're following us. Shit."

"How many?"

"Just one truck, looks like."

Katherine guns it, engine climbing. She turns the headlights off, the road and guardrails and fields and sweeping hills reduced to a blurred chiaroscuro.

"Might as well turn the headlights on, Katherine. It's the tail-lights they'll be following."

She turns the headlights back on. Things are easier now that she's decided. That glacier-like quality to her thoughts is gone. "You need to drive in a second."

"Why?"

"Just do it, okay? Real smooth. I'll stop and get out. You slide over, I get in. We take off. Cool?"

Peering out the back window, he nods. "Yeah, okay."

Katherine leans forward and takes her own pistol from the back of her waistband. She pulls over onto the shoulder, the truck rocking, and steps out.

She walks to the back of the truck and smashes out the taillights with the butt of the pistol. The crack of plastic and the fragile glass beneath. Dean's already taking off before the door's closed. Fluid as music, the way it worked.

He's a more erratic driver than she is, and faster. The only sound is the engine, the occasional rattle when they hit a swatch of buckled pavement or veer onto the gravel shoulder. Soon enough they see the twin coins of the headlights behind them begin to shrink and then disappear when they dip down into a low valley.

Another quarter mile and they're in Summerford; six or eight blocks of empty storefronts and abandoned cars at the curbs. Blip-in-the-road place. Dean wheels the truck off the main drag and pulls it into a narrow alleyway between two buildings, slowing to a stop when he finds an empty slot in a covered carport. He parks, turns off the engine, and they sit in a silence so sudden and pure that the tick-ing of the cooling engine feels loud.

Katherine says, "I think we—"

Dean holds a finger up to his lips. He slowly, carefully, opens his door. The dome light springs on and they both wince at the sudden illumination. There's no switch that she can find to turn it off, so she smashes that out too. More plastic falling down.

"Sorry," she says.

Dean puts a foot on the cement floor.

They wait. Him with one foot in, one foot out, gun resting on his thigh. "If they come down this alley, it's a shoot-out," he says quietly. She's not sure if he's talking to her or himself.

But no headlights pass by. No engine sound fills the mouth of the alley. It seems they've escaped.

Katherine steps out. She grips the edge of the truck bed and leans over, breathing. The panic makes her feel light, untethered from her body. She wills herself not to throw up.

"You okay?"

"Yeah," she says, and spits. She stands up, still gripping the lip of the truck bed.

"I think we ought to sit here for a bit," he says.

"I need to talk to you, Dean."

The truck between them, his eyes rove her face in the gloom. "Okay."

"Listen, when you asked me what I did? Back at the fire last night? Before the drift came."

"Sure."

"I wasn't square with you."

"I know," he says.

"You do?"

"I mean, yeah. We all got secret compartments in ourselves. It's not like you owe me anything, Katherine."

There's no way but forward. Better to make the wrong move, she tells herself, than no move at all. He turns and walks out into the alley, hands in his back pockets. She imagines it's the part of him that's a ragman, always looking for things to be salvaged from the wreckage of the world. Is that what she is to him? Salvage?

To his back, she says, "You know the song they played over the Message? 'I Won't Forget It'?"

He turns. "I remember hearing people talk about it afterwards. And before everything went to hell, yeah, there was a while there you couldn't turn the radio on without hearing that song."

"I wrote it," Katherine says.

He squints at her, smiling. "What do you mean?"

"I was in the Blank Letters. With my husband, a couple friends. We made some records, toured, all that. I wrote that song."

"Wait. You were in the *band* the Blank Letters? The actual band?"

"Yeah."

"Like you were the singer?"

"Yeah."

"Bull."

Katherine with a ghost of a smile. She steps out from beneath the carport. The world is so quiet they might be the only two people left. "Seriously. Went from tiny clubs to festivals with thirty thousand people. And then we split." And then my husband went mad, she thinks, and kick-started the end of the world.

"That's wild. Damn."

"Terradyne's the one that played the song."

"Like they meant to, you mean? Providence Initiative Terradyne. Played that song on purpose."

"Yeah."

"Why?" Dean says. "Why that song?"

There's the urge to bullshit; the truth, after all, is too strange. Too horrid. But to ask Dean to listen to her and then to feint and dodge with the truth? She can't do that to him. This will probably be good-bye between the two of them, anyway. Had he heard what she'd said when Matthew called her, rather than been off pissing at the side of the road, heard her ranting about cutting heads off, surely he'd have lit out. But now is the time for truth. Better that than to string him along, right into the mouth of whatever darkness lies ahead.

"It's a long story," she says. "And I'll tell you as much as I know.

But when you asked me why I wanted to go west, I wasn't straight with you. I want to go west because there's something I have to do there."

They walk for a bit. Dean processing. "Okay," he says.

"Okay?"

"Okay. Means I want to hear what you have to say."

"It's not just west," she says. "I have to go to Portland. There's something there I have to finish. I hoped, I've *been* hoping, that somehow Nick would get better. But he's not going to. I know that."

Dean keeps walking, shakes his head. "Portland, though, Katherine. Isn't that where everything started? They got a fever house there, right? A collation center?"

"Yeah."

"They're not letting anyone in, then."

She lifts her face to the scarred moon above, the alleyway drawn lunar-like in its chilly delineations of black and white.

"I don't give a shit," she says.

Dean laughs. "Well, maybe you will when you see that big-ass wall in person."

"I have a friend there." And then, for honesty's sake: "Well, an acquaintance."

"And you think he can get you in?"

"I hope so."

Katherine, you and your son, are you going home? I'm going there too. I'll meet you.

"But what's there, is what I'm asking. Why Portland?"

She thinks of Nick and realizes that she'll do this alone if she has to. Do it without Dean, without Bonner, without anyone. Just her against whatever wretched thing that moves through Matthew now, come what may. But again, Dean deserves the truth. "This story I want to tell you, it's pretty long."

"Well," he says, "we got a ways to Portland, if that's where we're going. Why don't you tell it to me on the way. Wouldn't mind taking a break from those tapes, honestly." He smiles at her, though she can tell he's unhappy. Worried. They've entwined themselves to each other with the thinnest of threads, and she's about to tell him a story that reels with madness, one that will end with her telling him *This is the man my husband was and this is what he became.*

Here is what he did to the world, and to my son.

And I'm going to Portland to kill him. Whatever he is now.

They get back in the truck.

Katherine sighs. Better to make the wrong move than no move at all.

"So," she says, relieved to finally begin, "when I was younger, in college, I went to a show. This was in LA. And I met this guy named Matthew and oh *shit,* the way he could play guitar, dude. To put it in polite terms, I was *moved.*"

And Dean is lifting his face to that buckshot moon and laughing, and that makes it easier still, and she keeps talking, and in her heart, she wants this telling to be worth something, she wants it to be as true as she can make it, even if it ends in death. She wants to tell it like a love letter to all the many things that she's lost—her husband, her son, her way.

JOHN BONNER

Portland, Oregon

The convention center.

The fever house itself.

He and Katz are up on the tongue, this long walkway that juts out into the middle of the ballroom, three stories up. The ballroom ceilings are high, vaulted. The tongue is, in essence, a steel beam that's been caged in wire mesh. To access it, you climb up scaffolding in the outside hallway and then go through a hole some op made with a reciprocating saw, and bingo, you're out on the tongue that leads out to the middle of the ballroom, way the hell up in the air.

Down below, three thousand fevered writhe and push and press against each other.

Bonner is terrified. The hell-house din of the place, the sighs and groans, their pressed-in bodies. The air stinks like an abattoir. Kendall greenlit the tongue years back as a deterrent to residents who gave Terradyne a hard time but, for whatever reason, couldn't just eat a bullet. A political tool. A motivator. There are three ballrooms in the convention center, all filled to the brim with fevered like this, all with their own tongue.

Katz holds a long loop of chain in one hand and his revolver in the other. He looks happy. He looks, unlike Bonner, entirely unconcerned about how the tongue wobbles and bends every time they move.

"Katz," Bonner says, unable to keep the plaintive quality out of his voice, "come on, man. We can figure this out."

"Where's Katherine Moriarty?"

"She's in Des Moines. There's a safe house there, she's got another ID—"

Katz rolls his eyes. "Shut the fuck up, Bonner."

Dave Kendall peers out from the other end of the tongue, safe on the scaffolding. The smell of shit and death fills Bonner's nose and through the steel weave of the beam he catches a glimpse of a face that turns up toward them, opens its jaws, then dips its head back down.

The tongue's caging is not quite large enough to stand up in, so both of them have to crouch. The body bag, with a chorus of riveted eyelets scattered throughout the top third of it, lies like a desiccated skin at Katz's feet. A pair of large lock hooks are set at each end of the bag. There's a hundred yards of chain, the links of which are as thick as Bonner's finger; they'll be run through each lock. The chain's hooked to a winch system that runs the length of the tongue, and operated out on the scaffolding.

You get in the bag and they lower you down.

Ops call it *dipping,* as in *dip a toe in.*

Katz gestures at the bag with his revolver. Bonner's frozen, rooted to his spot. Katz jounces on the beam a little, eyes on him, grinning. The tongue wobbles sickeningly. Bonner's heart rushes to his throat, and he sinks to his knees. "Fucking don't," he says, all shrill. "Jesus Christ, stop it."

Common knowledge: You have some recalcitrant fool dip a toe in, their attitude disappears.

"Where's Moriarty?"

"She's in Des Moines, there's a cabin there—"

Katz grins. "Get in the bag."

"I'm telling you—"

"You brought us out here. Made me get up on this thing. We could've fixed all this back at your place, but you screwed around. So let's dip a toe in, motherfuck. You can feel all your feelings."

Bonner just about crying. "Katz, I'm asking you, please don't make me do this."

Katz aims his revolver at Bonner's face. *"Get in."*

Bonner, taking little sips of that rancid air, his throat threatening to close, tears blurring his vision, crawls inside the heavy leather bag. It's hot, and clammy, and smells of sweat and piss and vomit and when Katz leans over him and zips the bag closed, Bonner starts keening like an animal. His hands push up against the bag. No leverage, his fingers tented right up near his face. Through the eyelets he can see the cage and the mesh and, above that, the ballroom ceiling. He hears Katz laugh and call out, "That winch all set?" Kendall's answer is lost.

Katz drags him to the lip of the tongue and then pushes him off.

There's a second where he's falling through the air and then the chain locks and he's aloft, the bag spinning madly. They start lowering him down. At some point he *feels* himself getting closer to the drift. There's a certain maddening deadness in the air.

It's hot inside, and when the first reaching hands brush the underside of the bag, he starts screaming. They keep lowering him and then the faces close over him, biting at the leather, at the chains, the empty, vicious road maps of their faces spied through the eyelets, the smash of bodies as they press against him, the stink as they lean into him, jaws snapping—

Bonner screams. Screams until he can't anymore, screams until some vital, necessary thing inside him breaks, and they're still there, still pressing against him. Trying to bite him.

4
WE GO WEST

THEO MARSDEN

Arlington, Virginia—I-84 West, outside of Ogden, Utah

When he'd told Jack Bonner that the Message wasn't his fault, he'd meant it.

There'd been a great number of machinations at work that night, the most monumental being the sudden vacuum created by the unexpected death of ARC agency director David Lundy. A death notably due to his head being caved in by his own dying asset, a mysterious and possibly extraterrestrial being referred to in surviving documents as "Saint Michael." Terradyne, still independent of the government at this point, had kept as close an eye as possible on Lundy's work over the years, both with Saint Michael and Lundy's "remnants," which included, purportedly, a severed hand that drove anyone in its proximity mad, and—more provocatively in Marsden's opinion—a short, digitized recording of a man speaking that drove people insane just by listening to it. Lundy reportedly kept the only copy of the recording on a USB stick around his neck. These were rumors, of course, whispers in the fog; Terradyne's intelligence-gathering capabilities before the Message were not absolute. Some of these rumors, Marsden assumed, were wildly exaggerated.

But when Lundy was killed by this Saint Michael in a flight over the Midwest, fleeing the volatility that the hand had wrought in Portland over a matter of hours, one of Lundy's colleagues, a woman named Diane Rodriguez, had taken the USB stick from around his neck and reached out to Jack Bonner with a simple offer: In exchange for future protection and a large cash payment, Terradyne could have the recording. By this point Portland, Oregon, had been overrun by the afflicted.

Clearly, Marsden realized, these remnants were things that *worked*, even if he and Jack didn't understand how.

He'd been at home in his Georgetown penthouse when Jack called to inform him of Rodriguez's offer. The Potomac steel gray and mist-shrouded outside the living room's picture windows. He was bouncing between phone and email, scanning intel reports, and talking briefly to a panicked President Yardley on an encrypted line. He remembers that intoxicating mixture of panic and feverish joy— that understanding that when things moved in one direction, they tended to move *fast*.

Jack had that same breathless, giddy quality Marsden recognized when they were on the cusp of closing a sale. He'd turned to the television, which was showing overhead images of downtown Portland: flames dotting the cityscape, threads of smoke climbing the sky, and then a cut to some jittering, handheld footage of someone on the ground, another body on top of them, biting at the face, the upturned hands.

The implication was clear, even among the confusion: The city was in ruins, a large percentage of its population somehow driven mad, driven to profound violence.

Marsden remembers walking over to his couch, the hard plastic shell of his television remote in his sweating hand. Next to the television was a framed photo of him and Barbara at some gala or another. Barbara in a crystal-blue gown that showed off her curves, Marsden with some black still in his hair, his arm around her waist. He walked over and straightened the photo. Her death from cancer the year before was like a tunnel housed inside him, a tunnel in which occasional rips of sorrow might pass through without warning. He shut his eyes, tried to come back to what Jack was saying.

"Theo, what do you think? I'm of the opinion we should move on this offer from Rodriguez. The situation on the ground is—"

"Give her whatever she wants," he said.

Jack paused. "You sure?"

"Absolutely."

"Good," he'd said, clearly relieved. It was perhaps the last time they were on the same page regarding anything of significance. And even this was moored in Marsden's deceit; if he was honest with himself, some notion of a plan was already forming.

"And Theo," Jack said, "I think we should use it." There had been no hesitation in his voice. "Portland is . . . fragile right now. We need a deterrent. If we can't contain it, we're going to be exposed and vulnerable, potentially on a national level—"

"Of course we'll use it," Marsden said. "Where are you?"

"I'm at the office."

"I'll head over now." He stood up, thumbing off the television and setting the photo of him and Barbara facedown. He would later marvel at the superstition of it, this childish desire that she not witness the things he was about to do.

Twenty minutes later, he entered the main control room at Terradyne's headquarters and had a brief discussion with Berliner, the head engineer tasked with overseeing Callista, Terradyne's global communications system. Marsden had already seen Jack, walking down the hall and flanked by a handful of techs, his face dazed with the weight of what they'd planned. Jack had wordlessly passed him the thumb drive containing the recording. Marsden held the USB stick in his hand for a moment before passing it over to Berliner, whispering his commands into the man's ear.

"Sir," Berliner said, "Mr. Bonner's already provided me with a list of targets." This, thankfully, was said in a cautious, whispered tone.

The control room was busy, cacophonous with people preparing for what was about to happen.

"The targets have changed," Marsden said.

Berliner had licked his lips. He was a thin, pale man, whose eyeglasses gave him a froggish appearance.

"Sir—"

"It's an order," he'd said into Berliner's ear, gripping the man's elbow. "Scrub your history after you do it, make it look like a systems error. I want the *program* to appear responsible, not you, you understand?"

"Yes, sir," Berliner croaked.

"I'll meet you back here in, what? Four hours? Do this for me, bury the order, and I'll come back here with enough money to insulate you from whatever might happen next." He offered Berliner a wolfish grin. "And I'm not talking stock options, friend. Cash, and no shortage of it."

He was sitting on his bed, holding Barbara's photo, when his phone buzzed.

UNKNOWN CALLER.

It was nearly six in the morning, dawn still just a suggestion beyond the shades.

Buzzing and buzzing, the call automatically disconnecting before leaving a message. Again, per his instructions. He wanted no lasting record of the recording; no voicemails, nothing that might be continually reactivated after this one time. He stood up, setting Barbara's photo facedown on the bed this time, and took his 9mm Taurus from its lockbox in the closet. He rode the elevator down to the garage. There was a feeling inside of him that was almost relief—he had crossed some irreversible point; everything of note had already taken place. Beyond this, they would only be reacting to events. And yet his pulse hammered at his temple, his hands were damp with sweat. A mix of adrenaline and fear striding through him.

People were already out on the street. He spied figures running through the dark, briefly lit under the cones of streetlights and then gone. The blat of a car alarm, the distant pop of gunfire. He saw his first body, a featureless hump at the curb, and then another in the middle of a parking lot, limbs flung out. He kept the Taurus on the passenger seat and took surface streets, afraid of getting stuck on the freeway. A car on fire, people being chased down the mouths of alleys. He parked in his private spot in the Terradyne garage, where he put the pistol in the back of his waistband and pulled his windbreaker over it. Taking his briefcase from the trunk of the car, he keyed himself into the building and took the elevator up.

The office was on full alert, everyone bustling. Yardley calling every ten minutes, demanding answers. He'd greenlit Jack Bonner's target list of enemy nations and wanted numbers. Wanted pie graphs and bullet points. Definable information as to how they'd just altered the world. But there was nothing to tell him yet. The Message was still an *idea,* even after the call had gone out. A caterpillar breaking from its chrysalis.

He found Berliner still in the control room. It was a massive place, air- and climate-controlled, filled with a labyrinth of tall-standing servers and flanked at the closest wall with an armada of screens and monitoring equipment. Berliner had been one of Jack's hires during Terradyne's earliest days; he'd been poached from the NSA, and Marsden took a single look at him and knew the man had kept his word. It was the way he held himself: He was at his desk, apart from the rest of the crew, looking queasy and stricken. Made insular with the burden he'd had placed on him.

Marsden, for once, was practically ignored. Engineers and systems analysts busy at their stations, the room filled with murmurs, men and women beginning to test the edges of the atrocity they'd just committed. Marsden had put a warm, fatherly hand on Berliner's shoulder. Berliner had looked up, his glasses catching the overhead light. The look on his face was one of drowning.

"Sir—" he said.

"Come with me," Marsden said, holding up the briefcase.

They'd walked out of the control room—people hardly giving them a glance, as far as Marsden could tell. Everyone bent to their work, trying to gauge the depth of the Message's results.

Down the hall, Marsden had held up a hand as another analyst came toward him, holding a tablet, his face frozen in horror.

"Take it up with Jack," Marsden said.

"Mr. Marsden—"

"Take it up with Jack." He led Berliner into the bathroom, where he knew there were no cameras.

Tile floors, a half dozen urinals followed by as many stalls. A mirrored bank of sinks on the opposite wall. Marsden surprised himself when he looked in the mirror—he looked good. Present, gathered. Calm. He looked for feet under the stalls, tried not to be obvious about it while Berliner chewed on a thumbnail. It was a tough call he'd made, following Marsden's command. Even Jack's original plan—play the Message over selected enemy nations, specific geographic locales—even that was still a death sentence that numbered in the millions.

But what Berliner had just done? What Marsden had *told* him to do?

It meant the ending of things. There was a madness in it, but a bravery too.

"Theo," Berliner said. His voice had wavered, Marsden remembered that. Sounding almost childlike. "I instigated all the commands you set. I just want Jack to know—"

"Did you tell him?" Marsden set the briefcase down. Took off his coat, laid it on the counter. His voice was soft, measured. He made sure he wasn't presenting his back, or the gun in his waistband, to Berliner.

"No. Like I said, I scrubbed everything, I—"

"You put the fail-safes in place? Covered your tracks?"

"I did everything, Theo, I understand the point of obfuscating it, hiding it, it makes sense—"

"Do you have the drive?"

Berliner reached into his pocket, handed the USB stick back to Marsden. It was like holding a small god in his fist.

Marsden dropped it to the ground and stepped on it until it cracked. The two of them stared at those shards of broken plastic for a moment until Marsden said, "Did you copy it?"

"You said no copies, Theo."

Marsden nodded. "And you didn't tell Jack? Or anyone on the team?"

"No! Theo, I—"

"Good," he said, "here's your money." He handed Berliner the briefcase. As Berliner went to open it, Marsden reached in his waistband and stepped forward, jamming the barrel of the Taurus under Berliner's jaw and firing. The round exited above his right eyebrow, an explosion of brain and warm blood that stippled Marsden's face and made him flinch. Berliner fell backward, knocking the stall door open and cracking the back of his head against the toilet. Marsden crouched, his knees popping, and set the pistol down near Berliner's hand. It wasn't as if anyone would be dusting for fingerprints, or running the gun's registration. As of half an hour ago, it was a different world.

It could be argued—Jack had certainly made the point often enough—that Marsden had killed plenty of people before. They both had. Death was what Terradyne trafficked in, after all. But this was the first time Theo had pulled the trigger himself. He'd quickly washed Berliner's blood and brains from his face and managed to cover his spattered shirt with his windbreaker moments before people ran in. An engineer, a few programmers. People he vaguely recognized from his infrequent sojourns into the control room. He crafted his face into a careful blankness, one that implied shock, horror.

People looked from Marsden to Berliner's body on the tile. The abstract spatter on the stall door, the growing pool of blood around his head.

"I tried to stop him," Marsden said, his voice shaking. Some part of him wishing Jack was there to see it.

"Sir," the engineer said. One of Berliner's subordinates. "Sir, we have a serious problem."

"I'd say *this* is a serious problem," Marsden had said, gesturing at Berliner, allowing a hint of righteousness to creep into his voice.

"Sir, he—it looks like he broke protocol. The, uh, the dispatch? The recording? Sir, it was issued *everywhere*. Something went wrong." The man had taken a deep, shaky breath, shoved a knuckle against his lips.

"I don't understand."

"The dispatch went out over the entirety of our networks."

"What do you mean, the entirety?"

"Everywhere, sir. All means of conveyance. Every satellite. Military, commercial, residential. The message went out everywhere, sir."

"What about other networks? Global networks?"

"They were all accessed. The message was piggybacked."

"You're telling me it went *everywhere*?"

A nod.

Marsden had allowed himself to look horrified. No one else had spoken. Everyone trying to gauge what it meant for the future.

Marsden, thrumming with adrenaline, thinking *Jack, this was the only way to do it. I had to. Wipe everything clean and rebuild. Lead firmly and with purpose.* Knowing that Jack would forever blame himself, would forever try to decipher *why* Berliner had done what he'd done. Or how the systems might have managed, accidentally or not, to bypass their own fail-safes.

Poor Jack. Wanting to destroy only part of the world, and instead upending the entire thing.

Now.

Katherine Moriarty is going west.

Most likely to Portland.

He's sure of it.

That's where John Bonner is, that's where Katherine's life had been before the Message.

She's going to Portland.

And he will meet her there. Then, with the woman and the girl and the child, Yardley will bend under Marsden's will.

Marsden leans against the Humvee, eyes closed, his face lifted to the sun. They are parked on the shoulder of the highway, and the world seems a fine thing, divided into the beautifully striated greens and blues of midafternoon.

The girl, Naomi, is changing the baby, who is fussy and loud. The two of them stand at the trunk, the girl doing what she can to clean him. Canino stands beside Marsden, as ever, tight-jawed and scanning the horizon for threats.

I don't want her near me, says the voice in Theo Marsden's head. *We need her, but I don't want her near me.*

A new development, this.

Matthew Coffin's voice is like a sigh that drifts down the crooked hallways of his brain. It's not frightening anymore, though he *had* been afraid, at first—there in that motel room with his eye flowering blood in front of the mirror, Coffin suddenly speaking inside him. He'd felt like he'd gone mad, was having some sort of a stroke. But no. Not mad. Not dying. Coffin is a passenger, and he bids Marsden to keep it a secret. Promises rewards for doing so. With that promise comes some measure of how he'd felt so often while gazing up at the body in the box: soothed, adrift, anesthetized. Swimming in the blood-churn of his thoughts.

You're doping me up, aren't you? Making me calm.

Coffin ignores him, says a third time: *I don't want her near me.*

"All right," Marsden says, cross, and Canino looks over at him.

Him neither, Coffin says. *The gunman.*

"You okay, sir?" Canino says.

"I'm fine, son," Marsden says.

We need the girl and the child, Coffin says now, his distaste obvious. *But him, not so much.*

"Antoine's hungry," Naomi says.

"Tough shit," Canino shoots back. He seems to hang on Marsden's every word—part of it, probably, is his belief that Marsden will lead him to the woman who killed his brother. But another part, Marsden knows, is that Canino is one of those young men who are just easily led. Probably an errant, brutal father in his past, a mother who withheld love, some kind of blockade to the heart that makes him—killer or no—desperately eager to please. Eager to be told *Good boy*.

Whether or not Coffin needs him, Marsden does. He is Marsden's bullet.

"We have MREs," Marsden says to the girl without turning.

"Dear God, please don't make me feed this baby any more packaged cheese," she says.

Marsden laughs with his eyes closed and Canino says, "Yeah, cool, I'll just dip down to the Whole Foods then."

They are parked among a throng of abandoned vehicles, their shapes softened with years of dust and discoloration. Marsden's eyes have been bothering him and he's pulled over to take a break.

He turns to Canino. "Go look," he says.

"What, for food?"

"Yes."

"Sir, it's not like we're gonna—"

Marsden quells a mild but interesting urge to rip the boy's tongue out and instead waves his hand at the cars around them. "Chris. Go look."

Canino mutters something but begins walking along the length of vehicles, trying doors, trunks.

"Do you even know what you're doing?" This from Naomi, who bends to the child in the back of the Humvee, her dark hair obscuring her face.

It's a fair question. The most recent call to his op, trying to pinpoint Katherine Moriarty's cell phone location, was met with a hang-up. Word is out on Theo Marsden, it seems. All they're doing right now is getting away—away from Rolla, away from Yardley's reach, away from grasping hands that might take his treasures from him. But all that will change with Portland.

In Portland, with Moriarty and the girl and the child, he'll break Yardley like wheat against a blade. Coffin has told him as much.

He turns away from the girl without answering her question and takes out his phone and the little piece of paper from his pocket. He calls Yardley.

It rings once, like Yardley's been waiting. "Theo, this has gone on long enough. Jack Bonner's on life support, he—"

"How about I kill them?"

Naomi turns, her eyes wide. Marsden frowns and shakes his head, waves his hand.

"What?" Yardley says.

"How about I kill them? The girl and the baby? Then you can ruminate on all that you had, Preston, and all that you threw away."

"Theo, come back to Rolla. Let's talk. This is not insurmountable. Have you prayed?"

Marsden grins at the horizon. "Oh, cut the shit. You and your God would meet me there with snipers on the rooftops. I'm not stupid."

"Theo, with Coffin dead, we've got nothing else but the girl. Please, reconsider."

"That's the thing," Marsden says. He turns his back to the girl and says quietly, "He's not dead, Preston. He's in here with me."

A moment, and then, "What? I don't understand—"

"Listen to me. You return my security clearance and dump more credits on this hunter's ration card, the one I'm with, or I'll kill the girl and the child both. You track this phone, you send a shock team after me, all you'll find is their bodies. I promise you."

"Theo—"

Marsden hangs up. To Naomi, he says, "That was bravado, dear, just to be clear. A poker game. I'm still operating under the assumption that you're valuable." The look she gives him is a mixture of shock and malice, and he delights in it.

Canino, some distance ahead, turns and comes trotting back. He hooks a thumb over his shoulder and calls out, "Can I have my pistol, sir? We got a couple fevered locked up in a car back there."

"Really?" For a moment, his vision suddenly blurs and he blinks it away. "Let's take a look." He motions toward Naomi. "All of us."

"I don't want to," Naomi says.

"If I gave a shit, that would be concerning," Marsden says, and grips her by the arm.

Some dozen cars ahead, they come to a maroon coupe rimed in dust; the driver's side window has a clean circle smeared among the caked filth. Marsden leans forward to peer in the gloom and a pale hand slaps at the glass. He jumps back, laughing a little. A face in there.

"The car locked?" he asks Coffin.

"I haven't checked."

"You said there's two inside?"

"Yes, sir."

He turns to Naomi. "Hand me the baby."

"No," Naomi says. Her face is set, her lip trembling. Again, Marsden feels an admiration for her. She lets out a kind of low moan when he unholsters the pistol and presses the barrel against her forehead. She hands the child over.

The baby's weight is surprising. Not only a bargaining tool, but a thing of blood and bone and chubby limbs. He presses Antoine to his chest—Coffin is suddenly animated inside him, clamoring to see the child. Marsden hands the pistol to Canino.

"Keep one of them intact," he says.

Canino stares at the car for a moment and then exhales. Pumping himself up. He tries to open the driver's side door but time has done its work—the door's sealed. The interior of the car is suddenly rife with noise and activity, the fevered in there sensing a change.

Canino pulls again and the door unseals with an audible crack and a fevered woman in a sleeveless blouse snarls at them, tries to lurch out into the world but can't. She's locked in her seatbelt. Marsden has a moment of dark wonderment, imagining her stuck inside that car for years, not even present enough in her own body to unlatch a seatbelt. Sitting there as day goes to dusk to night, snow and rain and the summer sun boiling the inside of the car. Hundreds of days and nights.

I did that, he thinks.

Canino leans in and shoots her through the eye.

He peers in over the seat. "The other one's like a kid. Like a teenager."

"Open the back door."

"And don't kill her?"

"No."

Canino holsters his pistol and pulls on the rear driver's side door—this one gives way easier, and in seconds she's on him, a fevered adolescent with frayed braids, her jaw snapping as he falls to the asphalt and buries a hand around her throat.

"Turn her," Marsden says to Naomi, still holding the child to his chest.

"No!" The girl in a half crouch, panic and anguish bending her.

Marsden flips the child upside down—Antoine squalling in outrage, limbs flailing. "I'll drop him." Coffin hissing with rage inside him.

The fevered teen's fingers skate across Canino's closed eyes. Antoine screams.

Naomi storms over and lays her hand on the back of the girl's neck. The girl arches her spine as if some current's been shot through her, lifting her gray, dirt-smeared face up to the sun. Every muscle is rigid, striated. She blinks, her own sclera going from red to newsprint yellow to white right in front of him. He *sees* it happen. She opens her mouth, her eyes roving among them, her gaze infused with a sudden *awareness,* and then, beneath her, Canino frees his pistol from his holster and fires three, four times into her chest. Birds caw and take flight. She collapses on him and then he puts the pistol against the side of her head and shoots her again.

Naomi sobs and turns away.

Marsden rights Antoine, holds him tight.

"Well done," he says.

"I fucking hate you," the girl gasps, tears tracking through the grime on her face. "I hate you so much."

FROM THE ARCHIVAL NOTEBOOKS
OF MATTHEW COFFIN

I've stopped walking in circles around Francis's table. Those weird fugues I fell into, they're gone. Like they served their purpose, allowed me to, I don't know, reach the right level of accessibility or something. Be open enough.

The tape with my voice on it—the one with DEVIL ROCK written on the label—that's all the proof I need. All that shit about making a fever house, a house of wounds? Where I'm the one that's talking but it's *him* telling me what to do? That's the key.

We've made a deal, see.

All these icons carved into me with steak knives.

That's the handshake. Sealing the deal.

I see it now.

Francis comes back from tour tomorrow. The apartment is far from what you would call pristine. Stinks of blood, frankly. My clothes stick to my skin a lot and I have to peel them off and then the scabs rip open again. Can't remember the last time I ate. Slept.

We've been *plotting*, me and him. Coming up with a plan.

I'm so sorry for all of this, Katherine. This grand waste of love between us. This journal, it's not an excuse, it's more like an explanation, okay?

I'm going to fix things.

I went out this morning, had to do some stuff. Was told to. By the thing in the loft—I keep wanting to name it, name him, like the naming of the thing will make it all somehow understandable. But he's unnameable, really. So old he's more an idea than anything.

And yet the visions he's offered me of what could be—me and you and Nick together again, the three of us starting over, without all this wreckage. The band still together, my kid not a stranger to me. Me as a husband who doesn't implode with resentment and boiling rage at the woman I've supposedly tethered my heart to. He's shown me a life with all of us together, but with me different and better and *more than I am now*—and that's what I want. That's what's been promised to me.

But first, I need to put in the work.

I went downtown, Burnside, near the giant bookstore and the pizza place and the other, smaller bookstore, one of those focal points in the city for me, those little pockets of what makes this place so great, and I put the DEVIL ROCK cassette in its plastic shell on a bus bench.

Why do you want me to leave this here? Will something bad happen?

And he answered, *Something good will happen. But not for a long time.*

His voice, it's right there, behind the curve of the skull. It's a voice of nothingness. It's wind beneath a door, I don't know how to describe it otherwise.

Will anyone be hurt? I asked. These things he needs me to do, I'm willing to do them to myself, but I'm dog-ass tired of hurting other people, and I want him to know that.

Life is full of hurt is the answer I get, which is a little too freshman-level philosophy for me, so I just tell him, a little firmer: I'm tired of hurting people. I'm doing this so I'll *stop* hurting people.

He doesn't respond to that, and I don't know what else to do, so I leave the tape on the bench. Getting rid of the tape makes the rest of it easier. I've gone too far to turn back now.

I walked east, crossing over the Hawthorne Bridge, and at the midpoint he made me stop and look out at the flat gray sheet of river below. It was raining, and miserable; rainwater dripped from my chin and wetted my socks and it felt so good. Life felt so good because I had something to look forward to.

I kept walking along Hawthorne, up to Thirty-ninth, and it continued to feel glorious. The rain, the traffic slicing through puddles. The headlights. There's a superstore there on Thirty-ninth and Hawthorne, boxy and imposing, and I went into their Home and Garden section, my footsteps squeaking on the floor. I only needed a couple things.

I walked out with my items in a paper bag—a hacksaw, a big pair of steel scissors. Twenty yards of rubber tubing.

Right by the front doors, I stopped in front of a rack of sunglasses.

I put a pair on and walked right out. No one said shit.

Back at the loft, I laid out my purchases on the kitchen table. Took off my shirt. Went to the kitchen drawer. Got out a spoon.

I took the spoon and the scissors into that cubicle of a bathroom and looked in the mirror. For a moment I felt profoundly sorry for all that I'd done to my body, or had done to it. My torso and arms were covered in these marks, some infected and bleeding, weeping pus. Some pointless riddle drawn across my flesh.

I lay the spoon and scissors on the edge of the sink.

Will it hurt? I asked.

Yes.

And then?

And then a period of waiting. Rejuvenation, and then you will be together. Be wed. United, to walk down the centuries.

What about my kid?

Yes, the child too.

And what do you get out of this? I asked. This drove him to an-other one of his silences, until he said, once again, the promise I've heard so many times: *Avail yourself to me. The hand the eye the voice. Build me a house of fever and wounds and you will have all you ever wanted.*

It wasn't an answer, but I had seen the happiness I might have with you, with Nick.

I picked up the spoon from the rim of the sink. With my other hand, I pulled down my eyelid.

Put the tip of the spoon behind the lid, beneath the curve of my eye. There against the hard bone of the socket.

Later, I bled.

Made a circle of blood on the floor. As necessary. Instructed.

It hardly hurt. A distant pulsing, like I'd been hit with some kind of numbing agent. It made it easier. Will make the rest easier too.

For you.

All of this for you.

And then, Katherine, you *came* here—came to the loft, and I jammed the socket where my missing eye had been, jammed it with scraps from a cut-up shirt, him telling me it would be necessary to stop the bleeding so you wouldn't worry.

You came and I tried to tell you that we could be together again, and I showed you the eye, separate from me now, and I held it in my palm and we both watched it move toward you—marking you, so that he and I could find you when it was time—and you ran.

God, my handwriting is so bad.

The hand, the eye, the voice, Katherine.

I did the eye. So one down, two to go.

And then he'll get his house of fever and wounds and I'll get you. Get Nick. All of us, without our shitty past trailing behind us.

I'll close the cover of this book.

I'll open these scissors. Put the blades against my tongue.

I'll pick up the saw and lay its teeth against my wrist.

The hand, the eye, the voice.

And I'll go to the bridge and step over, into the dark.

Waiting and rejuvenation and then we'll be together.

Me and you and Nick.

Better than before.

I'm sorry, Katherine.

I'm sorry for all of it.

I do love you. I'm sorry that love was so damn broken.

JOHN BONNER
Portland, Oregon

In the bag, there's no such thing as time. There's only sensation—the suffocating envelopment of the fevered. They snap at the leather, break their teeth biting at the chain that holds the bag four feet off the ground. He's screamed himself hoarse. The inside of the bag is slick with sweat, his own piss and expectorate. The hell of their snarling gray faces through the eyelets as they try to devour him.

There's no time in there. Just the press, the constant surety that the bag will fall, the chain will break, they will descend on him.

But no; at some point he starts his ascension. Minutes later? Years, maybe. The chains suddenly pull taut, his body bending in a slight V inside the bag, the twisting view of the ceiling as he slowly rises toward it, slowly spins around.

His throat aches from screaming. Cold piss tightens his jeans.

He rises enough that the hands slapping at the bag fade away. The clank of each link in the chain notching home above him as he's winched back up onto the steel tongue that sticks out into the middle of the ballroom. Finally, he feels more hands grip the bag—

Bonner squealing, trying to push them away—and he's yanked back up on the tongue. The zipper opens and there's Katz crouching over him, grinning beneath his mustache, revolver in his fist. Bonner's mind is a canvas with a single brushstroke on it: *Away away away.*

"How you doing, John? Ready to tell us about Katheri—"

Bonner pushes up on Katz's wrist and the barrel of the revolver shatters the man's front teeth. Katz drops the gun. It bounces off the edge of the tongue, falls down into the ballroom. *Away away away.* Bonner bursts up like some revenant from the bag, that pinched animal noise stuck in his throat, and he sinks his grip into the fat beneath Katz's jaw. The old cop's eyes go big with panic, with pain, and then Bonner twists, pushes Katz over, toward the edge.

"John, *no*—"

Bonner screeches and kicks him hard in the shoulder and Katz falls off the edge, gracelessly, screaming the entire way down. There's no thud of impact, but the animated quality of the fevered, the noise down there, kicks up a notch.

Bonner starts crawling toward the doorway at the base of the tongue, panting now. *Away.* Dave Kendall's stunned face looking back at him. Bonner feels the steel mesh flooring of the tongue beneath his palms, the wet fabric at his thighs. A bead of sweat makes the trek from his hairline to his nose, tumbles off. He settles on Kendall's face in that hole in the wall, there on the other side.

Kendall gets it. Sees the intent. By the time Bonner's made it through the hole and is staggering down the rickety, pieced-together scaffolding, his legs trembling like a colt's, Kendall's disappeared.

Bonner veers down the hall, trying to find an escape route. *Away.* Stops once to lean against the wall and gag, take big gulps of air. Finally finds an unmarked door that opens on a hallway that he follows until he sees another door at the end. The EXIT sign above the door is dark, but when he pushes it open an alarm goes off above his head, shrill and bright. He staggers through an empty parking lot trying to find his legs, trying to run.

Half an hour later, he cases his own house for a few minutes, front and back, before he hops the back fence and pushes open the sliding patio door. His mind has calmed a little, enough to move. Everything seems as he's left it. His car's in the driveway. They haven't swept his house—Matthew Coffin's notebooks are still spread out on the kitchen table. His Glock's still sitting there.

Bonner risks a shower, thirty seconds. To rinse off the horror of the bag, the cloying stink of it. He dresses in fresh clothes and grabs a duffel and throws what he needs inside—the eye in its gold-leaf box, Coffin's notebooks, a 12-gauge Ithaca shotgun with a shortened barrel, a box of shells. A curved hunting blade in a sheath. Puts his Glock in a hip holster that he clips onto his belt. Takes his phone, makes sure it's charged, that he still has Katherine's number. He calls her cell and it just rings and rings. Must've followed his suggestion and gotten rid of it. Prays—as close as he comes to such a thing—that she reaches out to him somehow.

He walks outside, puts the duffel in the trunk, gets in.

Feels like a robot, a machine, doing the next thing in front of him. Shoves his time in the bag way down. Almost clips a telephone pole hanging a right, has to will himself to calm down. To breathe. If Katherine really is coming here, there's little time to get things right. Every second matters.

The building on Eighty-second looks the same. Up the stairs, Bonner pauses at the landing before he puts the key in the door. He feels the hand calling out, and he steps inside, to the kitchen. He takes the box from the freezer and steps back outside before he can fall into its fog, before it can slow him, fuck him up.

Practically runs down to the parking lot. Puts the hand in the duffel bag in the trunk, next to the eye.

You are the harbinger.

Not me. I'm doing all this to *stop* it.

Destroy the hand, then. Run over it. Throw it in the Willamette.

Load up a burn barrel with scrap and drop it in. Hell, shoot the thing. Why not?

But he doesn't. Not yet. Not without Katherine. There's some instinctual part of him that knows to destroy the remnants now will spell disaster later. He saw the hand and the eye in his vision, after all. That and the strange, clotted mass of string, whatever the hell that is.

He starts the car. His phone buzzes.

He heads out of the parking lot.

Knows where he has to go.

And in the maelstrom of Bonner's mind, the hand crows, jubilant and mad.

Thrilled at finally being set free again.

THEO MARSDEN

Fairlane, Iowa—Boise, Idaho

Canino seems skittish. Nervous about entering Boise. By now he probably has some sense that Marsden is not quite right. Like Portland, Boise is one of the seventeen collation centers scattered throughout the country, and with that comes a certain solemnity. They saw their first warning fifty miles before, a billboard that read:

WARNING
GOVERNMENT COLLATION CENTER AHEAD
53 MILES
NO ENTRY OR EXIT
WITHOUT PROPER IDENTIFICATION

The girl has stopped speaking to them entirely. Questions are met with a stony, furious silence. Orders are followed, but mutely. She sits in the back of the Humvee, holding the child, who has grown listless too. The two of them falling into the dark stars of themselves.

But she showed him. She really can do it. She can turn them back. Matthew Coffin is afraid of her.

Keep her nearby but keep her away from me.

Are you scared of her?

I need her. We need her.

For what?

Silence.

You're not going to answer me?

We are becoming, you and I.

Marsden is not yet familiar enough with the blighted territory of their shared mind to decipher exactly what that entails. There is a sense of timelessness about the thing inside him. He's ascribed it a name—Matthew Coffin—because he doesn't know what else to call it. But Coffin is clearly only tangential to it. Trying to explore the thing's mind yields little: Its interior is lunar, darkly layered. Even the identity upon that top layer—Matthew Coffin, dead musician, distant father, poor husband—is simply a thread of dust on the edge of a blade. The thing inside Marsden is cagey and wise and old.

And its ambition matches his own.

They both desire power, he feels it.

Their enjoinment has brought about changes. *Marsden* is changing. He should be terrified of what's happening, and a dim, buried part of him is. But there's still that pleasant, *unhurried* feeling, narcotic in its purity.

The change began with his left eye, back in that motel room in Nebraska. The weeping of red, translucent tears that make him constantly dab at his eye with a rag. Then came an ache in his joints, a kind of heated throbbing. Nearly seventy years old, Theo Marsden was no stranger to the stiffness of the body, but this was different. This felt as if little beads of molten fire had been inserted into the spaces between the bones. First in his hands and feet, then throughout his whole body. Marsden remembered his mother massaging his shins and shoulders when he was a young boy, telling him the aches he felt were *growing pains,* that it meant he was getting bigger. Growing up. This is like that, only tenfold, as if his bones are reshaping themselves.

Then came the dryness of the skin on his cheeks. The skin on his elbows growing papery and thin, beginning to split open. Perhaps a hundred miles back, he'd looked down to see that the knees of his pants showed dottings of blood.

Now he squints against the sun and dabs at his eye and says, What are you, Matthew? Truly.

Coffin doesn't answer for a long time. Marsden thinks he's chosen to ignore him again, but then he says in that sullen voice of his: *I break time's back upon my knee. I skirt between the walls.*

The walls of what?

Of worlds beyond this one. Of lightness and darkness.

Which is not really an answer, is it?

All along, the Humvee eats the miles. President Yardley has, apparently, bowed to his threat—Canino's ration card still works at every Jane station they stop at. They rip across the countryside, Marsden calling out like some hellish tour guide when he sees totems to the world being reborn: They pass enough Terradyne farmland and processing centers behind their walls of razor wire and cyclone fencing and guard towers that it begins to feel commonplace. They spot a number of BUY, DON'T BARTER billboards, Jane's gaze glowering and fierce. It all feels good. Soon enough, he'll call Yardley and list his demands.

What *are* my demands, he muses. If his plan is to unseat the president, what's the wisest way to go about it?

Well, get him away from both DC and Rolla. Neutral ground, then wrest him from his throne. Kill him and assume control.

Easier said than done, perhaps.

"Sir, you sure you don't want to maybe go around?"

This from Canino, and Marsden jumps a little at the soldier's voice, snared as he is in his own musings. He turns and smiles. Feels his teeth wobble sickly in his gums. "Go around?"

Eyeing him warily, Canino says, "Around, you know, the city."

"Go around Boise? Just drive around it?"

A pained look on the soldier's face. "I just think, you know, going through a fever house, if we're trying to keep a low profile and shit . . ."

Marsden turns back to the road. "Have you ever been to a fever house before? Inside a collation center?"

"No, sir."

"You understand who I am, correct?" Canino swallows, and Marsden keeps on. "You do understand that I am the architect of this whole thing. This whole affair." He motions with a cracked, weeping hand at the expanse of the world outside the windshield. "What you see here, I *made* all this. You understand, don't you?"

Canino looking at him like he's gone insane. "Sir, it's just that—what if it's a trap?"

"What if *what's* a trap, boy?"

"Well, what if we go in there, over the wall, and they don't let us go back out?"

"Who is they?"

"I don't know."

Marsden points a finger at him. "No one's holding *me* captive, boy. I *built* this world. Remember that."

They drive on in silence. Marsden's mind is a maelstrom of visions—meeting Jack at UCLA, the closed-circle madness of kicking the man's face in five decades later. The spatter of Berliner's brains on the bathroom stall. Barbara lighting a cigarette in a black dress. Later, in her hospice bed, her hair the color of ash. He watches these visions with a cold detachment. Beneath all of it, there is the thin scum of Coffin's consciousness, a thing that grows louder as they get closer to the city.

Why are we going here? he asks that interior voice, Canino's question rankling his sense of control.

Gets no answer.

I'll stop the car. Answer me.

I need to see.

See what?

I need to see them.

Marsden has the feeling that were he to truly push back against Coffin's will, he might be surprised at how deeply this thing inside him has taken root. It might already be too late for any pushing back.

I want Yardley's position. I haven't done all this for nothing.

You'll have all you ever wanted, Coffin assures him, and for the moment Marsden lets that be enough.

Outside Boise there are yellow fields and the scattered markers of dead industry. Beyond the fields, brown and green scalloped hills. And then, there, where Highways 30 and 84 run perpendicular to each other: the wall.

The wall around Boise is massive. Fifteen feet high, a slapdash mix of lashed and repurposed telephone poles and sheets of steel, sections of cement, iron grating; filthy, tagged in graffiti, the whole thing topped with barbs and coils of wires and great gleaming hanks of glass.

The wall extends some hundred yards past the highways on each side and then is slowly drawn back; none of the walled cities' perimeters have a linear design, it's all catch-as-catch-can.

There's a guard station and an orange and white boom gate some hundred yards before the wall itself, manned by a pair of men in Terradyne fatigues.

Marsden slows, pins the girl's eyes in the rearview mirror. "If you try to get them to do something, I'll kill the child and then you. Believe it."

Naomi's eyes are chips of ice. "You talk too much," she says.

They coast to a stop before the boom gate and Marsden takes out his Terradyne ID, pistol tucked beneath his thigh.

He offers the op his ID through the window. The op nods at all of them, his eyes lingering perhaps a bit longer on Naomi and the baby than Marsden would prefer, then slides the ID through the reader hanging from a chain on his belt. The moment hangs on a wire and then there's the telltale beep of an accepted read—Yardley still keeping his word—and then the op notices the name on the reader, notices Marsden's title. His eyes pinball wildly throughout the interior of the Humvee, taking it all in. The old man's bedraggled appearance—to put it mildly—coupled with the fact that there's a fucking baby inside the rig. He clearly doesn't quite know what to make of it.

"My family," Marsden offers. A grin that aims for conciliatory but feels strained, mad. "We're traveling."

The op buys it or doesn't. Either way, questioning the CEO of Terradyne is way above his pay grade. He licks his lips. "Do you need an escort or anything, sir? Can I call ahead for you somewhere?"

"We're fine, son. We're going to the fever house."

The op's young, a shaving rash at his throat, and Marsden sees him pause and then take the leap: "Sir, do you need medical attention? I—"

Canino leans over from his seat to lock eyes with the boy. "Open the fucking gate, dude."

The Boise collation center is in a horse track.

Is a horse track. At the fairgrounds. LES BOIS PARK on the exterior of the building, which is ringed in sandbags and sawhorses, and monitored by Terradyne ops with guns hanging from their chests. They park and, after Marsden has an op read his card, the four of them are led through various checkpoints and into the track building by the confused warden of the house, a man with a comb-over and ill-fitting fatigues. There are some weak requests that Marsden might turn over his pistol, but he refuses and it isn't brought up again.

The warden's office is a cramped box with a window that looks out on the track, which is ringed in its own pieced-together fencing. There are two chairs flanking the warden's desk, a desk stacked high with documents—tallies and procurement sheets, ID logs, all that— but everyone stands clustered near the door. Marsden can see the fevered milling about between the slats.

"How many do you have there?"

"Approximately six thousand, sir."

"You just put them all on the racetrack?"

The warden's Adam's apple bobs. "Uh, yes."

The fence is blocking most of the sunlight through the window. Marsden feels Coffin, silent up until now, *lean* toward the fevered out there. Antoine gurgles, pats Naomi's chin.

The warden squares the papers on his desk, like he's looking for something to do with his hands, and says, "Mr. Marsden, we're thrilled you're here, of course, but is there something specific I can do for you?"

Coffin *leans.*

"I'd like to see a fevered," Marsden says.

"Um," says the warden. He smooths over his thin pastiche of hair, offers the other three a terrified grin, a man looking for rescue. "Ah. I see."

"Alone," Marsden says. "In a room."

"It's highly unusual."

"And yet." Marsden holds up his palms, smiles. That one bloodied eye. The papery, slowly splitting skin of his cheeks. "Here we are."

He's brought to a windowless room around the corner. A drain in the floor, the walls tiled up to the waist. Holes in the plaster where plumbing had once been.

An op brings a fevered in, a chain lashed around the throat. Each collation center is left to their own devices when it comes to how to dress them, or whether to dress them at all, and the Boise house seems to have little concern for such things: The fevered is narrow-chested and shirtless. Wearing the filthy pants and ragged boots he was presumably turned in.

The fevered sees him and lurches forward, the chain going taut. The op, a burly middle-aged man with a red mustache, pulls him back.

"You can leave us," Marsden says.

"Sir, he'll be on you the second I let go."

Coffin inside him, snapping to be let free.

"Go ahead."

"No disrespect, but the warden will have my ass."

Marsden steps forward, hooks a hand against the fevered's throat and walks him up to the wall, the chain hissing along the tiled floor. The flesh beneath his grip is cold with sluggish blood.

"We're fine here," Marsden says, and the op walks backward, palms up, his face carefully blank. He steps out the door, gently closes it.

The thing inside him steps forward—*truly* steps forward—for the first time. Marsden is pushed back, a passenger in his own body. There's a sense of tremendous possibility, as if the entity—*Coffin/ not-Coffin*, he thinks wildly—is merely testing the depths. Seeing what he—what *it*—might be capable of.

"*To your knees,*" it says, using Marsden's voice.

The fevered falls to the ground like a blade's been run across his Achilles tendons. The knobs of his spine rise like topography.

The Coffin-thing, with Marsden's voice and a minute sweep of the hand toward the closed door: "*Break yourself upon it.*"

The fevered, snarling, pushes up and runs headlong into the door. The sound of impact, the meaty thump of the skull against steel. Bashes his forehead against the door, again, again, the skull beginning to cave, the monster-thing in Marsden's hijacked body watching, considering. The percussive quality of the head against the door like a drumbeat until the fevered's tortured brain is pulped and he drops to the tile. Truly and finally lifeless.

A house of fever and wounds, rises the voice in his mind. *A house of the headless jaw. A house where I am king, and all before me is ruin.*

Marsden, pinned down in the dark of his own mind. The Coffin-thing stronger, so much stronger, than he could have imagined.

NAOMI LAURENT

Boise, Idaho

They're standing in the hallway outside the warden's office. There are few guards around, and the kind of psychic *hum* of the fevered milling out there in the grandstands and on the track, with just a few walls and a few dozen feet between her and them, makes Naomi edgy and cross. Marsden's been led further into the building, insisting upon his odd palaver with a fevered, whatever in God's name that's all about. Canino stands beside her in the hall, radiating unease. Even without his gun he's frightening.

He turns to her, shaking his head. "Going into a room with one of them? By yourself? Stupid."

Canino's loyalty to this strange man is like some code she can't decipher. Had Naomi been in his position, she'd have used that pistol the first chance she got, walked it up Marsden's body a dozen times by now.

"We could run," she says quietly, offering him a small smile. "The door is right there. He's busy. We could go."

A moment passes and then Canino looks away. "I ain't going anywhere."

"Why are you *with* him?" she asks, desperation sharpening her voice to a knife edge. Antoine stirs.

Canino turns, offers her his narrow face again, that arcing scar over his ear. "I'm not *with* him," he says, gesturing down the hall Marsden's walked down. "I'm not *with* anybody. He says he can get me the woman that killed my brother. I don't give a shit about him, about you, nothing. The lady that killed Jason's the one I want. That's all."

Naomi softens, almost in spite of herself. She knows what it means to have ghosts that are impossible to expel. "I'm sorry," she says, and means it. "I had a—my brother died too."

Canino sneers, contemptuous. "Everybody's got a dead brother. A dead somebody."

And then Marsden turns the corner and walks down the hall toward them.

Changed.

Even the way he *walks* has changed.

Naomi's breath catches in her throat. She turns to run out the doors, Antoine held to her chest, but she hears his wet chuckle, the sound of his shoes against the floor, and it's like something from a nightmare.

She's hardly moved at all—her body so *slow*—when he grips her shoulder and she spins, letting out a small shriek in spite of herself.

That shock of white hair the only thing familiar about him now. Both eyes shot through with burst veins, filled with blood. Small traceries of blood beginning to spill down the worn, wrinkled parchment of his face.

"We should make haste," he rattles, grinning. Gums bleeding and gray.

Somehow worst of all, he has a new voice, and it is like someone speaking from underground.

A man with his throat stuffed full of dirt.

They make it to the parking lot without incident, those few soldiers they come in proximity to giving them distance, one of them half-heartedly raising his rifle. Naomi is pushed into the Humvee with a writhing, shrieking Antoine. Marsden, his skin openly sup-purating blood now, red blooms on his shirt, his pants, gets in the passenger seat.

From around the corner of the building comes the warden. He raises an arm and trots toward them.

"How the fuck does this thing *start*—" Canino says in the driver's seat, his voice pinched with panic. Marsden reaches over and flips the toggle that starts the engine.

The Humvee roars.

Then the old man opens the passenger door and staggers out onto the asphalt.

Naomi sees the warden take in Marsden. From the backseat, she can see the seams at the back of his neck weeping blood, pinking his shirt collar. The warden holds up a hand, as if to keep him away. "Sir, what happened in there?" he says. He takes a step back. "What—"

"Help me," Marsden says. Still that terrible, dirt-clotted voice, but now there's fear in it too, Naomi realizing there's some internal war happening inside him.

"What?"

"Help me, I can't—" Marsden chokes out in that voice.

"*Go*," Naomi says to Canino, and for a moment it seems like he might do it, might leave the old man—he puts both hands on the steering wheel, turns around to peer at the parking lot behind her head—but then the warden turns and runs back toward the entrance and Marsden comes back to the Humvee and gets in. Whatever battle that was taking place inside him seems to have shifted—he has wholly become this new thing now.

He turns and looks at her. "Give me the baby."

His face a mask of blood. Both irises red now. In front of Naomi's eyes, knobs as big as robin's eggs rise from his cheekbones, stretch the skin tight and glossy.

Naomi shrinks back, makes herself and the baby small. "Don't touch him," she says. "You touch him and I'll kill you." Pure animal panic working through her now.

Marsden—whatever he is now—reaches back and lays a hand over the boy's head. Naomi shrieks, bats at it. He leans over the seat and takes the child from her with a tenderness made all the more horrible for what he's becoming. Naomi clutches herself and curls up into a ball as a single drop of Marsden's blood falls onto Antoine's cheek. The child blinks in surprise.

Canino reverses, heads out of the parking lot.

"West, boy," Marsden rattles, staring down at the baby. "We go west."

KATHERINE MORIARTY

Alice Lake, Oregon

She and Dean driving through the day and night and day. Southern Oregon now, both of them irritable, tired of shitty processed Jane food, tired of sitting in the truck for endless hours, tired of the tapes Dean lifted from the house off the highway. There are a few they haven't listened to yet, but for a time in Wyoming, of all places, they'd happened across an FM station, a live broadcast of a man and his young daughter talking, playing records, telling each other jokes. A crystalline moment of sweetness, she and Dean both enrapt as the miles unspooled. Transfixed by the girl's laugh, the easy way the two of them spoke to each other. Lacey, her name was—they never caught the father's name through the hours they listened—and she sang beautiful, lilting versions of kids' songs while her father played the guitar. "Twinkle, Twinkle, Little Star" and "The Cat Came Back" and "Puff the Magic Dragon." Katherine found herself weeping at times, weeping for herself and Nick and Matthew, Lacey and her father. Dean and his wife and son. The whole boundless dead world. Somewhere near Salt Lake City they lost the signal for good, and it felt like losing a friend when their voices finally succumbed to waves of static.

So now, midafternoon in a Southern Oregon town with prairie and field and cragged blue mountains beyond. Wild horses spotted here and there among the foothills, the gas stations and tractor trailers.

The tank's on E, and they find a station. Portland is close, less than five hours away if they don't hit a drift or have to backtrack. The sun warms her legs but her body feels stiff, locked up. "I open another can of anything with Jane's face on it, I'm just gonna curl up and die right here," Katherine says.

"I hear you."

They park in the lot. Dean sighs, drums his fingers on the steering wheel. "I want to give whoever's behind the counter an option first, cool?"

"Of course." Katherine makes a face like that's the most reasonable thing in the world.

After their first time strong-arming a gas station attendant, Dean has insisted that they actually try to barter for gas without sticking guns in people's faces. This, she figures, is what passes for morality in the post-Message landscape.

To Katherine's surprise, the gas station attendant, an old man with a glossed wooden cane and colorful rubber bands in the braids of his beard, is amenable to trade. He hobbles out and spends a few minutes cheerfully pointing at various things that Dean's collected, ruminating on his own personal experience with them. When Dean asks, "That mean you want it, then?" he answers with a wheezy, rheumatic "Well, nah, just saying I had one of them before."

After they've spent half an hour out in the parking lot, not another customer coming by, and Dean has pulled every bin out of the truck bed and put them back in, Katherine's halfway considering just walking into the station and turning the pumps on herself, old man be damned. Dean's kept up his patter, matched the old man's gruff-ness with his own upbeat salesman pitch, but even he's at the end of his patience.

"So I guess we can't interest you in anything after all," he says.

The old man hoists his cane at the truck cab. "Well, what you got in there?"

Katherine sighs and opens up the driver's side door, leans in. Picks up the plastic shell of cassettes. "Nothing, really, unless you're into albums like *Legacy of Brutality* or mixtapes with *Devil Rock* written on them."

"Devil rock?"

Katherine holds up the blank cassette.

The old man squints. "You got any George Strait in there? Con-way Twitty? That's real music."

"No, sir."

"Ah," the old man says, runs a gnarled, arthritic hand along the length of wiry beard. "I guess I'll take that propane stove and them canisters you got, then. That ought to be worth a tank."

"You mind if we load up on some water, few cans of soup?" asks Dean. "Been a while since we ate."

"I need a phone too," Katherine says. "You got any burners?"

"Surely do. I suppose that'll work."

Katherine puts the *Devil Rock* cassette in its slot in the case, sets the case on the passenger-side floorboard.

Twenty minutes later they're back on the highway and Katherine calls Bonner with her new phone.

"Yeah?" he says cautiously.

"It's me."

"Good. You ditched the phone. Where are you?"

"Southern Oregon. Couple hours away."

"And you're sure you want to do this?"

She cuts her eyes to Dean, driving. Her story of Matthew—of all of it, getting out of Chicago, Nick, all the madness and heartache of the past five years—was met with a calmness and acceptance that she never would have been able to gather if she were in his shoes. He's saved her twice—first from the hunters in Cape Winston, and then the drift. Saved her a third time by believing her story and deciding to stay. She knows he has his own reasons—the death of his son is entwined with all of it, and the fevered man in the chair, the man he couldn't kill—but gratitude floods her right now, the simple grace that she doesn't have to do this alone.

"I'm sure."

"Good," Bonner says. "Because I think I've got it. Some part of it, anyway."

"Got what?"

"The answer. It was in his notebooks all along."

"Wait, his notebooks? How did you get Matthew's notebooks?"

"Christ, that's a long story in itself. I'll tell you when you get here. But listen, the answer's here, what he's doing. There are sections in this notebook where he just lays it all out. 'Wed the wife, crown the son, devour the light.'"

She remembers that gravelly, strange voice on the phone: *Katherine, you and your son, are you going home?*

"Katherine, we can beat him. It's all here." He sounds manic, ragged. Strung out. Reminds her, honestly, of Matthew in those final hours, how he had crossed some internal line. It comes to her then:

"John, do you have the hand?"

"What?"

"Do you have the remnant with you?"

A pause, and then: "It's down in the car."

"Fucking *why*?"

"We need it."

"Bullshit," Katherine says. "Throw it back in the river. Get rid of it. The hell is the matter with you?"

"Let me ask you something. Is Dean still with you?"

"Yeah. Why?"

"He happen to be a Black guy, maybe forty-five, fifty years old? Slim? Got some gray going at the temples?"

She swallows. The sense of envelopment, of speed as the land whirs by outside the windshield.

"It's him, right?" Bonner says.

In a voice that feels almost disembodied, Katherine says, "How do you know that?"

"Because I saw it. I saw all this. Him, you, me. *Nick.* We all die, Katherine. Everyone dies unless we do this exactly right. He's aiming for hell, or some version of it. That's what he wants. We *need* the remnants to stop him."

"How are we supposed to get in? Through the wall?"

It's Bonner's turn to pause. "I don't know. But I don't think it's going to be a problem."

"What? You don't?"

"He wants us here. Wants *you* here. He needs you."

"Bonner, what was it? 'Wed the wife, crown the son, devour the light.' What does that mean? What's the light?"

"What," Bonner says, "or who. Call me when you get close."

"What are you going to do?"

He sounds, incredibly, like he's smiling. "Me? I got to go kick a nest."

5
KATHERINE AND
THE MONSTER

NAOMI LAURENT

Nevers, Bourgogne-Franche-Comté region, France — Portland, Oregon

Denis in that mud-choked field, after the fevered had stormed their sleeping area, everyone around them dead or overrun. After she'd touched him, pulled the fever from him, he'd looked at her with a mix of wonder and fear and revulsion.

What the fuck are you? Denis had said.

She didn't know then.

Still doesn't.

She had always felt herself a strange girl, with strange things that happened around her, so routinely and often that the strangeness became like another entity in the house. Not dangerous per se, but like a nosy neighbor apt to enter without knocking, suddenly just *there*. She and her father were always the recipients of the strangeness. Never Hugo, never Naomi's mom. It leant a closeness to the two of them; they shared this thing that no one else did.

They hadn't always lived in Nevers. Her father was from Alabama, in the United States. Her parents hadn't even actually married until Naomi was seven, and she kept her mother's name. They'd first met after he had gotten out of the army; he'd been injured at some point and the army had let him leave. Naomi would sometimes ask him if he was in a war when he got hurt, if he had gotten shot, and her father would laugh and say no, nothing like that. And then he would tousle her hair, or point out a funny bird, and the moment would change.

He was older than most of her friends' fathers, and the injuries he'd received still bothered him. He would have a hard time lifting her when she was young, wincing at the stiffness in his arms, and she learned to hug him around the leg instead, the waist when she got taller. He would have to work late sometimes—his job had quarterly deadlines, "boring things with computers and money," he said, and when these deadlines came up, he'd stay at the office. Naomi liked this because although she loved her father very much, with his tattoo and his eyes that crinkled when he laughed, his thin, white-blond beard, they got to go out to eat when he worked late. It was a family tradition, she and her mother and Hugo getting Chinese food, or going to Hippopotamus, which Hugo loved.

Strangeness, though. Once, when Naomi had just turned eight, her father had called to say that he would be working late. Naomi had been drawing at the kitchen table, Hugo in his high chair squeezing applesauce in his fist like he had just discovered magic itself. Her mother had hung up the phone and said, "Well, Nomo, it looks like the three of us will be eating out tonight."

"Daddy's working late?"

"He is."

Not an unusual thing, but as she continued to draw, she felt something itching in the back of her mind. Some unnameable insistence. She sat there, trying to understand, until a picture pushed its way to the front of her mind: her father, gasping, pressed against the steering wheel of their car, his body smashed and broken. Another car going through the stoplight.

A vision with shotgun clarity. She could actually smell blood, hear the *ping* of relaxing metal, the gritty sound of footsteps on glass as people tried to open his door.

She'd started crying, and then Hugo, goggle-eyed with applesauce in his hair, started crying as well. Her mother had run back into the room, flabbergasted. "What is it?"

She told her mother what she'd seen. Her mother, to Naomi's surprise, called her father right away and told him to take the train home. And he had, and had come into her room as she slept that night and hugged her. She'd awoken enough to smell his father-smell of cigarettes and aftershave, to murmur a *Hi, Daddy* into his neck, to be briefly flooded with relief before sleep claimed her again.

They never spoke of it outright, but she was always grateful to her mother for the unquestioning belief she'd shown. Her father took the train the next morning and then drove the car home the next night and everything was fine.

Still, strangeness stacked on strangeness.

On a car ride, Naomi once guessing what four consecutive songs would be on the radio and her father guessing the three following before he got the eighth one wrong. (This event, she remembered, had eventually made her mother cry for a reason that Naomi couldn't understand, and she would wonder later if he'd eventually picked wrong on purpose.)

A year before the Message, she developed an itchy spot on her leg, a few inches above the knee. She scratched and scratched. It was summer, and while the itchy patch grew to be reasonably large, the size of an apple, she assumed that it was a bug bite, infected or something.

She'd finally shown her mother, who had frowned at the red, pebbled patch for a long while, then given her an ice pack. When the area, still itching madly, didn't change the next day, Naomi had been given hydrocortisone. Still no change.

With the itchy patch came strange dreams. Glimpses of her father as a much younger man, his hair blond and short, no white in his beard. No beard at all. He carried a gun.

And a man with a shaved head—no, with no hair at all—and pale skin, curled up in a dark corner, with dark blood rippling down his back.

The last dream was the strongest. In this dream there was heat, screaming, a gray man with wounds scoring his body, a man without a hand.

Naomi woke sweat-soaked, her limbs throbbing, as if they were packed with chips of stone. She had a fever. Her parents gave her medicine and still she dreamt, ached, and finally cried out; the pain had become too much. Next her father was setting her in the bathtub, turning the shower on cold, and that's when they saw the mark on her leg.

Still the size of an apple, still red and pebbled, but now its shape had changed. Naomi, her body twisted in agony, had blacked out, but not before she heard her mother saying to her father the strangest thing: *You did this, damn it.* You *did.*

Her fever broke an hour later. They took her to the hospital anyway. It was busy there, but her pain had subsided enough that she could eat a popsicle the nurse offered her. The mark on her leg still itched a little. It was organic, yet strangely linear. Like a brand, she thought. A rough rectangle with a jagged runner through the middle, like a crook of lightning, or a saw-toothed mountain range. Her mother had wanted the doctor to look at it—she was crying, her fist pressed to her mouth—but her father downplayed it and the doctor shrugged, unconcerned. He sent them home, told her parents that Naomi needed rest, fluids.

Strangeness upon strangeness.

A month later, the mark on her leg had not gone away, but instead had become flat as a birthmark, as if it had been painted on.

"But what *is* it, Mama?" she would ask, and her mother would *tsk* her away. The feel of the house had changed since she'd gone to the hospital. Like she had done something wrong by getting sick. And then her mother, as if understanding what Naomi was thinking, would suddenly step forward and bring her in tightly for a hug.

Her parents argued more. She could never catch the exact words, but the tone and cadence would drift up from the living room like smoke.

She knew they were talking about her. About the mark.

Six months later and the house had grown tight with the tension of things unsaid. They called her Naomi all the time now, never Nomo.

The first time the *shout* happened, her father had been on a work trip. She was riding her bike home from school, down the narrow cobblestone paths between buildings, when a voice spoke inside her head, so strident and with such force it might as well have been spoken beside her:

stop cutting me

And then, louder:

STOP CUTTING ME

She swerved. Her front wheel caught in the narrow space between two stones and Naomi flew over the handlebars. Elbows scraped, one knee shredded, she lay on the ground blinking at the sky.

It wasn't her father they were hurting, though that had been her initial fear. No, it was the bleeding man in the dark corner. The bald, pale-skinned one, the one she'd dreamt about when she had the fever. She knew it without understanding *how* she knew it.

She knew something else: The bleeding from his back, they were wings.

They were his wings, and people kept cutting them off.

That night she scrubbed and scrubbed at her glyph, scrubbed until the whole area at her thigh was inflamed and dotted with minute beads of blood. Then she put bandages on her elbows and her knee, tried to forget about it all.

———

A month later it happened again. This time she was in her bedroom, doing homework. Her father was in the kitchen making dinner, Hugo watching cartoons while her mother did laundry. It was even louder this time, a heaving *shout* in the darkness:

stop it STOP IT STOP IT

Naomi cried out. Her body spasmed; she pushed her tablet to the floor.

Her father bellowed in the kitchen at the same time.

She walked in there, dazed, frightened, her legs trembling— convinced in some way that she would see the man with the sawn- off wings standing there next to him.

But it was just her father grimacing and holding a towel to his hand. He'd lost control of his knife. The smell of simmering onions and garlic hung in the air.

Her mother had burst into the kitchen then. She'd looked at the two of them and hissed at Naomi's father, "You have to tell her, Jer- emy."

"It's nothing."

Her mother was a small woman, but she stormed up to her father and squeezed the towel around his hand. "Tell her."

He winced. "She's too young. She won't understand."

"It *involves* her now. *Please.*"

"Shit, Daphne, alright. Let go, Jesus."

Naomi had stood there, frozen, the clearness of the voice still bright in her head. Her father had frowned down at the towel, cursed under his breath.

"After I clean this up," he said.

Dinner was abandoned. Her mother took Hugo out to eat to give them space. Her father made them quick cheese sandwiches that neither of them touched. Instead he went to the refrigerator and opened a beer, two fingers now wrapped awkwardly in large ban-

dages. He lifted the bottle and drank half of it. He had a worn manila envelope under his arm, the edges soft with age.

He gave her a smile like he was already sorry, then reached in the
envelope and pushed a photo across the table to her.

It was a picture of him. He wore a giant parka, the hood ringed in
fur; he looked like a doll with his face poking out of the jacket's
hood. Young and happy, he had wire-rimmed glasses and a big smile.
No beard. She looked up from the photo. The man in front of her
seemed so old in comparison.

He smiled, like he could tell what she was thinking. "Look pretty
good, don't I?"

"You look like a teenager."

"I practically was," he said, smiling. "I was twenty-three. Can you
imagine being twenty-three?"

"No," Naomi admitted.

"Me neither," her father said. "Not anymore." He smiled when he
said it, but she could tell he was sad. He took another drink of his
beer, those two bandaged fingers sticking out stiffly. The overhead
light cast sharp shadows across his face.

"I was stationed—I was with the army—in Greenland. An Air
Force base. See that jacket I'm wearing?"

"It's big."

"It's up in the Arctic, it's almost all ice there. You had to wear
jackets like that or you'd freeze."

"Wait, it's an Air Force base? But you were in the army?"

Her father nodded. "I was part of a unit there doing training. The
Air Force guys were teaching us things about their vehicles. Do you
know what a motor pool is, Naomi?"

"Like trucks and stuff. A garage."

He father winked. "You're smart, kid." He seemed a little more
relaxed and not as worried, and this made Naomi not as worried too.
"So, I was being trained in the motor pool, because the army wanted
my unit, my guys, to know how to make our vehicles run in cold

weather. The Air Force mechanics at Thule were teaching us. The idea was that we would train for three weeks, then get sent to our own bases to run the motor pools there."

"So you didn't fight," Naomi said, unable to keep the disappointment out of her voice.

"No, sweets, I didn't fight. Thank goodness." He drained his beer and got up to take out another bottle. She waited as she heard the pop and hiss of it, her father stepping on the garbage can and dropping the bottle cap inside. He sat back down.

"That picture was taken almost forty years ago. Crazy to think." He sighed and slowly exhaled, rubbed at his throat for a moment with his free hand. "I'm going to show you another picture now, and you're going to have a lot of questions. And that's cool, I'd have a ton of questions too if I were you." He leaned forward a little bit, and behind his glasses, his eyes were kind. She felt safe looking at his face. The tight feeling of the house the past six months seemed to loosen. "But you might also be a little scared, and I want to tell you that you shouldn't be. Mommy and I will protect you. That's our entire job. That's our most *important* job."

She smiled. He and her mother had said this bit—*It's our most important job*—since she was small, and they had started saying it to Hugo too when he got scared. She loved its simplicity, how they sounded both playful and very serious when they said it.

"More important than working at the bank?"

"Way more."

"More important than Mom making X-rays at the hospital?"

"Oh yes," her father said. "Like I said, the most important one of them all."

"Okay," Naomi said, and then smiled at him. "Can I have a beer?"

"No, you may not." He didn't smile back like she thought he would. "Are you ready? This is a scary picture, but I want you to remember that everything's okay now. Do you understand?"

"Yes," she said, all her good feeling suddenly gone, but it was too late to say stop. Her father reached into the manila envelope and pushed another photo across the table.

Him, still young, but in a hospital bed this time. Both arms in casts up to his shoulders and hung up by pulleys to keep them elevated. Dark stitches marring his lip. The camera flash turned his eyes red. A man in a white coat took up a third of the photograph, standing blurry in the foreground. Naomi's heart ran cold.

"What happened? How did you get hurt?"

"Hold on," her father said, and took out another photograph.

One of those old kinds, with the white frames—Polaroids. The image was washed out and pale, like it had been taken in a bright room. Her father was sitting in a folding chair, in army pants and an olive-green T-shirt. An ankle cocked on a knee, a cigarette between two fingers. He was growing out his beard. He was still young but he looked older here, with some of the careworn qualities to his face she would come to cherish so much as his daughter.

But his eyes looked frightened, somehow, drawn into themselves.

Her breath caught.

There on his arm was a raised, pebbled rash. The skin inflamed.

The same rectangular glyph on his forearm. The same swooping gesture contained within, like a mountain cleaved in half.

Naomi's scalp prickled with sweat.

"Your tattoo," she said in a voice that seemed to come from far away.

He held out his arm, showed her the tattoo of the knife, wings sprouting from each side of the handle. But then she squinted, pulling his wrist forward to get a better look, and beneath the tattoo ink, like a mirage, was something you couldn't see unless you were looking for it: the same image as hers.

She reared back, her eyes searching his face. "Papa, what *is* it?"

"I don't know," he said. And then, just when the silence became unbearable, he seemed to make some decision, and he told her the rest.

He'd been going into one of the garages, a large, cavernous room with tall steel shelves along the walls, shelves filled with parts and gear and materials. His team was fixing a snowplow, a huge one, working late in a nearby building, and her father had been sent by another mechanic to retrieve a part from one of the shelves. It was well below freezing outside. He wore that puffy coat with the furry fringe, and also gloves and goggles; you could go snow-blind in the space between buildings if you weren't careful. Frostbitten and dead ten feet away from a door.

He'd gone into that garage and hit the lights, the room flooding with illumination. Right away he felt something was off. Wrong.

He found the man hiding between two Jeeps.

The man had been crouched, one knee resting on the concrete, light gleaming off the blood smeared across his body. Entirely nude, his hands curled around his head, body thrumming like a loose wire. Drugs, her dad figured. Some grunt who got his hands on something and it had gone bad for him. But the *feeling* in the place, her father felt almost ill with it. Like being near a giant magnet, all your organs being throttled from the inside.

"Sir?" he'd said, some part of him resorting to formality when faced with the unbridled oddness of it all. While the man had an awful lot of blood on him, there was no trail, no pooling.

The man lifted his head and Naomi's father had taken a step back: The face was pale, beautiful, like something carved from soap.

"Hey," her father said, putting out a gentle hand, as if approaching a wounded animal. That was still the idea he was running with—the man was clearly not in his right mind. He crept closer again, keeping that hand out, then reached down and touched the man's shoulder.

"Listen, let's get you up—"

The man's mouth opened, and her father froze.

"There will be a grand leveling," the man said, clear and precise. "A depravity. A house of fever and wounds. And I am to watch, to *only* watch. And yet." His voice was plaintive and high, anguished. His eyes searched Naomi's father's face.

"Okay," her father said softly. One hundred percent a PCP run, he decided. But where was the blood coming from? He realized then, *Oh shit, what if it isn't* this guy's *blood at all? What if he did this to someone else?* He wanted to leave and get his CO, grab guys from the other building, but what if this guy wandered outside. He'd die in minutes out there. "Listen, why don't we—"

"And yet," the man said again. "The girl, if she is wise and careful, will make the house fall. Remember it."

"The girl, huh? Alright, man, what I need you to do—"

And then this bloody, naked man had risen, seized Naomi's father, squeezing his forearms until the ulna and radius bones broke as smartly as someone smacking a pair of dinner plates against the lip of a counter.

"Why did he hurt you?" Naomi asked that night at the kitchen table.

"I don't know," her father answered. "I've thought about it a lot, Nomo. I don't know if I needed to be hurt somehow so this could happen," and here he gestured at the tattoo, "or if he meant to, I don't know, convey something to me."

"I don't know what 'convey' means."

"If he meant to give me something, and either was too wounded to do it softly, or he had to hurt me to pass this along. Whatever this is." He shrugged, gesturing at his tattoo, the image beneath. "Or maybe it was an accident."

"Did he leave you there?"

"He sat back down. My CO finally came in looking for me and heard me screaming—I was in a lot of pain, rolling around on the ground—and then the MPs got called and they tackled him. I never saw him again."

"Who was he?"

Her father smiled. "You're asking good questions, sweets. I wish I knew. My CO just told me that folks from the Pentagon flew out and took him away. I got sent to a hospital in Washington, DC, and had to do a lot of interviews with people about what happened. And then there was that mark on my arm when I got my cast off. The same one you've got on your leg."

"What did the army say about it?"

"They had me do lots of tests, but the strange things that happened—the things that happen to you and me, like with the songs on the radio—didn't start until a long time later. After you were born."

She'd sat in front of her father then, feeling locked in, trapped. The story she'd just heard didn't make her feel any better. Made her feel worse, in fact.

"Is that him in my head? That's him yelling?"

He had raised his eyebrows. "I don't think he's talking *to* us, exactly. But yes, that's him."

"Why?"

Her father sighed, ran a hand down his face. "Because they're hurting him."

"Who is?"

Her father puffed out his cheeks and exhaled slowly, and any other time Naomi would have thought this was funny. "I think two beers is enough," he said, and then laid his palms flat on the table and lifted his eyes to her. "When I was there on the floor next to him? With my arms broken? He put his fingers against my neck, his bloody fingers. And I saw God, Naomi. I swear it. As close to God as I can understand. Everyone's gotten the idea of God wrong. A robe, a beard, all of that silliness. No, it's not like that. I saw God, Naomi, and I saw you. As a baby. As you are now. And older too. And as I saw all that, that man said, 'She is the light.'"

Her father stood up and went to the sink, poured himself a glass of water. He looked stooped and wrung-out but somehow less sad too. Like he was glad to have finally gotten it all out.

"So he was talking about me? When he talked about a girl who was wise and careful?" She found this idea both thrilling and terrifying.

"I think so."

"What does it *mean*, though? What's a house of fever and wounds?"

Her father had set his glass in the sink. "Again, you ask good questions."

She frowned. "That means you don't know."

He turned to her and smiled. "Oh, there's *so* much I don't know. But I know that you're loved, Naomi, and safe. You and Hugo, always. All this other stuff, we'll manage it together, the whole family. Okay?"

"Okay."

Strange things continued. Small things. Knowing exactly how many pages there were in a book she'd just picked up. The outfit a stranger would be wearing when she turned the corner. How many red cars on a street. It became less scary eventually.

And then the Message. Her mom, Hugo. The year of wandering, and then Denis. Naomi thought of it often: *There will be a grand leveling. A depravity. A house of fever and wounds. And yet the girl, if she is wise and careful, will make the house fall. Remember it.*

Things had become clear after she pulled the sickness from Denis. The automatic, intuitive way she knew how to do it.

And clearer still when she heard Marsden at the horse track. How he'd called the place a fever house.

Of course.

A house of fever and wounds, and she will make the house fall.

This is her purpose, then.

It's always been her purpose. To end all of this, somehow.

Impossible not to think of her father as they approach the walled city of Portland. How he and the image on her leg and what she can do are all bound together, all twisted, her past and present and future all hopelessly entwined. She is not so old that she doesn't wish that he was there with her now, that he might guide her toward some safer passage. As if there were a clear and right choice in all of this. She sees the same nightmarish mishmash of steel and timber and concrete that made up the wall in Boise. The same spikes and pyres of glass and wire on top.

It is night, and raining, and the sound of it hammers the roof.

Marsden, there in the dashboard light, has become a monster in the passenger seat.

He's had Canino root through the bins in the back of the Humvee and now wears a poncho with a hood, and as they slow to a stop at the guard station before the wall, she can hear its plastic creaking as Marsden's body shifts and changes. Hear the occasional *pap* of blood falling on it. He holds Antoine with hands more claws than anything now. She's almost acclimated to the adrenaline flooding through her, the way her brain keeps insisting she run, run.

But no. She won't leave the child. Not after all this. Even as tears blur her vision, as terror stills her.

They pull up to the gate and Marsden's arm creeps out—pale white, the sleeve of his dress shirt pink and wet. He hands Canino his ID.

The guard steps out of his tin shack, rain jumping off his helmet in fat drops, and peers in at them, frowning. "I don't know who you are, but you folks need to turn back. Authorized personnel only."

"Just run the card," Canino says. Naomi hears his own fear humming through every word.

The soldier looks at him sharply, but then takes in Canino's fatigues and the name and title on the ID he's just been handed. He runs it through the reader on his hip; they all hear the beep, and he hands it back. He trots back into the shack and after a moment, the wall begins sliding back.

And then the four of them are driving through that dark mouth, into the city beyond, and the wall is closing behind them.

THEO MARSDEN
Portland, Oregon

Marsden has been pushed to the edge of his own consciousness. A witness. The thing that moves *through* and *within* his body knows that this is the most vulnerable time, this halfway point between becoming and not.

He—the ancient, veiled thing that has occasionally managed similar hijackings of human bodies throughout the centuries—tries to hold on to the ID with Marsden's wet, misshapen fingers and can't manage it. It falls to the floorboard and Marsden makes no attempt to pick it up. The physical trappings of this place matter less and less by the minute.

Marsden's phone rings and he fishes it out. This, at least, he can do. "Yes," he answers, in a mouth slowly being crowded with more teeth, a shelf of jaw that's become nearly snout-like.

"Theo?" Yardley says.

"Hello, Preston."

Marsden tries to *push* to the forefront then. He's dismayed at how easily the thing shoves him back down.

"Theo," Yardley says, "you son of a bitch. The warden in Boise tells me you brained some fevered in there. That you're, I don't know. Sick or something."

"Sick," Marsden chortles. There are perhaps a dozen small yellow teeth growing in the dark flesh of his tongue and he clicks them against the roof of his mouth.

A pause, and then Yardley keeps going. "Theo, Jack Bonner's died from his injuries. I'm pulling the plug on the whole affair. Coffin's dead and I doubt that girl's actually capable of what intelligence claimed, or that she'll live too long in your care. I've issued standing orders to arrest you for sedition, and if you resist, I've greenlit to shoot your traitorous ass dead. Steve Stater's taking charge of the Providence Initiative, and you've stepped right into a court-martial. Pray to the lord for mercy, Theo, because you'll find none with me." He hangs up.

The thing laughs.

Not Marsden anymore, and never really Coffin at all. Coffin nothing more than a suit it wore for a while.

The phone rings again and it pokes at the screen with a taloned finger, hooting wetly. Gleeful at all this *attention*. The call connects and it makes some grunt appropriating a greeting.

"Matthew? Hi, this is John Bonner."

"Bonner," it says like a branch breaking.

"I don't know if anyone at Terradyne ever talked about me while you were hiding down in that hole in Rolla, but I'm the guy that's gonna put a fucking bullet through your teeth."

When the Marsden-thing laughs, the sound is like bones cracking apart.

"Oh, you like that? Great. Get a load of this: I know you got a lot of moving parts to make this little 'hell on earth' thing of yours work. I'm not gonna make it easy for you. You meet me at the loft—the one where you started all of this—or I take a hacksaw to Katherine Moriarty, how's that? Try 'wedding a wife' when she doesn't have a head, my man. Something tells me that's gonna put a monkey wrench in your shit."

It clamors with outrage now, with fear, and the baby curled in its broken, bloody hands opens his eyes wide and *howls* against the noise of it. The girl begins weeping in the backseat.

"The loft," Bonner says. "One hour, you sad little motherfucker."

He hangs up and the thing drops the phone to the floorboard. Arches its back against the seat and howls, everyone in the Humvee screaming along with it. "Sir," Canino says beside him, crying now himself, "do you—" and the Marsden-thing turns and vomits a great jet of black blood onto Canino's neck and arm and the console between their two seats. Naomi screams again, Canino letting out a kind of breathless moan even as he manages to keep driving. Marsden coughs and more blood sprays out from between his teeth like water through a sewer grate, splashes across the inside of the windshield, the child's face.

All this while Marsden's memories and Coffin's memories and the memories of a hundred others are rifled through and discarded like a man flicking through his suits. Marsden, the *true* Marsden, his essence a dying ember now, feels sorrow curl through him. Sees Barbara, sees Jack. Sees Berliner with his brains splashed on the door of the bathroom stall. Sees Coffin pressing his tongueless mouth to his own. The *transfer*.

Marsden tries to push forward one more time but manages nothing. What began in the Rolla labyrinth nears its completion. The thing vomits blood down its own chest again, onto the child. The skin along the backs of its hands splits. The wrinkles on the back of its neck open further, watery blood spilling down.

Canino, shrieking, has finally had enough. He opens the driver's side door of the Humvee, coasting, and the thing reaches out an arm and hooks a clawed hand around his neck. Pulls him back inside.

The creature leans forward, jaws drizzling blood. Gets right up into the gunman's face. It is so close to finishing now, it can feel it, can feel the nearness of everything here. The remnants, the wife, the son, the light, all this *time* spent waiting—

"The fever house," it says. Words like a bottle broken on cement.

Canino, gibbering, sobbing: "I, I don't know where it—"

"I'll tell you."

It leads them to the convention center.

Some interior pulse as its guide. It's a large building, a scatter of train tracks like sutures and the jagged teeth of downtown visible in the gloom. Rings of sandbags around the place, the windows boarded up. Entries blockaded. A building simplified, made into a box. A storage tank.

There are spray-painted arrows on the ground, lit up white and gleaming in the headlights, that direct them to the entrance. Marsden's body by this point is a scaffolding of ripped, split flesh. It gestures at the arrows, grunts; speech is becoming difficult now. Limbs elongating, the sound of cracking bone loud inside the Humvee. The baby's face is blood-spattered. The son. The son.

They stop at the entrance, the headlights lighting up the steel doors. It holds the child to its chest and turns to Naomi, pushing the hood of the poncho down. She screams, pushing her head against the back of the seat.

"Come," it rasps, ropes of black blood hanging off its jaws. It hoists the baby up by the wadded fabric of his outfit and rattles him a bit, a dog with a toy in its jaws. The implication is clear. The child's head wobbles this way and that, screeching in outrage.

The four of them step out into the rain and make their way to the doors. The thing rips the poncho off, drops it to the ground, where it catches the wind and skitters away. Marsden's body has grown taller by six inches or more, and the dress shirt he wore has ripped across the creature's widened back. Glistening sores salt its body, showing hints of yellow bone beneath. Curls of flesh hang loose. It's shedding.

It pounds on the door with a fist marred with an extra knuckle on each finger. The sound reverberates. The gunman and the girl crouch behind the thing. A slot in the door slides back and a man's face peers out at them from inside the building.

"What the fu—"

The thing makes a shelf of its hand, a flat plane with four shattered black talons at the end of them, and drives it through the slot and into the man's face. His eyes. He shrieks and falls back and someone else shuts the slot. The baby bucks against the creature's body.

It walks on legs grown stick-thin over to one of the plywood sheets placed over the windows. Setting the baby down with a surprising carefulness, it leaps up onto the sandbags bracing the plywood and wraps its fingers around the edge of the wood. Hangs there for a moment before it puts a foot against the outer wall and *pulls*. The plywood screaming over the sound of the rain.

A volley of rounds punch through the wood, and Naomi moans and covers her ears. The thing drops to the ground, fingertips tenting against the concrete, protecting her and the child both. When the gunfire pauses, it pivots, whip-fast, and jumps onto the sandbags again, then pulls on the corner of the plywood until a large section of it cracks and cleanly breaks off.

The interior of the building: floodlights, cement floors, everything carved down to a bare utility.

It senses the thousands of supplicants inside, their fever-rot like a song in its mind.

There is a hierarchy of devils and this one, this devil, minor and shunted to the side, has begun this ritual many times—*the hand the eye the voice a house of fever and wounds*—but has never come so close to finishing it. To bringing about a new and blood-lashed world, one of its very own.

It picks up the baby and clambers over the sandbags.

Turning, it looks at the gunman and the girl. "Stay," it croaks, and hoists the child. This will be the last thing it says. Its jaw gives one final crack, some final internal shift, now no longer capable of supporting speech. It walks inside.

Striding down the hall of the convention center, it holds the child to its chest. Most of the soldiers see it—the distended ruin of Marsden's face, its ragged clothes, the clots of flesh hanging from its body, wens and boils and elongated hands—and simply run. Some—not many, but some—fire upon it, even as it clutches a child. These are dispatched with a few bounds of its stick-legs, a clawed hand driven into their hearts.

Soon it stands outside the massive double doorways to one of the ballrooms, and the thing that was Theodore Marsden tilts its head and thinks, *Come to me.*

Thinks, *You will be my hounds.*

It is so near now. So close.

It hacks at the doors with the blade of its free hand until they are weak enough and its supplicants, the thousands of them inside the ballroom, are able to push through.

It walks down the hall to the next ballroom and its supplicants follow, single-minded as the blood through a beating heart.

Then to the final ballroom, and they follow still. The Marsden-thing turns and wends its way through them all, thousands of cold bodies trapped in their half-lit place between death and not death, passing among them like water around stones.

It returns to the front door of the collation center, the first dead man's body a scrawl on the ground. It lifts the steel panic bar laid across the door, throws it open.

Stepping out into the rain, the blood on the child's face washes away in threads.

The girl and the gunman are surrounded now by three soldiers in Terradyne fatigues.

It gestures—almost dismissively—and a dozen supplicants charge them and tackle the soldiers, knock them to the ground. Devour them amid their screams. The girl and the gunman both left weeping and untouched, cowering in the rain.

Some will stay with it, act as its army. Its foot soldiers. To the rest, it says, *Go. Go out there and make me a king's house.*

It gathers the girl and the gunman behind it with a sweep of those arms, a gesture of containment, as its thousands of supplicants begin moving out into the rain, along the arteries of the city.

KATHERINE MORIARTY

Portland, Oregon

They come to the eastern outskirts of the city. The truck moving along the freeway with its line of cars bracing the shoulders. Katherine dials Bonner again.

"We're here."

"Good," Bonner says. "Have you come to the wall yet?"

"Almost."

"If it's not open when you get there, I'll head over there and try to open it for you. But I think he's ready."

Bonner waits with her on the phone as they drive.

They come to the guard shack, the wall. She inhales sharply, the seatbelt tightening as Dean reflexively hits the brakes.

The wall is wide open. They see fevered roaming the dark, staggering along the street.

"What the hell," Dean hisses. "What the hell." Beyond the wall, inside, they glimpse dottings of flames, the sky glowing with them, and shapes of people bent and skulking in the shadows.

"Bonner," Katherine says. "It's open."

"Okay," he says. Dean slowly passes the abandoned guard shack, then they're through the wall. A fevered paces the truck for a moment, almost gracefully tracing lines in the window glass with her fingertips, and then they're past her. They're listening to the DEVIL ROCK mixtape that Dean had gotten in that house outside of Cape Winston, and "Sympathy for the Devil" is playing. It all seems cloyingly, maddeningly ironic now, a tape full of songs about the devil, and Katherine turns the volume down on the stereo. Her breathing's pinched, like her throat's been winnowed down to this narrow aperture.

"I need you to meet me," Bonner says.

"Oh, I can't do this," she says softly, terror blooming, thinking about how she's ruined everything she's touched, ruined her son, ruined her marriage, ruined—somehow, with that stupid fucking *song*—the entire world.

"You can," Dean says softly beside her. He stops the truck. Distant fire smears bands of light across their windshield. The fevered stalk and twist in the gloom; a string of perhaps a dozen of them spy some motion up the street and sprint after it in that shambolic, broken way of theirs. The close press of buildings on each side, the narrow alleys.

"I *can't*." She wipes at her mouth with her knuckles, hot tears spilling down her face. Her hands slowly come to rest at her throat. The panic feels insurmountable, like something pressing down on her shoulders, pushing her toward the earth. Rage is not enough, she realizes. She thought it could be, but no. Revenge is not enough.

Softer still, Bonner says over the phone, "You can, Katherine. You have to. There's no other way—"

"John, can you just give me a second, please? Jesus."

"We don't have time for this shit, Katherine. He wants to end the world."

She pushes down a sudden urge to laugh. Wants to tell him that Matthew Coffin couldn't balance a checkbook, that he played guitar like a savant but typed with two fingers, that he once wooed her by buying a handwritten Patti Smith poem off a rare books dealer in

Greenpoint. *Bonner, he fucking drank beer in the shower,* she wants to say. *And you're telling me that's the man who wants to end the world?*

But she knows he's right. That Matthew's gone. Been gone a long time.

"I'm just scared as shit," she says.

"I know," Bonner says. He leaves the rest unspoken, but it's there, freighted and irrevocable: It doesn't matter. We have to do it anyway.

JOHN BONNER

Portland, Oregon

Sitting in his idling car in front of the loft where Matthew Coffin dismembered himself so many years ago, Bonner listens to rain pounding the roof. Checks the time on his phone constantly, punctuated by the occasional *foomp* of an explosion, the off-time chatter of gunfire. He sees a truck approaching and flicks his headlights, his mouth sour with fear. The pickup comes to a stop at the curb opposite the loft and a man gets out of the driver's side. Cold goes through Bonner's body when he recognizes Dean from his vision. *That man's gonna bleed,* he thinks, then curses himself for it; fear making him ungenerous, but there's nothing to do about it now. And then, God, there's Katherine. Hair gray-threaded now, all the softness burned from her face. She crosses the street to his car. Another crumpling explosion drifts through the night and it's like the fever house has never ended. Like they're all destined to endlessly relive the post-Message hours. As if it will always be night and there will always be things ripping the night apart and Bonner will forever be feeling like he's just a little too late to stop whatever comes next.

She gets in the passenger seat. Dean gets in the back. Bonner, feeling foolish, sticks a hand over his shoulder. Dean shakes.

"Been a while," he says to Katherine. Aiming for a kind of off-handed casualness that belies the pants-shitting terror he's feeling.

"Did you kick your nest?" is all she says.

"Oh yeah. He's pissed. I don't know how he's moving around, but I gave him an hour."

"How long ago was that?"

Bonner looks at his phone. "Forty-five minutes ago."

"Jesus."

"I mean, I doubt he's got a watch on him. The sounds I heard made it seem like, uh, he's going through some shit. Punctuality's probably not real concerning." Casting a glance over his shoulder, he says, "Did Katherine fill you in on any of this, man?"

"I mean, as much as one could actually grasp any of this insanity, yes she did," Dean says. Bonner in the rearview sees him rub at a spot above his eyebrow. "But I'm wondering about this hand you were talking about. Is that what I'm feeling? Because I feel pretty fucking weird right now, man."

"That's John's doing," Katherine says drily. "He's got a remnant in the trunk. Just try to ignore it."

Dean laughs. "Devil hand in the trunk. Ignore it. Right." He lets out a slow, shaky breath.

Bonner pulls the notebook from between his seat and the console. Hands it to her.

"I don't want to read this," she says.

He takes it from her, opens it to a page. "The eye, the hand, the voice. The ritual he did, it needed these three remnants for Matthew to change. These three dismemberments. The carved symbols on the body, his fugue-states, all that. That was the first step. That let the thing in, let it inhabit Matthew after he, you know."

"After he killed himself?"

"This thing drove him to that, Katherine. I believe it." He flips to another page, dense with scrawls. "Now we have this: 'Wed the wife, crown the son, devour the light.' Whatever's coming next, that's the big thing. That's what it's going to try to do." He remembers the man in Katherine's apartment. *He's coming here, John, and you will be the one to open hell's door for him.*

Katherine shakes her head, closes her eyes. "Jesus Christ, Bonner."

"Listen," Dean says. "I am not doing great right now."

"Just hang in there," Bonner offers. "It's only got the one trick, just push it down."

"So if I'm the wife," Katherine says, "who's the son? Nick? Nick's not here. And what's the light?"

"I don't know."

"Well, those seem like pretty fucking vital questions, don't you think? Goddamn, that hand is driving me nuts. How do you stand it?"

"We need the remnants. I think if we destroy them while this thing's doing whatever it is it's trying to do, we'll hurt it. Kill it, even."

"But you only have two," Katherine says.

"The hand and the eye. Jack told me the recording was never found after the Message. I don't think there're any duplicates."

"So we're screwed. We don't even know what he *is* anymore." He sees the hopelessness on her face, remembers the flat, bombed-out look she wore when he trundled a bound and fevered Nick off the airplane years ago. Like all was lost.

"Listen," he says, "I think *he* needs all three remnants for this to work too. So if we get him here and we trap him, maybe destroying two's enough for us. Maybe that helps us. He needs all the remnants, but he *also* needs the wife, the son, the light. If he doesn't have them all, maybe he's too weak."

"Well, what happens if he gets them? What happens if he manages to, you know, *devour the light*? I mean, look around you. Look at what happened the first time. What can be worse than this?"

Oh, but that's Katherine bullshitting herself. She knows that it can always get worse.

In the backseat, with a dragging edge to his voice, Dean says, "It's great that you folks can be so casual about this feeling, but I am about to freak the fuck out. I got maybe another minute in this car before I do something stupid. What *exactly* is the plan?"

"The loft is right there. We take the remnants and go in—"

"What if he's already inside?" Katherine says.

"He's not. So we get him in there, we lock him in, and when he goes for Katherine, we destroy the hand and the eye. And then we drop him."

"Thin," Dean mutters. Bonner lets it go; the man's right.

Katherine looks at him, assessing. "And you're willing to do that?"

"Do what?"

"You could have destroyed them whenever, John. But you chose not to."

Bonner laughs, looks away. He feels a flare of defensiveness; but again, she's right. He rolls his window down a bit to get some cool air before he says something he'll regret.

And then they hear it, through the open car window.

A kind of monstrous sighing, a sound almost buried beneath the bleat of car alarms and gunfire.

"What *is* that?" Katherine says, almost whispering, eyes white in the gloom.

"That," Dean says, "is a drift. Big one too. Coming this way."

THEO MARSDEN

Portland, Oregon

t had been a man once. Before it became a devil, a thing that exists *between*.

Dim memories of that short period of life are buried there beneath the catalog of bodies it has inhabited, the lost, broken people it's convinced to perform its bloody rites. There had been some kind of life before all of that, blood and bone, sorrows and joys.

It had been a man once.

But the shambling string of centuries have hung a dark veil over that first, initial life. If there was a betrayal that brought about this strange transition, these exacting demands of ritual, it no longer remembers. What leap that took place from manhood to this half-life, it cannot recall.

It is almost entirely driven by *sense* now. Intuition, an innate knowledge. While waiting in that box underground, it had heard the man talk about the girl who could "turn them back," and understood immediately. *Moved* immediately, seized the moment. *She* was the light; the son was a malleable aspect of the ritual, the wife less so, but the light, the devouring of the light, was absolute.

It had lured the old man—his was a weaker body than the Coffin one, reborn as it was, but better suited for the task of traveling. It had gone forth with the girl, the light, and—perfect, perfect, a son ready-made—the child. All the touchstones needed to complete its becoming, and the world had fallen before it like fronds in a hurricane.

Now, here. All the remnants are near, all three of them.

This too is sensed, a glottal thumping in the spoiled meat of its brain, and the thing strides quickly down the avenue, eager to finish this long and complicated task. It had been a man once, and then it had been cheated in some manner, been wronged—the details are lost, distorted by time, but the *feeling* is there, a ghost of pain. It is a devil by name, by desire, one cowled in bitterness and fury, one forever seeking vengeance, a mantle of its own. By wedding the wife and crowning the son and devouring the light, it will forge a kingdom, a new and burning world culled from this one. It stretches its stick-legs along the street, eats up the distance, black froth lacing its split lips. It grips the weeping gunman by his arm; if the infant should die, *this* will be the crowned son. The girl, the light, struggles behind, but the army at her back demands she keep up lest she be swallowed.

It will be wed and will perform the rituals to continue its bloodline through the child it has carefully kept alive, and it will devour all that is lasting and pure of this strange and truculent girl's abilities, this envoy of the light, and then the world will become its house. A king's house, where fire ripples across the sky in sheets and it wears a necklace of heads and if it says *Offer your neck to me,* anyone will raise their throat for the cutting simply because it was demanded.

A place where other devils will court it for entrance. Will beg. Those same devils that once mocked and cajoled and flung it away.

It strides the darkened streets, drawn to that loft where Matthew Coffin spent his final days. Where he completed the first phase of the ritual—the hand the voice the eye.

Its army follows behind. Thousands deep, filling the streets, snaking down alleyways, stragglers distracted by the screams of human witnesses that peer stunned from doorways, the group as a whole remaining true and loyal.

It sees the loft, finally, that darkened doorway, the steel panels of the bay doors beside it. The egg-like knobs at its cheeks split open and spill a viscous, clotted yellow fluid. Wet, skeletal forms tremble inside the craters. The girl shrinks back, tries to turn away, but it holds on to her arm easily. Its tooth-studded tongue wipes the scud of blood and froth from its mouth and it looses a ragged croak of victory.

It has never been as close as this.

It will make a king's house, and it will rule them all.

DEAN HAGGERTY

Portland, Oregon

Bonner shoots the lock and Dean takes in their surroundings: a whirl of cement floors, a table and chair, a mouse-gnawed futon in the gloom, everything furred in dust. "Can't see shit in here," Bonner mutters, hoisting a duffel bag onto the table. He zips it open—that godforsaken clamor in Dean's brain kicking up a notch—and takes out a shotgun.

"Got a lantern in the truck," Dean says. "Electric one."

Bonner cuts his eyes to the door. "You got a gun?"

He gestures at the doorway. "I mean, the lantern's just right there, man. In the truck bed, even."

"You got a gun, though?"

Dean pulls the fever hunter's pistol from his waistband. Swears he can hear that tidal, rasping sound getting closer. They don't have much time.

"Alright," Bonner says, and Dean trots across the street, over to the truck. Rifling through his bins, he finds the lantern. Scans the street, smells smoke. Hears screams, gunfire. Someone runs by at the end of the block, their footfalls loud and distinct.

When this Matthew Coffin arrives, how's he gonna do it? Gonna pop out of a Chevy Nova? Arrive on a chariot pulled by a dozen flaming skeletons? Dean has the distinct sense that Bonner's out of his depth here, and Katherine, justifiably, is top-floor terrified. The rigidity of her face, the wooden way in which she's moving around. Dean's moving on a sort of autopilot himself: If he thinks about it too much, truly tries to discern why he's here at all, he's going to freeze up. He steps back into the loft, puts the lantern on the table. It's a sphere of white light that does little to illuminate the corners of the room, but it's better than nothing.

Bonner's taken everything out of the duffel bag, laid it all on the table. A couple boxes—one of them throbbing sickeningly in his mind—some cheap notebooks, a sheathed knife. Box of shotgun shells. Katherine touches the front of one of the notebooks, doesn't open it. She's taking her own pistol out, when Bonner says "Holy shit" at the doorway.

Dean's heart flips. He walks on watery legs over to the door. A few blocks down he sees a few stragglers at first, rounding the corner, and then a *sea* of fevered that spills out into the street, soon spanning from one sidewalk to the other. They keep coming. Dean's heart stutters—it makes the drift they saw on the highway look like nothing. This is a boundless wall of bodies ambling toward them.

Leading the fevered walks a man.

Man, though, seems a loose suggestion at best. It must be seven feet tall, a batshit-crazy amalgam of alabaster, stick-like limbs and clotted, weeping flesh. The thing's head stands on a pale stalk of neck. Even from this distance, a block and a half away, Dean can see strange organs thrumming beneath the drum-tight skin of its belly. It walks next to a weeping, shorn-headed man in Terradyne fatigues—*Jesus Christ, it's the kid from Cape Winston*—and it has a spider-like hand wrapped around the arm of a young, dark-haired girl. Dean squints in the meager streetlight. The thing holds something to his chest.

"Is that Matthew," Katherine says breathlessly, pressing in behind him, defeat and terror and a looming madness scribbled all through her voice. "Oh God, he has a baby, that's the *son*, John, he doesn't need Nick at all, he's got a *baby,* that can't be Matthew, can it—"

Suddenly the weeping soldier bolts forward, legs pumping, his eyes skating across the loft's doorway for only a second before he runs to the pickup parked across the street.

No one follows him. The creature continues its long-legged stride. The fevered follow at their own shambling pace. The shorn-headed man yanks open the truck's door and jumps in. Slams it shut. Turns the engine, slapping madly at the driver's side door lock. He scrabbles across the seat, slapping at the passenger door lock as well, his whole body infused with panic.

And then something happens.

The interior of the cab is suddenly filled with noise, the muted sound of someone talking. Loud.

The soldier in the truck suddenly sits up, goes rigid, presses the back of his head against the rear window and *screams*.

"What is that?" Katherine whispers, stepping back deeper into the loft, her fingers briefly squeezing Dean's bicep and then letting go. "What *is* that—"

"That's the Message," Bonner says, his eyes widening in horror, shot through with the sudden weight of understanding. "That's the last remnant, how the fuck is it here—"

"The tape," Dean says dreamily, his voice sounding like it's coming from underwater. They can't make out specific words in the truck, just the volleys of bass throb, consonants. He knows that if they could hear it any more clearly, they'd be clawing at their faces too. At each other.

"What?"

"He hit the volume knob on the stereo just now. The mixtape. We'd been listening to a mixtape—"

"I don't know what you're—"

"*Devil Rock,*" Dean says. Not wanting to believe it. Not wanting to *understand* it. "That's—that's the Message on there?" He looks over at Katherine. "I fucking picked that tape up in *Massachusetts,* in some teenager's *bedroom,* how in the *hell—*"

And then, at the end of the block, the stick-man swivels its terrible, bulbous head toward the door. The squalling child held cradled in one arm, the dark-haired girl dragged behind. Even from this distance, he sees its eyes settle on them. Feels ice flood his blood.

"We got to turn that shit off," Dean says. The man in the truck screams, claws at his face. He writhes, flails, and then, holy *shit,* Dean hears the telltale *thunk.*

"Dean—"

"He just pulled the hood release," he says. "Flailing around. Just pulled it with his foot, I guess." He looks back at them. "I can turn the stereo off."

"Dean—"

"I got this," he says, thinking of the man in the chair, Nichole on the day she walked out. Thinking of George, mostly. He runs across the street to the truck. Spends precious seconds opening the hood, and then he's scanning the interior, imagining George as if he'd lived, seventeen years old now, ready for his first car. *Here's the transmission, son, the radiator, engine, of course, but what* we *need, what we're looking for, is the spark plug cables, we pull all* those *motherfuckers and this truck dies sure as hell and that tape stops running, there they are,* right there—

He hears Katherine scream, his fingers grazing a cable, and looks up into a clotted, ruined face right next to his, white as milk, gore-spattered, something rippling in the bulbed flesh of its cheekbones, glistening sputum trembling from its jaws, it opens its mouth and *laughs* at him and Dean sees that there're teeth, dear God, there're teeth on its fucking *tongue—*

It runs a handful of jagged, splintered fingernails across his throat.

His pistol clatters to the ground as he reaches up to this new *space* at his neck, like his hands are going to hold together what's already come undone, Dean with an image of those summers at Nags Head, him and George, the way the waves could sneak up, pull your legs out from under you, the way he never let that happen to his boy, never ever, him holding tight to George always, but it's like that now, Dean's legs pulled out from beneath him, falling to the pavement, hands tight at his neck, the blood pumping hard.

JOHN BONNER

Portland, Oregon

How everything can go wrong in a fucking eyeblink. Across the street, the creature runs a hand across Dean's throat and he falls, scrabbling at the wound. The thing turns, still holding that baby to its chest, and walks toward them. Bonner and Katherine—just by the nature of the thing's monstrosity, its inhumanity—fall back deeper into the loft. A gray, handless Matthew was one thing, but this—this is shit exhumed from a nightmare. Within seconds, it's stepping inside, ducking its head beneath the sill. Its head swivels, finding Katherine at the back of the room.

At its cheekbones, a pair of veined, pale wings flare open weakly, clots of flesh tumbling to the floor. The thing's terrible jaw unhinges, clicks. The ruby eyes teardrop-shaped.

It cradles the screaming child to its chest and walks toward Katherine, who is crouched and weeping against the far wall, her pistol pointed at the floor. Bonner's brain insists he *move,* and he wants to, but just seeing this thing walk, it's like your gaze wants to turn away.

You are the harbinger.

At the kitchen table, where the duffel bag is splayed open, the hand pulses in its lead-lined box. Its pointless little cage. It cajoles, urges, sings to him, even in the middle of all this.

Dig out your eye, it says, *and stick the barrel of the gun in there and pull the trigger, bend your fingers until they break, find a shard of glass and cut yourse—*

At the table, Bonner opens the gilded box and takes out the eye. He holds it in his shaking palm. It weighs nothing. He thinks of Matthew Coffin holding this very same eye after scooping it out of his own skull. All the terrible power imbued in it, the countless deaths it has cataloged.

"Hey," he calls out. The thing keeps moving toward Katherine.

"Matthew," he calls again, "or whoever the fuck you are. Check it out."

Bonner drops the eye to the cement floor.

It lands, rolls a little on that dry, coiled stalk of optic nerve.

He catches a glimpse of lantern light reflected in its curvature and then stomps on the fucking thing. A wet *pop,* and he smears his sole across the concrete.

The creature curls, howling, hands curling over its skull. The flesh along its spine ruptures wetly, showing knobs of ridged bone beneath.

At the table, Bonner flips the latch of the lead-lined box that contains the hand. A grin on his face that feels maniacal, insane. Its blood-song rises, howls, shrieks inside him. He picks it up and drops it to the floor. He's panting like a dog.

Dropping to one knee—*You are the harbinger, John*—and with a wild, leaping triumph inside him, he puts the barrel of the shotgun against the palm of that ruinous, deadly hand and pulls the trigger.

Absolutely pulps the thing, nothing left of it but a loose scatter of gray fingers and fan-tailed gore on the cement.

The creature bellows, driven to both knees now, lacquered blood spilling from its wounds. Its smell is one of churned, fetid earth, the cloying sugar-stink of death, a fresh grave exhumed. Black blood threads its body from its countless wounds, its head dipped toward the floor. Liquid pops and snaps scatter along its body. Bonner, exultant, steps up beside the thing and presses the barrel of the Ithaca up to its head. The blast is thunderous, painful in the close room. He sees a red snarl of cleaved flesh fly off, the thing's head rocking against the impact. Another burst of ugly, savage joy twists through him. Nick, Sean Pernicio, Samantha Weils, all his dead, here's some penance for them, some measure of return on all that boundless guilt, we *got* you, motherfucker—

The thing turns to him, rising, its skull carved down to yellow bone on that side, and slaps the shotgun from his hands, shattering and nearly ripping off the finger still in the trigger guard. The shotgun slides across the floor, and Bonner feels its hand wrap around his throat. *Like cold rope,* he thinks wildly, as he's walked up against the wall. Katherine screams and Bonner sees her, finally animated, run toward the thing, raising her own pistol to the back of its skull. It seems to sense her nearness, and it lets go of Bonner, who falls gasping to the floor. It turns to her then, crouching so that their faces are level, and those bone-wings beneath its eyes suddenly spread like white, flexing hands, each phalange capped with a claw.

It wraps a hand around Katherine's throat, the bleeding, flesh-clotted skull tilting this way and that, those red eyes roving her face.

Here, Bonner understands, here is the *true* thing that Matthew Coffin pledged his fealty to. Gave his life to. The thing that in return offered Coffin some kind of succor with the monstrous bullshit lie of a second chance after death.

Its grip tightens around Katherine's throat. The child screams at the pale thing's breast.

Then it *leans* toward Katherine and opens its mouth, and the bone-wings beneath its eyes flare again and wrap themselves around her head, the claws snaring in her gray-black hair. Bonner hears her muffled scream, cradling his bleeding, broken hand to his chest.

The thing puts its mouth to hers. Closes its eyes.

Bonner thinks, *Wed the wife crown the son devour the light*—

The wedding begins.

KATHERINE MORIARTY

Portland, Oregon

The wings envelop her. Tangle themselves in her hair, curl one over the other at the back of her skull. An embrace. In the darkness, she feels the claws piercing her skin. She screams, or tries to, but the sound is muffled. The fucking unbridled *stink* of the thing.

And then Katherine is hung aloft in a dream.

A dream, or something close to it.

She is back in her apartment near UCLA, where she'll soon wind up dropping out in a fit of what she'll think is profound musical inspiration but is more likely a heady mixture of unmitigated lust and a desire to torch the strict perimeters of her life. She's just seen Matthew Coffin's band play a show at Raji's the night before, and they have slept together, which she enjoyed very much, and now the two of them are navigating that sometimes sweet, always awkward morning after. The dream has landed her in that nexus, apparently, where she found herself profoundly attracted to him—his crazed whirl of ink-black hair, that wiry, long-limbed frame scattered with stick-and-poke tattoos, his offhand arrogance that she would later discover masked a number of profound insecurities—but he was still, mostly, a stranger to her. She knows this is a dream, a kind of nightmare, actually, her body in stasis, still trapped in that hellscape of a loft, she and that monster twined in some sort of deathly kiss.

But the sense of *realness* here is profound, man. The way the sun falls in a stacked column of thin, precise rectangles on the kitchen counter as it shines through the blinds. The coffee-smeared lip of the coffee cup at Matthew's foot. She even hears the blurred *brap* of a scooter passing beneath the window of her apartment.

Matthew's sitting on the couch in his underwear, all ribs and flashing eyes, and when he looks at her, Katherine feels that familiar mix of lust and trepidation, like she knows for a fact that here is a guy with many hidden rooms inside him and not all of them great. Which, let's face it, had been part of the appeal. But for now, here in her apartment? They're young, the sun's out, and Katherine's got that easy, loose-limbed feeling after getting laid. All is well. The world is a flower that blooms for them.

Matthew takes a cigarette from a pack on the coffee table and lights it, scratching his chin with his thumb while he looks at her with those dark, unknowable eyes.

"What?" Katherine says lightly, smiling. Only a little self-conscious.

"I was just thinking," he says, and oh God, it all comes flooding back to her. How much she's missed that voice. The scratchy, sonorous way of it. The loss of him—all these years, all these ruinous mistakes. All this *death,* piled high. God, that voice. They had truly meant something to each other at one point.

"What were you thinking?" Katherine says. She'll say anything to keep him talking. She sits cross-legged on the carpet, the coffee table between them. Smoke from his cigarette curls in the air. Katherine wants to touch him even as she is dimly aware that this is what the creature wants. That it will bind her to it somehow, that this is the wedding Bonner's spoken of. But she doesn't care.

To hear his voice again. To be here, young and mostly unhurt. To be in love with him, to be close again to a version of Matthew not yet bitter at the world's shortcomings. A Matthew that doesn't blame her for his own failings.

She doesn't care, she'll torch it all, she is reaching for him, when he says, "I was thinking you should sing something." And then he leans over the side of the couch, and she thinks *There's a guitar back there, I bet* and she's right, that's what he's doing, pulling a battered acoustic from over the arm of the couch, so this isn't the aftermath of their first time together at all—it's their whole history being played out. They'd been together for a while before he asked her to sing, before he got hold of some battered guitar and brought it back to her apartment. The genesis of the Blank Letters. So this is instead an odd mishmash of their entire lives, everything pressed into a jumbled dreamscape. A fever dream.

"I don't want to sing anything," she says, remembering dimly that great ruin will come from their songs, one in particular, but Matthew's fingers skitter over the fretboard, the side of his palm damping the strings. He plays fast. He could always play fast.

He dips his head further down. "Sing it, Katherine."

"I don't want to."

She remembers it now. A song called "I Won't Forget It."

"You fucking sing it, Katherine," he says, and his voice is thick, something wrong with his throat, his mouth. He plays faster and this world, this moment, is so real she can see the paper of his cigarette smoldering in the ashtray, feel the weave of her apartment's carpet under her palms. Feel her heart banging against her ribs. She doesn't want to touch him anymore. She's afraid.

"Where's Nick," she says, this sudden bomb-blast realization that they will have a son together, and they will raise him and love him and then, each in their own way, fail him spectacularly.

It's the memory of Nick that frees her.

She starts to rise. She'll flip the coffee table, she'll drive Matthew's cigarette into his eye, she'll brain him with the ashtray.

And then he lifts his face and it is the face of the beast, broken and weeping blood, the snout almost doglike now, the bones pulled forward like warmed wax.

It peers at her with one weeping ruby eye. A dark cave where the other one used to be.

It plays the guitar but just open strings now, tuneless and jarring, because the hand that forms the chords is only a grayed stump.

A hiss of air from its mouth. No words, because it has no tongue.

But in her mind, the voice chortles and says: *Sing for me, Katherine. Sing for me, that we might be wed,* and then it reaches out, Katherine screaming and the guitar giving out one last tuneless twang, and *it* touches *her,* and all is lost.

NAOMI LAURENT

Portland, Oregon

She bends toward the man slowly bleeding to death beside the truck. She doesn't know if she can heal him—if the creature has given him the fever, she can fix that. But there is still that ragged, lethal-looking wound at his throat. He's pushed himself up against the side of the truck, sitting upright, taking small rabbit-sips of air, and the fevered man inside the cab, amid the bass-throb of another song, still bucks and screams. Naomi is reaching for the wounded man when the Marsden-thing howls inside the loft. Outside, a murmur ripples through the fevered. They fill the street as far as she can see, but are strangely still and unmoving, as if they're facing some invisible barrier they've been told not to cross. A shotgun blasts inside the loft and another ripple of unease moves through the gathered crowd. She stands, fear and doubt surging through her, not knowing what to do; she chances a look back inside the building where the Marsden-thing has its hand around a woman's throat, shadowed and half seen, when the man with the shotgun strides forth out onto the sidewalk. He lifts the gun as he comes at her, his eyes veering from Canino inside the truck to the fevered and back to her. There's normal music coming from inside the cab now, a man and a guitar.

"Who the fuck are you?" the man says, keeping his distance. He holds one bloody hand to his chest.

"N-Naomi."

"Naomi, okay. Why are you with him? Who is he to you?"

She stutters, panic seizing her, and his teeth pull back like an animal's. He pushes the barrel against her cheek, the cold press of it. *"Talk."*

"He took me."

"Why?"

Her mind veers wildly—the mark on her leg, her father's story, the memory of that voice shouting *STOP IT* in her head. "Because of what I can do," she says.

The man takes the gun away. "Well, if you can do something, Naomi," he says, peering back into the building, "now is the fucking time."

Naomi, relieved that the cold press of the shotgun barrel is gone, crouches down and touches the wounded man's throat. He gasps, his blood wetting her hand. The images of his life unspool—him, thin-limbed and laughing, young, kicking at waves that glitter with the setting sun as he holds a laughing little boy, his son. A closed drawer in a morgue, a letter on a table from what Naomi knows was the man's wife, saying goodbye. Endless stretches of road, the good feeling of his legs working as he rides down the miles. A fevered—horrible—with a sawblade stuck in its head, lashed there with wire. *One bullet one bullet I'm sorry.* She takes on these memories, owns them, ferries them into herself as she pulls the fever from him. He doesn't respond except to flutter his eyes, roll them up to the whites. He's far gone.

She stands and looks into the building, where the monster—that's what it is, there's no other name for it—has separated from the woman. Both of them closer to the entrance now, near the middle of the room. Her face is pocked, spilling dark runnels of blood where the bone-claws have punctured her.

She turns to them, and before Naomi's eyes, the skin of the woman's face, her arms, marble red and then blue and begin to split open like some sped-up stop-motion film of decay. She twists and bends with it. Her hair growing straw-like and white. Becoming another version of it, of the Marsden-thing. Behind her, it hoists the child to its face—Naomi has a heart-seizing moment where she thinks it is about to literally devour Antoine and she opens her mouth to scream—but it simply draws a line across the child's forehead with one of those jagged black nails. Antoine screeches in pain and surprise and the woman—whatever new thing inhabits her—hisses with something like pleasure.

She thinks of her father. Hugo. Her mother.

All these people she wanted to save and couldn't.

And then—*the house will fall*—she *knows*. Knows what to do next.

Naomi turns.

Stretches her arms wide, walks toward the street.

Toward the thousands of fevered there.

JOHN BONNER

Portland, Oregon

His brain a wild tangle as the girl wanders toward the fevered.

"Kid," he calls out. "Don't." But she keeps walking, approaching them, and the song inside the truck changes again and Bonner's drawn back to it. Two remnants destroyed and it's not enough. Not even close. Wed the wife, crown the son, devour the light? I have to destroy the recording, he thinks, if we want a fucking chance at this. Katherine turned, Dean bleeding out. Everything slipping away in a second, and here he'd thought it was going to be so fucking *easy*.

Dean looks bad. Dying bad. He has that telltale hand cupping his throat, just like the vision Bonner saw in the eye. The kid in the cab sees him and slaps at the driver's side glass, presses his face against it, leaving smears. Bonner puts the Glock's barrel up against the glass and shoots him twice. The kid falls back onto the seat. The window stars and Bonner, hurt shouting through his whole body from his crooked, bleeding finger, uses the pistol's handle to punch in the window. It takes precious seconds, and he realizes how badly he's fucked up when he chances a look back into the loft and sees that

Katherine's become even more transformed, almost canine in the strange arch of her legs, the architecture of her frame. A broken-mirror version of what Matthew's become. He smashes out a sizeable portion of the window glass—the song loud now, Johnny Cash's "Devil's Right Hand," Bonner almost laughing at the outright fucking lunacy of it—and shoves the pistol in his pocket. Puts his hand through the hole in the window and grabs at the truck's lock. Opens the door and is scrabbling at the tape deck in the console, trying to eject the thing, when the fevered man on the seat rises up, his hands spidering across Bonner's head, the collar of his coat, grasping for purchase. Bonner bumps his broken hand against the seat and howls, pushes himself up, scrabbling with his good hand for the pistol in his pocket. The fevered's shattered jaw hangs in a sheet of gore, another black entrance wound in his cheekbone, those blown-candle eyes, and Bonner's growling like an animal as he puts the barrel against the soldier's forehead and fires. The man falls back against the passenger window, stilled, spatter on the glass behind him.

Bonner ejects the tape and it spits out into his hand. He turns and drops it to the pavement and stomps on the plastic shell, grinds his heel against it. Gasping, lightheaded, his hand a starburst of pain, he crouches down and picks up the tangled spool of magnetic tape, holds it to his stomach, and rips at it, and he realizes that everything he saw in the eye, the totality of his vision, has come true. That strange, half-seen collection of string he'd seen had been *this,* this handful of tape that apparently traveled with Katherine from Massachusetts, and who knows where before that. Remnants like to move, he thinks sickly. Curls of shredded tape flutter on the breeze like joyless streamers.

More screams echo in the loft—Matthew and Katherine feeling the repercussion of the destroyed remnant. But they still hold the child, lean over it. Destroyed all three, Bonner thinks, almost petulantly, the fuck else do you want me to *do*? He can't see the girl anywhere, swallowed by the fevered, some half-assed attempt at getting away, at suicide.

Bonner runs back into the loft. He'll charge them, maybe, put himself between them and the baby. What else is there to do? The Katherine-monster and the Matthew-monster hover over the child like a pair of doting hellbound parents. Some part of him realizes that perhaps killing the child will stop what's happening, and even then he can't do it. He strides toward them, watching as Katherine's torso widens with the audible snap of cracking bones, her flesh splitting open, red blooms beneath her clothes. The Katherine-monster cradles the child's head with one distended hand while the Matthew-monster hangs its open mouth above the child, drooling a torrent of black blood into its screaming face.

Like it's feeding him, Bonner thinks.

Whatever the thing began with Matthew all those years back, it's close to finishing. Wed the wife, crown the son, devour the light. The two of them bent over the boy, enrapt.

I'm sorry, he thinks—though he doesn't know if he's talking to Katherine or the baby or Nick Coffin or Jack Bonner; there's no shortage of people that deserve an apology from him—and then he walks up and puts the Glock against Katherine Moriarty's eye. She has enough humanity intact to look surprised, and then the Matthew-creature, almost distractedly, runs a jagged line of claws across Bonner's guts and he sees his own intestines spill out in a great black and pink rush. He falls to the floor before them.

Fucking blew it, Katherine. He got us.

He lies there, the concrete cool against his cheek, facing the open doorway of the loft. The sky above the building across the street glows with fire.

Then he sees the strangest thing, the thing that lets him know he's definitely dying.

He sees people wandering past the door.

Dazed, coughing, weeping people. Wailing people. First one woman, then another. A man in a filthy suit. Then an entire crowd of people wandering past the door.

Speaking to each other. Crying out in confusion.

He sees the dark-haired girl wandering among them, her fingers brushing lightly over shoulders, touching arms.

The light, he thinks.

Above him, the monsters begin screaming like they've been scalded.

NAOMI LAURENT

Portland, Oregon

Is this wise and careful, she asks herself. Wishes profoundly for another minute with Hugo in his car seat beside her, holding his plastic dinosaur, asking his barrage of questions. Her mom and dad up front, arguing about directions, her mother looking pretty with her sunglasses on, like a movie star trying to be sneaky. *Papa, do fish have shoulders?* Her father laughing until he cried. One more minute there. One more hour.

She walks among the sea of fevered, this army the creature brought along with it. She touches them, and the touching is a missive sent out into the long dark night. It is a love letter to her father, her mother, her poor brother.

She walks into the sea of fevered and they reach for her, they hiss and claw, but then she touches them and draws the fever from them and then weaves her way through them to touch still more.

A love letter. A love song.

The house will fall, she thinks.

She draws the fever from them, and they stand there stunned, unspeaking, the humanity flooding back through them. Their eyes

flutter, a new awareness returning. Some begin howling in agony as
their injuries, long unfelt, are revealed. Others scream at the simple
strangeness and horror of it. And then she realizes that not only are
the people she is touching having the fever pulled from them, but
the people *they* are touching as well.

The thought comes to her: *I can change the world.*

She *feels* everything, the static-burst minutiae of their lives, and
rather than being overwhelming, like she experiences with one person, it's as if she's being held aloft on a wave. Buoyed by all their
gathered lives. Love, sorrow, hope, rage, faith, regret, shame, jealousy,
kindness. All of it, the *vastness* of life. The breadth of it. This wave
that ripples outward.

Then she hears screaming from inside the loft, and she turns and
runs inside, toward Antoine, toward the beasts, knowing that if she
hasn't entirely stopped them, she has hurt them somehow.

The creatures see her and hiss, crouching, Antoine still a form
pressed against the Marsden-thing's chest. It pushes up against the
far wall as if in revulsion. Fear.

"Katherine's the key," the man on the floor sputters. She can
hardly hear him. He's pooled in blood that looks black in the gloom.
"Turn her."

The Marsden-creature crouches lower, its fingers tracing softly
along the floor with the hand that is not holding Antoine. Black, fun-
gal blooms now rise from ruptures along its body. They gleam, catching lantern light, drip ichor. It's dying, she thinks. Katherine, perhaps
sensing Naomi's intention, hisses and charges her. They collide, the
two of them sliding briefly along the floor, Naomi's vision blurring as
her head smacks against the cement. Katherine's dog-like jaw opens,
her gums black, her face beaded with blood, scores of tiny cuts, and
then Naomi puts her hand to Katherine's face and feels a starburst of
longing and ache as she draws the fever out—the profound sorrow of
this woman. Naomi gasps and pushes her off.

The Marsden-creature screams; Naomi sees that it has fallen to
one knee now, and seems to be in the process of liquefying. Blood

suppurates from those blooms that rise from its body. It hisses like something serpentine. Through it all, it holds tight to Antoine.

Katherine blinks beside her, the red pulled from her eyes. A human gaze peering from that broken face. The Marsden-monster begins taking shambling, dragging steps toward the door of the loft, as if to escape. Katherine, her body changing back so quickly that Naomi hears bones cracking like falling dominoes, pushes herself up and staggers after the thing; on her way she hip-checks the kitchen table and Naomi sees the blade there catch Katherine's eye. She pulls Bonner's knife free of its scabbard and walks on.

Naomi stands up and runs toward the door to block the Marsden-thing. The creature lets out a nearly human cry of frustration and fear, caught between the two women.

It turns and holds out a stilling hand at Katherine as she approaches, a warning she ignores. It pivots, backs up until it's against the wall, and it screams again, and then Katherine, bloodied but human once more, her clothes a riot of rips and blood-spatter, lays a hand on the crown of Antoine's head. She pins the child's body between the two of them and drives the hunting knife into the creature's face so hard that Naomi hears the *thunk* of the blade against the wall behind its skull.

It lets out a last febrile hiss, its body sagging, limbs slowly drifting toward the floor, the screaming, bloodied child now held safely in Katherine's arms.

THEO MARSDEN

Portland, Oregon

The wife—no, she has a name, Marsden almost remembers it, there with the last sliver of his consciousness, her name that at one time had seemed so important—the wife drives a blade into his face, through the temple and the mealy, worm-rich pulp of brain. She pins it to the wall.

So profoundly close. All these years of waiting. Patience. And then the very forces it needed to enjoin and devour—the wife, the light—have ended it instead.

Marsden fades to nothing. Coffin fades. The rest of the thing's boundless dead, so many broken souls, rattle along for a moment like tin cans on a string and then fade as well. A chorus of sparks whirling in a funnel, swallowed by nothingness.

A man once. A lesser, cast-off devil. An exile.

It dies.

JOHN BONNER

Portland, Oregon

The eye had been right about everything. Shown him every-thing. God, the ripped-up spools of the cassette, how long that had thrown him. Mystified him. He smiles.

Katherine gathers the screaming child to her chest and steps back from the monster pinned like some sort of specimen to the wall. It's melting, looks like, and Bonner imagines it will soon be nothing but a heap of muck on the floor and maybe a crazed, nightmarish skull stuck on a blade. Let the next visitor to this shithole have fun figur-ing that one out.

"There's your harbinger, asshole," he crows, but it comes out phlegmy and nonsensical and he coughs, spits blood over himself. It should hurt—Christ, everything should hurt—and it does, but dis-tantly. Pain felt in another room.

The girl bends down before him, tucks a hank of hair behind her ear. Puts a hand to his face.

"You saved them out there," he says, and it comes out garbled too. She says something in response and he can't tell what it is, his hear-ing is not great at this point either, but he figures she's talking about the past, probably, how your past is like a coat you put on, something you carry along with you—the way people forget about the past even as it forms who they are, and maybe she's talking about Sean Pernicio, there on the Williamsburg Bridge, dumb, hopeful, angry, well-intentioned Sean, how Bonner would do it all so differently now, do all of it so differently, with Weils, and Uncle Jack, and Nick, ah, Nick is a big one, if only Bonner could have been faster, and he realizes then that the girl, this one right here, she could *change Nick back,* she could do it, and he tries to ask her if she'll do that, to tell her how much it would mean to Katherine. But he can't get the words right. Can't hear anything anymore. Darkness pressing on him, his eyes going bad, everything disconnected now, but yeah, if she could turn Nick back, oh, the weight that would lift from Katherine's heart, that such a thing is possible after the past five years, all this death, how it would pull that brittle, heartbroken, calculating rage from behind her eyes, how it would excise this woman's own useless guilt, give her the whole entire sum of her life back, Bonner knows it. Knows it for sure.

Seriously, though, he wants to say, if she could do that, it would mean so much.

But talking, it's so hard.

Bonner lies back. Closes his eyes.

Rests.

EPILOGUE
A SMALL ISLAND
OF LIGHT

NAOMI LAURENT

Portland, Oregon—Baker, Washington

Gunfire ripples around them. Screams. For a short time, a single siren that abruptly stops.

In the loft, Naomi says, "We have to get your friend to a doctor." There is a part of her that wants to run from this woman, Katherine, from what she was only minutes before.

"Okay," Katherine says stiffly, staring down at the dead man's body. "Okay," she says again, and turns, bending to pick up the shotgun.

They walk outside, Naomi cleaning Antoine's face as best she can. The child and this woman both blood-caked, like they've bathed in the stuff. They step outside and she watches as Katherine crouches and puts her fingers to Dean's neck, feels the dim pulse there. They load him into the back of the pickup. He's hard to lift, and even though they do a bad job of it, he doesn't cry out.

They get in the truck. Katherine drives. Antoine is pressed against Naomi's chest. There is the cut on his forehead, and she has pulled the fever from him a second time now, and what that might do to someone, do to a baby, she doesn't know.

They thread their way slowly through the wandering, growing throng of returned people. They number in the thousands now, shambling through the darkness. Talking to each other, trying to discern their shared histories. That's how Naomi is already thinking of them: *returned*. People brought back from that dark precipice. The truck wends slowly through the crowd, and people raise a hand against the headlights or stare down at the filth-caked clothes they were turned in. Some sit on curbs and weep. Some trot after the truck, if they're able, but not in the blood-maddened way of the fevered. Rather as if seeking an answer. That idea—that she is someone to follow—scares the hell out of Naomi. Makes her want to curl into herself. She's not a leader like that. She's too young, too afraid. She's as lost as any of them.

Finally they make it through the scrim of activity, and follow a line of vehicles to another exit, across the wall again, this time crossing over the Interstate Bridge into Washington State, the dark thread of the Columbia beneath their humming wheels.

It is late, and beyond the city no one is out. They've lashed one of Dean's shirts around his neck with his belt, a ludicrous attempt to stop the bleeding, and Naomi is sure they will find him dead in the truck bed next time they stop. She roves the radio constantly, twists the dial as if she'll happen across a station announcing where a doctor is, a hospital. But the radio is filled with static and a man woodenly touting the importance of something called the Providence Initiative and then more static.

The names of these towns are so different from the names of places she's familiar with. Cumbersome and blocky, like stones in your mouth: Vancouver. Hazel Dell. Salmon Creek. It is when they are nearing the small town of Baker, Washington, that the truck runs out of gas.

They step out of the truck onto the shoulder. The land awash in moonlight that renders the fields and highway and leaning fences in a gray half-light. Beyond the hill, half visible, a smoke-charred fast-food restaurant like a mausoleum.

In the bed, Dean is still alive.

"What do we do?" Naomi says.

"He can't walk," says Katherine. "We have to wait. We can't leave him."

Twenty minutes later, headlights pass them and then the vehicle pulls to a stop in front of the truck. It's a van, and Katherine trots up, shotgun in hand. Talks to the driver. She comes back and a heavyset older man in an orange knit cap gets out and follows her.

"He knows a doctor," Katherine says.

"How can we trust you?" Naomi says.

The man, maybe fifty, with a trim white beard and a limp, laughs outright—Katherine bloodied, them with a child, a man in a truck bed with a slit throat.

"I don't think you got much choice," he says.

He backs his van up and they transfer Dean into it—the three of them lifting him, Dean still silent—and Katherine gets in the back, Naomi up front. The man introduces himself as Ed, and they drive.

Off the highway and onto a side road, wheels jouncing in the ruts. They pull to a stop next to a field, a line of cars parked at the shoulder, a scatter of generator lights and fires. There is a tent city here, beyond a cordon of barbed wire hung with soda cans—an early-warning system against interlopers.

Rows of tents and canvas outbuildings, a half dozen burn barrels scattered throughout, flames leaping from the mouths. Somewhere a generator chugs along. Ed calls out and soon there are a handful of people cresting the hillside and ferrying Dean back down in a home-made stretcher, down to that island, that island of light. She and Katherine and Antoine follow.

They have a hospital of sorts. True, it's only a large tent with canvas walls and a few mismatched beds. And yet, hope floods through her—Naomi is sick of death by now. Sick of meeting people only to lose them. The doctor is a small, tightly strung woman with glasses and a rope of pink scar around her neck. But her efficiency—gently guiding a young man on how to place an IV into the back of Dean's hand—does much to calm her. The doctor has unbuckled the belt at his throat and is unpeeling the shirt from Dean's neck when she looks up and says, "Is that your baby?"

"Yes," Naomi says.

"I want to see you both after I'm done here."

"Yes," Naomi says again.

"Good. Now, if you don't mind, please get the hell out. There's nothing you can do at this point."

Ed grimaces, opens the tent flap for them. "Darcy, ever the gentle soul."

The doctor opens her mouth to speak, annoyed, and he holds up a hand.

He leads Naomi, Katherine and Antoine out into a night hung heavy with stars. A line of those blue toilets, what her father had called porta-potties. The whole affair ringed with barbed wire and sawhorses and blackberry brambles. Those residents with ration cards attempt to provide for the rest, Ed tells them, ushering the women over to a burn barrel to warm themselves. While others like him earn their keep by foraging in the bygone world, or try to barter for necessary things.

Even with Ed's approval, they're welcomed cautiously, grudgingly even; it's Antoine that finally makes the people brighten, and soon word gets out that there is a baby here and the camp stirs to life, hard-faced men with guns on their hips crouching before the child, babbling and making silly faces. Antoine laughs and laughs, his mouth split in a firelit grin. Someone hands them a bag of Jane bread, a hard heel of bologna, a knife. A mug of bean soup that steams in the dark. Water is passed around. Naomi eats, drinks, can hardly remember the last time she's done either. She feeds Antoine and he waves his arms and spits down his shirt and everyone laughs.

Eventually things quiet, people return to their tents, but the feeling has changed to one of welcome. She stays beside a burn barrel, gazing into the flames while Antoine sleeps in her arms, and after a while Katherine sidles up next to her. Sparks wheel up toward the sky. Katherine holds her hands out, warms them.

"Matthew wasn't there," she says quietly.

"I don't know what you mean," Naomi says.

"My husband. The one who started all this. I thought it would be him in that, that body. But it was just, I don't know, memories of him. A wish, all twisted up."

"I only knew Marsden," Naomi says.

Katherine laughs then, and Naomi prays that she never grows so old that her laugh sounds as bitter as this one.

The crackle of burning. Whirling. Antoine sighs, resettles.

"But we killed it," Naomi says, aware of the childish, plaintive quality in her voice, like she's trying to convince herself. "You killed it. Yes?"

"I hope so," Katherine manages. She bends down, picks up a handful of scrap wood from next to the barrel and drops it in. More sparks. "Matthew, my husband? He died the day after I talked to him in the loft, all those years back. He's been dead a long time. I've just been, I don't know. Hoping."

Naomi says nothing. She doesn't know what this woman's talking about, but knows a confession when she hears it. Like when she lays her hands on someone, when she turns them back, the way she catches the flitting ghosts of their lives—this is just another version of that. Naomi as receiver, Naomi as sounding board.

"I'm sorry," she manages.

Katherine turns to her, eyes bright with cheer that is almost fury, knuckling a tear away. "Oh, don't be, Naomi. Not one second of this is your fault. You saved us all."

"Not that man," Naomi says before she can stop herself.

"Bonner," Katherine says. "No. Not John."

"I feel so bad," she says, her voice growing thick.

"You can, Naomi. You can feel that way. I know I do. But Bonner, he did what he needed to do. And so did you."

Ed and the doctor approach them then, Ed's orange cap glowing in the gloom. Naomi remembers Dr. Suarez, how she'd been kind to Naomi in a frightening, murderous time. She hopes the woman is alright. Has somehow forged a bridge to safety within that place she was in.

"Will he be okay?" Katherine asks. "Dean?"

"Probably not," the doctor says.

Ed smiles, shakes his head. "Darcy, Jesus. Come on."

The doctor's mouth a small, knitted line. "Maybe he will. Massive blood loss, worry of infection, sepsis, these are all concerns. He needs a transfusion and that's just not possible. We have to wait and see." Her eyes settle on Naomi, down to Antoine. "Will you come with me, please?"

Naomi takes a step toward Katherine. "Why?"

"I just want to give you and your baby a checkup. Just a cursory thing. No shots or anything. But that cut on his head there? It should be cleaned. He needs fresh clothes. And honestly, we just don't get a lot of infants out here." She looks between the two of them. "If you want to do it tomorrow, fine. You want to tell me to beat it, great. It's up to you."

A sound in the distance then, a kind of thud that seems to tease the inner ear, and a soft murmur spreads throughout the camp. Naomi feels the memory of that sound in her bones. She thinks of Denis, of Emilie, the farmhouse. The mounded shapes of the dead cows.

It's a helicopter, and they all watch it pass by overhead, the lights on its underside shearing across the sky.

They're given a pair of sleeping bags. They find a cleared spot and Naomi falls asleep immediately. In seconds, it seems. She is dreaming of her father, and he is right on the cusp of understanding that strange red glyph on his arm and telling her what it means, when someone shakes her awake.

Katherine's face above her in the dark. She's crying.

Naomi's eyes widen, and she starts to rise in panic. "What is it? Antoine?"

"No, no, it's okay," Katherine says. "It's just . . . Naomi, I need to ask you a favor. Maybe the biggest favor."

And then Katherine talks about her son, a man named Nick. Her words coming haltingly at first and then faster, as if she's happy to finally be rid of them.

She wakes again the next morning, everything dew-heavy and gray. Tendrils of smoke climb from the burn barrels, and the camp, with its smashed footpaths and muddied tents, looks dismal in the light of day.

Beside her, Antoine's mouth wrinkles and puckers, and then his wide, coffee-brown eyes open and focus on her. Darcy has cleaned and bandaged his forehead and the bandage makes him look silly. He gurgles, coos, and then grasps her finger and grins.

She picks him up—oof, he needs to be changed—and stands.

There's Katherine at a camp stove by one of the barrels. Naomi walks over. Katherine has heated water and pours her a cup of coffee. Naomi thanks her, sips.

"Dean made it through the night," Katherine says.

"That's good," Naomi says, wiping sleep from her eyes. She sets Antoine down. Let him get muddy. Who cares. There will be no shortage of dirt in this world.

"We'll leave when it's okay for him to travel. Does that work for you?"

"However you want to do it, Katherine."

"Cape Winston, it's a long way away. The other end of the country. It'll be better to have more people." She sips her coffee; Naomi can tell she has been up thinking, thinking.

"Okay."

"They'll be looking for you, Naomi."

"I'm not afraid," Naomi says, and Katherine gives her a look like *Why not?* But it's true. She was wise and careful and the house fell.

I did my best, Papa. I have to go turn this man at the other ocean, a whole country away. Nick Coffin. Such a dramatic name, you would have loved it. I'll turn people along the way, whenever I see them. Always. The more the better.

Every time I do it, it will be for you and Mama and Hugo. My love letter to you.

I miss you all so much.

They hear a rattle and clank nearby and Naomi turns to see a fevered woman snared in the barbed-wire perimeter some thirty yards away. She has long black hair, knotted and tangled with weeds and leaves. She sees them and leans forward, her jaw opening wide as if to bite the wind itself.

Katherine sips her coffee. "How does it work, Naomi? How do you do it?"

Naomi picks up the baby and breathes deep. Antoine reaches up and pats her face like an old man offering reassurance.

"Come on," she says, "I'll show you."

And the three of them begin making their way toward the woman in the wire.

ACKNOWLEDGMENTS

Okay, look, if writing a book is tough—and oh, it usually is—writing its sequel can at times feel insurmountable. At least this one did. Writing a sequel to a book like *Fever House*, which ended with a very, uh, specific set of parameters and challenges, was tough. To put it bluntly, I ended that book with a number of wild-ass cliffhangers, and *The Devil by Name* took a few attempts to find its footing in early drafts. I owe a lot of people high fives, free drinks, or mixtapes for their guidance, patience, and kindness along the way. Undoubtedly I'm forgetting some folks, but the people mentioned here deserve credit for helping me find my way through the process of writing this book.

Caitlin McKenna, my editor at Random House, who more than once helped me navigate toward the beating heart of this story and away from its pitfalls. Grateful as hell that we get to do this, thank you.

Chad Luibl, my agent at Janklow & Nesbit. Guy is unflinching when it comes to advocating and making things happen for his writers. Let's do this fifty more times.

Greg Kubie, who is great at publicity *and* leading a half-blind guy through the utter madness of the Javits Center and 200,000 people dressed in costumes I'm too square to understand.

Profound thanks to the rest of the Janklow & Nesbit, Random House, and UTA teams: Roma Panganiban, Kristina Moore, Noa Shapiro, Celia Albers, Maria Braeckel, Claire Fennell, Windy Dorresteyn, Rebecca Berlant, Cindy Berman, Erica Gonzalez, Michael Steger, Lianna Blakeman, Stefanie Lieberman, Molly Steinblatt, and Adam Hobbins. To Lawrence Krauser for his clear-eyed copyedits. To Elizabeth Eno for the interior design. To Ella Laytham, who somehow managed to make the covers of both novels so uniformly striking *and* jaw-dropping and yet entirely their own things. Seriously, I'm forever in your debt for how rad these books look.

Once again, a huge bellow of gratitude to all the librarians and booksellers out there. With the world leaning the way it is, you are fighting the best and most meaningful of fights.

To Tricia Reeks, who put out my first four books via Meerkat Press and has never wavered in her belief in the work. Again, thanks for everything.

To the friends and writers and writer friends who dragged me out of the house and into the world, usually in spite of my best efforts: Jeffrey Arnsdorf, Stacy and Matt Baiocchi, Nathan and Brandi Cornelius, Michael Dolan, Lyndsay Hogland, Capella Lapham, James Mapes, Doug O'Loughlin, Shawn Porter, Jesse and Jill Stowell and their kids, Dan Tischler, Lisa Titan and the folks at St. John's Boxing, and Gordon B. White.

To Kenton. Never loved a neighborhood before, not really.

To EV and Rosie, forever.

To Robin, who steadies our ship, walks the world with a huge, wide-open heart, and still makes me laugh like the first time we met.

To the readers, for the grace and the chance. Let's meet again with the next one.

ABOUT THE AUTHOR

KEITH ROSSON is the author of the novels *Fever House, Smoke City, Road Seven,* and *The Mercy of the Tide,* as well as the Shirley Jackson Award–winning story collection *Folk Songs for Trauma Surgeons.* His short stories have appeared in *Southwest Review, PANK, Nightmare Magazine, Cream City Review, Outlook Springs, December,* and others. He lives in Portland, Oregon, with his partner and two children.

ABOUT THE TYPE

This book was set in Caslon, a typeface first designed in 1722 by William Caslon (1692–1766). Its widespread use by most English printers in the early eighteenth century soon supplanted the Dutch typefaces that had formerly prevailed. The roman is considered a "workhorse" typeface due to its pleasant, open appearance, while the italic is exceedingly decorative.